New York Times bestselling author J. B. Salsbury spends her days lost in a world of budding romance and impossible obstacles. Her love of good storytelling led her to earn a degree in Media Communications. Since 2013 she has published six bestselling novels in The Fighting Series and won a RONE Award. J. B. Salsbury lives with her husband and two kids in Phoenix, Arizona.

Visit her at **www.jbsalsbury.com**, find her on Facebook at **www.facebook.com/JBSalsburybooks** and on Twitter **@JBSalsbury**.

Immerse yourself in J. B. Salsbury's deeply emotional, addictive love sories:

'Heartwarming, raw, and sexy. J. B. Salsbury did an amazing job on this one! With pacing so intense, it knocked me off my feet' Tijan, *New York Times* bestselling author

'A brilliantly constructed romantic thriller you'll devour in one sitting! The *perfect* amount of sexual tension and sweetness rolled up with my favorite of all: a *dangerously* hot alpha male, makes this one addictive read!' Elizabeth Reyes, *USA Today* bestselling author

'Wow! My head is spinning and my heart is rejoicing. Sweet, tender, unexpected, heartbreaking, and so beautifully healing. It's like nothing I've ever read before' Mia Sheridan, *New York Times* bestselling author

'J. B. Salsbury crafts a masterful romance with *Split*. It grabbed me by the throat and punched me in the heart' Claudia Connor, *New York Times* bestselling author

More praise for J. B. Salsbury:

'An addicting, wild ride of epic proportions that will stay with you long after you've reached the end' Harper Sloan, *New York Times* bestselling author

'Visceral. Addictive. Out of this world intense. A roller-coaster ride from start to end, *Split* will take your breath away' Katy Evans, *New York Times* bestselling author

'Riveting and heartbreaking, *Split* is a must read and one of my favorites of 2016' Rebecca Shea, *New York Times* bestselling author

'A powerful punch of deep emotion, sexy characters, and ingenious writing – this is the book you've been waiting for' Pam Godwin, *New York Times* bestselling author

'5 stars! Highly recommend! I went into *Split* completely blind and at first had no idea what to expect. But then the book swept me away' Pepper Winters, *New York Times* bestselling author

Split

J. B. SALSBURY

headline
ETERNAL

Published by arrangement with Forever,
an imprint of Grand Central Publishing.

First published in Great Britain in 2016
by HEADLINE ETERNAL
An imprint of HEADLINE PUBLISHING GROUP

1

Cataloguing in Publication Data is available from the British Library

ISBN 978 1 4722 3861 0

Offset in 10.4/16.82 pt Granjon LT Std by Jouve (UK), Milton Keynes

Printed and bound in Great Britain by CPI Group (UK) Ltd, Croydon, CR0 4YY

Headline's policy is to use papers that are natural, renewable and recyclable
products and made from wood grown in well-managed forests and other
controlled sources. The logging and manufacturing processes are expected
to conform to the environmental regulations of the country of origin.

HEADLINE PUBLISHING GROUP

To Amanda
Because you believed I could...
So I did.

ACKNOWLEDGMENTS

First off, I want to thank God for allowing me the ability to tell stories. All good things come from you.

Thank you to my husband, who is and always will be the only hero in my life. It's your love that inspires me and your support that anchors me.

Thank you to my babies, who have made me feel like I'm the greatest novelist the world has ever seen, even though they have no idea what I write. I love their blind faith.

To my parents and my brother for being the best pimps and my number one fans, thank you. I'd never have the courage to do this if it weren't for you.

A huge thank you to Evelyn Johnson for always having my back and for allowing me to drag her all over the country for signings and events. Your friendship and loyalty are unparalleled.

Thank you to my dear friend Amanda Simpson. From the moment this story was conceived, you've been my biggest supporter. You went above and beyond the call of duty: reading, critiquing, brainstorming, and shoving me on when I had my doubts. I'll never be able to pay you back for all you've

ACKNOWLEDGMENTS

done for me, not only as a friend, but also as my business partner. I appreciate you more than words can express. To my friend Jonas Lee, thank you for taking on the hefty responsibility of critiquing this story for me. Your insight on this was invaluable. You could've easily blown me off but instead you worked hard to help me iron out all the wrinkles while being a huge source of encouragement. *Thank you* will never be enough.

Thank you, Sara Sellars, for your expertise in the inner workings of broadcast news that helped bring Shyann Jennings to life.

To my agent MacKenzie Frasier-Bub, thank you for believing in me and encouraging me to try something new. You are, like, totally, the most bitchin' agent, like, ever.

Huge thank you to Megha Parekh for not only believing in the writer that I am, but also in the one I have the potential to become. I will not let you down.

Always a huge thank you to the talented Elizabeth Reyes. I'd never have had the *cajones* to write if it weren't for your encouragement and support. Thank you for your time and, more importantly, your friendship.

None of this would be possible if it weren't for the readers who've given my books a chance. There are so many incredible authors out there, and I'm humbled and honored every time a reader picks one of my books. Thank you for taking a chance on me.

Last but not least and probably the most important, thank you to all the Fighting Girls who support me and my books with the kind of steadfast love only an FG is capable of. I'd be nowhere without you girls. You mean the world to me.

Split

PROLOGUE

Ten years ago…

It's dark. Like when I hide under my bed and can't see my hand in front of my face. But I'm not under my bed now.

Cold seeps into my body. My head rings; static blares in my ears.

I blacked out again, but this is different. Everything about this feels different.

There's shuffling…some kind of panic in the air. My heart pounds and with the rapid blood flow brings a sharp stabbing pain that explodes in my neck. I try to open my eyes, push at the dark and reach for light, but a sticky coating covers my face. I suck in a breath, cough against the thick sludge that clogs my nose and throat. The metallic tang of blood turns my gut. I retch, hacking up something thick, and agony slices through my jaw.

"Oh fuck!" A deep masculine voice rips through my panic. "This one's alive!"

I try again to open my eyes.

"We need an EMT!"

I need to get up, find somewhere to hide. Mom always gets angry after one of my blackouts and with the pain...*oh God the pain*...I can't take one of her punishments.

My arms ache but I force them to my eyes to clear the dark haze that clouds my vision. Weight presses against my shoulder, keeping me down. No, I have to get out of here.

"Don't move." The voice, I try to place it. A neighbor? I don't know who else—"ETA on the ambulance! This kid's gonna bleed out!"

"What..." My voice makes no sound, only a low gurgle within my chest. I try to push up, reach out. *Help me!* Shadows dance behind my eyes.

"God have mercy—we're gonna lose him!"

"Stay down!" A male voice is close. "Oh shit...don't move!"

I slip in and out. Voices frantic but muted in my ears.

"Neighbors said he's fifteen..."

"...fucking bloodbath..."

"Help..." I cough and reach for the fire blazing in my jaw.

A firm grip wraps my neck. I struggle against it as it cuts off what little breath I'm able to take. "Hang on, son." It loosens and I suck in a gulp of blessed air mixed with fluid that makes me cough.

"He's gonna drown in his own blood if we don't get him—"

"Son, can you hear us?"

I nod as best I can, reaching for the light. *Don't black out. Don't give up.*

"Did you do this, boy?" The thick growl of a different man sounds in the distance. His voice deeper. Angrier.

I'm in so much trouble. I want to tell him I don't remember. I have a condition. Lapses in memory. But I can't get the words to make it to my mouth.

"They're all dead."

My heart kicks behind my ribs.

Dead? Who's dead?

Dizziness washes over me and I don't fight it. Nausea rips through my gut. The biting taste of vomit mixed with blood floods my mouth. I suck air, fight through the mud for oxygen. My lungs burn. I absorb the words and pray for a blackout to come. The dark that takes away all the pain, the shadow that tucks me in and shelters me.

The pounding pulse in my neck slows to a dull throb. The static between my ears turns to a purr. Warmth envelopes me.

"Son of a bitch." More shuffling. "He's our only witness."

Words blur as I drift in and out of darkness. Not like the blackouts, but something different. Deeper. As if sleep pulls me, then releases me like a yo-yo.

"Dammit! We're gonna lose him."

The pain dies off. Peacefulness wraps around me. I drift back into night and welcome the dark I know will protect me.

ONE

SHYANN

Present day

There isn't a single moment in life that compares to this one. Eh...I suppose if one day I meet the right guy who doesn't mind playing second to my career goals, maybe a wedding would compare. Or not. I mean, weddings mean family and family means ripping open old wounds, and, well, that idea alone makes me want to barf all over my knock-off Jimmy Choos.

No, I was right the first time. This moment is a game changer. It's hit or miss, no room for second place. Five years in college, working my ass off and pulling in more student loans than I'll be able to pay back in four lifetimes all teeters on thirty seconds of live newsfeed.

I shift restlessly in my seat, squinting back and forth between my phone and the dark road through the windshield. "Should be right up here, less than a mile."

"Know that. Got the same address you did." My cameraman turns left into a residential area, a decent part of town, middle- to lower-class neighborhood. "Besides, the place will be crawling with police. There's no way we'll miss it."

I turn toward him and grin. "Police, but we'll be the first and only news van." I'm downright giddy! "This has to be perfect. We can't afford to fuck this up."

He grunts and I glare, annoyed by his nonchalance.

"I'm serious, Leaf. Make sure you get the right angle. I need this to be perfect. If the camera hits me funky, I look like a Cabbage Patch doll." I smooth my skirt and blouse, wishing the outfit brought me more confidence, but instead I feel like one of those assassin bugs that wears the corpses of other bugs as armor. Not what I'm most comfortable in but at least I look enough the part to be taken seriously.

Fake it till you make it, Shyann.

"I got just as much riding on this as you do." His voice is more animated than his usual lazy hippie drawl. He eyeballs me for a second. "Sure you're ready for this?"

I swallow my nerves. "Of course I am. I was born ready for this." My toes curl up, already cramping in my Timmy Shoos. Not sure they were even worth the eighteen bucks I paid for them.

"Good to hear, 'cause"—he squints at a grouping of emergency vehicles in front of a single-level home and slows to a stop—"it's go time."

I lean forward to gaze out the front window. An officer glares at our news van. Typical. An ambulance sits in the driveway, and the back doors are open and the cavity inside is empty. "They haven't brought her out yet?"

"Shit! Let's hurry!" Leaf scrambles between the seats into the back to grab his equipment.

"Do you have any idea what this means?" I pull the mirror down and frantically swipe on some lipstick. "It only happened, what, like—"

"Fourteen minutes ago." The van door slides open with a loud *whoosh*.

I was at the station the second the call came over the police scanner. Code 240. Aggravated assault. Female. Unconscious, strangulation, no sign of forced entry.

After a string of serial assaults on women in Phoenix, less than 150 miles from the mountain town of Flagstaff, the similarities of this assault were too unique to ignore. Assault on women wasn't unusual, but whoever was committing them over the last few months wasn't sexually assaulting his victims. They were, as the Phoenix police had announced, "unusual in nature." And now we had one in our town.

Possibly.

It's a long shot, but it's a shot worth taking.

Reporters from Phoenix won't be here until morning. If this is what I think it is, we'll be picked up live for the nine o'clock news. Only a few months out of school and I'll be live in a top-ranking—number eleven to be exact—media market newscast.

Hopping from the van, heart pounding in my chest, I circle the front to find Leaf lining up a good shot. Butterflies explode in my gut as I shrug on my Burberry raincoat. The tag says Blurrberry and the signature plaid pattern is off by a black stripe or two, but a chance at national exposure calls for my very best fake designer clothes.

"This is it." I pop in my earpiece and check the time. "Nine o'clock news starts in ten minutes. We have to be ready."

Leaf mumbles something I ignore and I start planning my intro.

"Ladies and gentlemen…" I clear my throat and lower my voice. "The scene before us…" No, more emotion. That's the key to this job, being completely emotionless, but infusing enough fake emotion so the viewers relate. Only the best broadcasters can do it, and I'm determined to be one of the best. "Big city terror ravages the town of Flagstaff, as what is speculated to be the eighth victim in a serial assault on women—"

"Shyann, you there?"

I adjust my earpiece at the sound of my producer Trevor's voice, then speak into my mic. "We're here."

"Leaf, move left. If they bring out the woman on a stretcher, we'll get a perfect view." I shuffle into position. "There, good. We don't have time to interview neighbors, but we'll do the live feed and then you two get some faces on video. Tears, fear, all the shit that makes a great story." He clears his throat. "Shyann, straighten your coat. You look like you just rolled out of bed in it."

I glare at the camera and at the sound of Trevor's chuckle, then roll my eyes.

"No smart-ass retort, honey? I'm shocked."

My body heats with embarrassment and anger, which is kind of nice, seeing as we're headed into the autumn months and my cheesy coat is doing very little to fight off the evening chill.

Trevor, my semi-boyfriend, loves humiliating me on-screen. He swears it keeps me humble. Says I'm hungrier than most, driven beyond what's healthy. He also says I'm ruthless and have the emotional capacity of a gnat. Maybe he's right, but I refuse to see my striving for success as a negative thing.

"Wake up, Shyann!" Trevor's voice powers through my earpiece.

"I'm awake, asshole." I press it and dip my chin to listen, not wanting to miss a single word of direction.

"There's my girl."

He's not a bad guy; matter of fact, he's a lot like me—motivated to do something big in order to make a name for himself. He's ambitious and detached from petty things that get in the way of success. Now that I think about it, that's where our similarities end. "How much time until we're live?"

"We're opening with your story. Tell us the basics, then stand by. We'll do the local news but pop in as developments unravel." He clears his throat and mumbles something to someone in the studio. "Be ready in five."

I flash five fingers and then roll one to Leaf and he nods. "In five. We're ready."

"All right, Leaf's feed, looks like he's got a good visual of the police and the front door. If we can get them bringing the body bag out, that's our money shot."

"Body bag? The victims in Phoenix all survived the assaults."

"I guess she could be alive, but if so, why are they taking so long to get her to the hospital? Either way, the shot'll be epic if we get it."

A fissure of discomfort slithers through my chest at the casual way we deal with death in the news. Sure, on-screen we're the caring and empathetic news reporter, but inside we're rejoicing to get a shot of a dead body? No, I push all that shit back and focus.

"Let's do this— *Whoa*!" The heel of my shoe sinks into the ground. I flap my arms for balance and barely recover. The earth is mushier than usual after a couple days of rain, and even though this is one of the more developed neighborhoods in Flag, it's still a city in the mountains, which means lots of natural ground.

"You better be all right. We're on in three."

Thanks for the concern, dick. "I'm good." I put on a mask of professionalism while my skin practically vibrates with nervous energy.

"Stand by."

I take my position, smooth my hair, and focus on my words.

If all goes well, I'll get out of this hole-in-hell town and into a bigger market, which is one step closer to anchor. No one just out of college gets this kind of an opportunity. My professors always encouraged me to go for an anchor job, my half–Native American blood making me look just dark enough to be considered a minority but light enough to be desirable. It's total bullshit, but I don't make the rules. Can't hate a girl for taking advantage, though. I have very specific career goals, and if using my ethnicity helps me to get there, so be it.

My momma always said I was meant for big things. I can still hear her voice in my head: *"You're too big for this world, Shyann."* Said I came out of the womb with goals and never stopped reaching for them. My chest cramps at the pride my momma would feel if she were alive today. She always pushed me to chase my dreams. God, I hope she can see me now.

"We're on in five…four…"

I straighten my coat and look directly into the camera as Trevor counts down in my ear.

This is for you, Momma.

"You're on!"

"Terror struck this quaint Flagstaff neighborhood as big-city crime moves north. After several assaults on women in Phoenix, all with identical trademarks, police have now moved their investigation to neighboring cities as another victim surfaces. The name of this most recent victim hasn't been released, but her age, socioeconomic profile, and details of the crime fit other victims of who Phoenix police are now calling the Shadow. All the assaults were committed in the evening hours, with no witnesses, and the perpetrator is masked and wears gloves, leaving no forensic evidence behind. The call to this house behind me came in shortly after eight p.m. when the woman who lives here was found bloodied and unconscious—"

"There's movement in the doorway," Trevor says.

"…after a frantic nine-one-one call."

"No! Let me go!" A young girl, a teenager, is practically carried out of the house by an officer. Leaf swings the camera to her. She's curled into the chest of an older policeman, her shoulders bouncing as she sobs.

"Shyann!" Trevor's voice booms through my earpiece, making me jump. "Keep talking. Leaf, get us a visual on the girl."

"Oh, uh, it seems a…" The girl's face twists in agony and I swallow past the thickness in my throat. "A girl who—"

"Mom, no…please, Mom!" Her guttural shriek pierces the air.

Another fissure slices through my chest and old feelings threaten to bubble to the surface.

Emotionless. Stay distant, Shyann.

"Seems to be the victim's daughter—"

"Let me see her," the girl pleads with police. "Oh, God, please…"

The girl's anguish reaches through my chest and squeezes my heart. My throat grows tight. The backs of EMTs shuffle out the door as they carry a stretcher.

"Mommy!"

I ignore the girl as best I can and try to trudge on. "It seems…um… they're—"

"No!" The girl throws her body onto the stretcher and it's then I notice the woman on it is covered in a white sheet. Completely covered. Even her face.

Oh, God. She's dead.

Trevor's voice growls in my ear. "She's dead! Get the shot!"

My stomach churns.

"Talk! Shyann!"

I nod. "It seems tragedy has taken a turn…um…for the…"

The young girl launches herself at the body again. The police hold her back while she kicks and screams for her mother.

My breath catches as memories flood my mind. I was just like her. Losing control of my body, kicking and wanting to inflict the kind of pain I was feeling. The heart-pumping panic, sudden coldness that blankets overheated skin causing uncontrollable shivers. And the terror, all of it shoots through me now like it did when I lost my momma.

"Shyann! Talk to her!" The levity in Trevor's voice ignites my blood, replacing my frigid panic. "This is fucking gold."

Leaf moves to get a better view and jerks his wide eyes for me to get into the shot. I turn back, studying the girl, remembering the confusion, the heartbreak, the all-consuming unfairness.

"Please don't die…" Her anger turns to sobs of devastation so palpable they shake my foundation.

I take a wobbly step forward.

"Don't be dead…"

"I swear to God, Shyann, if you don't get in there and grab this story…this is our ticket. You hear me, dammit? Get your ass in there!"

I open my mouth to speak, Trevor's demand in my ear pushing my lips to move, but there are no words.

I can't.

Everything becomes irrelevant. My stupid fucking clothes, dreams of becoming an anchor for a national broadcast, all of it pales in the light of this girl's recognizable anguish. Her cries rip through my unaffected façade and reach into my soul. It slices through vital organs and dives into the recesses where I've locked away my hate. Anger. Cruelty that a child would have to suffer through the loss of the single person in this world that ever understood her.

Trevor growls in my ear. "Shya—"

"I can't." The words come out with the force brought on by years of suppression.

"You *can't*? We're live! Talk!"

Leaf's free hand rolls frantically through the air, his camera lens zeroing in like a weapon ready to cause mass destruction.

My head moves on my shoulders, conveying the one word that won't leave my lips. *No.*

"Fuck it, she's done!" Trevor's voice shakes with fury. "Leaf, get in there now!"

Leaf moves before Trevor's even done talking and shoves the camera lens into the girl's face.

"No!" An impulse to shield her compels me forward. "Leave her alone." I stumble over loose rocks, but it's not enough to stop me. "Cut the feed!"

"Back off, Shyann! You're—"

I tear out my earpiece and throw my body between the girl and the camera lens.

Leaf gasps, "What the fu—"

"Leave her alone!" I grab the camera and slam it into Leaf's face so hard it sends him to his ass.

The firm clunk of the news camera rings in my ears and blood spills from just under Leaf's eyebrow, signaling me to a single truth.

My short career in broadcast news has come to an end.

***

Five years fit into a few boxes now packed in the bed of my Ford Ranger. I never thought much about my lack of belongings. Makes sense I guess. If it wasn't something I could wear or something I was studying, I had no use for it. The last five years of my life have consisted of meeting my basic needs—shelter, sleep, sustenance—and chasing after my career goals. Anything to keep from being forced back to the town I was raised in.

I had big plans when I left home. College, work, and get as far away from Payson as I could. Now here I am, a few months past graduation, and I made it ninety-four miles.

Not impressive.

I was looking forward to bouncing around from small market to small market, going from one furnished studio apartment to the other, ready to pack up and go when a job opportunity called. If it called. Which after last week's incident it probably never will.

"You sure you're okay to drive home alone?" Trevor's leaning against my truck, a coffee in one hand and wearing his stupid fucking aviator glasses that make him look nothing like Maverick. His styled dirty-blond hair doesn't budge in the wind and his pale skin screams of a man who spends most of his days inside and behind a desk.

Maybe it's growing up in a small town, or the closest men in my life being the build-it-yourself, hunt, and drink beer type, but his pleated golf shorts and lavender collared shirt tucked in like a good little preppy doesn't make me weak in the knees. He's handsome, gets plenty of attention from women, but all he's ever been for me is comfortable. He doesn't bring out my inner sex goddess, nor does he completely repulse me.

"You sure you care?" I slam the tailgate shut a little harder than I need to.

He sighs. Loud. "Honey…"

I cringe inwardly at that ridiculous pet name.

"I do care, but you knew this would happen."

Not even an ounce of sympathy, not that he'd understand why I did what I did. Trevor's one of those robotic guys, prides himself in having zero emotions and preaches the importance of keeping all relationships, business or otherwise, feelings-free. It's one of the things I dig about him—I mean, until now.

"This was your chance, Shyann. You blew it." He laughs, but it's more of a shocked I-can't-believe-how-stupid-you-are chuckle. "You gave Leaf an orbital fracture. You fucked this up for all of us."

"Thanks for the recap, Trevor." I split my ponytail and pull it tight.

"You can't expect to keep your job after that. You know better."

"Just like a bad little puppy, you're gonna rub my nose in it. I appreciate that." *As if I don't already feel like shit.* It's not like I did it on purpose; it just happened.

Truth is, I've always had a horrible temper. I've managed to keep it under control; being away from my childhood home and the small town I grew up in made it easy. I distanced myself from everything that made me *feel*, until the newscast heard 'round the world. For me, there was no holding back.

He hooks me by the waist and pulls me into a one-arm hug, pressing our hips together. "Aw, don't leave mad." He kisses me and the smell of coffee on his breath mixed with his overly sweet cologne turns my stomach. "I wish you didn't have to go back to that hick town."

"It's not a hick t-town. It's a quaint m-mountain community."

His eyes narrow. "You're stuttering. You always stutter when you lie."

"Whatever." I press my hand against his chest to get some distance, and a small fire burns in my gut. "Besides, it's only temporary until I figure out what my next move is."

Trevor's the one who got me the job at FBS. *Job* is a bit of an exaggeration, seeing as I only made enough money to pay for the necessities. Now I've got sixty-eight dollars in my account and my rent was past due until Trevor paid the six hundred dollars so I could get out of my lease. I'd feel bad for taking his money, but my only other option was asking my dad. Trevor was the lesser of two pride-squashing evils, and Lord knows I have little dignity left to spare.

He releases me and opens the truck door. "Drive safely and call me when you get there." There's a tiny hint of the man I remember meeting in my comm classes back when we had mutual respect for each other and our career goals. "Let me know what you decide."

"Will do." I slide into the driver's seat and strap on my seat belt. "And…uh…I'll send you a check as soon as I get some money."

He shuts the door and leans down to poke his head through the open window. "I'm sorry I couldn't give you somewhere to stay while you figure all this out. It's just—"

"Are we really doing this? Don't act like you give a flying fuck where I end up, Trevor."

Disapproval twists his mouth. "That mouth'll keep getting you into trouble if you're not careful, honey."

I fight the urge to shove my finger down my throat. "I like my mouth. It's honest."

His lips brush across my cheekbone. "Get your shit together, then bring your dirty mouth back to me. I'll see if there are any job openings in town. Maybe the coffee shop's hiring." There's a hint of humor in his voice.

"You're an asshole." How I ever ended up naked with him is a mystery. I mean, if lots and *lots* of tequila can be considered a mystery. After that it just seemed like an easy way to scratch an itch.

"You love me."

I stare at him for a few seconds, realizing that I don't love him. I care about him as much as a person who cares about nothing can, but that's the extent. We established the ground rules from the beginning—no attachments, our careers come first, don't get in each other's way.

"I'll be in touch." I avoid his eyes and step on the gas, forcing him to step back from the truck. I don't even look in the rearview mirror as I pull away.

I hit the road, grateful for the one thing my dad gave me besides my blue eyes that earned me my middle name—my truck. It's small, only two seats, but it has four-wheel-drive and even though it's the color of baby shit—the dealership calls it champagne—it's been the most reliable thing in my life.

The highway stretches out before me, and talk radio blares static through my speakers. I punch off the obnoxious noise and force myself to sit in my own silence.

Stupid, stupid, Shyann.

Five years of college for what? I worked my butt off to get where I was, got handed the opportunity that would catapult my career, and killed my chances in a few seconds of live newsfeed. Now there isn't a broadcast company in this country that will touch me. And I'm broke.

I know better than to let my personal feelings interfere with my work. As much as I regret what I did to end my short career, I can't say I'd do anything differently. There's no way I could exploit that young girl's suffering.

The girl's mother had a heart defect and the severe beating put too much stress on her heart and killed her. Not a painless death, I'm sure, but at least it was quick.

Unlike my momma's.

No, she had to suffer for over two years, her body giving up at an agonizing pace, leaving her mind for last so she'd be completely aware of how she was dying. The memories slice through my mind's eye, my dad holding her limp body, roaring his anger at God.

It was sitting in that cold church, watching every person in our town filter past me with words they hoped would ease my pain. That was when I decided I'd get out of Payson the second I graduated and never go back. I was angry, starving for a fight. Desperate to have my dad back rather than the empty man with the dead eyes who she left us with. He hated that I was leaving, never understood my need to run, to do all the things I promised my momma I'd do. We fought. Hard. Unforgivable words were exchanged, and we haven't managed to patch our relationship since.

Now I'm crawling back to beg for mercy, the prodigal child, broke, jobless, and with debt hanging off me like dead weight. If there's one thing I know for sure, Nash Jennings will never let me live this down.

He might be a proud man, but I'm just as proud. I'll need time to save money, figure out my options, and the second I do I'm out of there. Yeah, this is my best option.

I'm meant for big things. This is simply a speed bump.

TWO

LUCAS

"Yo, dreamboy!"

I jerk my head up from my tape measure to see Stilts struggling to secure a rafter to a tie beam.

"Mind helping me out?"

A quick nod and I climb up the ladder, taking two rungs at a time, the red on the middle-aged man's cheeks getting redder like an alarm that's about to blare. "Got it." I hold the beam steady on my end while he levels and secures it into place.

Sweat drips off the tip of his bulbous nose. "Thanks, kid."

Kid. The word grates along my spine. I've lived through more in my twenty-five years than most guys twice my age. Not that he'll ever know that.

"No problem." I jump down and head back to working on the partition wall that will eventually be a kitchen. This type of work has always come easy to me. Cuts, angles, levels, everything in construction is a math equation with only one right answer.

Easy, predictable, and safe. At least, safe for me.

Carving is what I love most. Taking a salvaged piece of wood and turning it into something new and beautiful, giving it a new purpose. A different life.

My mind works through the project before me, my hands securing lumber with every pop of a nail gun, but in my head I'm somewhere else. Creating, always imagining. The wood's grain patterns twist and swirl, inspiring intricate pictures that I try to remember so I can sketch them later. It seems stupid, but even the simplest inanimate objects hold fascination when I look at them long enough. Maybe it's a vivid imagination or maybe my brain doesn't work like most.

"Looks good."

I peer up at Chris, my foreman, who's checking my levels. "Thank you, sir."

He regards me with very little concern, the same passive nonchalance he always does. "Nash is looking for you." He tilts his head toward what will eventually be the garage of this home, then turns away.

That's the other nice thing about working construction—there's not a lot of idle chitchat among men. They communicate in basics, need-to-know only, even eliminating words completely with the occasional grunt. I'm able to keep my head down, get lost in the project and earn a paycheck with little to no problems at all.

I rip my baseball hat from my head and give it a good shake, then do my best to smack the sawdust and wood shavings from my T-shirt and jeans as I head out to find Nash.

Seeing him at the far end of the garage, I'm reminded why the man commands the respect of not only his employees, but also from the entire town, far as I can tell. The guy stands over six feet tall, his silver and black hair a little too long to be considered clean cut and a little too short to be considered long. His eyebrows are dropped low in concentration that makes him appear to be cursing the hell out of whatever he's looking at.

"Lucas."

He doesn't even look up, but the firm way he says my name quickens my pace until I'm right up to him. "Sir?"

He doesn't take his eyes off the blueprints rolled out on a makeshift table constructed of two sawhorses and a sheet of plywood. "Clients called. Interested in a specialty piece for the fireplace." His thick, calloused finger runs along a line on the blueprint. "Here. Told 'em we got a guy who does some pretty good work. You interested?"

"Is that…" I squint at the blueprint, figuring out the numbers. "Eight feet? Roughly?"

He sets his steely gaze to mine and I fight to hold his stare. The color is so light blue they're almost white and, set against skin that's been exposed to the sun and the elements for what I'd guess to be close to sixty years, gives him an eerie and intimidating look. "Seven and a quarter."

I fidget, tugging my hat down to my eyebrows. "I can do that."

"I'll need a mock-up for approval."

My hands go into my pockets as nerves and excitement war in my chest. "Did they want something specific?"

He rubs the back of his neck, still studying the blueprints. "I showed 'em your last piece. They want something along those lines."

The last one I did was an outdoor scene, a river flowing with deer drinking and a family of black bears grabbing fish from it. It was inspired by the view outside my front door, so coming up with another one should be easy enough.

"Same wood, sir?"

He shakes his head and exhales heavily. "Been here for two months now.

You can call me Nash. Local pine will work." He makes a frustrated growl-ing noise, then shifts his gaze to a few men unloading supplies from his truck. "Cody!"

His son snaps to attention at the booming of his father's voice. "What's up?" He takes in his dad and gives me a chin lift that I return.

I'd never tell them, but Nash and Cody Jennings are the closest people I have in my life. They helped me out when I had nothing, and although it doesn't seem like much, this little powwow is considered a pretty deep con-versation for us.

"I need you to take a guy to the Wilson homestead and get as much of the wood you can fill in your truck."

Cody pulls off his work gloves and shoves them into his back pocket. "Wilson place? Why?"

"Hippies from the valley. They want as much repurposed woodwork as we can provide. Wilson property is owned by the bank; they said we could take what we want since they're gonna level it all anyway." Nash pulls the blueprint and rolls it up.

"Can't take my truck." He throws a thumb over his shoulder. "They're unloading the siding and have to go back for more."

"Take Lucas and his truck. See what you can salvage." His tone implies this is not a suggestion.

"Sure thing." Cody sets his black eyes on mine, so different from his fa-ther's, which makes me wonder what his mother looks like. From the little I've picked up in the two months I've lived here, she's not part of either of their lives anymore. "You ready?"

I pull out my keys and we move to my navy blue pickup. It's an older model, nothing fancy, but it's full-sized and built for hauling.

Luckily the Wilson homestead isn't far, so I won't be forced to talk much. Between Nash and Cody, the younger seems to be the most talkative of the two. Although he gave up asking me about anything personal after only a few days of knowing him.

It's better that way.

Too much sharing would lead to stories of the past.

Stories would lead to feelings.

Can't hold back the blackouts unless I stay numb.

SHYANN

Ain't this a bitch.

Sitting outside the old double-wide portable office with the Jennings Contractors sign slapped on the side, my stomach ties in knots. It's not facing off with one of Payson's most respected citizens, which isn't saying much for a town with a population of 15,000, and it's not my dad's disappointment I'm nervous about either. It's the satisfaction I'll be giving him once he sees he was right.

"Good luck makin' it out there on your own, Shy. You don't belong out there. You belong here in town close to your momma."

"Pretty sure she doesn't give a crap where I go, Dad, seein' as she's dead. Besides, she left home when she was my age, found you. Don't be a hypocrite."

I cringe at the memory of our last conversation the morning I left town, his glare practically shoving me out the door along with the parting words that sliced through my gut.

"You're nothing like your momma."

He's right.

She was strong, resilient, walked away from her childhood home and never looked back.

I came crawling back just as he always said I would.

"Fuck!" I slam my open palms against the steering wheel. "Ouch!" Gasping in pain, I shake out the nerve sting, willing myself to calm down.

Almost two hours in the truck that included a very long lunch break at an old café just outside of town and I still haven't perfected my speech, which I managed to put together in my head without even a sliver of suck-up to the Great Nash Jennings.

"I'm back, but it's only temporary. I'd love a place to stay while I get back on my feet. I'll find a job, save some money, and then I'll be out of your hair."

He'll have to torture me to get me to beg or admit I screwed up. He can't know how close I was to making it big only to make an even bigger ass out of myself on live television.

A tiny part of me whispers that maybe he already knows. He wouldn't get my old news channel here in Payson, but he'd get the Phoenix feed. Shit, how many people in town saw me make a complete fool out of myself and will know when they see me that I've been fired?

I swing out of the truck and go to wait inside. Chances are the old man forgot to lock the door.

The familiar feeling of rocks and dried pine needles crunch beneath my feet as I drag myself up the steps. A gust of crisp, dry mountain air whirls through the tall trees and I can't deny the comfort I find in it.

Reminds me of when my mom would walk me through the forest and tell me old Navajo stories about the tricky coyote who slayed a giant or the boy who became a god. She always made it easy to believe I was capable of becoming so much more than a small girl in a small town.

I reach for the door handle, but it's locked. I'm about to drop down on the steps and wait when the roar of a truck engine and spinning of tires in dirt sends my stomach plummeting.

Pulling together every bit of pride I have left, which isn't much, I square my shoulders and watch my dad's truck jerk to a halt.

The engine cuts off and my dad studies my truck in confusion. He must see me move from the corner of his eye, because his glare snaps to mine. I hold up one hand, maybe a wave, maybe an alien "I come in peace" greeting, which would make sense judging by the scrutiny of his cold stare.

His eyebrows drop low and he opens the door, swinging out his long, denim-clad legs tipped with massive steel-toe work boots. He leans back against his truck, arms crossed over his chest.

No welcome-home smile, arms open in acceptance? No, in typical mountain-man style, Nash Jennings is not going down without a fight. Shit.

I drop heavy footsteps down the stairs. "Hey, Dad."

"Shy. Everything okay?" As hard as he is, I detect the edge of worry in his voice.

My dad never has responded well to subtlety, and I agree it's a waste of time. "Lost my job."

He remains stoic, not giving away an ounce of what he's feeling. "This visit, it temporary?" Translation: *How long till you take off running again?*

I close a few feet of distance between us but stay at arm's length. I hope he sees it as me being brave, standing on my own, rather than the buffer zone I need to keep from throwing myself at his mercy.

Fact is, I'm desperate. And, hell, I miss having someone to lean on. Trevor was okay, but it's hard to lean on a man who's more concerned about me crinkling his *New York Times*.

"I don't know. I'm broke, don't have anywhere else to go." I shrug one shoulder and dig the toe of my white Ked into the dirt. "Thought maybe you'd give me a place to stay while I get on my feet." So much for my tough-girl speech. One look from my old man and I'm back to being sixteen years old.

His glare tightens, making his pale blue eyes even more daunting. "Then what?"

"Try to get back into broadcasting, I guess. If I can find someone who'll hire me."

He scratches his jaw and the corner of his lip curls into a half-smile. "Who'd you piss off, Shy?"

Only my dad would find my highly sensitive temper funny. "Everyone, basically."

"Shit, can't say I'm surprised." He dips his chin and rubs the back of his neck, but I can see the curl of his lips is still there.

"Gee. Thanks, Dad." Salt in the wound, the old Jennings way. Man up or shut up.

A small chuckle rumbles in his chest before he pulls it together and pierces me with a glare. "What the hell are you wearin'?"

I peek down at my khaki capris complete with cuffs that hit me midcalf and the mint-green polo shirt that makes me hungry for butter mints. "Only thing I got."

"Haven't touched your room since you left. All your clothes are still there." He motions to my feet. "Don't wanna get your purdy shoes dirty slummin' out here with the rednecks."

Back for all of three minutes and he's already picking a fight. I hold on to the growl and string of powerful words that itch for release and submit with a nod.

"The house is unlocked. Supper's at seven." He pushes off the truck and moves past me.

That was fairly painless. No dragging me back through the night I left for college, reminding me of all the shitty and unforgiveable things I said, no throwing in my face all the promises I'd made to cut him out of my life completely. Nothing.

"That's it?"

He stops and peers over his shoulder. "You're my daughter, aren't you?"

I don't answer since I obviously am.

"What kind of man turns away his daughter?"

My eyes flood with heat and if I were the crying type I'd probably shed a tear. But I'm not.

"Besides...knew you'd be back," he mumbles as he moves to the door.

My spine snaps straight and an uncontrollable, and rather pathetic, growl gargles in my throat. My dad's answering chuckle works to further infuriate me.

"G'on now. Go unload. We'll talk more tonight." The door to his office slams behind him and I stomp my foot so hard pain shoots up my leg.

Arrogant, hardheaded, bossy...ugh!

I march back to my car, but rather than follow Dad's orders, I drive around for another hour exercising my free will. Yeah, it's a waste of gas. It's also irresponsible because I have no money, but I do it all smiling.

Everyone else in this town might bend to the will of Nash Jennings. Not me.

THREE

LUCAS

I run my fingertips along the grain of the near hundred-year-old wood. The rich, dark patina speaks of seasons upon seasons of life. Snow, rain, and sun have all contributed to the dense color that will soon lend its personality to a modern home.

This old pine was probably harvested from the acres of wooded land surrounding this homestead. On three acres there are five different structures: the main house, which is gone except for the old stone fireplace, stands like a tombstone and four small structures probably housed the Wilson's adult children.

Cody presses both hands against the exterior wall of one of the smaller cabins and it creaks, then sways. "Shouldn't be too hard to knock down."

I nod and slide my gloved hand over the wood and rusted nails. "Shame to take it, though."

"Banks just gonna sell this land. We're doin' them a favor." He runs the back of his hand across his forehead, pushing his sweat-soaked black hair off his face. "If we don't take it, it'll end up in some junkyard. 'Least we take it we reuse it."

I shrug and wedge the flat end of a crowbar between two pieces of wood. The wood slats have aged dark, but it's the posts behind them I'm interested in. Leveraging with my weight, the old nails give way easily and I start a pile of salvageable wood. Cody does the same, throwing out pieces that are fragile and cracked. We fall into silence working side by side until our shirts are wet and our forearms and necks are pink and sting from the sun.

Once there's nothing left to the structure, I motion to a small pile of rocks that is all that's left of the cabin. "Not much more we can get out of this one."

"Thank fuck. It's hot as hell out here." He tosses his crowbar and I load the first of a healthy pile of salvage wood into the back of the pickup. "Watch your back." His eyes grow wide in mock fear. "Old Man Wilson might be lurking."

I strong-arm a large pile of wood into the truck carefully to avoid splinters the size of pencils. "I thought you said the bank owned it?"

He chuckles and fires a few long planks into the truck bed, tossing up dirt. "I'm talking about the dead one." He wiggles his gloved fingers and makes a haunted *Ooooo* sound before laughing.

"You mean a ghost?" I attempt to inflect humor into my voice and fail.

"Ahh…that's right. You've only been here for a couple months. You're not familiar with Payson's history." He tosses in an armful of planks and leans against the tailgate, breathing hard. "Wilson family. One of the first homesteaders in town, back in 1880 or some shit."

I listen, but just barely, preoccupied with separating and loading wood.

"Old man Wilson was hard on the boys, used a horse whip on 'em, or so rumor has it."

My head buzzes and vision blurs.

"One night they banned together, busted into their parents' bedroom while they were sleeping." He motions to the stone chimney of the main house. "Right over there, man. Those boys slit their father's throat."

I brace myself against the truck. Cody doesn't seem to notice, or he just assumes I'm exhausted. Maybe that's all it is, that combined with the heat.

"In the man's own bed. Got their payback by watching him bleed out all over their own mother."

My eyes focus on the wood, studying every intricate curve of its grain to keep in the present and fight off the gray haze edging my vision. I blink and wipe sweat from my eyes, hoping it's the cause of my blurry view.

Not a blackout. Please, do not black out.

"They buried the man's body somewhere on their land. When people started to figure things out, family said he'd been attacked by a mountain lion. Their mom carried that to her grave, never would give her sons up." He chuckles and the sound of his boots crunching against dirt cuts through my near-blackout fog. "Story goes, the sound of their mother's screams can still be heard in the night."

I cringe. The tailgate slams shut.

Gunfire.

Blackness flickers before my eyes.

"Whoa, dude, you okay?"

I blink back the darkness to find Cody, his hands on my shoulders and his concerned expression less than a foot from my face.

I blacked out. But only for a second.

"I'm fine, yeah." I step back and dip my chin to wipe my sweaty face on my shoulder. "Hot. That's all."

"Freaky-ass shit, man." His gaze moves over my face. "Your eyes, they…" He motions to my eyes. "Your face got all serious and your eyes…" He grins and starts laughing. "Oh, I get it!" He shoves me and shakes his head. "Real funny, asshole."

"Ha, yeah. I was just messin' around." I reach into the cab of the truck to grab my water. My pulse pounds in my neck and I slow my breathing.

That was close. Way too close. Luckily this one was short enough to explain away. If I had a real blackout in front of Cody, he'd know my secret. I can't afford to get too close and let my guard down. I slipped up. That can't happen again. If I screw this up and they find out who I am, what I've done, I'll never be able to stay here.

He comes around to the passenger side and hops in, still chuckling. "Remind me to never play ghost stories with you, freaky bastard."

Freaky bastard. If he only knew how true that is.

SHYANN

God, this house is oppressive.

My feet are planted in the doorway of my old room. Everything seems so small. I'd think the most successful homebuilder in town would build himself a bigger house. I step inside to sit on my bed as guilt rushes to the surface and threatens to suffocate me worse than the tiny bedroom I grew up in.

My dad would never leave this place. It's the first and only home he lived in with my mom. They built it after they got married, raised my brother and me in it, and my mom breathed her last breath just two doors down from where I'm sitting.

I drop back on the twin bed, bashing my head against the log wall. "Ow, son of a…" I rub my pounding skull and take in the white eyelet curtains and pink wicker furniture. "And suddenly I'm ten again."

Boxes line one side of the room, mostly knock-off designer clothes that'll do me no good up here. Just as the dust in this room clouds my vision, so, too, does exhaustion fog my mind as the reality of my situation presses down on me.

I'm a twenty-three-year-old woman living with her dad because I couldn't do my job. No matter how many times I've checked my phone for the we-made-a-mistake-firing-you e-mail from the network, it never comes.

Shit, that reminds me. I should message Trevor and let him know I'm here. I dig into my back pocket and pull out my phone, hit the text icon, and groan.

"No service. Shocker." I could call him from my dad's landline, but I was hoping to avoid a lengthy conversation that would only serve to remind me how far I'd fallen.

I toss the high-tech, now-useless piece of crap to my bedside table, scrunch my pillow under my head, and pray for sleep to take me. Maybe when I wake I'll realize this is all just some bad dream and I didn't fuck up my entire future and land right back where I started.

With nothing.

***

"Shy."

The booming voice pierces the thick solitude of sleep.

"Hmm." I nuzzle deeper into my pillow.

"Hungry?" There's a concern in his voice that I instantly recognize. "Food's ready."

My eyes snap open.

Ahh, yes. I'm home. Crap.

As my mind comes to, so does my belly. I roll to my back and stretch. "I'm up."

"Come on, it's getting cold." The thump of his boots against the hard-wood floor retreats down the hallway.

"So much for waking from this nightmare." I yawn and stretch again, noticing the sun that was outside the window when I nodded off is now dipped below the tree line, turning the sky vibrant shades of pinks and purples.

I shuffle to the kitchen, where I'm hit with the mouthwatering scent of my dad grilling. If there's one thing my dad does well, outside of building beautiful homes, it's cooking meat over fire.

He plates a steak the size of my head next to a loaded baked potato with all the grace of a Neanderthal.

"Smells good." I grab a glass and fill it with water from the sink, then sit at the table in the spot I'd occupied as a little girl. The seat at the end where my mother used to sit has a light coating of dust, whereas my seat along with my brother's across from me seems to be used from time to time.

He drops the plate in front of me. "Eat up."

I stare wide-eyed at the meal that's big enough to feed a family and my stomach rumbles. "I'll do my best."

He sits in his seat with a plate and a cold beer in front of him, but his sterling-blue eyes are fixed on me. "You're skinny." His chin dips to my plate.

I roll my eyes and grab a fork. "You say skinny like it's a bad thing."

"Winter'll eat you alive up here." He shoves a bite of potato that's drip-ping in cheddar cheese and bacon into his mouth.

"Not planning on sticking around till winter." As soon as the words leave my mouth, I wish I could suck them back in. I don't want to fight with my dad, but he always manages to bring out my argumentative side.

His jaw ticks. "Either way, need to put some meat on your bones." The words filter through a cheekful of food.

It's pointless to explain that I'm an on-air personality and appearances mean everything. One, because my dad couldn't give a shit. Two, because I'm no longer anything but a mountain man's daughter who is currently eating steak that tastes a lot like crow.

We eat in silence and I shovel bites into my mouth, chew, and swallow all while scanning the cramped room in search of some semblance of life. Instead, everywhere I look I see death. Momma hunched over the dinner table in her wheelchair, her spine protruding beneath her thin nightgown while strings of drool soak her chest. My dad sitting exactly where he is now, his head in one hand and a mostly empty bottle of bourbon in the other while my momma sat, staring at nothing, and her mind understood everything.

I force myself to banish those memories in favor of good ones. My brother and I racing around my mom's legs, hiding in her apron while she made fried bread and the best refried beans I'd ever tasted. Just as the scent of her Native American cooking hung in the air, so did the love she had for her family. She was the thread that held us together, and once she was gone, we all fell apart. My dad retreated into his work, my brother retreated into himself, and I couldn't get away from it all fast enough.

Couldn't get out of this *house* fast enough.

Because as much as I love her, the memories of her last days are all that seem to remain here. Just a few waking hours in this house and my skin is practically crawling for me to escape.

"Wanna tell me what happened?"

"Not really." I shovel a bite into my mouth, hoping he doesn't press.

"Saw the newscast, Shy." He shrugs like it's no big deal. That's because they cut the feed before I broke Leaf's eye. "You froze. Happens. Don't see what it's worth firing you for."

Pushing food around my plate, I avoid his eyes. "Yeah, well…personal feelings don't mix with news reporting. I blew it."

The room falls silent except for the sounds of our eating. I study the kitchen, trying to avoid seeing what might be disappointment on his face.

The clank of his fork on his plate calls my attention from a row of colorful kachina dolls that line the windowsill above the sink. "You got a plan?"

I nod. "I'll call some old friends, see if any of them know of someplace that's hiring."

He laughs, but it's far from the ha-ha funny kind. "Never was good enough for you," he mumbles.

Well that didn't take long.

I wipe my mouth and take a sip of water, then lean back, clearing my throat. "Suppose I should be impressed that it took you all of five minutes to bring that shit up."

"Mouth."

"I'm twenty-three years old. My mouth and how I use it are no longer your business."

"In my house, you bet your ass it is."

I cross my arms over my chest, my blood firing with irritation. "Oh, so *ass* is okay, yeah? Mind passing me along the list of approved curse words so I can keep from offending your delicate sensitivities during my short stay here?"

He growls and drops his chin, Nash Jennings's universal body language for "this conversation is over." His chest expands with a deep breath, causing me a twinge of regret.

Hell, all we've ever done is fight. Mom used to say it was because we were so much alike, which would just infuriate us both and we'd fight more.

He sits back, breathes deep, and shovels a heaping forkful of baked potato into his mouth, chews, and swallows. "Talk to the girls but know your job at Jennings is always open."

"Thanks. I…" I'd rather slap myself in the face until I pass out. "We'll see."

He nods and tosses his napkin onto the table, then pushes out his seat enough to prop a heavy-booted foot on one knee. "Office could use you back. Shit's gone to shit since you left."

My jaw drops at his blatant cussing, but he doesn't respond to my shock. Typical.

"I've sent out close to fifty résumés. Might get a bite here soon." Probably not, but he doesn't need to know that. I sent my résumé to every broadcasting station in the country that's hiring and haven't heard a word in response yet.

He tilts his head. "Been gone for five years, Shy. How long do we get you before you take off again?"

"I don't know, but I don't plan on living *here* long if that's what you're asking."

His expression is impassive, but his eyes register the blow and reflect pain.

"Dad, it's nothing personal." That's a lie. It's always been personal. *You're nothing like your momma.* "I could crash with Cody."

"He's living in a trailer down by Kohls Ranch."

Damn, that won't work. I love my brother, but I'm not cramming into a trailer and sleeping on a couch.

That leaves one other option. I hate bringing it up. Dad hasn't been rational about it since momma died, but I have to try.

My teeth run along my top lip as nerves prick my gut. I shrug and pick at the worn edge of the rustic kitchen table. "What about the river house?"

I expect the air between us to string tight with tension, to feel the power of his glare on the top of my head like a physical touch, but instead there's nothing.

I peek up to find his expression blank.

The river house was my mom and dad's dream cottage. They'd started building it together a few years before mom got sick: the plan to move down there once my brother and I were out of the house. Unfortunately, the construction was halted when she lost the ability to use her hands, walk, and eventually became paralyzed. Since then my dad has all but pretended the place doesn't exist. Last I checked, it wasn't totally livable yet, but it has walls, running water, and electricity, and it's not crawling with memories of her death.

"I know all the finishing work needs to be done, and it still needs some exterior work, but I can—"

"No."

I jerk back and glare. "Why not?"

"It needed work—"

"Right, and I said I'd do the work." He knows better than to treat me like some fragile flower that can't handle a little labor. Hell, he taught me how to frame when I was twelve. My face burns with anger.

"It's not that."

I push back from the table, the harsh scratch of the chair legs on the floor intensifying the moment. "What is it, then?"

"It's occupied."

My stomach drops and I blink slowly. "I'm sorry…what?"

"Got a guy livin' there now." The way he says it, so unapologetically, like he didn't deliver a verbal sucker punch, inflames me.

"How…?" No, he hasn't set foot in that place for eight years and now he's got a fucking tenant? "That's Mom's place." The high pitch of outrage tints my words.

"Shy…"

"No." I shake my head. "Kick the guy out. Evict him. I'm her daughter! If anyone deserves to live there, it's me."

"No can do, baby."

"I can't believe you'd do this." I slam my palms on the table. "That was Mom's dream house and you let a stranger move in? Was Cody okay with this?"

His failure to answer says all I need to know.

"I can't fuckin' believe this!" I push up from my chair, not sure where I'm going, only that I need to get the hell away before I say something I can't take back. A voice in my head whispers that he's not the only one who's irrational about that house, but I ignore it. "You had no right. How could you— No, forget it." I grab my keys off the counter and storm out the back door. "I don't care."

If he thinks I'm going to live here with the memory of my mom's death hanging off the walls like décor, he's fucking crazy. I'd rather sleep in the dirt.

FOUR

LUCAS

Nothing is as peaceful as a quiet day in the mountains when the only sound is the wind through the pine trees. It's one of the reasons I settled in Payson.

It's the absence of that silence, the complete opposite of serenity that has me stuck frozen outside Nash Jennings's home. I could hear it as I pulled up the dirt drive, and the sound has me nearly paralyzed in fear.

The angry and shrieking voice of a woman.

A woman.

I haven't known Cody and Nash for that long, but not once have I heard of my boss having a woman. Not that he'd talk about it if he did; he doesn't strike me as the type to share the details of his personal life.

Cody leans forward in his seat and registers the tan-colored truck parked outside the house. "Oh shit…" He grins wide, humor in his voice. "She's back."

I swing my gaze between the house and Cody. "You okay with me droppin' you off?"

He tilts his head toward me. "You kidding? I wouldn't miss this for anything." He grabs his tool belt off the floor and pushes out of the truck. "Thanks for the ride."

Right as he's about to shut the door, the slamming of a different door echoes from the rustic old house.

"I don't care!"

A woman, or rather a girl, as she looks to be more my age than Nash's, stomps across the gravel toward the truck. She trudges down the path, then stops with a yelp and cradles her bare foot. She hops on one leg, cussing like I've never heard a woman cuss, then drops to her butt. Her sleek black hair falls over her face as she inspects her wounded heel.

"You're clumsy as hell, you know that, right?" Cody yells at the girl, and her eyes dart to him. Illuminated by my headlights, I watch her hateful expression instantly soften.

I suck in a breath when I catch the full force of her face. Maybe it's the dimming light of sunset, but her black hair and olive skin are an intense contrast to the palest blue eyes I've ever seen. I turn to Cody to avoid the intensity of her. The yelling, anger, and the fact that she's female send sirens of retreat through my central nervous system. She's overpowering.

"Oh, thanks a lot for the help, you piece of shit!" Although her words are harsh, they're laced with affection, which is confusing.

Cody must pick up on it, too, because he barks out in laughter. "I'm coming, you big wuss." He finally shuts the door to my truck and leans into the open window. "Come on, I'll introduce you to the delicate angel over there."

"No, I better—"

"Take your time! My bloodstream's flooding with tetanus, but you go ahead and have a chat." She throws up one hand. "I'll wait...*fucker*." She mumbles the last word and yet manages to still make it sound like a powerful curse.

He shakes his head but thankfully lets me off the hook. "Thanks for the ride. I'll see you tomorrow."

He makes his way toward the girl and says something I can't hear but it makes her smile. Who is she to him? Cousin, girlfriend, sister?

Not my business.

I throw the truck into reverse and back out of the drive, but not before looking up one more time to see those pale eyes staring right through me.

***

Five minutes down the road from the Jennings's house is my refuge. Hidden deep within the trees at the end of a single-lane dirt road is the little A-frame house I've managed to secure as home for the last seven weeks.

Its front porch pushes right up to a creek that turns into a river during the rainy season, or so I've heard. It's functional; the only exceptional thing about the place is the location, but it's better than the campsite I was at with nothing but a sleeping bag to keep me warm, a tarp to keep me dry, and a lake to bathe in. But even camping was a luxury compared to some of the places I lived before. At least the outdoors doesn't come with bars, locks, or psychopathic roommates.

I park my pickup under the juniper tree by the back door and hop out, feeling the tightness in my muscles that always accompany a hard day's labor. I grab a box of scrap that was left over from the last house we built. A few pieces of random, mismatched electrical plates, hardware, and doorknobs, all given to me by our foreman.

The trickle of the creek and wheezing of a soft wind through the trees calms my nerves and I'm reminded that I'm alone. Safe.

Halfway up the stairs, I sense movement from beneath the porch. I set down the box and lean around the railing but it's too dark to see anything. Chances are it's a raccoon or a possum. A high-pitched whine filters through the dark. Whatever is down there needs help.

I jog back to the truck and grab a flashlight and shine it under the porch to see a set of sad brown eyes staring back at me. It's a dog. All the way out here? His fur is dark, but it looks like there are some spots that might've been white once upon a time.

"Hey, puppy. It's okay." I reach out, but the animal recoils as if my hand is a weapon. "I won't hurt you." I put down the flashlight but keep the beam shining in his general direction, and rest my elbows on my knees. "Come here, you're okay."

He whimpers and readjusts to lying down, claiming his spot and not budging.

"You hungry?"

Another sad whine, as if he can actually understand what I'm saying. I take all four porch steps in one stride and let myself into the house, turning on the single bulb that hangs in the kitchen, and pop open the fridge. Mayo, mustard, peanut butter…no. I grab a package of hot dogs and head back down to peer beneath the deck.

Ripping off an end, I squat and hold out the meat. He stares at my hand but doesn't move. I toss the piece back and he sniffs it a couple times before swallowing it in one bite. "Yeah, you're hungry."

I rip off another piece and strings of slobber drip from his jowls. It's as if tasting food ignited his hunger even more, a feeling I can relate to. One after another, I toss pieces and he inhales each until he's consumed five hot dogs, all of what was left in the package.

"Full, Buddy? Come here." I pat my thighs and he retreats deeper into the shadows.

The weather is nice enough. He should be fine for the night as well as be protected from larger animals under the porch. I've got too much work to do tonight to try to coax him out.

If there's one thing I know about being scared, it's that trust isn't given out freely, and the dark is your best friend.

I head back inside and take a quick shower, bringing my clothes in with me to wash them and hang them to dry. The room I sleep in is mostly empty except for a bare mattress one of the guys at work gave me. With some sheets and a pillow I got from a garage sale, and my sleeping bag as a blanket, it's one of the most comfortable places I've ever slept, and that has little to do with the bed.

Pulling on a pair of sweatpants, I drag my feet against the cold hardwood floor into the kitchen where I've laid out a jar of peanut butter and half a loaf of bread.

Expiration on the jar is two years from now.

Bread is fresh, free of mold.

I check the food one more time. Again. And once more before I make myself two peanut butter sandwiches.

"It's good. It's safe." I say the words aloud to myself and it helps.

Tentatively I take the first bite, rolling it around in my mouth to test the flavor before swallowing. It's been ten years since I was forced to eat the food given to me, and even still the hazy memories of violent food poisoning coupled with laughter haunt my every meal. I shove down the sandwiches with no enjoyment, meeting the base need quickly before I can talk myself out of it, then clean up and move to the single piece of furniture in the house.

A small table and chair I made from scrap wood after the first build I worked on with Jennings. It's pieced together by two-by-fours in random lengths but sanded smooth and stained to the color of maple syrup. The chair is much of the same, and although the wood is unforgiving and aches my back, the pride in what I've created makes it seem like goose down.

I crank open the casement windows and note the scent of pine and fresh dirt. So much better than the sterile, recycled air I was breathing for most of my life. At least, the most I remember.

I grab my sketchbook and flip open to a blank page. Pencil in hand, I toy with ideas for the mantelpiece but find focus difficult, as my thoughts are on today. That episode with Cody was too close. Since the morning I woke up here, I've only had a few minor blackouts that lasted just hours, but thankfully I've come back to consciousness here in the cabin every time. Safe.

But the story of the Wilson family homestead triggered the blackness. I felt the veil tickling the edges of my mind, threatening to fall. I can't get so comfortable that I forget to protect myself. If I blacked out in front of Cody, he'd probably tell his dad and I could lose my job. Or worse, Cody would see a side of me that even I know very little about.

If I go black, I can't be responsible for what happens and I'll be back to living my life on the run.

FIVE

SHYANN

"Miss Shyann Blue Jennings, I cannot believe my eyes!" Dorothy from the 87 Café, aptly named for its placement right on I-87 that runs through Payson, presses her palm against her robust stained-apron-covered chest, feigning shock. Chances are she knew I was back in town the second my front tires crossed Main Street.

She's been living in Payson since she was a little girl and I'd swear her roots run so deep under this town she feels the earth shift when someone new steps into it. And once they do, she's the bullhorn that spreads the good news and she doesn't gossip the modern way with text messages and social media. No, she's old school. She's all about the face-to-face gab session, which I swear is the only reason she even works in the town's busiest restaurant that doubles as Payson's social hub.

Smacked right in the middle of town, the 87 Café isn't your typical city diner. Trading in chrome and red pleather seating for wood and faux cowhide, old horseshoes nailed to the wall for decoration, and a signed head shot of Garth Brooks displayed proudly at the entrance. With a daily special of BBQ whatever, the place is a cowboy's paradise. I've barely made it through the front door and my mouth is watering from the scent of smoked meat and sweet sauce, and it's not even nine o'clock in the morning.

"Hey, Dorothy— Oh!"

Her arms wrap around me in a tight hug and her plump little body seems to have filled out a little more since I last saw her. She pulls back and studies my face, her smile turning sad and her dusty brown eyes shiny. "You look so much like your momma." She pulls me back in with such force it momentarily knocks the air from my lungs.

"Good to see you too." I pat her back, hoping she gets the hint to release me.

After a few seconds, she does. "Come on." She jerks her head to the counter that's sprinkled with a few people. I feel their eyes on me, but I keep mine on Dorothy as I drop down on a stool at the far end. She pours me a cup of coffee without asking. "What brings you to town?" She props a hip on the counter. "And what in God's name are you wearing?"

I rip open a few sugar packets, grinning. "It's Dolce and Gabbana." Or Dolce Gambino, but she doesn't need to know that.

"Dole-say what?" Her gaze roams my midnight-blue silk blouse. Trevor always loved this top. Said on-screen it really brought out my eyes. "Nash see you in that getup?"

"I'm a flatlander now, Dorothy." I busy myself by stirring my coffee, a little nervous to acknowledge the flash of disappointment in the woman's eyes. "Got a college degree, a real job...er *had* a real job."

Her drawn-on brows drop low over her eyes and she leans in. "Heard 'bout that. Shame they let you go."

Of course she did—the woman smells gossip like a wine taster does wine, shoving her nose right in it. *Mmm...smells fresh with an aroma of as-*

sumptions and hints of half-truths, but it'll make a good story, so let's fill up the glasses and share.

I take a sip of coffee and straighten my shoulders. "Thanks, it was p-probably time to m-move on anyway. Figure I'd come home for a bit, um…r-regroup." I rein in my stutter. No use giving her the real story littered with pathetic weakness I don't need spread around town.

Her face breaks into a smile so big it deepens all her wrinkles. "That's wonderful. I know your daddy must miss you. Be nice to have y'all together working the family business."

I clear my throat and shake my head. "I don't think Jennings is the best place for me."

"Don't be silly. It's the perfect place for you; it has your name all over it. Literally." She laughs and nods to an older man a few stools down when he flags her for a coffee refill. She fills his cup and returns to me, still grinning.

"I was hoping to, ya know, expand my résumé."

She uses the pencil stabbed behind her ear to scratch her scalp, which is hidden beneath a helmet of graying brown hair. "Expand your…résumé?"

"Yeah, I thought you'd probably know if anyone in town is hiring."

She turns and grabs a few plates heaping with eggs and a variety of breakfast meat, then drops them to a man with his nose buried in a newspaper and the man closest to me.

"I don't understand."

She wouldn't. I shrug. "Are Deirdre and Sam still in town?" I cringe at her sharp look. I haven't spoken to my two childhood best friends since before I left. I shouldn't be surprised that Dorothy knows that. "College was busy and I…I just lost touch, ya know?"

She doesn't respond to my lame excuse, her silence speaking volumes of displeasure, then turns to a steaming bowl the cook just put up in the window and places it in front of me.

"Deirdre moved to the valley…"

Oatmeal with a scoop of brown sugar, raisins, and a side of cream. She remembered.

"Thank you."

"…got married and is pregnant with her second kid."

I blink, shocked. "Wow, didn't realize she was in a such a hurry."

"How long has it been since you were last here?" She's asking, but she knows. She just wants to hear me say it.

"Five years."

She lifts a brow. "What else would she do?"

My inner feminist clenches her fists. "Um…I don't know, go to college."

"Not everyone is itchin' to run away from their past, Shy."

My spoon drops hard against the bowl of oatmeal. "That's not what I've been d-d-doing." I slam my mouth shut to avoid spewing the lies that threaten to burst free.

Her eyes go soft and she nods. "No one would blame you if you were. God knows after your mom—"

"What about Sam?"

She allows my subject change and blows out a long breath. "Sam's been working at Pistol Pete's. Still single, although she's stickin' like glue to Dustin Miller…" Her mouth twists as if she just sucked on a lemon. "If you know what I mean."

"He's like Payson royalty. I'm not surprised."

Dustin's family owns the feed shop here in town. We dated in high school and I had a feeling he and Sam were into each other. I wonder if they even waited for my back tires to cross the county line before hooking up.

"He's doing well." She makes a clicking sound with her mouth. "Got promoted after his grandfather passed away two summers ago."

"Impressive." Born into a family business and taking over the reins.

Takes absolutely zero skill or motivation. *And yet* I'm *the loser for leaving town to get an education.* "I need to get ahold of Sam."

"She works the early shift during the week. They open at eight in the morning, so you should be able to find her over there, although…not sure why you'd bother looking for a job when you got familial ties to the most successful business in town, but that ain't my concern."

I fight the urge to roll my eyes. Everything in this town is her concern.

I spoon a few bites of warm oatmeal into my mouth, and the creamy sweetness reminds me of my childhood, coming here on Sundays with my family. I sink into the memory and can almost smell my momma's lavender-scented lotion.

Dorothy and I small talk about the past while I eat enough oatmeal to be polite, even though memories of my mom fill my stomach. I change the subject to the Payson job market. It seems my options for work are the local bar or mucking stalls at the local ranches. I consider Pistol Pete's. It's a bar, yeah, but it also hosts live bands that come up from Phoenix to play on the weekends and draws a pretty good crowd. Not the best of opportunities, but I need to keep my eyes on the goal. Save up enough money to move to the valley, get myself set up in an apartment with enough cash to live on while I beg my way back into broadcasting.

My phone vibrates in my pocket and practically sends me out of my seat. I fish it out and look to see Trevor's name on the caller ID.

"Shit." I hit ACCEPT and press the phone to my ear. "Hey, sorry I didn't call you last night. I don't get service out at my dad's place."

"Hey, honey. No biggie. Figured you'd be getting all caught up with the local hillbillies." He chuckles. "What did you guys do last night? Cow tipping?"

What a dick. I mean, I make fun of Payson people, but I'm allowed to. They're *my* people.

"Nah, just…" I dip my head and spot Dorothy across the diner, far enough away that she can't hear me. "Got in a fight with my dad—"

"Did you hear about the redneck who got married?"

"What?"

"Yeah, he took his wife to the honeymoon suite, found out she was a virgin, so he kicked her out and had the wedding annulled."

"Trevor—"

"Said, 'If you're not good enough for your own family, you're not good enough for me.'" He cackles obnoxiously.

I pull the phone away from my ear. "Funny."

"Right?" He sniffs and I'd swear he was wiping tears from his eyes. "You figure out when you're coming back?"

"The station gonna offer me my job back?" Not that it paid that much, but that wasn't the point. It was the opportunity to make a name for myself, to move on to a bigger and better market.

"Not likely. But still, I miss you. I mean, everyone at the station is giving me the cold shoulder since you left, like I had a say in your being let go, ya know?"

Typical Trevor only cares about how the end of *my* career affects him.

The bell over the door rings and there's movement to my right as a man takes the stool next to me. His baseball cap is pulled low over his eyes, but he tilts his head and peeks in my direction. He's young, my age, but I don't recognize him as a local. I smile politely, then frown when he quickly turns away from me. My gaze slides down his arms to see his knuckles are pale from the grip he has on a thermos.

"Trevor, um…" I dip my chin, feeling uncomfortable with the present company and not wanting to be overheard. "I should go."

"The usual?" Dorothy calls to the man while making her way toward him.

"Yes, ma'am." He pulls the lid off the thermos and places it on the counter.

"You sure you don't want something to eat?" She grins and pours his coffee.

"No, thank you," he mumbles.

His voice is deep, making him sound manlier than his baseball hat and shy demeanor imply.

Dorothy sighs and returns her coffeepot to its warmer, then turns with her hands propped on her hips. "Boy, you never eat. What would your momma say about you skipping a healthy breakfast?"

His frame locks. "I...I don't have a momma—" The thermos drops to the floor between us, spilling its heated contents all the way down. We both jump up at the same time and I swoop down to grab the thermos, colliding with the guy's shoulder.

He jerks away, as if my touch burned like the coffee would. "I'm sorry. I'm—"

"No problem." I put the rustic metal container back on the tabletop and dry my hand on a napkin.

Dorothy scurries around the counter with a handful of towels. "Don't worry about this. Sometimes I think if we never spilled anything on the floor it'd never get cleaned."

The guy grabs the towels and bends to wipe up the mess. "I got it." He cleans the spilled liquid with a speediness I've never seen, as if he can't finish fast enough.

Dorothy refills his thermos, screws the top on, and wipes it down. She looks at him, her lips turned downward. "Sorry about that. I didn't know."

He nods and slides a few dollars onto the counter, but I don't miss how his eyes dart to mine before he quickly walks away.

He lost his mom too.

It's then I realize I still have my phone in my hand. I press it to my ear.

"...so the redneck said, 'Why would I do *your* cousin when I got my own?'"

"Trevor, listen, I'm sorry to cut you off, but I have to go."

"If you get bored, call me. And really, honey, come on down for a visit. I miss you and—"

"Yeah, sure, sounds good." I end the call and watch the guy who spilled his coffee move across the parking lot to a faded blue truck, the tires and wheel wells coated in dried mud. There's an invisible string that connects us, a kinship in the pain of losing a parent, and although I don't even know the guy's name, he feels like a friend.

"Can I grab you a refill?"

I turn to find Dorothy smiling with her hot pot of coffee in hand.

"No, I'm good." I pull my wallet from my fake Versace purse.

She places her hand over mine. "Don't even think about it. Breakfast is on me."

"You don't need to do that."

She nods and smiles sweetly. "I know, but I want to."

I hide a few bucks under my bowl when she's not looking. "Thank you."

She comes around and pulls me in for another hug. "Don't be a stranger, okay, Shy?"

I nod into her shoulder, feeling a little awkward. After all, it's been a long time since I've been hugged like this. It feels maternal and makes my chest ache.

Just another reason why I hate this town.

Everyone here makes me miss my mom.

***

"Well I'll be dipped in dog shit and crowned prom queen." Sam stares at me, her arms crossed under her chest, plumping her breasts up to her neck and accentuating her already extreme cleavage. Judging by the scowl twisting her pretty face, I wonder if I should've taken a day to think about how I'd approach my old friend rather than coming directly from the diner. It's pretty obvious she's not happy to see me.

Her heavily lined and painted eyes roam the length of my body and her thick lips purse with disgust. "What in the hell happened to you?"

Note to self: Dig out some old jeans and flannels from my closet and pray they still fit.

"Good to see you, Sam." We give each other a quick hug that lacks the warmth of friendship.

Her tiny cutoff denim shorts and cowboy boots make her look like every dime store cowboy's wet dream. She doesn't look to have changed much since high school except for maybe a little sluttier, which is saying something since she already took the prize for most likely to end up pregnant at eighteen.

"You look good."

She waves me off. "This place makes me dress like a whore for my shifts. If I were home, my shorts would be, like, a half inch longer." She winks. "You in town for the weekend visiting the boys?"

"Eh…I mean, yes and no. I'll be staying for a while."

She tilts her head, the mahogany corkscrew curl of one of her pigtails dipping down between her breasts. "No kidding, you're back?"

"It's temporary. But um…" I swing my gaze around the dark bar, the stench of booze-stained wood and dry roasted peanuts competing with Sam's pungent perfume. "I could use a job."

Her eyebrows pop. "Here?"

"What can I say? I'm desperate."

She chuckles low and throaty, like maybe those years of sneaking off to smoke cigarettes when we were sixteen became more of a habit for her. "City life made you bitchy."

I can't help but grin. "Huh, and here I thought I was just being direct."

She ties on a short apron and shakes her head. "I'll talk to Loreen and see what she says. We might be able to use you for backup on the weekends, but during the week we're already fighting for hours."

Shit. A few weekends here and there, it'll take me twenty years to save enough money to leave town. I drop my chin and ignore the tiny voice that whispers I'll end up at Jennings eventually.

"Hey, Sam?" I shift on my ballet flats, feeling the mud between my toes from the mix of dry earth and sweat. I really need to find some more appropriate clothes. "We should grab a drink sometime. I need to get caught up on what's been going on the last five years."

"Ha!" Her once-cocky expression turns almost sad. "Like you care." She shoves past me and walks away.

I don't really care, but I miss my friend. Hell, she's the only real friend I've ever had. "Sam."

She stops but doesn't turn around.

"Look…I'm sorry, okay? I…" Probably should've called or tried to reconnect. I don't blame her for blowing me off. "I am a bitch."

"I get off at four-thirty." And with that she disappears into the back.

Great. An awkward drink with an old friend who practically hates me. This should be fun.

Before heading back to my dad's house, I swing by the bank and withdraw the last of my money. It's not much, and I'll be lucky if it'll get me through the next week even with living at home. I'm almost out of gas, have no job, and my dad's just waiting for me to come back begging.

SIX

SHYANN

It's almost four-thirty when I pull into the single paved parking lot outside Pistol Pete's. After a quick pass through the tiny ten-car lot up front, I hit the dirt lot that's used for overflow.

Pretty busy for a Thursday. Must be the happy hour crowd, or it could be the larger part of the labor community that can't end the workday without a cold beer.

I find a spot at the far end and I'm grateful for the old cowboy boots I found in the back of my closet. They're a half-size too small, but the black leather is so worn and soft, slipping them on felt like coming home. But this time in a good way.

I check my face in the rearview mirror. Wanting to look somewhere between trying and not giving a shit, I'd put on a light layer of makeup, straight ironed the fuzz of humidity from my hair, and threw on a kickass pair of skinny jeans, pairing it with a tank top and an old flannel.

Just enough to look like the old me but with a big-city-girl flare.

The sun dips below the pine trees enough that although it's still light, it's muted and comfortable with a soft breeze that reminds me fall is on its way. A song about a lost lover and a pickup truck filters through the big barn doors as I kick up dirt through the lot. I push through the double doors and wait for my eyes to adjust to the dim light. Voices at all levels, from murmurs to obnoxious yelling, round out the audio-intrusion and the heavy scent of booze and dirty boots mix in a way only a country bar can.

I scan the room without lingering too long on faces, and don't see Sam, so I take seat at the bar.

A woman with unnaturally red hair that's shaved in a buzz cut on one side tosses a cocktail napkin in front of me. "What'll it be."

I lean in. "I'm looking for Sam. She still here?"

Her eyes narrow and she turns to the guy beside her who just showed up with two six-packs of Heineken under each arm. "Monty, you seen Sam?"

He squats to a cooler fridge and mumbles, "Out back having a smoke."

The woman nods, jingling the dozen little hoop earrings in her ear. Not your typical Paysonite. She doesn't look familiar either, so she's probably a transplant. "She'll be out in a minute."

"Thanks." My fingers drum against the bar, and feeling eyes on me, I keep my gaze forward. Maybe this was a bad idea. Last thing I want is an impromptu high school reunion.

"Sit at my bar, you drink." The fire of hair on her head matches her lipstick. "So?" She lifts one eyebrow and waits.

"Do you have Grey Goose?"

The guy stocking beer snorts.

She scowls and looks offended. "You know you're in a bar, right?"

"Grey Goose and water. With a lemon, please."

She studies me for a second, like she's trying to figure me out, then shakes her head and moves to make my drink.

The feeling like I'm being watched weighs heavy on my back. Another reason to hate small towns—there's no hiding from anyone. Ever.

My shoulders curl and I consider begging Sam to hit up the diner or a coffee shop, someplace other than—

"Shyann? Is that you?"

Fuck.

I pinch my eyes closed and take a deep breath, mustering up every ounce of fake-happy I have on reserve and turn to…

"Adam Bleeker. Wow, it's been a long time." The guy is twice the width he was in high school, but even with his face being a little rounder he still looks the same. I take in his plaid button-up and baggy jeans, realizing he also still dresses the same. Not a surprise. People who stay in town end up on permanent freeze frame.

Adam grins and leans against the bar next to me. "I haven't see you in—"

"Five years, yeah." Everyone in this damn town seems so intent on reminding me.

"Five years…wow." His brown eyes shine with friendliness. He always was a decent guy, the token nice guy who hung around a bunch of stuck-up jocks. "How the hell are you?"

The bartender comes back and drops a small glass of ice water down in front of me, then a shot glass filled with clear liquid, and a napkin topped with a mushy lemon slice. "There ya go."

"Oh…" I take it all in, thinking I underestimated this woman.

"It's—"

"Yeah, I get it." Grey Goose and water with a lemon wedge. "Clever."

A small curve hits her lips. "Thanks."

She walks away and I look over to see Adam's eyes darting between the drink and me. Oh for shit's sake. He's waiting.

I throw back the shot of vodka and my throat ignites.

"Never did back down from a challenge. Nice to see Shyann Jennings hasn't changed." He holds up his pint glass, half filled with beer, and I clink my water glass to it.

"Ooooh, sure she's changed…" Sam presses into the bar on my other side, an unfriendly smirk on her face. "If she were the same Shy, she'd have run away about ten minutes ago."

Bitch. Yeah, coming here was definitely a mistake.

"Unless…" A sick but gorgeous grin paints her already painted face. "Maybe there's a little bit of fighter in you yet."

"You gonna test a theory, Sam? If so, I'll need a couple more of these." I slide the empty shot glass to the bar and it gets the Strawberry Shortcake on Acid's attention.

"Another?"

I fix my eyes on Sam, waiting.

Mountain kids grew up kicking the shit out of each other. I'm too old for it, but I'd rather maintain my dignity than cower. Besides, blowing off a little of this tension I've been carrying around doesn't sound half bad.

I give myself a mental shake. I'm not a mountain kid anymore; I'm a fucking news reporter. Someday if I'm lucky I'll become a news anchor in a top three market. That means no bar fights!

She tilts her head and holds my glare for a few silent minutes before her expression softens. "I'll have the usual."

The bartender pulls out a light beer in an icy longneck and pops the top. "And you?"

Light beer is hanging out booze, not fighting fuel. It's Sam's olive branch.

Thank God.

"I'll have the same."

I exhale as the tension that surrounds us, along with a few gawkers who had drawn close, dissipates.

With a tilt of the bottle, I swing the watery beer and Sam drops onto the stool next to me. "See you've been reacquainted with Adam."

"He hasn't changed much."

She shakes her head and brings her bottle to her lips. "Not a bit. Probably still picks his boogers and eats 'em too."

I snort, stifling a full-blown belly laugh.

"Enjoying your stay in our fair city?" She swivels toward me, her long, tan legs crossed.

No, I hate it. "Sure. What's not to enjoy?" I tilt my beer to my lips.

Silence builds between us for seconds that stretch into a minute. I don't know what I was thinking would happen between us now that I'm back. We've been friends since we were kids. Don't think either of us missed a birthday party or sleepover. I don't have a single memory that doesn't involve Sam to some degree. Then I left her behind without a word.

Fuck, I wouldn't blame her if she hated me.

"Been by to see Dorothy I guess." She must know that's how I'd find her.

"I did."

"So I'm sure you know about me and Dustin."

"No big deal." I push away a tiny twist of betrayal. What did I expect? Dustin would stay single forever, pining for the one who got away?

She nods and presses her lips to the bottle.

"Sam, taking off like I did, it wasn't right. I should've kept in touch."

Her eyes narrow. "I don't do the hiring, Shy. You don't gotta kiss my ass."

I pick at the peeling label from my bottle, avoiding eye contact. "I'm not apologizing to get a job. I'm really sorry. After Mom died, I just…I don't do feelings. At least, not well."

She nods and turns back to her beer, almost as if she's giving me some privacy to put my tough girl mask back on. People in this town are rugged;

they don't cry in public and they certainly don't get mushy over beers and apologies.

Having said what I needed to say, I pull my shit together and drown the rest of my apology with a healthy swig of booze.

"Loreen!" she calls, and the bartender moves to us. "This is Shyann Jennings. She's looking for some work."

The redhead studies me and blinks. "Jennings...as in—"

"Yep." Sam chuckles and props her elbows on the bar.

"Why the hell do you need a job? You've got the richest last name in Payson."

Is there not a single person in this dirt hole who doesn't know who my dad is? "It's personal."

"I can respect that." She wipes her hands on a bar towel before shoving one corner of it into the waistband of her jeans. "You have experience in a bar?"

Not unless drinking in one counts, but how hard could it be? I contemplate saying, *No, but maybe a degree in journalism and media communications might suffice,* but I bite my tongue. "I'm a quick learner."

"Don't got much, but if you're willing to work a few weekends here and there, we'll see how you do, maybe add more hours as the ski season picks up."

Ski season. It's the one time of year where the streets of Payson look more like the streets of Beverly Hills. The dirt and pine trees become the backdrop to thousands of vacationers who line the city's pockets with enough cash in three months to sustain the nine-month slow season.

"That'd be great. Thanks." I'm lying. Maybe I should consider swallowing this putrid lump of pride. Taking back my job at Jennings is an easy in, good money, and it's something I already know how to do. One night every other weekend waiting tables won't pay me what I'd make at Jennings.

And as much as I don't want to admit it, I'm getting a little sick of the dull twisting feeling in my gut that resembles—but certainly cannot be—guilt at choosing the local bar over the family business. What would Momma think of me turning my back on Dad? I frown at the thought of her disappointment.

Sam leans into my shoulder and whispers, "It's a shit job, Shy."

"Then why do you work here?"

Her expression turns sad. "I have no choice. If I did, I'd take—"

"Hot damn, look what the big city dragged in. Is that…?"

I drop my chin and groan at the deep baritone of my ex-boyfriend Dustin's voice.

"Shy Jennings…" He pushes in next to Sam, throwing an arm over her shoulders. "I thought you were kiddin', babe."

She seems to shrivel a little.

"Dustin." I nod. "It's been a long time."

His thick blond hair is shorter than I remember, but no less gorgeous. Tan skin, dark brown eyes, and the height and girth that epitomizes the mountain man appeal, but I remember too well how all that pretty is only for show.

"I didn't notice." He twists his handsome face in confusion and looks at Sam. "How long has it been?"

The bartender hands him a short cocktail glass with what looks like straight bourbon on ice.

Sam mumbles, "Don't be a dick."

"What up, Dustin?" A dark-haired guy who looks like a lumberjack, with his dark beard, beanie, and flannel shirt, slaps Dustin on the back. "How'd you end up with— Oh my God!" The guy's wide eyes point at me.

Crap.

"Is that Shy Jennings?"

Another man overhears him and moves toward us.

My feet burn to run, to get the hell out of here and accept the job back at Jennings, probably what I should've just done in the first place.

I flash a weak wave. "Hey."

"Dude, I haven't seen you since…" His gaze flickers up to the ceiling and then his eyes snap to mine. "The graduation party at Dustin's house."

On instinct, my eyes dart to Dustin's and his go wide before he catches himself and squeezes Sam to his side.

Dustin had a huge party out at his parents' ranch. We'd made love in the barn on a bed of hay like a couple of hicks. He'd told me he loved me and was looking forward to our future together, the Jennings and Miller family names joining to be some kind of small town nobility. I told him I was leaving to go to Flagstaff for school and that I'd hoped to never come back, thus ending our romantic interlude. Thing is, I'd loved Dustin once, as much as I was capable of, but I didn't love anyone as much as I hated Payson.

The reunions go on like this for another few hours. The liquor keeps coming and before I can control myself, I'm falling into old stories with my ex-best friend, ex-boyfriend, and kids I'd gone all through school with. Most of them seem to understand why I left, with the exception of Sam and Dustin, but as the drinks come, so does their eventual forgiveness.

At one in the morning, we stumble out of the bar. Too drunk to drive, we sit in the parking lot talking until half of us decide to call Henry, our resident cabdriver, and the other half chooses to walk home in the cool night air. I hop in the cab and because my dad's place is on the outskirts of town, I'm last to be dropped off. It isn't until Henry pulls up at the house that I get a bright idea. It'll be the first time since I've been back and I'll need the drunken lubrication to endure it.

Sober would be torture.

Come to think of it, drunk might actually be worse.

LUCAS

The room is dark except for the glow from my flashlight. My shoulder aches from a wayward spring poking through the thin layer of cushion on my secondhand mattress. I run the light back and forth along the edge of my bed, casting a yellow glow on three action figures propped between my bed and the wall. They serve as a tribute and a reminder of their death.

Spider-Man, Batman, and Pinkie Pie.

These weren't actually owned by my siblings. I wasn't able to return home after the night they died. I found those in one of those stores where everything costs one dollar shortly after I was released. I didn't have much money, but I knew I had to have these so I'd never forget.

It's all I have left of them; the only memories I've managed to hold on to are wrapped in three cartoon characters. I have no home videos or photos, only three pieces of molded plastic that have *Made in China* stamped on their feet.

Alexis loved the pink pony with the balloons imprinted on her flank. She never had a birthday party, but one of her teachers gave her a Pinkie Pie My Little Pony birthday card when she turned six. She coveted the stickers inside and ever since then my baby sister was obsessed.

Mikey was always trying to convince us that Spider-Man would win in any fight against any superhero, but Dave swore nothing could top Batman, even though we all agreed the guy wasn't technically a superhero but instead a rich man with a lot of gadgets. I mean, it's not like he had X-ray vision or could spit webs from his palms.

The corner of my lips tug at the memory even if it's only one of few. My blackouts have robbed me of the majority of my childhood, and I hate them for that. I want my brothers and sister back. I suppose it was a good thing I was practically blind with my own blood the night they died. At least what little I do remember was of their life rather than the image of their death. I spent their funeral behind bars, so even their half-sized caskets can't haunt me.

Just these three palm-sized pieces of plastic along with a handful of fading memories are all I have left.

With the joy that comes at remembering them, there's also pain. As much as it hurts to stare at the plastic and paint, I must. I face off with the sorrow and welcome it. It's important I remember what I can. The horror of what can happen if I don't keep my feelings in check. If I don't hold on to my restraint.

Always remember.

The tiny painted faces of— I jump at the sound of something outside my window. Crunching gravel and…humming?

I click off my flashlight and close my eyes to concentrate, sure I misheard.

No, that's definitely humming and…a giggle? Yeah, a feminine giggle.

I sit up and crawl across the floor to the open window. Listening close, I determine the sound is coming from the creek on the other side of the house.

With the lights off, I'm able to move freely without being seen, but all the windows are open, so I go light on my feet to avoid being heard. I make it to the living room and lean over the small table to peer out the window.

Squinting, I can barely make out the form of a person. A woman.

How in the hell did a woman get out here?

I search the surrounding woods for a car, another person, anything, but find nothing. It's as if she just appeared out of thin air.

It's at least a five-mile hike out here from the main road. The moon is high, so I'd guess it's sometime after midnight. Luckily it's close to full, so the woman is able to see in the thick darkness.

She stumbles, lists, and drops onto a boulder with a trill of laughter.

Huh… maybe she can't see.

Talking softly to herself, she reaches down and pulls off one boot, then the other, followed by her socks. With what looks like effort, she pushes back to standing and hooks her fingers into the waistband of her jeans. Her hips shift from side to side and— Oh God.

I drop my gaze, blinking.

Why is she taking her pants off?

I don't want to invade her privacy. I should just turn and go back to bed, protect her modesty and honor, but… my teeth run along my bottom lip and my stomach flips with anticipation. Her light humming and giggles continue to filter in through the open window. I shouldn't look. It's not right.

She screeches.

My gaze jerks back to her.

"Oh my God, it's freezing!"

I turn my head, try to avert my eyes, but it's impossible, as if they're tethered to her.

She slowly wades into the water, the soft curves of her body on full display beneath the moonlight. Toned legs meet the round globes of her backside and her hips sway with each step. Long black hair falls down the length of her back, the tips reaching for her bottom as if they're just as desperate to touch its softness as I am.

Images of my hands caressing her thighs and opening her legs flood my mind. A sickness stirs in my gut, but this isn't the illness that comes with food poisoning. No, this is something dangerous. A need that makes me restless, overcome with wanting. My fingertips itch to touch, my mouth waters to taste, and between my legs I'm heavy and aching.

This is bad. It feels wrong. Dirty.

Yet I'm helpless to look away.

She's not quite in the deepest part of the creek, the water only hitting her at midthigh, and she turns to face the house. For a second I fear she might see me, but she doesn't startle, only continues to sway, at ease, as if she's become one with the current.

Her face is cast in shadows and my eyes travel down the long column of her neck. I lick my lips and imagine what she'd taste like, what her soft body would feel like. The creamy skin of her full breasts stand in extreme contrast to her dark tight nipples. A low groan falls from my throat as my gaze slides down her soft belly to the thin strip of hair between her legs.

My hips flex uncontrollably and I dip my hand into my sweatpants, gripping myself so hard it hurts.

As much as I'm desperate for pleasure, I shouldn't use her to take it.

She isn't mine.

It's not right.

My hand pumps on its own accord and disgust and shame roll through me.

I've never seen a naked woman this beautiful. Just watching her is doing things to my body that are impossible to control. Although I've felt the unwelcome draw to a woman, wrestled with the burning need that coils between my legs, it's never been this extreme. This demanding. There's safety in my anonymity and my shame takes a backseat to my yearning.

I bite my lip against the pleasure-pain of my grip as I watch her drag her fingertips along the surface of the water. She sways back and forth and I feel her body moving in my arms. My lips soaking up the moisture from her bare skin, my hands in all that long hair. What would it feel like to be skin on skin, to have the warmth of another body pressed against mine?

She steps out of the shadows, and my eyes, lids half-mast and vision lust-fogged, move up to her face—Oh God!

I stumble backward. Rip my hand from between my legs.

It's her.

The woman from the diner and Mr. Jennings's house.

I squint. She's crying.

I crouch low and watch. She's staring at the house and her cheeks are wet with tears. What was once the gentle sound of her humming has turned to quiet sobs.

Maybe she saw me and she's upset?

But she's still standing there, completely exposed. It's as if the house itself is making her cry.

I blink against the strange urge to comfort her. As if women aren't intimidating enough, emotional women trigger a darkness in me I can't allow myself to acknowledge.

Who is she? The night I dropped Cody off, she was terrifying, but today at the diner she was kind. Gentle even. And with that piercing stare that sends my pulse racing, she's the kind of pretty that makes my chest hurt.

Without another thought, I turn and scurry back to my room. I crawl beneath my sleeping bag and try to ignore the still heavy weight between my legs and the painful throb that begs for my hand. No. I push away images of the naked woman in the creek.

The room shrinks around me and I slam my eyes closed, begging for sleep to take me.

SEVEN

SHYANN

"So no one will hire you and now you're desperate enough to come by and ask for your old job back?" My dad doesn't look up from his newspaper and takes a sip of black coffee.

The smell turns my stomach, even though I had four cups *and* a plate of eggs and bacon in an attempt to cure my hangover. It didn't work. After last night, I'm never drinking again.

Had I actually cried? The details are fuzzy, but I remember being naked in the creek. The lights were off in the river house; whoever Dad has living there was sound asleep while I stared and imagined the future my mom had planned to build in it. It was too much. The cold water sobered me up enough that a wave of pain and anger crashed over me.

But I don't cry.

Not since she died.

So what the hell was that?

I swear this town is fucking with my head. I pinch the bridge of my nose and pray for the ache between my ears to fade. "If you wanna be all techni-cal about it, then…yeah."

I hate this, I hate this, I *hate* this.

The fact is, I have no choice. I need money *now*, and the job is available *now*. Necessity shoves aside my pride. Sooner I make some money, sooner I'll be gone.

"Fine." He folds up his newspaper and smacks it down on his desk, kick-ing up a flurry of dust that lights up in the sunlight through the window. "But things have changed since you worked here in high school. Job now includes pickin' up supplies from town when we need 'em. Didn't want you driving to the city back then, but figure you're a big-shot career woman now; you can handle it."

"Okay, but—"

"Also might need you on job sites. Been spreading myself thin and we've been busier than ever."

My head throbs. Is he yelling?

"And the pay, you'll get twenty an hour to start. If you prove your salt, I'll raise that." His eyes go over my shoulder at the sound of the office door opening and he waves in whoever is behind me.

"Whoa, Native American Barbie." My brother plucks the shoulder hem of my blouse. "Nice threads."

I smack his hand. "Shut up."

He chuckles and drops into the seat next to me, propping his work-boot-covered feet on my dad's desk and dropping a decent amount of dirt off the tread in the process.

My dad stands and grabs his tool belt from a nearby table that's in no bet-ter shape than his desk. "Get started out there, then in here. Cody and I'll be out most of the day."

"Aw, shit…" Cody's voice is laced with laughter. "She caved." He pushes his black hair off his forehead. "Less than twenty-four hours. That's gotta be a record."

"Cody, up." My dad's growl erases my brother's cocky grin. "Got work to do, so does your sister."

My brother pushes up to stand. "Hell yeah she does." He whistles low and his gaze moves around the room. "Dad, I don't know how to tell you this, so I'm just going to come out and say it."

My dad drops a stack of overstuffed file folders into my lap, spilling their guts to the floor at my feet. "What's that?" How he's managed to run a successful company and not know the first thing about organizing paperwork is a damn mystery.

"You're a whore."

My dad freezes and glares at my brother. "Fuck does that mean?"

"This." Cody holds his arms out, motioning to the entire room. "You're hoarding."

"Code, someone who hoards is not a whore." The rumble of irritation is heavy in my dad's voice, either from impatience or from my brother's idiocy.

"Of course they are." Cody laughs.

"No. They're not, dumbass." I wrangle the file folders back into my arms and carry them to the reception desk.

Cody ruffles my hair, pushing it into my eyes, and I'm stuck unable to clear it.

"You dick!"

"What the hell is wrong with you two?" Dad snags his keys and pops on a faded baseball hat with the Jennings Contractors logo on it. "Both of you talk like you were raised by bikers."

My brother grins. "Crabby ole mountain man'll give a biker's mouth a run for its money."

Dad mumbles something that makes Cody laugh and they leave without saying goodbye.

I finally blow the hair out of my eyes and study what is supposed to be a lobby, or it was when I worked here years ago, but now resembles a storage unit. Blueprints scatter every available tabletop, both rolled up and spread open, held down by wrenches, screwdrivers, even a can of WD-40. I plop down at my desk and groan. It'll take me forever to get this all straightened out.

Only days ago I was at the jumping point of a career-changing event. I chose to drop-kick my own ass right off a cliff rather than do what had to be done and this is my penance. Cleaning up a half decade of crappy book-keeping and housekeeping for a man who always made me feel like my dreams were too big and my place was in a small pond.

Nash Jennings might be right about a lot of things, but not that. This is a temporary setback that I will rectify as soon as I figure out how. I'm not giving up. Not without a fight.

***

Several hours after my dad and Cody left, I'm knee-deep in paperwork and contemplating my shitty situation. My blouse is wrinkled and sticks to my skin, suffocating my body like Saran Wrap, and my gray slacks are probably black on the butt from sitting on the filthy carpet, but it was the only clear space to lay everything out.

I flex my fingers and paper cuts hatch-mark my aching digits from rolling blueprints and sorting through invoices. Hunger rumbles in my stomach and I'm about to grab the granola bar from my purse when I hear a vehicle pull up out front. I can't see it from my position on the floor, but I'm hoping it's my dad with lunch.

I peek up just as a man comes through the door.

Not Dad, and sadly he's not carrying a bag of deli sandwiches, so I hoist my body off the ground. "Sorry, I— Oh…" I blow a loose strand of hair from my eyes. "You." The guy from the diner. The one who lost his mom. My chest aches.

He stares, his face unreadable.

"I'm sorry, I just…" I take a step toward him and have to tilt my head up to see his eyes. "I saw you yesterday."

He makes a choking noise and looks away.

"At the 87 Café? You were grabbing coffee."

His baseball hat is pulled low over his eyes—similar to how he was wearing it at the diner—and his chin is dipped to his chest so I can't get a good look at his face. He shifts on his feet. "Yeah, I remember."

"Um…" I peer behind me, then back at him. "Is there something I can help you with?"

"Ma'am." He pulls his hat off and runs a hand through a thick mass of dark hair, avoiding my eyes. "I'm here to see Mr. Jennings."

"Mr. Jennings?" I tilt my head and study him. Faded jeans coated in dirt and sawdust. The scent of mountain air and pinesap wafting off of his solid frame speak of time working manual labor. And I remember his truck. "You work for Jennings?"

"Yes, ma'am." He pops his hat back on and pulls it low. He has to be in his midtwenties, but his body language is more like a teenage boy. None of the bloated confidence like the men I'm used to. His timidity is kind of charming. His hands fidget in front of his thighs. He catches me watching and quickly shoves them into his pockets.

"Shyann."

He lifts his chin, showcasing a square jaw and full lips. He really is beautiful. "Ma'am?"

"Call me Shyann." I hold out a hand and swear the movement makes him jump, even if only minutely. "Shyann Jennings."

He stills for a second, registers my name, then grabs my hand for a quick, firm shake. His palm is warm, clammy, and calloused, and as soon as he grabs mine, he releases it. "Nice to meet you."

"You're not from around here." Growing up in a small town I know everyone there is, including their relatives, but that's not what gives away his flatlander status. He's not a natural-born mountain man. His skin is tan, but it's not from spending his youth working land or maintaining a farm. Kids like me who grow up country spend the majority of our lives outside. This guy's tan is new, without freckles or the grooves most men get around their mouth and eyes.

Then there are his manners. He's overly polite, overly respectful. Hell, he took his hat off when he addressed me. Again, not uncommon in small towns, but the way he does it is more militant than genteel.

"No, ma'am." He shoves his hands deeper into the pockets of his jeans.

"Where you from?"

He shrugs and his eyes dart to the front door. A patch of puckered skin mars the slope of his neck just below his jaw. "Little bit a'everywhere."

"Are you a felon?"

His body jerks back and he tenses. "No, ma'am. No, I…I'm not…"

I slide a stack of invoices and purchase orders into my arms and hope taking my focus off him will relieve his nervousness. "Most people who wind up in a small town are hiding something. I don't judge."

He's stock-still, staring, and as I pass him to the file cabinet, I do it close to try to get a glimpse of his eyes, but he steps back to maintain his distance.

"Would it be all right if I left something for Mr. Jennings on his desk?"

"Sure." I motion toward my dad's office. "Have at it."

He nods, then shuffles to the office where he must drop off something small. I didn't see him with anything in his hands when he got here. Before I know it, he's passing me, headed for the front door and rubbing the back of his neck.

Maybe it's his mysterious demeanor or the fact that we share a common loss, but I'm not ready to see him go.

"What is it?" I blurt the question, grateful when he stops just shy of the door.

He turns to me and my heart stupidly thunders in my chest. "What?"

"What did you drop off? Just, ya know, so I can tell Nash." *Smooth, Shyann.*

He seems taken aback. "A mock-up."

"Mock-up for what?"

His jaw tightens as if my questions are irritating, and I wonder if my irrational desire to know more about him is coming off as annoying and nosy.

The groan of a truck kicking up dirt filters into the office. I peer out the window just as my dad slides from the driver's side.

"Looks like you'll be able to give it to him yourself." I turn back to the filing cabinet as the heavy footfalls of my dad's boots hit the threshold. And for some unexplainable reason, I'm thankful my dad's presence will force him to stay.

LUCAS

She's Nash's daughter.

And I've seen her naked!

Even imagined myself *with* her naked.

This is so wrong.

I clear my throat and force myself to breathe through my desire to run. The office isn't small, but this girl seems to take up all the air in the room.

Her presence has me edgy, her shocking blue eyes are impossible to hold, and the way she tilts her head to study me feels like she can see through to my soul. She's pushy and forward, a complete contrast to the girl I saw last night. That girl had been vulnerable both physically and emotionally, and the strength I see in her now makes my skin prickle. If I were a stronger man, I'd confess what I saw, apologize for intruding on her private moment. But I'm not.

"Lucas." Mr. Jennings's gaze moves around the space and I realize his daughter has his exact same eyes, but whereas his are intimidating, hers are probing. "Wow, look at this place." He studies the brunette with a knowing grin and she rolls her eyes. "Can see the desk again."

"Four years of college and I'm pushing paper." She huffs and shoves a file into a drawer with enough force to crinkle the pages.

His lips twitch as he swings his gaze to me. "I assume you met my daughter, Shy."

Interesting name for a girl who is anything but.

I pull my hat off and nod. "Sir, yes, we met."

"Shy, this is Lucas." Mr. Jennings motions to me and her eyes follow.

"Lucas." She says my name as if she's tasting it on her tongue.

My pulse pounds in my neck. I need to get away from her, from the feelings her presence evokes.

I take a step toward the door. "I dropped the mock-up on your desk."

"No shit." His eyebrows rise. "Done already?" He doesn't wait for my response but heads the few yards back to his office and returns with my sketch in his hand. He unfolds and studies the page. "Sheezus, son...this is good."

Pride swells in my chest and I force my eyes to the floor to avoid them seeing my smile. "Thank you, sir."

"What is it?" Shyann's light steps move across the room. "Holy shit..."

"Shy, can you go a day without cussin'?" The disappointment I hear in his voice calls my eyes to her, expecting to see the familiar expression of dejection that every child feels when scorned by a parent, but she appears calm. Confident even.

"All I'm saying is this is some good *shit*, Dad." She curls her full lips between her teeth as if fighting a smile while her dad ignores her.

Brave. I'd be terrified to talk back to a man like Mr. Jennings.

"Good work, Lucas." He shakes out the loose-leaf page. "This'll look great in wood."

His daughter's probing glare comes to me and my chest tightens. "Wood? You carve this into wood?"

"Yes, ma'am."

Her eyes narrow. "Shyann."

"Shyann." Heat warms my neck. I attempt to drop my gaze, but it's as if it's drawn to hers by some magnetic force.

The walls seem to close in on us, the surrounding air becoming almost too thick to breathe. The same need from last night stirs deep in my gut. It's new and so forbidden it makes me nauseous and excited in equal parts.

Her cheeks take on a pink that stands out against her olive skin, and again I wonder what it would feel like against my hand, my chest, my lips. The thought evokes images that I feel in the front of my jeans.

I blink, breaking our bond, and with a full, deep breath I step back. "Better go," I whisper, and nod before turning away.

My stomach roils with the tinge of regret for rudely running off, but unnerved, I have to get some space. More air. Clear my head.

In the couple months I've been here, I've managed to keep my emotions in check and Shyann Jennings is threating to take down everything I've worked so hard to build. This stability and assuredness she projects doesn't match the woman in the creek last night. I push her out of my mind and resolve to keep her there. But my head struggles with a single question I can't seem to let go.

What would make a woman that strong cry, naked in a creek, alone in the middle of the night? I'm pulled in two different directions.

Half wanting to bolt.

Half risking to know more.

SHYANN

I watch Lucas's retreating frame as he practically runs to his truck. "Is it something I said?"

My dad pulls his eyes from the mock-up and follows my gaze. "Nah. Don't worry about him. He keeps to himself. Think it's an artist thing. Don't take it personally."

My mind flickers back to the patch of scarred skin on his neck that should make him unattractive but instead adds a dangerous edge to his good looks. "What's his story?"

"Don't know. Don't ask. He showed up at a job site 'bout two months ago, offered a hand, did good work, could tell it wasn't his first time on a job site. Kept showin' up, so I hired him."

"Hmm." I take another peek at the pencil sketch in my dad's hands.

The scene is of the mountains, Payson mountains. Douglas fir and blue spruce trees peppering the edge of a creek where elk graze, some drinking from the stream while others stand at attention, as if on lookout for predators. The different shades of gray cast shadows and give the sketch a three-dimensional quality that will become two-dimensional in wood.

"How'd you know he could draw?"

"Didn't. One day while he was on a break he just picked up a piece of scrap wood and starting whittling away. Next thing we knew, he was holding a wooden bear. Got my attention, so I asked if he could do more. He did a mantel."

The man barely speaks, seems close to terrified in benign situations, and he creates masterpieces with his hands.

It's official. I'm intrigued.

EIGHT

SHYANN

How does anyone survive without Wi-Fi?

I drop my cell to my side on the bed and groan. Stuck in my old room surrounded by frill and dusty eyelet curtains and I've got nothing to do. Even the crickets have gone silent, mimicking my boredom.

I've raked through my boxes and pulled out my mountain-friendly clothes for the week. It's not much, but with a few tank tops and some old flannels I found hanging in my closet, it'll do.

After the long day I had, I came back to my dad's place where he made Cody and me another meal consisting of the only two food groups he's ever acknowledged: meat and potatoes. If his intention is for me to pack on some pounds, a few more meals like that should do the job.

Tonight was the first family dinner I've had since my brother and Dad came to Flagstaff for my graduation. But tonight's dinner was not as awkward as that last. After all, my dad hated the fact that I gave up Jennings Contractors to go to college. It's not that he begrudged my getting an education as much as he despised that I wanted to do it in another town. Away from him, my mother's memory, the Jennings legacy. What's more, it drove him nuts that I refused to take his money for the five years I was gone.

Momma used to say I was like a dog with a bone. Once I had my sights on something, I went for it. It would have to be pried from my cold dead grip for me to let it go.

Which is why crawling home begging stings like a bitch.

I roll to my side, shove my hands under my pillow, and stare at the doorway. Even with the door closed, I can see my mom standing there. She'd lean a hip against the wall, tilt her head, and listen to me complain about the stupidest shit. She was vibrant, opinionated; she'd yell using her hands and laugh with her whole body. But those are the memories I have to dig for. As soon as I find them, they morph into haunting images of the end. Her useless arms curled into her body, her regal Native American cheekbones overly pronounced and standing out against her sunken, pallid cheeks. Her skeleton protruding beneath paper-thin skin. Heat burns my eyes, but not a single tear falls.

"Knock knock…" Cody raps twice on the door. "You decent?"

"Yeah, sure." I sniff and sit up, rubbing my eyes. "Come on in."

He cracks the door and peeks inside. "I'm takin' off."

"Game's over?" I push up off my bed.

"Yeah." His eyes narrow. "You all right?"

I shrug. "Sucks not having service out here." I snag my phone off the bed. "This thing's useless," I mumble.

He purses his lips and for a moment I see Momma. Cody got most of her Navajo genes—darker skin, black hair, and compassionate eyes. "What's really bothering you?"

I hold up my phone and give it a weak shake, avoiding Cody's stare. "Trevor's annoyed he can't get in touch with me…"

"So? That guy's an idiot."

"...could be getting e-mails back from all the résumés I sent out, but I can't check..."

"Not sure that matters at ten o'clock at night."

I huff out a breath.

"Come on." He rolls his hand through the air. "We can do this all night or you can spit it out."

I sag in on myself, knowing he won't give up until I fess up. "Just hard, ya know, being home."

He drops his gaze and nods. "Yeah."

"I just...I see her everywhere and I don't see the healthy her, but—"

"The sick her." He pushes into the room and props a thigh on my old desk. His massive leg, dirty denim, and a sheathed hunting knife clipped to his hip are laughable against my pink desk covered in hand-painted butterflies. "Me too."

"How do you do this, Code? How can you stand coming here to this house or even living in this town? Everything reminds me of her."

"Easy." He swivels and jerks his head in the direction of the living room. "I do it for him. Whatever we went through, he went through worse. He sheltered us from the worst of it. Nobody sheltered him. He held her when she lost the ability to talk but needed to scream. Talked to her when everyone else treated her like she'd already gone. We may've been her life, Shy, but she was *his* life. That's a lot of burden for one man to carry." He shrugs. "Can't leave him. I'm all he has now."

I cringe at the truth in his words as guilt ravages my gut. "He has me too." It comes out as a defense, which only intensifies the grip on my stomach. Fact is, I ran as soon as I was old enough to do it legally. I went against everything he wanted and did what I could to save myself. It was selfish, but it was survival. I had to get away from the hurt.

Fuck, it's been over six years since she died, and being here is still torture.

But did I ever stop to consider how badly my dad was hurting? He's the bravest, strongest, most stubborn person I've ever met. I figured he'd be fine. Eventually.

I lean against the desk next to Cody. "How'd you know about all that? He never talked about it."

"We've had a few father–son talks over a case of beer." He wraps an arm around me for a quick squeeze. "I don't blame you for leaving, Shy. You act tough, but it's just to cover up all your mushy insides."

I tilt my head and study my brother's dark eyes that have flecks of gold just like Mom's did. "I'm your big sister. I left you behind when you needed me."

His lips curve up a hint at the ends. "You might be older in years, but I'm way more mature."

I rock into him with my shoulder and he chuckles.

"It's good to have you back." He stands and moves to the door but turns before passing through it. "When these newspeople call and start offering you your dream job, do us a favor this time and stay in touch."

"I will." I drop my chin, unable to hold my brother's eyes as the pride and sadness in his gaze tightens my throat.

"Good. G'night."

The old door closes with a whine that matches my own. I never really stopped to think about how badly my dad was hurting after losing Mom. So lost in a tornado of emotions, I couldn't see beyond my own grief. But still, why stay here in this house of death when he could be living in Mom's dream home surrounded by memories from when she was healthy and they had their entire lives ahead of them? To allow it to be lived in by a stranger, someone who has no idea what a privilege it is to be so close to the last thing that was important to her. The thought makes my muscles tense.

If anyone deserves to live in that house, it's me. And with my open-ended stay, there's no way I can stay in this house indefinitely.

Dog with a bone, right?

I'm getting my momma's house back.

LUCAS

"Come on, Buddy. Aren't you hungry?" I hold a handful of dog food on my palm.

He recedes deeper beneath the deck and growls.

"Okay. It's okay." I toss the kibble back into the plastic bowl and push it deep beneath the porch. "It's yours. I won't bug you."

Despite my best efforts to lure him from his hiding spot, he hasn't left since he first showed up almost a week ago. Every night I get back from the job site, I peek down to see those terrified brown eyes peering back at me. I have to assume he comes out while I'm gone, or maybe while I sleep, but when I'm here, he tucks away in his shelter.

My guess is he's been hurt before and struggles with trust. I don't want to push him and scare him away. It's actually been kinda nice to have someone to take care of again.

I take a seat at my table and open my sketchbook. It's nothing fancy, just a pad of blank drawing paper, the kind they sell to kids. Even if I had a television, I don't like to watch. Fearing a story on the evening news or a few minutes of a crime show will trigger a blackout. I have a stack of comic books, but I've read them over a dozen times each, so sketching is how I pass the time.

My hands hurt from putting up drywall all day, but it's not enough to keep them from moving over the page. With quick strokes and some gentle shading, an eye takes shape. Wide but turned up at the edge, followed by eyelashes, thick and the color of coal. The irises stay light, only a touch of blended lead to illustrate powder blue.

Shyann.

The girl has been stuck in my head since we first met. She's at the job site at least once a day, usually to drop off coffee for the crew or to swing by and have Nash sign something important. I've come so close to walking up to say hi, but my nerves make it impossible, so I do the next best thing and try to ignore her. But even my best attempts can't keep my gaze from searching her out.

Those first few days I'd catch her watching me. She'd smile and her show of friendliness would send me deeper into my work. Yesterday I caught her glaring at me, as if my refusal to acknowledge her conveyed my disinterest. Little could she possibly know she's all I think about anymore. For someone like me, obsession can be dangerous.

Today was the worst, though. She never even looked my way, acted like I didn't exist. And that hurt, which is stupid because I hardly know the girl.

Outside of what she looks like naked.

My fingers clamp the pencil tighter.

I also know Shyann has an explosive temperament and as much as that scares me I can't keep myself from imagining what it would be like to know her better. But I've never been friends with a woman before. Never had the opportunity to even know a woman. The females I've known in the past were heartless; all of them seemed to want something from me. Something I was never able to give. So they'd take it by force, or try. I shake my head and drag myself back to the page only to find the image of Shyann's naked body sketched in pencil.

This is exactly why it's best for Shyann Jennings to ignore me. I'm not like other guys and she's the type that's probably attracted to friends who're confident. Safe. Stable.

Every single thing I'm not.

NINE

SHYANN

"Thank you for your interest but the position has been..."

"Fuck." I slam my phone down on my desk and bite back a string of colorful curses. *"Filled."*

It's been almost two weeks since my stellar fuckup, and after sending out my résumé and applying for every job I could find, from field reporter to research assistant, at every news outfit in existence, I've got nothing.

Trevor said I'd most likely get blackballed after I assaulted my cameraman. "You were emotionally volatile. It's a class-A no-no in the world of broadcast news," he'd said, but I didn't think every broadcast business in the country would've gotten wind of it.

One mistake. One assault— Oh, who am I kidding?

I'm stuck in Payson for the foreseeable future. Until I figure out how the hell I'm going to pay off the fifty-thousand-dollar education I can't use.

I could claw my way out of my skin I'm so mad. I hoped for another chance. I don't want to come home to the house my mother died in after working a long day as a secretary at the family business to watch *NCIS* reruns with my dad every night.

In the short time I've been here, all I've done is fall back into the day-to-day I lived my senior year in high school, but with fewer friends and a much more depressing future. I'd been speeding toward my goals and now I'm stuck in the sludge of discouragement that looks an awful lot like Payson dirt.

I bury my hands in my hair and squeeze. "I need to get out of here."

"Good." My dad's gruff voice is beside me, and I glance up just as he shoves a purchase order in my face. "Get out of here and pick this tile up."

"Tile?" I snag the yellow paper from his hand. "This is a lot of travertine."

He shrugs. "Client insists on having the entire house done. I need someone to drive the flatbed down and bring back the pallets. Besides"—he runs a finger along my desktop until it squeaks—"you're dustin' holes in my furniture and Windexing the Windex bottle."

"It was dirty." Like it's a crime to keep cleaning supplies clean. Okay, even I can admit that's a step too far.

"There's nothing left for you to clean." He nods to the purchase order. "Need some air, pick up some pallets while you're doin' it."

I stand up and grab my purse, thankful that I'm wearing a comfortable pair of worn jeans and soft NAU T-shirt that'll be perfect for a road trip to the warmer Phoenix temperatures.

"I'll go. Where's the flatbed?" It's usually being driven from job site to job site and rarely parked idly at the office.

"On its way." He turns to trod back to his desk. "I'm sending someone with you."

"What?" I follow on his heels. "Why?"

My quiet time to reflect will now be monopolized by country music and the methodical spat of chewing tobacco.

"Two reasons. One, not safe for a woman to travel alone with that Shadow guy on the loose. Two, might need some extra muscle with those pallets."

I blow out a long breath, praying for patience. Number two is total bullshit. The pallets are loaded by forklift and tied on with ratchet straps. Knowing my dad, it's all about number one.

"It's broad daylight and the Shadow only hits at night. I don't need a babysitter."

He lifts a brow. "Never said anything about you being babysat."

"Then why not let me go alone?"

The rumble of the diesel-fueled flatbed sounds from the open window.

My dad pushes past me and I follow him out and into the sun. My eyes adjust in time to see the driver's door swing open and two long, denim-covered legs extend from the truck cab followed by a faded red T-shirt and a baseball hat.

Is that...?

"Lucas!" My dad waves the guy over and I smooth the front of my shirt, wishing I'd worn something a little nicer.

It's not because Lucas is ridiculously good-looking, which he is. Or that he's built like a man should be built, not overly swollen with muscles sculpted in a gym but lean and strong from hard work. Wide shoulders, cut biceps, and narrow hips. It also has nothing to do with the way he acts like I don't exist, all but throwing up the challenge for me to prove to him that I do. And it certainly isn't those rough hands that can create delicate works of art as well as swing a hammer. Even if those are the kinds of things that are bound to bring on the butterflies, they're not it.

It's just, we share something. The loss of a parent. That kind of mutual experience makes me feel exposed when we're fifteen feet apart, let alone locked in a truck together.

Lucas adjusts his blue ball cap and closes the distance between us in long strides. "Mr. Jennings. Sir." He tilts his head my way but avoids my eyes. "Ma'am."

"I'm sending Shyann with you."

Lucas's frame goes rigid. He's inconvenienced by the sudden company. Why the hell does that piss me off?

"She has the purchase order and will handle everything. You make sure those pallets are secure." My dad fishes a credit card from his pocket and hands it to me. "For gas and lunch."

I nod and shove it into my purse. "Great."

"You two keep me posted. We need that tile on-site first thing in the morning, so do your jobs and don't fuck up."

"Yes, sir." Lucas pivots and climbs back into the truck.

"But it's okay for *you* to say *fuck*."

His lips twitch. "Get gone now. Be safe. Don't be too hard on my boy there. He's fragile," he says under his breath.

"Whatever." I drag my feet to the passenger side of the truck and climb in.

The cab smells like soap with a hint of spice, sawdust, and diesel fuel. Lucas has his eyes forward, his hands fisted on the steering wheel. "Want me to drive?" I try not to stare at the scar on his neck.

He reaches down and fires up the engine by way of answer.

"Suit yourself." I prop my feet on the dash and scoot down in my seat, making myself comfortable. If I were the type who could sleep while my life was in the hands of a virtual stranger, I would just to make things less awkward. Unfortunately I'm not.

We ride in silence for a good fifteen minutes and the strain grows between us with every passing mile. I reach forward and fumble with the radio dial, hoping sound will dull the roaring stillness. Everything is static coming down through the mountains, so I give up quickly and adjust the AC vents to blow on my suddenly heated skin.

"No radio." I drum my fingers on my thighs. "So…listen, this trip is going to be hard enough; we may as well get to know each other to kill time." His head is covered by his hat, and all I can see is thick hair the color of weak coffee that peeks out around his ears and neck. He's in desperate need of a haircut. His mouth is set in a tight line, and his jaw ticks ever so slightly, but he remains silent. "Where did you learn to draw?"

He doesn't take his eyes off the road. "Don't know."

"You don't know?"

"No, ma'am. Just always could."

Man of few words.

I slap my palms on my thighs. "Where are you from?"

The muscles in his forearms jump. "Why?"

"Just trying to make conversation."

He clears his throat, and his Adam's apple bobs in those few seconds of silence as he contemplates his answer. "San Bernardino."

"California. Very cool. Okay your turn."

He plays statue, his jaw hard.

"Ask me a question. Anything you want."

"I don't—"

"Oh come on, just throw something out there."

His hands flex and release on the wheel.

"First thing that comes to your mind."

He chews on his bottom lip for a few seconds. "What is…uh…" More silence and I wonder if he'll clam up on me and I'll be stuck staring out the window for the next hour and a half. "Your favorite, um…color?"

"Green. See, that wasn't so bad, was it?"

I swear I can see the side of his mouth lift in a grin. "No, ma'am."

"Why do you insist on calling me ma'am?"

He looks over at me, and for a moment I'm stunned to catch a glimpse of his eyes. They're gray. Dark gray like storm clouds. But I don't get a chance to look deeper, as he goes back to the road. "I..."

"Were you in the military?"

"No."

"Butler at some fancy estate?"

Another tiny smile. "No."

"Spend any time around the royal family?"

"No." He curls his lips between his teeth to stop his smile.

"Hmm...slave?"

His face turns to stone, and I swear it's like an invisible wall drops between us. "No, ma'am."

"Well good, because slavery is illegal. I'd have to report it; people would get arrested. Our small town doesn't need the scandal." I grin, but he doesn't respond as I fight desperately to get through the tension that separates us. "Okay, I just asked a bunch so you get some freebies. Go 'head."

"Why are you doing this?" he mumbles, and it takes me a second to figure out whether that was his question or not.

I grimace. "Really? That's all you got?"

He doesn't respond.

I tuck my hands under my knees to keep from fidgeting. "My dad says I've never done well with uncomfortable silence, but my mom would say I never did well with *any* kind of silence. I guess I just figure rather than sit here we may as well get to know each other. It's no big deal. Friends do it all the time."

"I don't have friends."

I laugh, but the sound is sadder than I intend. "I don't either." Another commonality between us.

The stillness again builds and the air in the cab is alive with an almost tangible energy.

"Your mom, she's..." His lips press together and the muscles in his forearms jumps.

"She died when I was sixteen. Lou Gehrig's disease."

He nods but doesn't give me the usual sympathy speech about being sorry and knowing my mom is in a better place, and for that I'm grateful.

"How about yours?"

His breath hitches. "How—"

"I overheard you at the diner."

His eyelids flutter, then abruptly squeeze shut in a grimace.

"I shouldn't have asked."

With his eyes back on the road, his jaw tenses and he shakes his head as if clearing away a memory.

"One-way street. I get it." I opened up about myself, but he shuts down when my questions get personal.

"Ma'am?"

"Shy. Ann. Shyann. It's not that hard."

"I know..."

I turn fully to him. "Then why do you keep calling me ma'am?" *And why won't you talk to me?*

Heat builds in my chest, as does frustration at his insistence to keep me at arm's length. He ignores me at work, goes out of his way to avoid me. It takes a whole hell of a lot of self-control to give someone the cold shoulder and I can't for the life of me figure out why he's giving me his.

"If I did something to upset you—"

"You didn't, I'm...I'm not good with"—he waves his hand back and forth between us—"this."

"This?"

"Small talk. Or any kind of talk. I'm not good with people."

That's more than he's given me so far. Maybe the whole getting-to-know-you thing was too much.

"Wanna play Would You Rather?"

"What's that?"

"I'll state two things, and all you have to do is pick which one you'd rather do. Easy enough?"

"I guess so."

"Okay, so, Lucas, would you rather hike naked through the snow or naked through the desert?"

He turns to me, his eyebrows dropped low, but there's humor in his expression. "Why am I naked?"

"No reason, just pick one."

His face twists adorably in disgust. "Gosh, um…guess I'd rather be naked in the desert."

"Me too. Okay, your turn."

"Oh, um…" His left leg jumps up and down in a nervous rhythm. "Would you rather, uh…get attacked by a shark or…" He's back to chewing his bottom lip and I try not to stare.

"A shark or…?"

"Or a…bear?"

"Ooooh, that's a good one. Hmm…" I tap my chin, thinking. "Shark would mean water and the added fear of drowning, which, if you think about it might be a good thing."

He peeks over at me.

"Quick death."

"Ah." He nods.

"Bear you'd probably be awake for the entire attack. I mean, unless he snapped your neck right away. In that case I'd say bear, but what if he didn't and you were forced to watch while he ate your insides." I shiver. "Yeah, I'm gonna go with shark. What about you?"

"I was gonna say bear, but…you talked me out of it."

For the first time since we met, he *really* smiles. Big, wide, and so bright it's almost blinding. It's childlike, the kind of happiness rarely seen in adults who've been so jaded by life that they no longer have the capability to experience pure joy. It's breathtaking. I sit still, taking a mental snapshot, totally captivated.

LUCAS

She needs to stop staring at me. As if her eyes aren't hard enough to avoid, magnetic and curious all at the same time, there's also her scent. Out in the fresh air it's assaulting, stuck in the cab of the truck it's penetrating. It reminds me of clean sheets and fresh flowers. Pure, yet complex. Comforting and intoxicating. I resist the impulse to relax in her presence, determined to get through the day without the blackout I feel shading my mind.

We're almost to the warehouse to pick up the tile, and we can't get there soon enough. Her get-to-know-me games and light laughter had me more at ease than is safe.

Maybe it's her no-BS way of communicating. Her ability to come right out and say whatever she's thinking, damn the consequences. She is who she is, lays herself out there, and makes no apologies for it. She's brave, and regardless of her gender, I can't help but admire that. It's when her curiosities are aimed at me, when she looks at me like I'm a puzzle to solve, my fear instincts flare and the darkness closes in.

We round the corner of a large brick building.

"If you can back up there." Shyann points to the loading dock of the warehouse. "I'll run up and ring the bell."

I back in easily and she hops out, but rather than sit in the truck I follow her up to the door. She lifts her hand to ring the bell and jumps a little when she notices me behind her, but smiles.

My chest throbs with the force of her small show of affection. God, I'm pathetic.

The door swings open to reveal Jim, the warehouse manager I've met a couple times before. "Afternoon, sir. We're here for the travertine Mr. Jennings ordered?"

"Oh, sure thing, Lucas." He waves us inside. "Come on in. I'll get it on the forklift."

She aims an annoyed glare over her shoulder at me, and just like when we were playing Would You Rather, that strange tingly feeling in my face has me grinning so wide my teeth get cold.

Then something amazing happens. I watch as her gaze slides to my mouth and the irritation in her expression softens and turns into a brilliant smile. A tiny flush hits her cheeks, a kiss of pink against her olive skin. The myriad of emotions that play so openly across her face is the most fascinating thing I've ever seen. Staying neutral around this woman is proving harder than I thought.

"If you want to check this out…" The man's voice jerks my gaze from Shyann, and he motions to the pallets stacked on top of each other, piled high with beige and dark brown marbled travertine tile. "Make sure this fulfills the order."

Shyann heads over with her purchase order and makes quick work of counting and referencing the slip. "It's all here."

Jim slaps the stack. "'Kay, let's get 'er loaded."

Thirty minutes later we're pulling away with several hundred pounds of tile strapped tightly to the flatbed.

"I don't get it," Shyann mumbles.

"What?"

"Why my dad insisted I come along. I mean, you had it totally handled out there."

I shrug but don't offer any opinions on the issue. I was equally shocked when I realized Mr. Jennings was sending her with me. I mean, he knows nothing about me, my past, what I've done. If he did, he'd never trust me around his daughter. Most likely he'd gather the townspeople and run me out with pitchforks. Which is why I need to keep my mouth shut and my head down in order to keep what little I've managed to attain.

"I'd kill for a green chili fry bread taco." She turns those piercing blue eyes toward me so quickly it sends a lock of her shining black hair over her eye. "You hungry?"

My stomach twists, a combination of hunger and fear, but I nod.

"Do you like Native American food?"

"Never had it."

"You wanna try some?" Her expression lights with excitement.

I tend to stay away from food that's prepared for me and stick to what's bland and safe, but I fear saying no will wipe that look off her face, and I kinda like it there.

I nod.

"There's a great place we can stop on our way out of town. I used to go every chance I could, which was only when Trevor and I were covering stories in the Valley. They make the best—"

"Who's Trevor?" The question flies from my lips before I can think better of it.

She purses her lips. "Eh…he's no one really. Coworker. *Ex* coworker."

My skin suddenly feels too tight as I consider her spending time with this man Trevor. It's unjustified and completely ridiculous; a beautiful woman like her probably spends time with a lot of guys. It's not my concern.

She gives me directions that take us to a tiny shack of a place just off the highway. Its bright blue paint is chipped in places as the sign on top reads THE FRY HOUSE, but the *F* is merely an outline of the letter that is no longer there. Its parking lot is nothing more than a flat spot of dirt and there are a few old wooden picnic benches scattered around the simple structure.

Fragrant spices fill the air along with the hint of fry oil and sweet dough. My mouth waters and not necessarily in a good way.

"Don't freak out. It looks shady, but it's safe. I promise." Shyann lifts an eyebrow as we make our way to the single window of the building. "Do you trust me?"

I don't trust anyone. "Not really."

She bursts into laughter and I feel the sound in my bones. "I'll order lunch. You find us a spot in the shade." With a flick of her wrist, she shoos me toward a picnic bench that happens to be under the shadow of a large paloverde tree.

I wipe my palms on my jeans and try to shake off this woman's effect as I sit on the tabletop with my feet on the bench. The light, tinkling sound of Shyann's voice carries toward me on the breeze and it does little to calm my nerves. I peruse my surroundings for a diversion.

Four men dressed in sweat-stained and dirt-covered clothes speak Spanish and eat like they've worked a long day in the sun. It looks like they're eating tacos, but these are bigger than a standard taco, fluffy and wrapped in yellow paper. One of the men catches me looking and studies me.

I drop my gaze and pull down my hat, my heart thudding in my chest. No matter how much time passes I can't shake the paranoia of being recognized. Even though I look nothing like the emaciated boy I was ten years ago, and this is a different town, different time, different me.

"Don't look so sad. I promise you're going to love it." Shyann steps up to me with a paper plate in each hand and a can of soda under each arm. She shoves a plate into my lap and drops down beside me before handing me a Coke.

I study the yellow paper that cradles a puffy circle of bread and what looks like shredded meat, cheese, sour cream, and lettuce. "What is it?"

She cracks open her Coke and takes a long swig, smacking her lips. "Fry bread taco." She motions to my plate. "Try it."

With her plate balanced on her knees, her long, slender fingers delicately unwrap the end of her taco and she brings it to her mouth, bites, and moans. "Oh wow, it's even better than I remember."

I stare down at mine, wondering where to start.

"It won't bite you," she says through a mouthful of food.

"I…I got food poisoning when I was a kid." A lot.

She licks sour cream from her finger. "From a taco?"

"No, but…" There are very few foods that didn't at one point make me deathly ill. "I don't eat food I didn't make myself."

She hums and I'm afraid to look at her out of fear that she'll see me as the freak that I am.

But then my plate disappears. I watch as she unwraps the end of my taco and takes a bite just like she did hers, chews, and swallows. "There." She returns my plate to my lap. "Now if we get sick, we do it together."

My cheeks ache before I even realize I'm smiling. She risked getting food poisoning for *me*. As much as the thought of ingesting this food is enough to make me sick, I refuse to disappoint her.

Imitating her, I peel the paper back and bring it close to my mouth, praying if the poisoning hits, it does it when I'm back home so I can be miserable in private.

"Go ahead. It's fine, I promise." She presses her fingertips to my hand, guiding the food toward my lips, and the heat of her touch has me squirming in my seat.

Slowly I place the taco into my mouth, bite, and chew. The flavors explode against my tongue. "Good."

"Right? My mom used to say that Mexico stole tacos from her people. She said the Navajos owned all things made of corn, and that included tacos, although"—she holds up her food and studies it—"pretty sure this is all flour."

Her mother was Navajo. That explains her complexion compared to her father. "You and Cody, you guys look like her."

She smiles sadly. "Mom said Navajo genes are always dominant. Said my eyes are a fluke."

As if responding to being called, the clear blue orbs light with acknowledgment.

"They're pretty." I suck in a breath and drop my gaze to the dirt ground. *Stupid, stupid, stupid.* "I mean, as far as color...goes?"

"Thank you." There's a smile in her voice, but I don't dare look because the way she stares at me sometimes I'd think she knows how often I've thought of those eyes. How many times I've mimicked the curves of her body into my drawings. The gentle dips and feminine flares of her form are masterpieces, like a playground for the eye. I've considered carving her into wood, dreamt of using her bare body as a canvas. I've fantasized about more than I'd ever be willing to admit.

My stomach tumbles with that same uneasy feeling I had when we first met. Flutters mixed with something dark, a need that makes my toes curl and my skin electrify. No, this can't be good.

If this is me being uninterested, I'm in so much trouble.

TEN

SHYANN

Every bite of taco Lucas takes is like watching a kid discover ice cream for the first time. He was nervous at first, then tentative but willing, and now ecstasy. He chews each bite, and it's hard not to stare at the fierce muscle of his jaw as it contracts and releases beneath smooth, tanned skin. I study the tips of his hair that stick out around his hat, straight mostly but with a slight curl at the nape of his neck. I wonder if it's as soft as it looks.

His chewing slows and his gaze moves to mine. "What?"

"Huh? Nothing." I swig from my Coke, hoping to hide my face behind it.

His eyebrows pinch together but he goes back to his food and I know he won't press me.

In the few hours we've spent together, I've come to know Lucas never pushes or instigates. He's content to roll with the punches, more of a follower than a leader, prefers to be told what to do, and if my attempt at conversation on the ride up was any indication, Lucas probably wouldn't even speak unless spoken to.

I never thought that would be an attractive quality in a man. My whole life I've been surrounded by bossy men who think they can make all my decisions for me. Hell, I dated my producer for crying out loud. All he ever did was tell me what to do, both at work and in our relationship. I don't remember a time when I was able to be with a man without needing to be on guard or preparing to go to battle over something. My dukes raised, so to speak.

That's why Lucas is so refreshing.

He places his empty paper plate in the space between us. It's stupid, but a twinge of irritation flares in my gut at him separating us with garbage.

"That was good. Thank you."

"I'm glad you liked it." I grab our empty plates and fold them into a detritus taco, walking it to the nearby garbage.

The woman who served us says something to me in Spanish—most people confuse my half Navajo, half Caucasian blood for Mexican—and holds up a white plastic bag filled with the food I ordered to go.

"Thank you." I snag the bag and nearly trip over a little girl who darts past me, running away from a young boy as an older woman scolds them in Spanish.

Turning toward the truck, I find Lucas checking the ratchet straps and securing the pallets of tile for the trek up the hill. His shoulders and back muscles flex beneath his shirt, and my eyes are drawn to a strip of tan skin where his jeans sag just below his hip. His clothes are worn thin but in a way that is more nonchalant than unkempt. He sees me coming and I motion to the bag in my hand, hoping it'll distract him from my blatant gawking.

"Dinner. Figure my dad, Cody, and you could use a good meal tonight."

His eyebrows pinch together and he blinks. "Me?" He looks genuinely shocked.

I lightly smack his upper arm. He jerks and his gaze darts to where I'd hit him. "Yes, *you*."

Still studying his arm, he mutters, "Why?"

I prop my hands on my hips and tilt my head. "You liked the taco, right?"

His charcoal eyes finally slide up to meet mine, but the relaxed and elated glow from earlier has been replaced by something different. He seems guarded but curious. "Yes, ma'a—um … Shyann."

"So let me treat you to dinner." Buying extra tacos seemed like an innocent gesture at the time, but judging by the intense way his eyes are locked on mine, I'm thinking something heavy just happened between us.

Without warning, he quickly drops his chin and stomps past me. "We better go."

I stand there for a few seconds too long but startle when the flatbed engine roars to life, and I scurry around to the passenger side.

I climb in, placing the bag at my feet and trying to settle in for the drive home amid a tension that rolls around and pricks my skin. I watch the minutes tick by on the clock. The truck's engine seems too loud in the quiet cab, and at the fifteen-minute mark I can no longer take the silence.

"So … what did you do before you moved to Payson?"

His eyelashes flutter, but his lips remain closed.

"Do I make you uncomfortable, Lucas?"

He blinks and the tight lock he has on his jaw softens. "A little."

"Why? Because I get the sense that you'd rather me shut up so you can get this time stuck in a truck with me over with."

He doesn't confirm or deny it.

I don't like the way that feels one little bit. "Okay." I won't make him say it.

Turning my head away from him, I lean my temple against the window and decide closing my eyes will help to get me through the last leg of the trip without unleashing hell on the poor guy.

But really... I've done everything I can to dissolve this unexplainable strain between us, but he refuses to let it go. I don't expect him to kiss my ass, but it would be nice if he made a little effort to engage. He's one of those quiet artsy types, antisocial and awkward, but still! I can tell he forces himself to talk to me and even that is giving me the bare minimum. What pisses me off is why I even care.

Whatever. He can have his tortured and brooding artist bullshit.

"Why do they call you Shy?"

I glare at him and have to remind myself that he didn't do anything wrong, so sending him the death stare probably isn't cool on my part. "Because it's my name." *Duh.*

"Hmm." His thoughtful eyes scan the horizon.

I go back to watching the scenery.

"But you're not *shy*."

"No. I'm not." I sigh heavily. "My mother's name was Annika. In Native American culture, you name your child after they're born and according to who they are, how they act, or what they look like. The Ann was taken from my mom's name, and my grandfather believes by naming me Shy I was cursed to be the opposite."

He makes a sound, somewhere between a chuckle and a huff.

"My middle name is Blue Eyes." I motion to my eyes. "Obviously. It's a little much so I dropped the 'Eyes' and go by Shyann Blue."

He smiles. It's subtle but warm.

"If you think that's bad, my brother's name is worse. My dad named him Cody. My mom gave my brother his middle name. Shilah."

"What does it mean?"

"It's *brother* in Navajo. His name is Cody Brother Jennings." A snort of laughter brings Lucas's eyes to mine. "You must think we're crazy."

"No." He looks uneasy and pulls his hat lower to shield his eyes. "You miss her."

The way he says it, his words dripping in a childlike fascination as if he wants to understand me, makes me want to pour out my deepest darkest secrets. "Sometimes so bad I can't breathe."

"I can tell. I hear it in your voice when you talk about her."

I wish I remembered more. As much as I scramble to recall the simple things like the way her hands looked after a morning in the garden or the way her arms felt when she'd hug me, they slip through my fingers as soon as I bring them close. But I'll never forget the softness that would touch my dad's face when he looked at her. Nor will I forget the look on his face when he watched her take her final breath, and certainly not the expression he wore when he stared at her, seated at her bedside for hours after she died.

Even worse is what *she* looked like, her brittle hands curled up against her rib cage, paler than the sheet covering her emaciated body, her eyes slightly opened, lips parted, totally void of life. Of spirit.

My eyes burn and frustration rolls through me. Why does every positive memory I have morph into something ugly? I can't have one thought of her without it leading to her death.

Irritation at being robbed of good memories makes me want to jump out of my skin.

A blue sign comes into view in the distance. That's exactly what I need. I'm sure Lucas will hate it, but right now I don't give a fuck; I just want the pain to go away.

I point to the sign. "Turn off there. I need to do something. It'll only take a second."

LUCAS

That was too close.

When she asked me about what I did before I moved to Payson, darkness flickered at the edge of my vision. Stuck in the truck, I couldn't run, so I turned the focus on her and asked about her name. But learning about Shyann is a double-edged sword because the more I learn, the more I want to know.

Now I'm in foreign territory.

The sign ahead says DEAD MAN'S DROP.

We're forty-five minutes between Payson and Phoenix with nothing around for miles and she wants to make a quick stop at Dead Man's Drop?

"We told Mr. Jennings—"

"I know." Her words snap with impatience. "We'll get there fifteen minutes later than planned and we've made good time so far. I don't think it'll be a big deal."

"I—"

"Please," she whispers, her eyes cast out the window.

I flip on the blinker and take the exit.

"Thank you." She points. "Right, then follow the dirt road. I'll tell you where to stop."

I do what she asks and after five miles, she motions for me to pull over. Before the truck comes to a complete stop, she's out and charging through the thick brush of forest. I lock up and chase after her. Losing the boss's daughter in the woods seems like a sure way to get myself fired, if not killed.

Luckily she's stomping, so following the sound of crunching underbrush makes it easy to find her. I keep a good distance and hope she knows where she's going and how to get back because I'm not paying attention to anything but avoiding the swing of her hips and her tight jeans.

After a few minutes I see a flash of green from the corner of my eye, like fabric being thrown. When I peer up, I stumble hard over a rock and catch myself on a tree to gawk at the view before me.

Shyann has removed her shirt and is standing in a black bra and jeans while hopping on one foot to remove her boot.

She's getting naked.

I blink to the dirt floor and force my eyes to stay put.

"Come on, Lucas!"

At the sound of my name, instinct has me jerking, peeking, and— *Oh dear God, she's sliding her jeans down her thighs.* Just like that night at the river.

I turn my back, my entire body rigid and one very particular part throbbing. "I'm uh…I'll just…um…"

"Oh, come on! It'll be fun!"

What will be fun? Getting naked in the forest? Is this a Would You Rather thing? Before it was being naked in the desert or in—

Her hand grips my shoulder and I whirl around. Unblinking, I can't tear my eyes away from Shyann standing before me in nothing but her bra and panties. My mouth goes dry, but that's because my jaw is hanging wide open. I slam it shut.

I've memorized what's underneath those strips of fabric. I'm heavy and tingly between my legs, and if she looks, which thank goodness she hasn't, there's no way she wouldn't see it.

"But um…" I nod to the flat, soft plane of her belly that is rounded just enough to make it look like the softest thing on the face of the planet.

She reaches out and takes my hand. "Hey…"

My eyes dart to hers.

"You don't have to jump if you don't want to."

"Okay." I lick my lips and hope she can't feel how bad I'm shaking.

"But you've gotta see this." She turns and drags me a few yards through the forest until she stops and points. "There."

I move closer and the trees part to reveal a decent-sized pool at the bottom of a cliff. "Wow…"

"This is Dead Man's Drop. I used to come up here all the time over summer…"

She's talking but my mind is on pause at the closeness of her body.

"…stay all day and swim…"

I can feel the heat of her skin against my forearm.

"…and Sam would—"

I blink and focus on her. "Sam?"

"Yeah, a friend—"

"You said you don't have any friends."

"I don't. Not anymore. She works at Pistol Pete's and even though we parted on bad terms…" She blinks and shakes her head. "Anyway, we had some good times here."

"No." I take a step back, pulling her with me. "You can't jump."

She narrows her eyes on me. "Of course I can."

"Is it safe?"

My grip on her grows tighter and she steps close enough that I can feel the heat of her breasts brush against my ribs. "Lucas, do you trust me?"

"No." The word comes out on a shaky whisper.

A gentle grin softens her face and with both her hands she works to relax my hold enough for her to slip free. Seconds later she turns, takes four long strides, and disappears off the rock cliff.

A holler that can only be described as guttural exhilaration echoes off the canyon walls and slices through the trees.

I race to the edge and there's nothing but a circle of white bubbles marring the once shimmering pond.

I wait for her to surface, and just when I'm about to jump in and rescue her, she pops up out of the water with a feral howl.

"That was amazing!" She waves at me. "The water is perfect!"

With adrenaline coursing through my veins, I allow myself a moment to wonder what it would be like to be as free as Shyann. Everything I do is weighed against the danger of doing it. The threat of blacking out always pulling me back to walk the safer, less risky side of any situation. But something about her makes me want to try harder, makes me want to take a risk like other twenty-five-year-old guys. The sound of her squealing lights a fire in my chest that has me wanting to jump.

Risking a blackout might be worth the few seconds of euphoria I haven't felt since…I can't remember.

I think of backing away and yelling for her to meet me at the truck, but something pulls me toward her. Part of me wonders if it's nothing more than wanting to be close, to keep her safe, because she belongs to Mr. Jennings and I owe him. But even as the thought enters my mind, so do others.

I want her to like me.

I want her to see me as brave.

I want to know what it's like to be normal.

I drop to a rock and untie the laces of my work boots, kicking them off and stuffing them with my socks. In my hat I put the keys to the truck, my wallet, and my shirt. Unbuckling my belt, I pull my jeans off and a rush of adrenaline fires through my veins.

"Lucas! Are you still there?"

I don't answer but instead shake out the numbness in my arms and bounce on my toes. "I can do this. I can do this." I check the depths of my mind and find no darkness lingering at the edge.

"Lucas! Where'd you go?"

Before I can change my mind, I take off running and push off the edge of the sharp cliff.

I'm weightless.

My legs kick and my arms flail as my body responds on instinct, in an attempt to fight gravity.

Another long howl from Shyann and my stomach goes to my throat as I plummet, then hit with a cool sting that enlivens me.

Water rushes around me. Not knowing how deep I've gone, I thrash to the surface.

I'm still here. No blackout.

I break through with a rebel yell I never knew I was capable of, followed by a gasp of air.

"Holy shit!" Her eyes are wide and I grin at the blatant shock playing across her face. "I can't believe you jumped!"

She swims closer to me, her black lashes dripping with water drawing my attention to her light eyes that seem to reflect the sparkle in the water. I'm hit with the force of her excitement and a wave she sends over my face. "That was fucking awesome!"

That's when it happens. A howl of laughter I didn't know I was capable of comes barreling up from my chest and echoes off the stone walls, and in this moment I'm free. She can't possibly know the victory I feel, but the way her gaze finds mine and her expression softens I can't help but wonder if she does.

My laughter dies as I tread water to stay afloat, tangled in her eyes.

"I didn't think you'd do it! Did you see how much distance you got?" Her chin dips in and out of the water as she kicks to stay afloat. "Did it hurt when you landed?"

My skin feels sensitive, but I don't think it's from the hit. "Not really."

"Did you like it? I mean, you had to have loved it, right?"

A smile practically slices my face in two. "I liked it."

"You're full of surprises, Lucas." She splashes me and swims off laughing toward a rock that's exposed to full sunlight.

Hoisting herself up, she lies back, and not in a graceful way like I'd imagined when I'd read Hans Christian Andersen's story about a mermaid on a rock. No, she drops back, legs and arms outstretched, panting heavily.

"You should get out in the sun." Her eyes are closed and the light makes her skin glow. My gaze follows the path of her slender neck that leads to dip between her breasts that are round and beaded at the tips.

Black peppers my vision.

No! I push it back with my mind. Why now? I'm not in any danger and feel better than I have in a long time. *I'm safe. She's not a threat.*

"Helps to dry off so we can hit the road." Her inky black hair falls across the rock all around her shoulders.

I close my eyes and focus on holding back the dark. Shyann, mostly naked before me, is too distracting and if I don't concentrate, there is no way I'll be able to hold off blacking out.

My legs kick to keep me from sinking and I welcome the cold water, praying it cools my heated blood so I can reinstate my walls.

A voice in the back of my mind whispers its warning.

I'm too close. Too exposed to this woman. In her presence all my defenses evaporate and the blackouts are a constant threat I'll have to fight to hold off.

I'd never want to hurt Shyann.

But if the blackouts return, there's no doubt…I will.

ELEVEN

SHYANN

"We're here."

I blink up and realize that I'd completely zoned out for the last thirty minutes of the trip. I'd like to say it was the come-down from the adrenaline that did it, but that'd be a lie.

My zoning out was more like a daydream. A fantasy playing on a loop, over and over, and it starred the insanely sexy and frustratingly complex man at my side.

I imagined what he'd look like shirtless, but what I saw today put my imagination to shame. He's built, I noticed, like a swimmer. Broad, powerful shoulders that taper into narrow hips, dips and valleys created by long firm muscle, and his ass…Let's just say watching Lucas crawl out of the water was even better than watching him jump in.

But that's not his most impressive body part. As much as it made me feel like a dirty old woman, I couldn't help but check out his crotch, and the sight was as sexy as it was terrifying.

Oh, who am I kidding? The man is packing and as much as he tried to hide it, there was no way he could. His white boxer briefs clung to every part of his body and even after being in cold water it was impossible not to notice.

"…you can have it."

I choke, then cough to clear my throat. "What?"

He stares at me through narrowed eyes. "The taco. You got three, right? I was saying if you want to keep it for dinner with your family, you can have it." He pulls the truck up to the work site, backing it into a spot close to the two-story board and batten home with a wraparound porch.

My face is on fire, but luckily he's too busy parking to notice. "Oh, right. No, it's okay, I got it for you."

My brother looks up from a table saw and pulls off his safety glasses before heading toward us.

We hop out and meet him at the flatbed.

"Nice job." Cody inspects the stack of pallets. "It's all here?"

I open my mouth to speak.

"It is." Lucas hands over the paper that I swore was in my possession. Or did I give it to him? "Checked it against the purchase order."

It's possible that being around his near nakedness may have screwed with my short-term memory.

"Great." Cody shoves it into his pocket. "We're finishing up here. You're welcome to head in and see what you can do."

"Oh, I need a ride back to the office. My truck—"

"Dad took your truck in." Cody grins like he lit the fuse to a firework and he's sitting back to enjoy the show.

"He did *what*?"

"Yeah, said it needed some work done."

"He didn't even ask me!" Controlling, pushy mountain man! I groan and let go of the fight that has me fisting my hands. The adrenaline rush and subsequent fall from the jump at Dead Man's still simmers in my veins and cools my temper. "Whatever."

"I can take her home."

All eyes go to Lucas, who's fidgeting with the bill of his baseball hat. "I need to work on my carving anyway. I'll drop her off at Nash's on my way."

Cody slaps Lucas on the shoulder. "Sounds good. Thanks, man."

"Um…hello?" I wave my hands between my brother and Lucas. "Believe it or not, I've managed to get myself through the last five years with zero help from y'all. I'm sure I can handle the decision on how I get home." I cross my arms over my chest.

Lucas stays silent, but Cody matches my stance in a direct challenge. "Oh yeah? Go ahead."

I take a moment to peruse the job site and see every available man engrossed in something. I clear my throat and throw back my shoulders. "I've decided to have Lucas take me home."

My brother shakes his head and flicks my shoulder with his dirty hand. "Good idea, smart-ass." Then walks away.

"Smart-ass? Guess I'll just keep the fry bread tacos I brought you from—"

"Whoa…" He holds up a hand and whirls back toward me. "Did you say what I think you just said?"

"Oh I said it, and I'll eat it if you don't tell me I'm the best big sister in the world and that your universe would cease to spin without me in it." I tap my foot, waiting.

"You are the best big sister ever." He wraps me in a hug and groans. "Oh my God, I can smell it on you! Green chili?"

"Uh-huh."

"I love you, I love you, I love you!" His eyes narrow on my head, then dart to Lucas's, which is hidden mostly under his hat. "Shy, why are you wet?"

It's a simple question with an easy answer. We stopped at Dead Man's Drop, but for some reason it feels scandalous. I clear my throat and play it off casually. "Hot as hell out. Lucas hasn't been, so we stopped at Dead Man's." I play off the weirdness I'm feeling with a grin.

Cody's eyes grow tighter. Lucas shuffles his feet beside me as we agonize through the few seconds of pregnant silence.

"Cool." Cody shrugs, all evidence of accusation erased from his face. "Don't forget to leave me that taco, favorite sister of mine."

I exhale, relaxing a bit, and turn to Lucas. His full, soft-looking lips pull into a smile. Something I've decided I really like seeing on him. He notices me staring and drops his gaze, but I don't miss the upward turn of his lips intensifying. I celebrate a small victory at being the person who put it there.

LUCAS

After tossing the keys to the flatbed over to Cody, I wait for Shyann to get her bag of food out of the truck's cab and grin as Cody tries to snatch it from her.

I leave them to their argument, a little uneasy about their fighting. They seem to be joking, but I can't help but feel edgy and tense when they do it. Like at any moment one of them is going to decide it's not funny and it'll become a real fight. That, I can't handle.

Shyann is on my heels as I reach my pickup. She climbs in and I turn over the engine.

"Thanks for the ride home. Sorry you have to do it."

"It's fine. It's on the way."

Her eyes come to me and I force myself to stay focused on the road because looking into the crystal-blue depths could drown me.

"My dad's house isn't on the way to anywhere. It's miles off the highway in the dirt."

"Oh, I…uh…I live about five miles past that. By the creek."

She gasps and quickly covers her mouth. I can't avoid looking any longer and once my eyes find hers, I wish they didn't. Her face is pale and she's glaring right at me.

Panic flares in my chest.

My pulse races.

My hands fist on the steering wheel and I try to regulate my breathing.

"*You.*"

She's angry. I can't take her anger. Not without risking a blackout. My skin gets hot and clammy. My vision blurs.

"This whole time it's been *you.*" Her voice is softer now and it helps my fear, but only a little.

What is she talking about? The question freezes in my throat and darkness flickers at the edge of my mind

"He said one of his guys, I thought…" A defeated sigh falls from her lips. "Makes sense I guess."

My foot lays heavy on the gas as I speed down the highway toward the turnoff that leads to getting her out of the truck. "I'm sorry." I'm not sure what I did, but it's clear I've done something horribly wrong.

"No." She shakes her head. "Don't be—"

"I am. Don't be mad. I don't want to upset you." Where are the words coming from? They're pouring out on instinct.

"You didn't."

"Yes. I did."

Heat hits my biceps and almost sends me through the roof. Her long slender fingers squeeze. "Lucas. Listen to me. You didn't do anything wrong. It's..." She blows out a breath. "Can you take me there?"

"T-t-to where I live?" Nerves explode in my stomach as I remember the last time she got close to my place. "I...uh..."

"It belonged to my mom," she whispers, and her hand drops from my arm to her lap.

That must've been what the tears were about that night she showed up in the creek.

"Your dad said I could live there in exchange for my finishing it up."

"I know."

Silence builds between us.

"I didn't know it was your mom's."

She flashes a sad smile. "I know that too."

By the time we get to Nash's place, she's calmer, the hardness in her eyes replaced by a blank stare. I wait in the truck so she can drop the fry bread tacos into the fridge, and she comes out holding a Styrofoam box. She climbs back into the truck and I reverse out of the dirt drive and point the truck toward home.

We don't speak and once the tiny house comes into view, she visibly tenses.

I pull up under the juniper tree and her fingers quake as she reaches for the door handle. She doesn't wait and drops out of the cab. I follow her, keeping my distance as she moves slowly around to the front of the house, but doesn't move any farther.

I feel like an intruder. Unwelcome not only in this house, but also in this private moment. As she's stuck in some kind of memory, somewhere between past and present, I realize we're not all that different.

I know what it's like to mourn.

Know the pain of loss.

My mom is gone too.

But whereas it seems Shyann lost an angel, I was freed from the devil.

"I came here." She talks to the front door. "The other night, I walked here and—"

"I know, I saw you." I cringe and drop my chin, unsure why I confessed and wishing I could take it back.

"You...saw me?"

I nod.

There's a shift, the slight crunch of gravel beneath her boots, and I feel her eyes on me without actually seeing them. "*All* of me?"

This reminds me of when I was a kid being questioned by my mom, knowing I needed to tell the truth but being terrified of the consequence.

"It was dark, but..." My shoulders touch my ears and I whisper, "Please, don't be mad."

"Oh..." She's quiet, reflective. Not what I was expecting, reminding me that Shyann is different. *She's not like Mom.*

I don't tell her what seeing her naked body did to me or how I responded, but that stirring between my legs is proof the memory is still fresh. "I'm sorry."

"Stop saying that." She lets out an exasperated breath. "I should be the one apologizing. I'd been out drinking and...it's your home now. I had no business being here. It's my fault."

"I should've looked away." My face ignites and I'm sure she can—I suck in a breath as her hand grabs mine.

Her eyes are gentle with compassion and understanding. "It's okay, Lucas."

My fingers squeeze hers without my permission and it brings a small smile to her sad face.

Pride pounds behind my ribs. I'm glad to erase even a tiny bit of her grief.

She holds up the Styrofoam container. "Can I put this in your fridge before it goes bad?"

I nod, and fear that this means I have to let go of her hand.

Her warm, firm grip is reassuring. Comforting. I don't want to lose it.

She moves and—"Oh shit!" She leaps behind me and her hands fist my T-shirt at my sides. "What the fuck is that?" Her arm shoots forward, her breasts pressed to my back. I fight the weakening in my knees at the overload of her touch. "There! Under the deck! Oh my God, it's a mountain lion. Is it a mountain lion?" She claws at my abdomen, tugging me backward. "Is there a gun in the truck? We need to get—"

"No." The mention of a weapon snaps me from the fog of her touch and intoxicating floral scent. "It's a dog."

"What!" Her muscles relax, but her grip on me tightens. It's almost enough to make me laugh. "Are you sure?"

"Yes." I place my hands over hers at my waist. "It's okay. Far as I can tell, he's harmless."

"Oh, okay." Her forehead presses into my shoulder blade and she exhales hard. "Right. A dog. I'm good."

She drops her hold and steps back. I immediately miss her heat and the suppleness of her body, but it's for the best. She bends over and picks up what's left of the fry bread taco in pieces over the ground.

"May I?" She motions to the dog. "Figure you're not going to eat it now."

"You can try. He's not mine." I follow her as she walks to the porch and crouches low. "I've tried to get him to come out, but he won't budge."

"You scared, little guy?" The light, almost singsong tone of her voice is tender and calming.

"I call him Buddy." My face warms for some reason I can't name.

"Hey, Buddy." She holds out the food. "I won't hurt you."

She waits and I drop to sit on the step, leaning back on an elbow to watch her try and entice the dog out with her gentle encouragement. I close my eyes for a moment, listening to her voice and enjoying this peek into her personality. Such a contradiction to the cursing, teasing, tenacious woman I'd glimpsed before.

"Atta boy, come on."

I push up and see the dog has his nose and two front paws poking out from beneath the deck.

"There ya go, boy." He licks Shyann's fingers and waits while she grabs more. "Oh, you're hungry."

The dog inches out a little more and I take the opportunity to inspect him for injuries. His snout is filthy, chest and neck the same, but I don't see any wounds or dried blood. His coat is longer than I originally thought, but he doesn't seem to match any particular breed, probably a mutt.

I lean in, propping my elbows on my knees. "How'd you do—"

The dog retreats back into the shadows.

"Sorry."

She twists around and grins. "It's okay. He's skittish. Probably a man who traumatized him. He seems okay with me."

"Yeah." Funny, I find it's women who are far more dangerous.

"I'll just leave this here." She dumps what's left of the taco in the dirt. "Mind if I toss this in your trash?"

My heart pounds. Shyann in my house? "Uh…sure."

TWELVE

SHYANN

My fingers are covered in dirt, dog slobber, and the remnants of a green chili taco. Probably not the best meal for a dog, but he seemed hungry and I couldn't let the food go to waste. Chances are, if that dog has been homeless for as long as his dirty fur dictates, he's probably eaten much worse.

Lucas gets up from the front steps and walks stiffly to the door.

I assumed my dad had rented the river house to one of his buddies, down and out, probably kicked out by his wife for being a drunk asshole. It would take someone as defenseless as Lucas, young and desperate but hardworking, to crack my dad's protective shell. Looking back, Lucas living here makes perfect sense.

I trail behind him and the wood deck creaks beneath my weight. I try to push away the images of my mom laying each plank by hand with a nail gun. My dad would say, "Don't fuck those hands up, darlin'," then kiss her on the head. Little did he know there was something way worse working inside her that would fuck up a lot more than her hands.

"It's under the sink." Lucas stands in the open doorway and studies me through narrowed eyes. "Garbage." He nods to the messy Styrofoam in my hands.

"Right." I step into the open living room and my breath catches.

The wood floor has been stained, the walls painted in an earthy taupe that accentuates the bright white molding. A woodstove acts as the centerpiece, loaning its rustic look to the modern space. My muscles release a bit of their tension.

"You do all this?"

He shrugs. "It's no big deal."

"It's beautiful. She…" I swallow hard. "My momma would've loved it."

To avoid looking like an emotional wreck, I stick to the task of finding the garbage and move to the small kitchen.

The cabinets are white and the countertops and backsplash are black and white checkered tile, like something out of the 1950s. But that's not the most remarkable part.

Every single handle pull is different. From cupboards, to drawers, to glass-encased shelving, all of it is a mix of hardware. Wrought iron, gold, silver, and even ceramic, and all in the shape of something found in nature. A gold leaf, a silver sand dollar, bronze stick, some of them are even animals. There's a fish on one, a bear on the other, and— A flash of turquoise catches my eye.

I squint. "Is that…Oh, Lucas." At the far end of the kitchen is a small pantry and the door handle is something I've seen so many times before it's practically haunted my dreams. "It's her pendant."

My mom had an amazing collection of Navajo jewelry, including large pieces that were weighted by enough silver and turquoise to sink a boat. As much as she loved them, she never wore them. She always said they'd make better decorations for houses than people and swore she'd put them to use here at the river house.

I run my fingertips along the smooth blue stone and silver sculpted in a horseshoe shape. "This is…" Too much. Too perfect. Too…*her*.

"Your dad gave it to me. Told me just to make sure it ended up somewhere." Lucas's voice is close; I must've been so lost I didn't hear him move. "I tried the bedrooms, but then it'd be hidden. It was too small for the front door. Figured the kitchen was the best place for it to be seen."

I nod and my vision swirls with tears. "She lived in the kitchen. It's perfect—" I cough to clear the lump in my throat.

Times like this I wish I could cry, that I could release the pent-up emotions that are constantly hovering below the surface. And this…it's beautiful and being in this space is overwhelming. It's only a piece of jewelry turned into a doorknob but it reminds me of her life rather than her death. Everything about this place is like a snapshot from happier times. Before our family was touched with sickness and loss, a time when possibilities were endless.

Just like her, this place is beautiful and unfinished. The thought is so brilliantly sad that it brings me crashing to my knees…

Or it should've.

But Lucas catches me.

"Shyann?" The warmth of his strong arms wraps around me. His eyes, so dark and full of tenderness as if he can read my mind and feel my pain.

I can't think of all the reasons why I shouldn't be helplessly gripping his shirt, all the repercussions for allowing him to see this side of me. The side I'm always shoving back and covering with ironclad strength. The reason I ran and the reason I didn't want to come home.

I'm weak.

I always have been. What most see as aggression is really a reflex to protect how fucking pathetic I am.

Even now, the scent of spice and pine swirling my senses, my body pressed into the broad masculine chest of a man who's shown me more compassion in these few minutes than four years with Trevor, something inside me shifts.

Heat blooms in my belly and I splay my hands on his stomach, finally releasing my death grip on his clothes. His abdomen flexes quickly, as if my touch delivers a physical burn. The air around us becomes alive with tension and I want to crush what little space is left between us. My lips tingle with the desire to taste his, to suck that full bottom lip into my mouth and see for myself if it's as soft as it looks.

I shouldn't. I know I shouldn't, but every single reason why pales against the way he's holding me as he loans me his strength.

My mouth goes dry as a new need flames bright and hungry. He stares down at me, his eyebrows pinched together and his lips parted. His pulse pounds beneath my palm, matching the race of my own.

He feels it too.

"Lucas…?" I wet my lips and panic flashes in his eyes. "Kiss me."

"I…" He blinks, slow, heavy lids passing over the slate-colored orbs. "I can't…"

My skin tingles with every whisper of his breath. "Please."

His expression softens and turns sad as if he's apologizing. Right when I think he's going to deny me, he lowers his mouth to mine.

In a brush so featherlight I wonder if I imagined it, he kisses me. Just as I'm about to kiss him back, he pulls away. His breathing slows and his muscles grow tense.

Seconds pass in loaded silence.

He refocuses on me and I startle at his change in demeanor. He glares at me from beneath heavy eyelids, and his lips are set in a flat line. His once timid, almost terrified expression is replaced by something sinister. I lurch in his hold, but he only clutches me tighter.

"What are you—" I gasp as his hands grip my ass and I arch away from him.

Full lips lift into a crooked grin and he bares his teeth. "Women. Always out for something, aren't you?"

I flinch at the frigid tone of his voice. All traces of the tenderness I'd felt before are gone. "I—"

He flexes his hips into mine, silencing me with the stab of his hard-on at my belly. "You like the effect you have, don't you?" With two long strides he presses me to the wall, his hands fisting my flesh to the point of pain. "Don't need to hear you say it. I can see it." He licks his bottom lip and practically snarls. "He won't give it to you." He leans down and runs his teeth along my jaw, his breath hot at my ear, and bathes my skin in goose bumps. "But I will."

"No, I—"

"Shhh…" His arms convulse with what feels like barely held restraint. "Don't be a cock tease."

"Stop it!" I press against his chest, my legs tense and ready to run. "You're scaring me."

His tall frame locks up and he nips my earlobe hard enough to make me whimper. "Good." He steps back, glowering, and seems even bigger now.

I tingle all over and try to remain upright. My limbs shake with adrenaline and with the distance between us I take my first full breath.

He casually leans against the counter as if nothing happened. Seemingly unaffected, he kicks his feet out and crosses them at the ankles. "You're scared, run." He motions to the door with a big sweeping stroke of his hand. "No one's keeping you here."

"What's wrong with you?" The words fall out on a whisper as my mind tries to make sense of I'm seeing.

His gaze turns predatory and his casualness dissolves. "Leave."

"But…" I struggle to find the right words. I was about to kiss him and he completely turned on me. "I thought…"

"Shy. Ann. Not so *shy*, Shyann." He chuckles. His voice sounds different, darker and teasing in a way I don't like at all. My cheeks flush with embarrassment as he mocks my emotions. "Not so shy, *Shy*. Ann." He continues to roll my name around in his mouth as if he's tried it and doesn't like the taste. "You thought you could flash those baby blues, shove your tits in my face, rub your pussy against me, and get what you want." He tsks and grins. "Shy. Ann?"

"Stop it!" God, who is this guy? One minute I can barely get him to speak and now he's being downright cruel.

He scowls and his jaw goes rock hard. "No! *You* stop it!"

"I'm leaving." I don't need this crap. One minute he's caring, then indifferent, and finally flat-out mean. I go to move past him, feeling like a total ass for thinking Lucas was different, that we had a connection, but I stop and look him in the eye. "You could've just told me you weren't interested."

He tilts his head and his eyes blaze a trail from my lips to my chest to…between my legs? I shiver from the visual assault and he must notice as he rubs his upper lip, grinning. "Oh no, Shy. Ann. He's interested. *That's* the problem."

What is this? It's like he's been injected with sex and crazy. He's the total opposite of the Lucas I've come to know. Disappointment washes over me and tightens my chest.

"G'night, Lucas." I trudge through the living room with my eyes to the floor.

Embarrassment and shame carry my feet faster and as I pass through the front door, he mumbles, "Call me Gage."

GAGE

I roll my head on my shoulders—his shoulders—what-the-fuck-ever. Same thing.

It's been a while since I've come forward, which says a lot about Luke. He's managed to avoid people that'll hurt him.

'Bout time. Only took twenty years to figure that out.

But then he had to go and fuck it all up by getting close to this chick. He tried to hold himself back, keep his shit together, but the little pussy fell dick, heart, and balls for a girl.

A woman.

Makes me sick to think he could actually enjoy the company of a female after what that bitch-whore of a mother put us through.

I'm not saying he should be gay—hell, I'm just as turned on by big tits and a tight little pussy as he is—but beyond what they can offer sexually, women are disgusting, evil, wretched creatures.

Even now that I buried him in the dark I can still feel the effect she has on him stirring his insides. I rub my chest in an attempt to push back that tingly shit left lingering behind my ribs. Fuck a woman, yeah. But this shit Luke feels is not okay.

The sickness of lust mixes with an airy sensation that, I'm not gonna lie, feels really fucking good.

But so does heroin.

Just because something feels good doesn't make it safe.

Bitches get off on causing pain, especially to Luke. And falling in love with a woman has the potential to be disastrous.

They're straight from the pit of hell, all of them except Alexis, but she was seven and was dead before the infection of womanhood could disease and ruin her.

I won't allow him to be hurt again. Ever.

My entire existence revolves around keeping him safe. And the things I've done, the unimaginable lengths I've gone to in order to protect him, are what nightmares are made of.

Luke doesn't need to be daydreaming about a woman who will only rip out his heart and destroy whatever good is left in him. Best to keep women in one category, and the only dreamin' they're good for is the wet kind.

Even now, as I watch that hot piece of ass storm down the dirt road, my cock stiffens. I coulda fucked her. She wanted it bad enough. I would've made her beg for it, just like all the rest. But I know her feelings for Luke run deeper than a quick fuck and there's no way I'll be able to keep him safe if I chum the waters with my dick.

Once Shyann disappears around the bend, I do a slow scan of my surroundings. I haven't been needed this badly since we were run out of a little town in Nevada, but I've been keeping tabs. Luke got himself a place to live, nice and quiet, perfect for him.

I notice his sketch pad on the table, those three stupid toys he drags with him everywhere he goes, and in the corner there's a large piece of wood that he's in the process of carving, wood shavings littering the floor.

"Busy, busy, boy. *Mother* would've beaten me silly if she'd seen that mess." I grin, slow and deliberate. "Good thing she's worm food."

I saunter over to the table and flip through pages of his drawings. I can't draw worth shit. Luke's always been the artist. I tilt my head and study the countless pleasant forest scenes, individual renderings of different trees, animals, leaves, and— "A fucking bunny, Luke?" I shake my head and flip through more when I come upon a page of different parts of a human face. A female face with…"Well fuck me runnin', if it isn't our little Shyann. You're in deeper than I thought, brother." I turn the page to find more sketches of her, her profile, jawline, lips, and—nice, her naked. "When your memory *is* working, it serves you well. Nice tits."

I pick up a pencil and scribble my other half a note, then slam the book closed and move outside. Surveying the area, I drop to the top step of the porch. A whine sounds from just under my right foot.

"Good, dog. You stay hidden. Nothing can hurt you if you stay in the dark." I lean back and my jeans pull tight between my legs. "Fuck, bitch left five minutes ago and I'm still hard." A growl of frustration gurgles up from my chest.

That won't do.

Looks like I'll have to stick around for a while, take care of some of Luke's basic needs while putting an end to this Shyann bullshit. When my work here is done, he won't be thinking with his dick and I'll have this Shyann bitch flushed out of his system. For good.

THIRTEEN

SHYANN

It's after nine in the morning when I finally pull my truck—with, thanks to my dad, four brand-new tires, an oil change, and new air filter—into the lot at Jennings.

After my fight with Lucas, I had over an hour walk home to think about all that happened. I may have pushed too hard. He didn't want to talk on the drive to Phoenix—I pushed. He didn't feel comfortable eating tacos—I pushed. And Dead Man's Drop...I shouldn't have pushed him. After kicking through the water with a near-naked Lucas, then breaking down at my mom's house, the way he held me...I suppose I let my hormones take the lead to my logic.

I spooked him, backed him into a corner until he was forced to push back.

But still. How quickly he swung from being almost mouselike to viper was scary. I shut off my truck and try not to think about how pathetic I looked in his arms, gazing up at him and begging that his lips find mine. Pushing him again.

I saw the look in his eyes when our lips were just a breath apart. He was scared. I pushed. His rejection stung, but it's what I needed.

I have better, more important things to focus on. Spending the day with Lucas and seeing Mom's old place totally derailed my plans. I didn't think about moving or my mental to-do list once. Typical girl easily swayed by an impressive chest and a pretty face. I give myself an internal shake.

Back on track.

Save money. Move the hell out of Payson, this time for good.

"Mornin', Dad!" I drop my purse off at my desk and hear the ruffle of his newspaper.

"Guess you slept in?"

I pour myself a cup of black coffee and dump in a ton of sugar to make it high octane. "Yeah. Didn't sleep well last night." Replaying every second of my day with Lucas trying to pinpoint where it all went wrong makes for a lousy sleep aid.

Dammit! So much for my self-imposed ban of all things Lucas.

"I'll be out most of the day. Things should be pretty slow around here, so if you want to forward the calls, I can find something for you to do at the job site."

No thank you. "Oh, um…I'm sure I'll be able to keep myself busy here."

Age and sore muscles have him groaning as he pushes up from his rolling chair. "You sure?"

"Yeah, I have a lot of…organizing I can do." I take a sip of the bitter hot coffee, hiding behind the cup.

"Suit yourself. Get bored give me a call." He shoves his cell into his pocket and snags his keys off the hook I hung on his wall so he'd quit losing them. "Oh, that reminds me…Sam called."

"Oh." I wave my cell phone before plugging it into the charger. "My battery died."

He leans a shoulder to the wall in front of me. "You working at Pistol Pete's?"

I shrug. "Just picking up some weekend shifts here and there if they're short staffed."

Disappointment shadows his eyes, but he nods. "Sounds good. Guess this weekend they need your help."

I try not to show how happy that little piece of information makes me. After all, every opportunity to work is one step closer to getting out of here.

"See ya." He scoops his tool belt off another hook I put in for that specific reason and leaves.

More time alone with my thoughts. This is good.

I plop down at my desk and check my phone. Once it's charged enough to make calls, I'll get in touch with Sam and take whatever shift she hands me.

I click on the outdated PC at my desk and go to Internet Explorer to pull up a map.

The cursor moves across the map of the United States. "Hmm...where do I want to go from here?" *As far away as possible.* I close my eyes and skate the cursor around, then stop and open my eyes. "Alabama. What the hell is there to do in Alabama?" I close my eyes and repeat the process. "Oregon." Yeah, I could do Oregon. Mountains, cool weather. "Put that on the list." I close my eyes one last time, move the cursor, and..."You've got to be kidding me." Arizona. No. "Okay, Oregon it is."

Now that's done. I lean back in my seat and stare at the ceiling.

My phone chimes that it's powered up followed by the ping of an unread text.

Are you in for the shift tonight? You're getting first dibs. Loreen seems to like you. ;)

It's not like I have anything better to do on a Friday night, and after my last trip to Pistol Pete's, I don't think it's smart to engage in any kind of social drinking. Lucas tolerated my skinny-dipping outside the river house before he really knew me. Something tells me if I showed up for a second swim, he'd be less courteous. I punch out a quick text telling her absolutely, I'll be there tonight.

Perfect! 4:30 don't be late.

If it's a busy night, Sam assured me I could make a couple hundred dollars in tips. That's two hundred steps closer to Oregon.

* * *

"Your *good news* is you got a job as a bar wench?" Trevor's condescending laughter crawls across my skin like a rash. "I mean, you're college educated for crying out loud. Couldn't you at least snag Head Bar Wench? And who the hell is Sam?"

Why did I think calling him would be a good idea? *Because you were hoping he'd say something sweet that would take your mind off Lucas.* Gah!

"Sam, short for *Samantha*, was my best friend growing up. She went out of her way to hook me up with the job. The more money I make, the quicker I can get back to living my life." I doodle on a piece of scrap paper, stick figures who're stabbing each other and crying over their bloodied limbs. "And take it easy with the *wench* stuff."

"Shy, I'm sorry, but…" He clears his throat, as if it helps him to avoid another fit of laughter. "You're better than that. I mean, you have a job at your dad's place. Why belittle yourself at some hillbilly bar with *Sam*?"

"Figure I'm going to be here, I want to spend every minute I can working toward getting out of here." It's not like I have a ton of friends banging down my door for shopping and girls' night out. What else am I going to do?

"I may have a way to help you do that."

I sit up tall and stare across the office, my ears perked. "How?" He has my attention.

"I got an inside word that Los Angeles is looking for people. They're taking reels and going over them at the end of the month."

Hope explodes in my chest. Trevor thinks I'm good enough for LA? I bite my lip against a high-pitched squeal.

"Trevor, that's amazing!" I rip a fresh piece of paper from the printer and ready my pen. "Do you have the information? I could send my reel over today!"

"Oh no... That's not what I meant."

"What?"

He blows out a long breath. "I wasn't talking about you, sweetie."

Not talking about... His good news is that *he's* going to be applying for a job in Los Angeles?

My shoulders slump. "Oh."

"Yeah, I'm sending in my reel, and, well, I was thinking that if I get the job, get settled in, I could pull some strings to see if we can get you back into the field."

Pull some strings. As in, I couldn't get the job on my own merit. As in, I'm not good enough to overlook one stupid mistake.

He doesn't believe in me at all.

"Right, yeah, that's uh... that would be awesome." One stick figure disembowels another with a big fat smile on its face.

He goes on to say more but I'm dead inside, far removed from whatever he's squawking about to listen.

My good news is I'm working a shift in a cowboy bar.

His is he's applying for a job at the second biggest media market in the country. Fuck my life.

"You know, you could send your reel in as well, but Los Angeles knows about the live newscast heard 'round the world."

I bet they do, and why do I get the feeling Trevor's the one who told them? God, how could I be so stupid? He probably sold himself by using that incident, probably bragged about how he saved the newscast and got me off the air immediately with his super producer skills.

Selfish prick.

Why am I even surprised?

"…and when I do, and you know I will, I'll make sure to—"

"I'm sorry, I gotta run."

I don't wait for him to reply. Nothing he says will help at this point.

I'm on my own, have been for a very long while now, and that's exactly the way I like it.

* * *

As I'm standing at the service bar in Pistol Pete's, I have a whole new respect for cocktail servers. Whereas before I figured they dressed like sluts because they were out to screw the able and willing, I've now come to realize clothing choice in this field is a valuable marketing strategy.

I'm not dressed in a miniskirt that the average woman would need a hairnet to wear, nor am I in a tank top that's cut to my belly button, but Sam is.

I'm wearing skinny jeans, boots, and an old Hank Williams T-shirt I found in my brother's closet that I cut the neck and sleeves off of so it'll hang off my shoulder. Not overly sexy, not completely unsexy, but far from slutty.

I'm also not pocketing a twenty-dollar bill every ten minutes like Sam.

Maybe a few hours of slut acting is worth it if it means making double what I've made so far, which is still nothing to dismiss.

The Undertow, a rock-country band from Phoenix, has just finished their first of three sets. The room is thick with bodies and trying to negotiate beverage service through the crowd is like trying to get upstream in a mud river while balancing a tray of full glassware.

"You doin' okay?" Loreen, who is accompanied tonight by two more girls and two guys to lift the heavy stuff, studies me.

Knowing my job would consist of mostly running drinks through thick crowds of people, I pulled my hair back into a sleek, straight ponytail. Not only is it giving me a headache from hell, but also it's not nearly as sexy as Sam's "innocent" pigtail braids.

"I'm good."

She nods and moves back to the bar that's stacked three deep with patrons half on their way to being hammered, if not there already.

I grab the couple beer bottles she set down, hooking them with my fingers. Someone bumps into me as if on cue, but I manage to keep the beer from spilling. I find Nick Miller and Justin Boathouse, two guys I knew from grade school. One is my brother's age and the other a year older than me.

"Thanks, Shyann!" Nick slips me a ten. "Keep the change."

Easy.

Moving around the room, I hardly see Sam or the other two girls working the floor. I met them at the beginning of my shift; they seem nice enough, but I'm not here to make friends or socialize.

I motion to a group of six at one of the high-top tables in my section and hold up one finger, then point to their drinks, international sign language for "Do you want another round?" They all nod and I head off to put in the order.

Loreen pulls and pops the caps off beers and I place them on the tray in a way that ensures ultimate balance. "You see Sam around?"

I throw a thumb over my shoulder. "Last I saw her she was in her section. I'm sure she just got busy."

She leans to the side to look around me, her bright red hair looking purple under the blue glow of a Bud Light sign. "Don't see her. Mind finding her and telling her I need a word?"

Yes, I do mind. Since when did I become Sam's keeper? "Sure."

I put the last two cocktails on the tray and carefully balance it, keeping it close to my body to try to avoid anyone knocking into it. After distributing them, the guys all pay up, separately.

Ugh...it should be mandatory for all people to work in a service industry like this before they're allowed to become adults so they understand how fucking annoying things like separate checks are. Next thing you know they'll be sending me back to the bar because there's too much ice in their drink or the hops-to-barley ratio on their beer isn't quite right.

After making change for six drinks, I storm off to the opposite end of the bar in search for Sam. She fits in well at a place like this; every girl around looks like some porno version of Daisy Duke. I think the best I could pull off would be a slutty Pocahontas.

"Hey, Tammie, have you seen Sam?" I ask the other cocktail server, and then panic because I think her name might be Tara.

Her eyes widen along with her smile. "Oh, you haven't seen?"

I shake my head. "Seen what?"

She lifts a brow, then leans in. "There's a super-hottie in the back corner. She's been hanging around him all night. I think he's with the band!" There's a frantic fangirl pitch to her already-high voice.

"Why does that not surprise me?"

She leans in to whisper, "Just wait till you see him! If I weren't happily married, I'd ride that fine stud like a rodeo cowgirl."

I can't help the laugh that bursts from my lips, but I'm determined to find Sam and send her to Loreen because every minute I'm not working is a dollar out of my pocket.

I shove through clusters of people and weave around those who are having way too much fun to notice me.

My eyes search the surrounding area until finally I see Sam in a tangle of body parts against the back wall. As I approach, the man she's leaning into slides his big paw up the back of her miniskirt and my jaw drops at their blatant fondling. I'm not a prude or anything, but it doesn't take much of an imagination to know what his fingers are doing between her legs. I force my eyes to their heads. The lighting is dim and if my ex-best friend's body language is anything to go by, I'd say either he's magnetic or she's sticky, like fly tape.

"Um…Sam?"

She doesn't respond, but her hand that was on his ribs moves to slide in between them and down and…Oh boy. This is awkward.

"Sam!"

She tilts her head, apparently going for his tonsils.

"Samantha!" I move to tap her shoulder but snag my hand back and freeze when the man's face comes into view.

Lucas?

His eyes lock on mine and he rips his mouth from hers.

"What do you want, Shy?" She sounds irritated but continues to gaze up adoringly at him. He doesn't take his eyes off mine.

He tilts his forehead down and without his baseball hat, his hair falls over his forehead to reveal glaring, cold-steel eyes. The shadows play off the angles of his face, making him terrifying and alluring at the same time.

"Oh, uh…" I point toward the bar. "Loreen wants you."

Lucas's hold on Sam tightens, crushing her to his chest so much that she has to grip his biceps to keep from folding backward.

Okay. Message received. He wants her. I'm interrupting.

The rejection boils beneath my skin.

"Tell her I'm busy, cover for me." Her hand glides up over his shoulder to sift through his hair, which pulls at his attention.

"Yeah, sure." Any excuse to get away, but I'm not fast enough.

He pulls one of her pigtails almost violently, tilting her head before he smashes his lips to hers. I spin around, but not before I'm witness to the perverse joining of their wet and greedy tongues.

My heart pounds with unwelcome anger. I try to convince myself for the millionth time that the Lucas I came to know doesn't exist. That he's not the same man I saw fumbling in the diner who'd lost his mom. He's not the man who'd smile at the most innocent jokes, who called me ma'am and blushed when I held his gaze a second too long. This man is someone else. So fuck him. Fuck them both. I don't need this shit. I'm moving to Oregon, dammit!

Halfway to the bathroom, I'm fighting the urge to double back and rip Sam's hair out piece by slutty piece and feed it to her when something snags my arm.

"Hey, slow down there, Turbo!"

I glare at a grinning Dustin.

He runs a lazy gaze over me. "Where are you off to so fast?"

Shit! Dustin's here and less than a few yards away his semi-girlfriend is mouth-fucking my…er…another guy! If I were half the bitch I wish I were, I'd lead him right to her, but I'm not. Besides, Lucas is allowed to kiss whoever he wants.

I catch my breath and calm my breathing. "Working." I point to my apron.

"No shit." He holds up a mostly empty beer bottle. "Grab me one more." His heavy eyelids, flushed cheeks, and soggy mouth indicate he probably doesn't need another. "Chop, chop." He smiles, as if ordering me around gets him off.

"Whatever, it's your hangover."

I reach for the bottle, but he pulls it up higher. I stare at him, unamused, and go for it again, but he snags it just out of my reach. Asshole! With a final huff, I jump to grab it and he moves so that my body crashes into his, chest to chest, belly to belly.

His arms wrap around my waist before I'm able to find my footing and his mouth brushes my earlobe. "Ahh, finally. Miss feeling you in my arms, Shy."

Is he fucking kidding?

I tilt my head to speak directly into his ear. "You didn't miss feeling me when you were fucking my best friend, did you, Dustin."

"Of course I did." He holds me tighter. "I wanted you, but you left. She was a placeholder until you came back."

"You're sick." I try to pull away, but he doesn't release me. "Let me go."

"No. Not until you kiss me."

"Fuck off." I shove again, but the six-foot-tall dickhead who lifts bags of feed all day is too strong.

"One kiss, Shy. I won't tell Sam, I promise." He dips his lips to mine and I turn my face so he slobbers on my cheek. "God, even your skin tastes the same."

"Get the fuck off!" I shove at him again, his hold so tight now I can't catch a full breath.

My eyes search frantically for help, but the noise of the bar combined with the way he's holding me wouldn't look like anything more than a couple hugging on the dance floor, drunk and swaying to the music.

He nuzzles my neck and the wet heat of his tongue bathes my throat.

"Please." I try to get my hands between us to push him away. "Dustin, stop it—"

His body jerks off me. The momentum sends me to the ground. Heat slices through my knee. My palms sting from slapping to the floor to catch my fall.

Dustin jumps to his feet, moves fast, and stands nose to nose with Lucas. "What the fuck is your problem, man?"

Shit.

Lucas threw him off me?

I hop up, and a sharp pain in my knee makes me limp to stand.

Lucas's eyes dart from my leg to my face, worry flashing behind a deadly glare, asking a silent question.

"I'm okay."

He blinks rapidly and seems to relax a little as he turns back to Dustin with the casualness of a lounging tiger. Calm, but deadly.

Dustin shoves Lucas. "Who the fuck do you think you—" His eyes become tight slits. "Oh, wait a second. I've heard about you. You're the retard working at Jennings." He shoves Lucas again, but he doesn't budge and seems completely unfazed.

"Leave him alone!" I push Dustin with two hands, only to have him grab my wrists and pull me into his chest.

"This what you want, retard?" He flips me around to face Lucas, his hands locking my arms at my belly.

Lucas's eyes grow impossibly darker.

From out of the crowd Sam appears, takes in the scene, then curls up to Lucas's side. Her arms wrap around his waist like pythons, but he seems totally unaware of her presence. "Give it up, Dustin. We broke up." Her eyes land on me apologetically. "You can have him back. I don't want 'im."

I shake my head and struggle to get away.

"Release her." An angry growl comes from Lucas's mouth but sounds nothing like him.

Sam peers up at him, frowning.

"Make me, *retard*." Dustin nuzzles my hair behind my ear and it's all I can do to keep from heaving.

"You're disgusting! Just leave him alone!" I kick my feet, but it's useless; he's too strong.

His beer breath fans my face as he laughs. "I can't believe it. You're stickin' up for the retard? You like the dumbshit, don't you, Shy?" He jerks me in his hold. "You want him? He'll have to take you from me."

Lucas's eyes slide to mine and practically glint with excitement. The hint of a smile curves his lips.

"Don't listen to him, Lucas!"

He jerks his gaze to Dustin and shrugs off Sam so hard she yelps. Stepping into Dustin's face, leaving me the only thing that stands between them, Lucas grins, cocks an arm, and punches my ex with lightning speed.

Blood sprays across my cheek.

Dustin drops like a sack of pig feed. I would've gone down with him if it weren't for Lucas's hold around my waist.

Sam rushes to Dustin, kneels, and shoves him. "You idiot!"

I move to check on him, but Lucas cuffs my wrist in an unforgiving grip and drags me away. My feet have no choice but to follow as he turns down the nearby hallway and pushes out the back door.

"Lucas, I—"

He whirls me around. I stumble and my knee screams before I'm slammed against the wall, nearly knocking the air from my lungs. "Not Lucas. *Gage*." His lips crash against mine and I gasp as his tongue slides into my mouth.

No, no! I don't want this. I beat his chest with my fists, but he growls, presses me deeper into the wall, sandwiching my arms between us. His tongue lashes against mine, powerful lips demanding my cooperation and draining me of my will to fight. My eyes flutter closed and I moan, helpless against the euphoria.

His lips are smooth, strong, and greedy. I wiggle my arms free and hook my hands behind his neck. My nails rake across his flesh. A growl rumbles in his chest and he pulls at my shirt, balling the front in his fist and pulling so tight it bites into my skin. The kiss is like nothing I've felt before—animalistic and primal.

This is not the Lucas I know. Not the timid, shy, almost scared man I've come to care about.

He bites my upper lip and reality comes crashing down over me.

Gage.

He called himself Gage.

I rip free of his lips, panting, and he runs his nose along my jaw. His breath hits my overheated skin in quick bursts.

"Who is Gage, Lucas?"

His body tenses and he slowly pulls back. His chin is down and he glares at me through heavy-lidded eyes that are on fire with an emotion I can't name.

A tendril of fear winds its way up my spine, racking my body with an intense shiver. I can't explain how I know, and it makes no sense, but… "You're not Lucas," I whisper.

He shakes his head, slowly, deliberately keeping our gazes locked.

"Where is he?"

His eyelids flutter and he pushes off me, putting space between us. "Stay away from him."

What is this? His face and body say Lucas, but he's carrying it so differently that… "I want to talk to Lucas."

His head jerks and he rushes at me, his big hands pinning my shoulders to the wall. "Do not *fuck* with him. Stay away, or I'll bury you." He turns on his heel and stalks into the parking lot, disappearing between rows of cars.

I want to chase after him, but fear has my feet cemented to the ground.

I run trembling fingertips along my lips. My pulse pounds in my ears, making me dizzy. "Who are you, Lucas?"

FOURTEEN

LUCAS

I'm flying. No, not flying, falling. Air whips around my body and a feeling of weightlessness lightens my chest. My arms and legs flail, but not in panic.

In exhilaration.

The howling laughter of a girl makes my heart pound.

Blue water comes into view just below my feet. It grows bigger as I plummet.

I brace to hit.

My body lurches. I gasp. My heart thuds heavily and I blink as my eyes adjust to the sunlight.

I'm in my room, on my bed. I hold my head in my hands, the light confirming what I already know.

"Blackout." I rub my temples as my senses flare back to life and do a quick mental check of my well-being. "Headache." Not uncommon after the blackouts.

I peer down at my body. Still wearing clothes, even though I'm in bed, or more like on top of my bed. My work boots are still on and...I open and close my right hand. "Sore knuckles?"

I check the window from where I'm sitting. My guess is it's early morning. A groan rumbles in my chest and the weight of discouragement threatens to push me back into sleep.

My memory. I have to try to pull up as much as I can. I lie back and throw my forearm over my eyes.

Work, picked up tile. Shyann was there.

The jump!

My dream, it really happened. My lips pull into a tiny smile despite the worry about my going dark. I dropped her off at home, came home to work on my carving, and—a flash of her in my kitchen sends me upright. I didn't take her home. I brought her here.

"She was here." Looking at the fixtures and…the feeling of her body in my arms, warm and so sad. I held her and she—

"Dammit!" I slam my fists into the mattress at my sides and wince as pain rockets through the right knuckle. *What did she see?*

I haven't blacked out in front of anyone since I moved here. Had a few in juvie, but they were short and never drew any attention. I even went years without a single blackout; then I moved into a halfway house and they came back with a vengeance. I'd wake up to so much anger, people I'd hurt, they'd demand answers and I'd have no recollection of what happened. Eventually I ended up having to run.

I moved to different cities, kept to myself for as long as I could. The more I exposed myself to people, the worse the blackouts became. It wasn't until I moved here that they let up.

The blackouts are back. And in front of Shyann of all people.

I search the surrounding area for evidence she'd been here, in my room, when a whiff of something pungent and foreign filters through my post-blackout fog. I try to follow the scent to find where it's coming from and don't have to go far. With two fingers, I lift the front of my shirt to my nose and cringe.

Perfume.

I was with a woman. Disgust rolls through my gut. Not again.

I jump up and dizziness washes over me. My stomach protests the movement but I push through it and head to the bathroom. I brace my hands on either side of the oval mirror above the sink and stare at my reflection. Most of my jaw is covered in scruff except for the spot on my neck, the scarred skin too damaged to grow hair. I run my fingertips along the puckered flesh and curse my condition.

It's the thorn in my side, my cross to bear.

I rip my shirt off over my head and throw it in the shower so I can wash it. The smell of perfume always reminds me of my mother and I can't risk another blackout this soon after coming to.

Pushing the lever to hot, I let the water work on my clothes while I shave. I lather up, wipe the steam from the mirror, and make the first few passes of the razor when something in the mirror catches my eye.

What the hell?

I lean in, tilting my head to inspect the large purple circle on my neck. *Is that…a hickey?*

Sweat breaks out on my skin and I kick off my jeans and check between my legs. Nothing seems out of the ordinary, not like times in the past when I've come to naked, sticky, and sore.

I power through the rest of my shave and jump in the shower. I don't know how long I'm in there, but by the time I'm finished I'm out of soap and my skin burns. As hard as I try to reach back and remember anything about what went on during my blackout, it's impossible to pull a coherent thought.

And what I do remember leads to my worst fear.

Shyann was here.

She was upset.

I went dark.

Now I have a hickey on my neck.

Did I...? No. I wouldn't, but— Oh God. *He* would.

I toss on a gray T-shirt and a clean pair of jeans and my stomach growls. When was the last time I ate? I grab my work boots and scramble to the living room. My eyes scour the area for clues. Anything.

But everything looks as it did, nothing out of place.

I move to the kitchen to grab a quick peanut butter sandwich and there in the windowsill are Spider-Man, Batman, and Pinkie Pie.

I didn't put those there.

My sketchbook lies open and my heart pounds as I move to it with apprehensive steps. The drawings on the open pages come into view. Shyann nude in the river. Her light eyes stare back at me from the page along with a warning. Scribbled in childlike handwriting...

Time for another sacrifice.

I drop my sandwich and grab my hat and keys.

Shyann.

Everything is a blur as I race down the dirt road, sending a wall of dust into the air. I pull up to the Jennings home and desperately search for her truck, but it isn't there.

I speed toward the highway, my pulse pounding in my throat, and hit the pavement with a squeal of my tires. My stomach growls again and hunger combined with worry for Shyann makes me dizzy.

She's not at the diner, and a quick pass by the Jennings office and there's no sign of her truck. My worst fears unfurl and I blink hard to keep my focus on the road and not give in to terror.

My head swims as I whip my truck around the corner and a little farther down the road to the three-acre lot we're building a two-story home on. Immediately I see Nash's truck and hop out to go fumble through some made-up excuse for being late and frantic.

Lying is something I've always been good at.

It's kept me out of the mental institutions, and if I pull this off, I can stay in Payson and keep my job. I just need to know she's safe.

A few of the guys give me a quick chin lift and Stilts crosses to meet me halfway through the site. "Hey, kiddo. Feelin' better?"

"Uh…" Feelin' better? Was I sick? "Yeah…?" I search for Nash or Cody, hoping they'll be able to tell me if Shy is okay.

He throws a thumb over his shoulder, pointing at someone who must be somewhere in the vicinity behind him. "Heard what happened."

Great, you mind filling me in?

"Oh yeah?" I'm cautious, not sure if we're talking about the same thing, but either way I need answers.

He leans forward. "Must say, happy to hear you knocked that little shit Dustin down a few notches. Kid needs to get his ass beat."

My eyes grow wide and I nod. It's all I can do because screaming, *What in the hell are you talking about?* would draw too much attention. If what he says is true, that means I was out.

Out as in gone, *and* out as in out in public.

"Anyway, too bad about the food poisoning." He slaps me on the shoulder. "You're still looking a little run-down. Might wanna take another day."

"Another day…yeah." My voice is vacant and the room spins.

"Whoa, easy there." He grips my shoulders, his bushy dark brows settling over concerned eyes, and encourages me to sit. "Put your head between your knees, or…shit…Can we get Lucas some water or something?" he calls over his shoulder.

I stare off in front of me but see nothing. This isn't like a blackout where I go from light to dark like a flick of a switch. This is—

"Lucas…?" A soft, feminine voice rings in my ears seconds before my field of vision is filled with liquid-blue eyes. "I got 'im, Stilts."

Shyann. She's okay. Just seeing her alive and healthy clears my head a little.

My eyes dart to Stilts's retreating feet and then back to her. She's wearing a baseball hat backward and there's white paint splattered across her cheek and some on a few long pieces of black hair that escaped her hat. Maybe it's just the relief at seeing she's okay, but in this moment she's never looked more beautiful.

"Hey..." She cups my jaw and forces my gaze to hers as her eyes search mine. "Lucas...right?" She angles her face away, but only slightly, like she's bracing for something.

"Yeah."

"Good." She lets out a long breath and her expression relaxes. "You're back," she whispers, and a tiny smile tilts her lips, but I can't return it.

She knows.

I survey our surroundings, and once I'm certain we're alone, I ask what I've been dying to know. "What happened?"

"Are you okay to walk?"

I nod.

She helps me to my feet, and I sway.

"Lucas, are you sure you're okay? When was the last time you ate?"

The last time I remember was... "Tacos."

Her head jerks. "Tacos? With me?"

I nod again. "Yeah."

She frowns and dips her shoulder under mine, wraps her arm around me, and holds me to her. "Come on."

We walk through the half-constructed home into the back that opens to dense forest trees. I'm grateful that she's strong, and as we pass by a few of the guys, she makes it look like she's holding on to me rather than holding me up. If I didn't feel so weak, so confused, I'd absorb the feel of her soft body pressed against mine, the warmth of her at my side. After a few yards through the brush, she stops at the base of a large Douglas fir.

"Here." She guides me to the ground, where I drop with my back against the trunk.

"Sorry, I don't know why I'm so messed up. Must be the food poisoning."

She ignores me, or it's possible she didn't hear me. "Be right back." She takes off and her retreating figure blurs to mix with the evergreens.

Sleep begs to take me. A cool breeze combines with the warm sun that filters through the boughs and settles against my skin. My eyelids grow heavy, but before they fall shut, a hand grips my chin.

"I need you to eat." She shoves a sandwich into my hand.

I push it back to her. "I can't. I—"

Her face comes close to mine, so close I can feel her breath on my lips, see the tiny flecks of gray in her eyes, and smell the sweet scent of her shampoo. "Do you trust me?"

"No."

"Eat it." Her eyes are cold and hard; this isn't a request, and I'm too tired to fight.

I take a bite of the sandwich and groan as the flavor floods my mouth. I'm suddenly ravenous, as if all my internal organs just realized they were starving.

She relaxes a little as I swallow bite after bite, until finally she drops next to me to lean against the tree, legs cocked, forearms resting against her jean-clad knees.

As soon as I finish the sandwich, she hands me a bottled water. I drink it in seconds, and she hands me another.

"I'm sorry. I don't know why—"

"You haven't eaten since Friday."

"So?"

Her head tilts and she pins me with a glare that has me dropping my eyes to avoid it. "It's Monday, Lucas."

My head whips around. "What?"

She shoves a bag of green grapes in front of my face. "Eat."

I do as I'm told. Fear of getting sick tickles the back of my mind but my hunger overtakes my unease.

"I don't know what's going on with you, but I get the feeling you're just as clueless as I am."

I stop chewing, shocked at how well she can read me, and then shove more grapes in my mouth.

"Thing is, a lot happened and…" She turns her eyes toward mine and hurt shines through them. "We need to have a serious talk."

FIFTEEN

SHYANN

Thank God he's back.

As much as I want to tie him up and interrogate him about what all went down on Friday night, what the hell he did for two days holed up in his house, I can tell he's scared. That lost look in his eyes I feel in my chest.

A flicker of the terrified boy I've seen before is back and the confusion on his face is enough to rip open old wounds.

I spent all weekend in the office researching what I thought was going on with Lucas, and after collecting as much information as I could, I'm afraid to be right.

Oh, Lucas, what have you been through?

After I feed him my entire lunch, including my midmorning and midafternoon snack, as well as my emergency chocolate stash, his color seems better. He's more alert and has the energy to hold up his own body.

We're tucked back far enough into the forest that no one can see us, but saws and nail guns can be heard beyond the trees. I turn to him and catch him staring at me, his eyebrows pinched together, and he's chewing that bottom lip that I know feels even softer than it looks. He studies the ground.

"Who's Gage?" *Ugh…smooth approach, Shyann.* Then again, finesse has never been my thing.

"Gage is…me." His shoulders drop and he shakes his head. "It's complicated."

I knew it. He's in there, both Gage and Lucas. "What *do* you know?"

He licks his lips and pulls his knees up to rest his forearms on them. "Ever since I can remember, I've had these…blackouts."

I swallow, nervous more for him than myself.

"They were random at first, or at least I thought. But when I got older, I noticed a pattern, like, they never happened at school or when I was home alone with my sister and brothers. They always happened when I was in trouble for something."

"How long do they usually last?"

He digs the heel of his boot into the dirt, raking out a hole it seems he'd rather crawl into than keep talking.

"It's okay. You can trust me."

"When I was ten, I went dark for days. When I came to, I couldn't remember anything."

I turn my head away, attempting to hide my shock, hoping he doesn't see my reaction to the disturbing information. "You always lose days? Like this weekend?"

"No, on average they last a few hours. Sometimes less. Depends on how bad things are." He grimaces.

"What kind of things?" I'm terrified to know the answer.

"Back then? The punishments." He gazes at me with troubled eyes. "Now? The threat."

"What did it this time?"

He shrugs and whispers, "You were upset. I wanted to…comfort you. That's the last thing I remember."

My gut churns, a sickening feeling only rivaled by my sadness. "You felt threatened…by me?"

"Women. They trigger them." He cringes slightly away from me as if he's expecting me to lash out.

I clear my throat and try to relax. If his need to comfort me triggered him before, my panic might do the same and I can't risk losing Lucas now that he's finally letting me in.

"What about the punishments?" I fight a swell of nausea, fearing his answer.

He rubs the back of his neck. "My mom."

I allow the silence to settle between us, not wanting to scare him from telling me more by blabbing the four thousand questions I have swirling through my head.

What if I trigger the violent side of Lucas just for being female? A spike of adrenaline speeds my pulse, and I'm suddenly hyperaware of my surroundings.

My instinct tells me to run, but deep down inside I believe Lucas wouldn't hurt me. He's had me alone, had the opportunity, but the only thing he hurt was my feelings. And even his more aggressive personality protected me from Dustin. That has to mean something.

"Sometimes I'd come to, curled up on the floor, aching all over. Others I'd wake up to her standing over me. She'd scream. I'd go from black to her face twisted in anger and the words…" He is staring at nothing but seems to be seeing everything.

My heart lodges in my throat at how he must've suffered. I scoot closer, place my hand on his back, and rub up and down in long firm strokes. His muscles flex beneath my touch but after a few dozen seconds he seems to calm.

"Did your parents ever take you to a doctor?"

He shakes his head but doesn't elaborate. Guess a woman who punishes her son so extremely that he would black out wouldn't seek medical attention. Too easy to get caught.

"My little brother Michael used to tell me about Gage. He'd say, 'I got scared but then Gage came' and 'If Mom gets mad, it'll be okay because Gage will take care of us.' I thought he was an imaginary friend, their version of a guardian angel."

The broken sound of his voice makes my eyes and sinuses burn.

"It wasn't until later that my little sister was looking at my class picture. She kept pointing at me saying, 'Who is that? Lucas or Gage?' After that, when he'd show up, he'd leave me notes."

"Notes, like on paper?"

"Yes, and also here." He flips his hands over, palms up.

I swallow past the tightness in my throat. "Anything this time?"

He opens his mouth, then quickly closes it and shakes his head. "No."

I fold my arms around my stomach, feeling a sudden chill in the breeze. His mother was abusive; that much is true. I can see why he's avoided my questions about her. Did she abandon him rather than die like I originally thought?

To think her abuse was so severe Lucas became a completely different person to protect himself is tragic beyond comprehension.

"What happened that night, Shyann?" He sounds so broken, as if he already knows the answer and he's apologizing for it.

"You were at a bar."

His wide eyes turn to me. "I was at a bar?" He drops his head into his hands and groans.

"Gage was. He punched a guy I grew up with." No need to go into details; something tells me the less information for Lucas to process the better.

His right hand flexes.

"I didn't know what was going on when you didn't show up for work this morning. I told my dad you were sick to keep him from coming to check on you. Hope that's okay."

"Why would you do that?" he whispers, then turns toward me. "Why would you protect me?"

"Lucas? Have you ever heard the words *dissociative identity disorder*?"

"I think so."

"It's an identity disorder. Some call it *multiple personality disorder*."

His ears get red. He tucks his chin and locks his hands behind his head. "If you're telling me I'm crazy, don't bother. I already know."

"You never got help—"

"I tried. He'd never let me." He studies the tops of the trees. "Don't you see? I can never be trusted because he'll always be part of me."

I blink, memories of Gage, his hate-filled stare, his threats, and that punch he delivered that hardly seemed to faze him.

"Do you want to hurt people?"

"Of course not."

"Maybe you have more control than you think." I shrug, as if it's as simple as that, hoping he feels encouraged even though I haven't the slightest idea if it's true. But I have to believe his goodness would win out.

I run my sweaty palms against my thighs, embarrassed to admit that maybe he's not all that different from me. When I lost my mom, a part of me died with her and I became someone else to avoid feeling the pain—career focused, selfish, hell-bent on leaving the memories behind no matter the cost.

"I don't expect you to understand."

I lean over and place my hand on his arm, begging him to look at me. He doesn't. "Then explain it."

"Why did I smell like perfume?" There's a hardness in his voice I've never heard before and I don't need to ask to know he's talking about Gage.

"He showed up at Pistol Pete's. I saw him kissing a girl and—"

A sound like that of a dying animal falls from his lips and he grips the back of his head. I can't imagine how terrifying it would be to have your body taken over and wake up having no idea what you'd done.

By the slump of his shoulders, I'd say he's assuming the worst. "Nothing happened, Lucas. I'm pretty sure you two never made it past second base."

"This is wrong…"

"It's a mountain town, bar hookups and fights are as common as four-wheel drive."

"…could've really hurt someone…"

"Lucas, you're overreacting."

"…so much worse." He freezes and peers up at me, his gray eyes shining with sadness. "You were there."

My face flames and his eyes dart to my cheeks, then widen. "Did I…Gage, did he…"

I open my mouth to tell him that he kissed me, that his hands roamed my body with a force that managed to terrify and excite me in equal parts. The words dance on the back of my tongue, ache to confess just how much I want him to touch me again, just how much I long for another possessive kiss that robs me of coherent thought.

Whatever he sees in my expression causes him to recoil.

"I gotta go." He pushes up fast and takes a retreating step before turning back to me. He seems to struggle with whether or not to help me up, but eventually gives me his hand and pulls me to my feet. "Thanks for the food.

Tell your dad I'll have that carving to him by the end of the week. I'll finish it at home…I mean, your mom's home…I—"

"Don't worry about that. My dad cares about you. If you need help—"

"No!" The power in his voice seems to scare him and makes my heart leap. "Please." He gets close and the proximity makes me want to pull him into my arms. "Don't tell anyone."

The dark fury that was in his eyes that night is replaced with painful innocence, a vulnerability that makes my arms desperate to soothe. He's broken, achingly beautiful, and—

"Shy."

His calling of my nickname rips me from my thoughts.

Eyes, smoke-gray and pleading. "Please."

"I won't. I promise."

He exhales hard and his shoulders slump. "Thank you. I'll…uh…I'll see you around." He jogs back to the work site, and I give myself a moment to regain my composure.

Lucas is unstable.

There's no denying it.

As much as he should terrify me, he doesn't, and that's what worries me most.

SIXTEEN

SHYANN

It's Friday afternoon. I'm sitting at my desk sorting new bids and am antsy as hell. It's been exactly one week since Lucas—more accurately Gage—kissed me outside Pistol Pete's and four days since I've seen him at all. I've thought about going down to the river house and checking on him, use food as an excuse, bring dog food for his porch-dwelling pet, claim I have some important message from my dad, but I hold back.

He gave me the impression he needed space, and I don't blame him. I can't imagine what it would be like to wake up and realize you've missed entire days, and what's worse, your body is walking and talking and kissing on your behalf. A kiss he doesn't remember and I can't seem to forget.

My cell phone chimes with an incoming text from a number I don't recognize.

It's Loreen. I've got a girl out tomorrow. You interested in picking up a shift?

I chew my lip and contemplate her offer. I made a hundred and fifty dollars last Friday. Even after Dustin got dragged out of the bar and banned for the rest of the night for fighting—funny when he didn't even throw a punch—I doubled what I'd made the first half of the night. Everyone wanted the play-by-play. I may have conveniently forgotten most of the details, knowing whatever blanks I left open the town gossip would fill with their own version on the truth. Good news is, I ended up pulling in some serious dough.

Sam pouted the rest of the night and when she wasn't pouting she was glaring at me. Guess having Lucas blow her off and drag me out of the bar was enough to dissolve whatever bridges we'd built and land me back on her shit list.

My phone rings in my hand, and thinking it's probably Loreen, I move to answer it. Trevor's name in big letters on my caller ID catches the corner of my eye and I send him straight to voice mail. As much as I need Trevor to keep my finger on the silent pulse of my postmortem career, I don't need to jump every time he calls.

"Shy!" my dad hollers from his office. "Pack your bags. We're going up to the lake to fish this weekend. Bass are bitin' and we wanna grab some while we still can without freezin' our balls off."

I cringe and spin my chair to face him. "Oooh, yeah…I don't have balls, so I'm gonna pass."

"Family time, it'll be fun." The skin around his eyes crinkles with a semi-smile.

"As enticing as a weekend in a crappy little cabin while you and Cody fart and drink beer sounds, I'll have to pass. I picked up a shift at the bar." *Or I just decided I would.*

"That's not how it is and you know it." He sorts and stacks some papers. "Only sissies get a cabin. We camp."

I roll my eyes and he laughs in his usual grumbly way as I punch out a quick text to Loreen confirming that I'll take the shift. "Fish guts, chewing tobacco spit, and no bathing for forty-eight hours. Sorry to miss it."

"Suit yourself." He kicks back and studies me. "If you're staying home, I'll have Lucas check in on you while we're gone."

My eyes go wide, but I spin and give him my back before he notices.

"...such thing as being too safe."

"I'm fine, Dad. You don't have to do that. Lucas is busy on his piece for the McKinstry place. I don't need a babysitter."

"He's right down the road. I'll just ask him to pop in and make sure you're okay."

"*Make sure I'm okay?* Dad, that's insane. You do realize I've lived alone before and managed to survive, right?"

"It'll make me feel better to know someone's checkin' in on you."

"I'm not a little girl. I can take care of myself." Anger wars with panic. My dad pushing Lucas at me again might spook him. After all, the last time this happened ended with Gage.

"It's not a big deal. Do it for me, okay? Give your old man some peace of mind."

"But Lucas—"

"He doesn't mind, Shy." I hear the loud thump of his work boots as he moves across the small portable office to my desk.

"How do you know? Just because you give him a place to stay doesn't mean you can take advantage of him."

His eyes narrow and he tilts his head. "Not taking advantage. I'd ask Cody to do the same thing."

"But he's my brother. Lucas is my..." I throw my hands in the air. "Nothing." The word tastes sour in my mouth.

He leans close. "You sure 'bout that?"

"Dad!"

"Lock up when you leave." He stomps past me and out the door, calling over his shoulder as he goes, "I'll see you Sunday night."

Ugh! Does the man ever friggin' listen?

LUCAS

"…so I'd appreciate it if you'd stop by and check on Shy while we're gone." Nash stands with one heavy boot on the bottom step of the porch, leg straight, as if he's holding the house back to keep it from attacking.

I grip the V-groove chisel and force myself to set down the mantelpiece I'd been working on when he showed up. The air is cooler in the evenings and there's a time just before the sun dips below the tree line when everything in the forest seems to come into focus. Shadows dance and light bounces. I'd moved my chair to the porch to work, having no idea my quiet evening was about to get interrupted.

"Yes, sir." I nod while my body aches to yell no.

I'm not ready to face her inquisitive eyes, her probing questions; I've barely managed to swallow all that I did, that Gage did. One thing I do remember and could never forget is the moment our lips touched before Gage threw me into the dark. I've relived it in my dreams, the subtle breath she took when I pressed my lips to hers. I felt the black come, thought I could hold it off. I was wrong. But I remember that kiss. As for what happened between Shyann and him, I'm still in the dark.

I can't be trusted around Shyann.

But Nash Jennings believes in me. He's given me a job, a place to live, and helped me to find my talent and use it to make money. He's done more for me than the California juvenile detention center, more than the halfway houses with all their good intentions, more than I could ever accomplish on my own. He deserves what very little I have to give.

He peers up from the dog bowls that sit just left of the bottom step. "Got a dog?"

"Stray."

He merely shrugs. "Good. Dog'll keep away the critters."

I nod.

He slaps a hand on his thigh, signaling the end of the conversation, but holds up one beefy, calloused hand, like he forgot to tell me something. "Fair warning, Shy isn't keen on bein' looked after. If you could, I don't know, make your checkin' in seem casual, that'd help your cause." He nods without sparing even a single glance to the house and turns to move back to his truck. "Be back Sunday."

"Yes, sir." He can't hear me, and I'm stuck on the porch trying to figure out how the hell I'm going to manage dropping in on Shyann.

My palms sweat and my pulse pounds. Anxiety floods my veins and marks me with insecurity. I'll just drop by. Easy. Knock, make sure she's okay, then leave.

"I can do that." I suck in a shaky breath and sink into my chair.

There's not much daylight left, so I pull the piece of wood to my lap, bend over it, and angle my chisel. The sharp metal edge thumps wildly against the lumber.

I'm shaking.

Defeat casts over me. I slide the piece to the floor and close my eyes.

"Dammit, Shyann. You're going to ruin everything for me."

SHYANN

"*...officials have yet to comment on what is predicted be an economic—*"

Click.

"*...the CDC reports this year to be the worst flu season since—*"

Click.

"*...plane went down after pilots radioed in—*"

Click.

"*...Kanye West is at it again—*"

Click.

The television flashes and fades to black and I toss the remote onto the coffee table. My dad refuses to get cable television, so my options for six o'clock on a Friday night are news or entertainment news. Lucky me.

I'd rather watch dust settle than other people live out what should have been my future. The good news is, feeling sorry for myself and wallowing in my own mistakes has kept my mind from wandering to Lucas. But sure enough, the second the distraction is gone, my thoughts are back on the beautifully broken man.

What must life be like for him? He'd talked about his brothers and even a sister. He has a family, so why is he here alone in Payson? Maybe he was forced out because of his condition?

I push up from the threadbare couch and move to the kitchen. My heart squeezes as memories of cooking for my mom push thoughts of Lucas from my head. She had a passion for cooking, which made her last few months with a feeding tube feel like a cruel joke. She was so young, not even forty years old, when she was diagnosed and died two years later. We—no, *she*—deserved more time.

Slamming cupboards, I decide that after dinner I'll go into town, maybe catch a movie. Anything to get away from this house and its depressing memories that never seem to let up.

A quick once-over of the freezer and I settle on frozen pizza. I rip open the packaging and toss the icy disk into the oven without waiting for it to preheat. The kitchen timer ticks loudly, breaking up the dreaded silence. I drum my fingers against the countertop. This'll take forever and every passing second of quiet feels like a century. I crank up the heat to defrost my dinner faster—

A knock sounds at the door and I jump.

My instincts scream, *Murderer!* until logic reminds me it's probably my babysitter, but if good looks could kill, I'd be a goner. As embarrassing as it is to be checked in on, I'd be lying if I said I wasn't a little excited about seeing Lucas, getting my eyes on the subject of all my thoughts.

"Coming." I pad across the kitchen floor in sock-covered feet and take a steadying breath before swinging open the door.

"Hey, Lucas."

My heart kicks behind my ribs at seeing him, standing there looking as timid and handsome as ever in jeans that seem to hug his long body in all the right places and a long-sleeved blue T-shirt. The top half of his face is shadowed beneath that damn ball cap I'm starting to wish I could hide so I didn't have to fight to see his eyes.

He shoves his hands into his pockets. "Your dad, he—"

"I know. He's a little overprotective." I move into the doorway and lean a shoulder against the frame. "You didn't have to do this. I'm fine here alone."

He looks around, everywhere but at me. "Promised Mr. Jennings I'd do it."

"Gotcha. But as you can see…" I motion to myself, from my faded Jennings Contractors tee to my pink pajama pants. "I'm good." It's then I realize I didn't hear him arrive. Here in the mountains where the earth is covered in rocks, dirt, and pine needles; it's impossible to get anywhere without making noise. "Did you walk?"

He looks down the path that leads to the river house. "Yeah."

"Lucas, you shouldn't walk that far this late at night. At least, not without a rifle."

For the first time, his eyes meet mine. "Don't like guns. Besides, it's not that far."

"I know how far it is. I walked it, remember?" As soon as the words leave my lips, I curse.

"Remember what? Why were you walking it?" His voice is pained, and the sound makes my chest ache.

"Never mind. I'm sorry." I blow out a long breath and step back into the house. "You wanna come in?"

He doesn't answer verbally but takes a retreating step.

Okay, fine. I walk outside and close the door behind me, then drop to an old iron bench my mom brought home from a garage sale when I was ten. The thing weighs a ton and Dad said he'd get rid of it if he were strong enough to lift it. He'd smile at her because we all knew he loved the damn thing for the simple fact that it made her happy. The bench was covered in Tupperware the week Mom died. It became a drop-off for the town do-gooders. Food for the mourning, as if we could eat when our entire world had been ripped apart.

I tuck my feet up under my butt and dust the dirt from my socks.

Lucas moves a little closer to lean against a large pine tree. "Tell me why I'd remember you walking miles through the forest, Shyann."

I contemplate lying, but something tells me he needs my honesty more than my protection. "That day in your kitchen, Gage he, uh…sent me home."

He leans his head back hard enough that it thumps against the trunk. "I'm sorry."

"He's protective of you, Lucas."

"I know."

"He doesn't need to protect you from me."

His eyes look almost black as he zeros in on mine.

"I'd never hurt you," I whisper.

"There's all kinds of hurt." His hands fist against his thighs and he stares at me as if he wants to say something, to confess something, but can't.

"What is it?" I turn my whole body to face him. "Tell me."

"Did we, I mean, did Gage...*do* anything?"

The cool air does nothing to temper my cheeks. "He kissed me."

There's a sharp intake of breath and then he drops his gaze. "I'm sorry." He doesn't sound apologetic. He sounds...angry.

"I'm not."

His head whips around to face me, his jaw tight. "How can you say that?"

"I don't know, I mean, I'm trying to figure it all out, too, but..." My stomach tumbles with nerves. I've never had a problem speaking my mind before, but with Lucas everything means more. "I like you, Lucas." There, I said it. Now he can run or fess up.

"Wha...why?" His eyebrows drop low over his eyes and he takes a few steps closer and into the light so I can see the curiosity on his face.

I almost laugh at how genuinely shocked and interested in my answer he seems. He's not fishing for compliments; it's as if he really can't believe I'd have any kind of good feelings toward him. Which is as heartbreaking as it is endearing.

"Why not?"

He grimaces, and I fear he might take off at any second, so I may as well get it all out.

"You're sweet, polite, and you don't try to push me around or control me."

His expression grows more intense.

"You've been through something and I get the feeling that what you've shared is only a small fraction of that." I stand and move closer to him, not enough to touch but close enough that he can see my face in the dim light.

"But sometimes, when I look at you, I see a hurt that is so familiar. I can't explain it more than to say I feel like I understand you."

He shuts down, closes himself off by turning away from me, so I'm stuck with his profile. "You don't know me."

"I know, and the little I do know about you scares me."

"It should." He looks down at me and there's a glint of danger in his eyes, as if Gage is simmering just below the surface. "I can't do this."

"We're not *doing* anything, Lucas. Can we just try being friends?"

"I told you, I don't have friends."

"And I told you, I don't either. So we'll be each other's first."

This time it's him who blushes, a crack in his guarded demeanor. I breathe in a sigh of relief, hoping he'll give us a shot.

An awkward silence builds between us and I'm so afraid if it stretches out any longer I'll lose him.

I clear my throat. "Have you eaten?"

"I'm not hungry."

"Okay, tough guy." I grab his hand and for a second he tries to pull away, but I refuse to let go. "Come on, let me feed you. Then I'll take you home."

He seems conflicted, but I ignore it, hoping it's not me he's conflicted about but that it's this situation he's unsure how to handle. I drag him through the door and he freezes.

"Something's burning." He pushes past me and races toward the kitchen. A few tendrils of smoke slither from the oven.

"Aw, crap."

He grabs a dishtowel and drops the oven door, pulling out a blackened pizza and dropping it into the sink. With a flick of his wrist, he turns on the water and I move around, opening all the windows, hoping to air it out before the smoke detector alerts the entire mountain to the fact that I'm a crappy cook.

He coughs a couple times and continues to fan the smoke toward the open window.

I use a dishtowel to do the same, as if I'm sending smoke signals for take-out. "I hope you like your pizza thin and crispy with extra cheese."

"And charcoal."

My jaw drops and I prop my hands on my hips. "My goodness, Lucas...did you just make a *joke*?"

His lips twitch and he shakes his head. "No. I was being serious."

Even his barely-there smile makes my stomach flip.

I fake gasp and point at him grinning. "Two jokes!"

He shuts off the water and tosses the towel on the counter, then turns, leans against it, and crosses his arms across his chest. It's one of the few times I've seen him act comfortable, almost confident. "Now what?"

I chew on the inside of my mouth to hold back my smile. "Hmmm...I suppose since it's your job to make sure I'm taken care of we better grab some food."

He drops his arms and shifts on his feet. "Oh, like...out?"

"You afraid to be seen in public with me or something?" Not that I'd blame him. "The rumors will fly, and the gossip circles will buzz, not to mention it'll give Sam a reason to hate me even more—"

"Your friend Sam?"

Oh shit. "Uh..." I wave him off, saving the Sam story for later, fearing it'll spook him. "Better yet, let's hit a drive-through and take it back to your place."

His eyes grow wide.

"I've gotta drop you off anyway, right? It's a nice night; we'll eat in the truck by the river. It'll be fun. That way I don't even have to change my clothes." I wink and head back to my room to grab my boots and my wallet before he can protest.

I can't explain this overpowering need to be with Lucas. The more I learn about him, the hungrier I am to know more. In so many ways we're nothing alike, but in all the ways that matter we are. He's complex, has the potential to be dangerous, and I'm putting myself in his path no matter how many times he pushes me away. There's also my draw to protect him. The strange pull that makes me want to follow him around and keep him safe. I blame it on the sexy vulnerability he possesses, the mysterious brooding that calls to a woman's need to soothe and heal.

Then there's Gage.

A man I know little about other than the fact that he's volatile. If I want to spend time with Lucas, I'll need to tread lightly to avoid triggering Gage. That means I'll have to keep my distance, work on being friends until Lucas trusts me enough to let me in.

Patience has never been my strong suit, but I'm willing to give it a shot.

LUCAS

"Burgers, Mexican, or…burgers?" We're at a red light and Shyann's leaning forward over her steering wheel to peek at all the fast-food places that converge at the main intersection in town. "Oh, there's Chinese, but Chinese drive-through?" She purses her lips. "Seems fishy if you ask me. Amazing how many places have popped up since I lived here." Her eyes meet mine and even in the dim light of the truck cab they practically sparkle. "Preference?"

"No." The angry roll in my stomach would prefer peanut butter sandwiches, but I keep my mouth shut. She knows about Gage and invited me into her house, made plans for us to have dinner together alone, and friendship. She offered me friendship. I'll eat whatever she wants to keep from screwing this up.

The light turns green.

"Burgers it is. This place has the best double cheeseburgers in town." She pulls her truck up to a building I've seen before. Bright red and blue sign and the parking lot has spaces where you can get service in your car by a girl on roller skates. She moves past all those and to the drive-through. "What looks good?"

I stare at the menu but see nothing. Fear of trying something new pricks at my nerves, and although I know I'll most likely be fine, I fear choosing something that will make me sick. "Whatever you're having. Please."

She studies me for a second through narrowed eyes until the speaker crackles and a static voice comes through. "Welcome to Sonic. Can I take your order?"

Shyann leans out the window and my eyes immediately trace the outline of her small waist as it flares into feminine hips. Her shirt slides up a little to expose a slice of olive skin that's flawless and probably soft to the touch.

"Two double cheeseburger meals, fries, and two Cokes." She drops back down to her seat, robbing me of the view. "Sound okay?"

I nod and she pulls the truck around to pay. I grab a twenty from my wallet and hand it to her.

She waves me off. "No, it's on me."

I shove the money at her. "Doesn't feel right. Let me."

Her eyes narrow. "If you pay, it'll feel like a date." The way she looks at me with an eyebrow raised in challenge makes my heart thunder in my chest.

I want this to be a date. I pass her the money and she takes it, a soft blush coloring her cheeks. "Thank you."

"You're welcome."

I turn away to hide my face as heat crawls up my neck. She clears her throat and an awkward silence fills the truck cab. I've never been out to dinner with a woman, nor have I ever been this close to one as pretty and caring as Shy. I'm able to relax a little around her now without a hint of threat from Gage, which is progress.

Seconds tick by but it feels like so much longer when finally the drive-through window slides open to reveal a woman wearing a shirt that matches the sign out front and a visor she's wearing more like a headband.

"That'll be fourteen-fifty— Hey, wait..." She puts her elbows on the windowsill to get a closer look. "I know you."

I would think she's talking to Shyann, except her eyes are firmly settled on me. Shyann's gaze whips back and forth between us.

"No, ma'am."

Her glare is tight and she manages to lean out more so that her head is practically inside the truck. "Sure I do. You're the new guy. Girls at the beauty salon were just talking about you the other day." She props her chin in her palm. "Everyone's dying to know your story. You single?"

My heart races and I struggle for a polite response.

"Ahem!" Shyann waves her hand in front of the woman's face. "I'm sitting right here." She turns her body, making herself a human barrier.

I stare in shock at the back of Shyann's head. She's protecting me.

My chest expands with a breath of relief.

The woman waves off Shy with a smile. "No disrespect, honey. I was just asking." She blinks a few times and grins. "Shyann Jennings, is that you?"

She sighs and her shoulders slump. "Yes."

The nosy woman flattens her palm to her chest. "Mary Beth Stewart. We had history and chemistry together."

"Oh, yeah. You look so...different." The way Shy said it didn't make it sound like a good different and I have to bite down to keep from laughing.

Mary Beth pats the ends of her shoulder-length hair. "Thank you, I've been trying to stay young." She cups her breasts. "Got these last year, and—"

"Okay, well..." Shy shoves money at the woman. "This should cover it."

"Oh, right!" Mary Beth smiles and takes the offered cash.

Shy turns to me, shock painting her expression, and mouths, *She grabbed her boobs!*

Battle lost. Laughter shoots from my lips, the sound so shocking, I turn away to muffle it into my hand. By the time I manage to get control, I find her looking at me in that soft way that I feel in my chest. Our gazes tangle and for a moment I'm trapped in the intensity of it.

"You laughed."

I clear my throat at the emotions whirling through me and thankfully no darkness. "Yeah."

"Drinks? Hello?"

Shy blinks and I suck in a breath as she turns to grab our Cokes. I take them from her to put them in the drink holder so she can get the rest of our order.

"Shyann, how is your brother?" She rests her forearms back on the windowsill, settling in. "I always did have the biggest crush on him."

"He's fine. Thanks!"

"It was great seeing yo—" We don't hear what else she has to say because Shyann pulls out of the drive-through and right onto the road back to our part of town.

I turn to see the woman hanging out the window, her lips still flapping. "I don't think she was finished talkin'."

"Huh?" She feigns shock and innocence. "Oh, was she talking to me? I couldn't quite hear her through all the slut."

I pull down my baseball hat and hope she doesn't see how much I'm enjoying her jealousy. "She seemed okay to me."

She rolls her eyes. "Of course you would say that. She practically crawled over my body to get into your lap."

A tiny smile ticks my lips. "You're exaggerating."

"Puleaze." She holds her palm up. "Don't even bother defending her. Poor girl can't help herself. Lord knows you don't make it easy," she mumbles.

"I didn't do anything."

"Besides be insanely charming and handsome? No, you're right, you didn't."

I direct my face-aching smile out the side window.

This woman, Shyann Jennings, smart, funny, kind…She thinks I'm charming and handsome and if I'm not mistaken she implied that she and I are a couple. "Thank you."

She digs her hand into the bag set between us to fish out a cluster of French fries. "You're welcome." She smiles, then shoves the fries into her mouth.

I gaze out the window and watch the darkness fly by, gratefully aware that the pitch-black only lingers outside of my head.

Gage is distant for now and Shyann is safe.

All I have to do is keep it that way.

SEVENTEEN

LUCAS

The ride back to the river house is silent, which is surprising considering the woman I'm with. There's a longing I haven't felt before, an urge to ask her a question just to hear her voice. I don't, though, committed to holding back and squelching urges in order to keep myself under control.

She pulls her truck up to the river's edge, rolls down both windows, and cuts the engine. Handing me my food just like she did with the fry bread tacos, she settles in with one fluffy boot resting in her open window.

I stare down at the burger and fries in my lap, building up the courage to eat.

"What's the story behind that?"

I turn to find her probing eyes darting between my face and my food.

I shrug. "Already told you. Got food—"

"Poisoning, I know, but it must've been pretty traumatic to turn you off food how many years later?"

I clear my throat. "Fifteen or so."

She whistles. "Were you hospitalized or something?"

"No." My mother would've rather us drown in our own vomit.

"What happened?" Her voice is so soft, and I want to tell her.

I want to evict even this small piece of myself, purge it from my system and feel lighter with it gone. But bringing up the past could provoke Gage and I won't risk her safety. I search the recesses of my mind, reach out with my feelings and sense nothing. No dark presence looming or fear for my well-being. Only contentment.

"Hey..." She squeezes my forearm. "You don't have to talk about it."

I don't take my eyes off her long delicate fingers on my skin, something in the past that would send Gage to the surface, and I still sense nothing.

My heart rate is steady.

I'm not afraid.

I lick my lips and turn to her. "When we were kids—"

"We? As in...um"—she picks at the paper napkin in her hand and avoids my eyes—"you and Gage?"

Surprisingly, a tiny smile ticks my lips. "No, we as in me and my brothers and sister." Just mentioning them makes my heart cramp violently.

She grins, as if the information brought her some satisfaction. Unease twists in my gut at the knowledge that what I'm about to tell her will wipe that smile clean off her face.

"My mother would punish us in *unconventional* ways."

Her dark eyebrows pinch together. "What does that mean?"

"She'd withhold food."

Her face twists with repulsion. "She would *starve* her kids? As punishment?"

I wince at the anger in her voice.

"I'm sorry. Go on."

I blow out a heavy breath and check for fear but feel nothing but relief at unloading. "We'd be so hungry that when she'd finally decide we'd been punished enough, she'd feed us. The meat would taste so good. I mean, we were starving, so we'd eat anything." Saliva floods my mouth as I recall the variety of things she'd have me eat. I keep the details to myself.

"Part of her punishment was our belief that the food was a reward, only to later find out it was all part of the punishment." My gaze slides to the windshield, staring out at nothing but seeing memories in Technicolor. "She had to have left the food out for weeks. Even now, I have a hard time smelling cooked meat." My gut tightens as I remember going from full to sick in a matter of hours.

I peek over at Shy, her eyes light with interest. "I know it's safe now, but it happened so many times it's like my stomach just can't accept the fact that I'm not being tricked again."

"How many times did your mother do this to you, Lucas?" Her voice shakes, but from anger or sadness I don't know and by her expression it's hard to gauge.

"Too many," I whisper. "Too many times to count."

"God, that's awful. Is that when you, when Gage…um…"

"I don't remember life without the blackouts." I don't explain that he rarely showed up for the food poisoning. That was minor compared to her other punishments and I'd only black out when things became too much for me to handle.

Gage hasn't always been my curse. Most of the time, he's been my savior.

She shakes her head before dropping it back to the seat. "I had no idea, the tacos, and now…I feel horrible."

Why do I have the intense urge to comfort her?

To pull her to me and hope my touch can erase the images I put in her head.

She gazes at me with more compassion than I've seen from another human being, and the intensity of it threatens to unman me.

"Don't. I'm okay now," I whisper, wanting to reassure her, because for some unknown reason I'd rather go through the sickness and the pain a hundred times over rather than be the cause of her discomfort.

This is when I wish I were a stronger man. If I could lay my feelings out, be brave like the strong woman sitting next to me and just tell her I like her. That I think about her all the time and fantasize about a life with her in it. I wish she knew how much I want to be normal for her, how much she deserves and how desperately I'd try and ultimately fail to be the kind of man who could make her happy. I want her. More than I should and enough that she has the potential to destroy me completely.

I open my mouth to speak, but slam it shut when she jumps in her seat.

"Well, then..." She grabs the burger from my lap. "What about French fries? You cool with those?"

I blink at the sudden change in her demeanor. "Yeah, I think so."

"You sure?"

That's it? I spill the ugly of my past and she absorbs it, then shakes it off like she doesn't see me as pathetic or damaged? "Yes."

She hops out of the truck and I watch as she rounds the bed to the front porch of the house. I follow behind her and get there just as she tosses both burgers into the dog's bowl. She wipes her hands and peers up at me. "No more meat, okay? I promise."

"You didn't have to—"

"I know. But I wanted to." An emotion flickers behind her eyes and she schools her expression before I get a good hold on what it was. "Can you control it? I mean, have you tried to control it, him? Gage?"

"If I stay alert, I can usually feel it coming. I've been able to hold off the blackout, but only for seconds. When he shows up, it's...abrupt, like getting hit on the head. One minute I'm there, the next I'm not."

She steps closer, searching my eyes, and the proximity makes my pulse pound. "Can he hear me?"

"I think so. We're the same person. If I can hear you, he can too."

"But you couldn't hear me when Gage was here."

I jolt at her confession. "You tried to get to me?"

"Not at first. At first I just thought you hated me and wanted me to leave you alone, but then, after the ki—" She rubs her forehead, her eyes downcast. "Crap, maybe...never mind."

I pull her hand from her face, unable to bear her hiding from me. "Tell me." My stomach tumbles and nerves make my palms sweat as I anticipate her next words.

She exhales in defeat and fixes her eyes on mine. "It was the kiss, Lucas. That's when I realized it wasn't you."

"How?"

"It was rough, aggressive, demanding. Everything you're not."

I swallow and try to avoid dropping my gaze. "Did he hurt you?"

"No," she whispers, and there's a longing in her voice.

"Did you like it?"

Her breath catches. "Yes."

My eyelids slide closed when I feel the warmth of her palm on my jaw and her fingers absently brush the scar on my neck, sending goose bumps down my arms.

"Talk to me."

"But...he scared you, right? You said he kicked you out, that you walked home." I blink, a war of emotions tumbling around in my chest. "I can't believe you'd kiss me."

"Gage kissed me."

"But you kissed him back. I mean, you kissed me back?"

She shivers and peers up at me with molten-blue eyes. "I did."

My pulse kicks wildly and I tremble as Shyann moves to erase the distance between us. She doesn't touch me, but she's close enough that with every inhale the heat of her breasts warms my ribs. "What are you doing, Shy?"

She smiles softly and closes her eyes. "I like it when you call me that."

That wasn't an answer, but the way she said it makes it feel like one.

"I don't know how." The words rush out, a defense of some kind.

"You do, trust me. You *really* do."

"I don't want to disappoint you." I blink and search the backs of my eyes, the depths of my head, hoping I don't find Gage there waiting to come forward. Other than the quick brush of our lips in my kitchen, I've never kissed a woman before. I've been kissed, every single time against my will, but I've blacked out before things went further. I've woken to naked women lying next to me, used condoms littering the floor, and an ache between my legs, but it's always been Gage.

"I won't be disappointed, Lucas. But I won't push you into doing something you don't want to do." She takes a step back, but my arm shoots out to hook her around the waist.

I didn't think; I just didn't want her to distance herself and reacted. She stares up at me with wide eyes, shock, which I recognize immediately because it's exactly the way I'm feeling.

Her expression softens and she guides my other arm around her waist so that I can interlace my fingers at her lower back. "Is this okay?"

The warmth of her body seeps through my hands and stirs my hunger. "Yes." I want to roar that it's better than okay. That I've been fantasizing about her like this since the night she showed up in the river, but every passing second where my lips aren't on hers feels like wasted time.

Sliding her hands up my forearms, she blazes a trail of heat to my biceps. "You're shaking."

"I'm nervous."

"Don't be. Just tell me this is what you want, Lucas. This is your kiss, not Gage's. If I'm pushing you—"

"You're not."

She pulls herself even closer and my erection meets the soft flesh of her stomach. My cheeks flame with embarrassment, but she doesn't seem to care. Instead she bites her lip and her breathing picks up.

I lick my lips, suddenly starving for her mouth but unsure how to proceed. In my limited experience, kisses have been violent, a rough meeting of mouths and teeth. That's not what I want with her.

What I want is to freeze time. I want to record how she feels in my hands, the longing in her eyes, the heat of her breath. I want to slow every single moment with her down so seconds last hours until her touch is branded into my memory.

A slight breeze carries the scent of her shampoo to swirl around me. My head dips for more, to breathe her in, absorb this little part of her. She smells so good, my mouth waters to taste her. A flash of insecurity gives me a moment of pause, but the draw is too much and I press my lips to her forehead. Her skin is like velvet against my mouth and I moan at the sensation. Her muscles go loose beneath my hold and she sighs, a message meant for only me. My breathing speeds and I lock my hands together even tighter as a tremor of nerves washes over me. I search my head and find nothing but peaceful anticipation.

"You're okay, Lucas." Her fingertips sift into my hair at my nape, and her thumbs run along my neck, gently encouraging.

Her touch brushes against my scar, shooting pulses of electricity to coil between my legs. My mouth waters and I swallow hard as I focus on her lips—plump flesh ripe with color, slick from her tongue and calling for my attention. I tilt my head, and our breath mixes as we come together.

The first touch of our lips is tentative, testing. Her mouth is warm against mine and she teases me to take more. My eyelids feel heavy, but I refuse to close them, fear that the dark will steal this from me before I can taste. One sample of her is likely to rob me of what's left of my sanity, but it doesn't keep me from wanting it.

Needing it more than air.

I run the tip of my tongue along her bottom lip and she opens enough that our lips converge. They mold together and move slowly as if the world itself has stalled, that time has frozen so this kiss will sear itself into our DNA, become the standard to which all beauty in life will be held against.

She pushes up on her toes, running the softness of her body against the hardness of mine. Having no clue what I'm doing, half following her lead and half following my gut, I dig my fingers into her hips, holding her to me. She moans, low and throaty, and the sound flips some switch inside me. Instinct takes over, and a knowledge I didn't know I had has me sliding my tongue against hers in a gentle rhythm. It must be what she wants because her fingers bite into my neck and she makes a sound that vibrates against my chest and sets fire to my blood.

More. I need more.

My hands unlock and the desire to learn her every curve, feel the heat of her bare skin against mine, overrides all common sense. I duck my hands under her shirt and the soft skin of her lower back is silk on my palms.

Her mouth devours mine and she fists my hair in an iron grip. I lift her to her toes and back down, rubbing her breasts against me, her body against the hardness between my legs that strains toward her.

God, yes. I've craved this, craved her.

A hunger rages within me. I grasp the back of her head and her body bows as I take control and deepen the kiss. A frenzy I've never felt before unleashes within me. Every fantasy I've had of this moment is nothing compared to living it. Her willing body in my arms spurs my imagination and I picture us twisted together, powering inside her—my vision flickers black.

No!

I rip my mouth away, panting. My pulse thunders in my ears.

"What happened? Is everything okay?" Her voice is heavy with worry and impatience.

"Fine." My forehead rests against hers, trying desperately to catch my breath. "I'm okay."

"Lucas…"

"Really." I flutter small kisses along her jaw, wanting so badly to do more but fear Gage will take this away from me. Focusing on my desire, my control, I try blindly to communicate to Gage and hope he doesn't see Shyann as a threat.

She doesn't seem as worried and turns to meet my mouth with hers. Unable to deny her, or myself, I groan and give in to this kiss. The warmth of her lips wraps me in security. My fists tremble with the effort to stay still as her fingers explore. She brushes against my nipples. I suck in a harsh breath and my hips jack forward. She grins but continues her delicate assault. My chest heaves, part of me wanting more while the other begs for reprieve from the overload of sensations. Her nails rake along my T-shirt and heat fires in my gut.

More.

My mind envisions her naked in the river while I explore every inch of her body. I imagine my mouth between her legs, her arching beneath me and my name falling from her lips.

Our kiss grows frantic. Blood powers through my veins. Darkness descends, but I push it back, hold it off for as long as I can because I'll even fight with my own head if it means more time with Shyann.

Naked, wet, heated, and those blue eyes begging.

Her hands slide lower, dip into the waistband of my jeans.

Tunnel vision presses in.

I want this. Want her. Never wanted anything so badly in my life.

I slam my eyes shut.

Focus.

Stay present.

I push back with everything I have.

But I'm not strong enough.

The veil falls.

EIGHTEEN

GAGE

Will this woman ever fucking learn?

I rip my lips from hers and she whimpers. Greedy little bitch.

Apparently my message to leave Luke the fuck alone wasn't understood.

I drop my hands, which had been locked so tightly to her my muscles ache, and step back, seething.

She gasps, and I keep my eyes to the dirt to avoid having to see the pathetic look women get when they're rejected. Weakness is revolting.

"Hey, I'm sorry." She reaches out and I smack her hand from the air before she can touch me. Her arms wrap around her belly.

I slowly move my gaze up her body. Baggy-ass pants that wouldn't flatter even the sexiest woman, a worn shirt that showcases her heaving breasts, and then…ta-da! There it is.

Recognition.

I grin.

She scowls. "Gage."

I hold out my hands and bow. "At your service, whore."

She jolts at my verbal stab, but her glare tightens. "Why are you here?"

I chuckle and look up to the stars. "Hmm…I was about to ask you the same thing, but seeing the condition I found you two in, I'd say I know exactly why you're here, *Shyyy* Ann."

She shakes her head, long strands of her midnight hair swaying with the movement. "I'm here with Lucas…"

"Not anymore."

"You weren't invited." The last word is spit like venom, but I don't miss the quiver of fear in her voice.

How fucking dare she.

"I'm not invited? *I'm* not invited!" I step into her face, rage making my muscles tense and shake. "You're the whore who isn't fucking invited!"

I gotta give it to her. Despite the hurt that works behind her eyes, she doesn't back down, which seems to harden my dick even more. Bitch.

"You didn't listen when I told you to leave him alone."

She squares her shoulders. "I don't want to leave him alone."

"What do you think is going to happen here? What delusional little girl fantasy do you have swirling in that tiny brain of yours, huh? You think he'll fall in love with you? That the two of you'll ride off into the sunset and live happily ever after?"

"What…no!"

"That's what you want, isn't it? You want Luke because he's easy to control. You love the power you have over him, don't you? Using that pussy to control the poor bastard."

She cringes.

I lurch at her and as much as I'd love to wrap my hands around her pretty little neck, I ball my fists at my side. "Stay away from him."

"I don't want to." Her voice is quiet, timid. She's losing her fight. Finally.

"I don't give a damn what you want. Do you have any idea how many women have tried to fuck Luke? How many times I've had to keep him from being raped?"

Her lip trembles and she shakes her head. "You're lying."

A low chuckle reverberates in my chest. "You don't know shit. And thanks to *me*, neither does he."

"Tell me."

"Why? So you can pity him more than you already do?"

"I don't pity him." Her full lips turn down as she most likely realizes the lie in her words.

"The fuck you don't. Everyone does. I'm only going to say this one more time." I breathe deep, trying to get a hold on my rage. *"Leave him the fuck alone!"*

She advances, pushes up on her toes, and gets directly into my face. "If you want me gone so badly, why didn't you let Dustin have me that night at the bar?"

Her words knock me in the chest. I was hoping she'd forget that night. All of it.

"Go home, Shyann." My growled demand doesn't move her an inch. Stubborn bitch.

"Tell me. If you hate me so much, why did you protect me from Dustin?"

I pull off Luke's stupid hat, run a frustrated hand through my hair, and fist it until it burns. "If I tell you, you'll leave?"

"Not a chance."

My gaze darts to hers. "Do you have a death wish or something?"

"I'm not afraid to die if that's what you're asking." Her body shivers, betraying her words. "I'm not afraid of you."

Aah, false confidence is such an easy tell.

"You're in the middle of a dark forest. No one home to make sure you get there safely. I could bury you and be rested by morning if I wanted."

She takes a retreating step. "You wouldn't."

My lips curl back over my teeth. "You know nothing about what I would and wouldn't do."

"That's where you're wrong." She straightens her shoulders in a pathetic attempt at confidence. "You protect Lucas. You'd never hurt me because you know it would hurt him."

I blink, considering her words. "A little pain now to save him from a lot of pain in the future would be worth it."

"Yeah? Is that why you starved him?"

Touché. The bitch is smart.

"I knew it. You let him starve as punishment. Just like his mother did."

I grip her arm and shove her back. "You fucking bitch! Don't you dare compare me to that useless piece of trash." I shove her again, making her stumble. "You think because Luke shared one little story with you, you know us?" I shove her again and she loses her footing and falls. I tower over her, glaring down at the pretty little bug that I could so easily squash under my foot. Be rid of her forever. "Stay the fuck away from him. Do you hear me?"

She sniffles but pushes up to her feet. Her eyes meet mine, and although hers shine with unshed tears, her gaze is steel. "Fuck you."

My nostrils flare. My pulse rages and static fills my ears. I reach around and grab her by the back of the head, her hair a handle as I stomp a path to the creek.

Bitches. Every fucking one of them deserves to die.

The water hits my boots, seeping in above my ankles as I drag her deeper into the frigid water.

Her wet boots slip on the rocks and she cries out when her weight drops. Her hands grip my forearm as my hold on her hair is the only thing that keeps her standing. "Gage, stop!"

Ha! Not until she understands.

We're waist-deep in the water when I pull her around to stand in front of me. My muscles shake with anger and a bunch of other shit I refuse to dwell on. The glow of the moon our only source of light, her lips appear blue and her eyes crystal clear.

"On your knees."

Her entire body quakes. "Don't do this."

"Get on your fucking knees!"

Her eyes dart to the sides, her head unable to move as my knuckles ache from holding her tight. "But…" Her eyebrows pinch together and then pop up.

Yeah, she understands now.

The water is waist high on me and hits her rib cage. Dropping to her knees will effectively put her underwater and silence her forever.

I step in close, tilt her head with a vicious yank. A cry of pain rips from her throat and I bring her lips to mine.

"I want you on your knees, Shyann. Don't worry, I won't make you suck me off. I prefer my whores breathing."

I tug and use my free hand to put pressure on her shoulder, lowering her against her will. She fights, but the cold water and fear must get the best of her because slowly she drops to one knee, then the other. The current tries to pull her away, but my firm hold keeps her right where I want her.

"Please, don't do this." She tilts her chin up, the water rising above her jawline and trickling into her mouth and nose. She coughs, gags.

Her mouth opens and closes like a fish gasping death-bringing air and I feel her body fight for life beneath my hands.

"Lucas…come back…" Her words trail off into gags as she struggles. Then finally water covers her face and she's completely submerged.

My mouth breaks into a smile and I bend over so she can hear me through her freshwater earmuffs. "You're going to die now, Shyann, and your last fucking thought will be how Lucas failed you. He failed to rescue you, and he's responsible for your death."

She flails in my hold, her body's last-ditch effort at survival.

"*Never* underestimate me."

NINETEEN

LUCAS

Light blazes before my eyes and I'm thrown forward.

Cold water fills my nose and mouth.

I frantically search for footing. My boot hooks on a rock and finally I push up, gasping air.

I'm breathing heavy and shaking, but not from the cold. My muscles are fueled with the aftermath of adrenaline. I search my surroundings. I'm in the river.

There's movement at the water's edge. Coughing.

Shyann!

I race to her, but being waist-deep in water makes me move in slow motion. "Shyann, are you okay?"

She whirls around to her back, and even in the dark I can see the fear flooding her eyes. "Don't touch me!" She crab-walks backward in an un-coordinated scurry, her soggy pajama pants sliding down and tangling her legs.

I hold up my hands and take a few steps back. She's soaked. Her thin shirt clings to her body, and she kicks free of her pants to move farther away from me.

"What—" The truth slams me in the chest and I stumble back into the water, nearly falling in it. "Gage did this."

"Stay away from me!"

"Okay, I will, but…" I take in her form, so small and helpless and scared. My mouth floods with saliva and nausea turns my stomach. "What did he do to you, Shy?"

She peers up at me. "Lucas?"

"Yeah." I'm ashamed she even has to ask. What have I done?

She relaxes, but not by much. "Oh God…" she whispers. "I think he wanted to kill me."

My head goes light and the overwhelming desire to run overtakes me. This is what happens when people get too close. I let her in, enjoyed her company, kissed her beautiful mouth, and he punished her for it. I can't leave her. Not like this. Not after whatever Gage did to break her down. I have to fix this.

"I want to go home." She sounds so defeated.

"I know." I hold out my hand and she flinches away. The heat of tears builds in my eyes. "Please, it's okay. I'll get you home."

Mr. Jennings is the closest thing I have to family now. Once he finds out what I did to his daughter, he'll have me arrested. Or if I'm lucky he'll give me what I've been wishing for for years and put me out of my misery.

"You scare me."

A single tear falls from my eye, but with the water I hope she doesn't see my cowardice. "I know." The confirmation rips through my soul.

Shyann is the brightest thing I've seen in my life. She's not mine, but God, I want her. Her friendship, her smile. That would've been enough. No, that *should've* been enough, but I took more. Way more than I deserved.

She walks down the river to a shallow spot and crosses slowly. Her bare legs wobble as she tries to balance on slippery rocks. I keep my distance but draw close enough to help her if she needs it. Her teeth chatter, her long wet hair plastered to her back, and her body curls in on itself.

"Let me grab you a towel."

She doesn't answer.

I jog inside to grab a clean towel. When I return to the porch, I prepare to find her gone, but instead she's on the bottom step crouched into a little ball.

"It's only me." I announce my approach to avoid upsetting her and when she jumps at the sound of my voice, I recoil.

I drape her shoulders with the towel, my arms itching to pull her back into my chest and hold her close, keep her safe and feel her breathe. She doesn't move to hold the warmth to her but stares off into the distance with the towel falling limply around her.

"What happened, Shyann?" I whisper.

She blinks, the only proof she's not a statue. "I can't believe you don't know."

"I don't."

"Gage, he..." She finally moves and pulls the towel around herself.

I search her bare legs for injury. "Did he hurt you?"

"No. He threatened me and scared me, but I'm okay."

"Your pants, when you were...did he—"

"He didn't touch me...like that." Her voice is dead, robotic and cold.

"I'm so sorry, Shy." My voice cracks with emotion. "I'd never want to hurt or scare you."

She turns her head slowly, and her blue eyes search mine. My heart cramps to see the light that usually shines so bright is dark. "I don't think we can be friends anymore, Lucas."

It hurts so badly, the pain of hearing those words, so resolute, from her lips. But I wouldn't expect anything less. "I understand."

She nods and stands, moving to her truck; she climbs inside. There are no goodbyes, no shared glances, not even the slightest acknowledgment between us.

"I'm sorry." This is all my fault. I got lulled into a false sense of security and after my last blackout I should've known things could get worse.

I tried to stay away, tried to keep my distance, but I wasn't strong enough.

Gage is. He always has been.

The truck backs up and peels down the dirt road, kicking up rocks and leaving dust in its wake.

I have two days before Nash and Cody get back. I'll stay up all night and finish the mantelpiece and then pack my stuff and move on.

Better to do it now before it's too late.

Before someone dies.

TWENTY

SHYANN

I can't close my eyes without seeing his face. Lying in bed with the sun just peeking up to warm the forest awake, I can't get the last image of Gage to stop haunting me long enough to sleep.

Anger and fury twist his handsome features, transforming the timid Lucas I know into someone terrifying. And as much as it scared me, as much as I was convinced my existence would be erased from this earth, a voice whispered that he wouldn't kill me. But I didn't listen. I gave up. Gave in to the terror rather than fight for what I wanted. Prove that I'm strong enough to handle anything Gage throws at me.

I walked away from the one person who's reminded me what it's like to feel again, and Lucas let me go.

It's as if he's been through this before, heard the alarm and knows the drill. And beyond my close call with death, that's what saddens me most.

People hate what they don't understand, shun those who are different. When my mom lost her ability to walk, stand on her own, when her hands were curled in on themselves like gnarled tree roots, the looks people gave her were unforgivable. They assumed her mind was gone, that she wouldn't notice, but that's the thing about ALS; her body fell apart and her mind was fully aware of every fucking second of it.

Lucas can't help who he is, what he's become, and yet he's forced to live in exile, unable to form relationships, fall in love, have a future that consists of someone outside himself.

I wonder what Lucas is doing now, if he's missing me or grateful I'm gone.

I roll to my side and my eyes fix on a warrior kachina my mom gave me when I was young. Its vibrant black and red face is dull with a light coating of dust and the eagle feather headdress is muddied with age and no longer displays the brilliant brown pattern. Holding a bow in one hand and an arrow in the other, he still appears fierce, prepared for battle.

She told me he was a protector. A great warrior who would keep me safe.

She was wrong.

The carved wood holds no more power to protect me from pain than I had to keep my mom on this earth.

Stupid Navajo myths and their ridiculous promises.

If only my mom were here now. She'd tell me what to do about Lucas. Why don't I just let him go?

There's something about him that's impossible to walk away from. Like an injured boy being held captive by his abuser. But Gage isn't his abuser; he's his warrior kachina. His real-life protector made of muscle and bone and capable of inflicting damage on anyone who stands in his way. Pushing anyone who has the potential to hurt Lucas away, but also everyone who has the potential to love him. If I want to spend time with Lucas, I need Gage to stop seeing me as a threat.

I don't know how to convince him I won't hurt Lucas. But I suppose pain to them is different than it is to me. It's possible I've been hurting Lucas this entire time and not even known it.

So many questions tumble around in my head, but in order to get answers, I have to see Lucas and, worse, risk triggering Gage.

If that happens, do I trust him enough not to hurt me?

Would I bet my life on it?

***

I wake with a start. A firm hand on my shoulder shaking me.

Oh no, he's back!

"No!" I thrash and kick. "Don't touch me!" My fist connects with something soft.

"Oomph!" My bed dips. "Fuckin' hell, Shy. You didn't have to hit me."

Cody?

I blink open my eyes and the room is dim, but there's sunlight from behind the curtains.

"What time is it?" I rub my eyes and try to calm my racing heart. "What're you doing here?"

He works his jaw around a couple times, wincing. "It's almost noon, Merryweather." His expression grows dim and he sets his dark eyes on me. "Some assholes broke into the McKinstry house last night. Fucked it all up."

I sit up. "What?"

He shakes his head. "Yeah, probably a bunch of kids. Anyway, the security company called and I told Dad I'd come check it out. He's gonna stay up there one more night, come back in the morning."

"Why didn't security call me?"

"Said they tried, didn't get an answer."

I rub my forehead. Shit, that's because I was being drowned by the alternate identity of the guy I kinda like. "Damn, I'm sorry, Code. I can go down there and take care of it and you can head back to the lake." I swing my feet over the bed, but he stops me.

"Nah, go back to sleep. I got it. Got a guy coming with me. Between the two of us, we should have it done in no time. Besides"—he stands and peers down at me—"you look like shit."

I throw a pillow over my head and shove my middle finger into the air.

"Dad said you're working at Pistol Pete's?"

"I am. Which is why I need my sleep." I shoo him away with my bird-flipping hand.

He chuckles. "Sweet. I'll see you there. No way I'm missing my big sister serving a bunch of drunk-ass mountain dicks. What time…"

The bed dips again and the sound of the curtains over my bed being opened make me want to throw something at my brother. "You said I could sleep. Shut those—"

"Gotta go, my guy's here." The bed bounces and his heavy footsteps retreat.

His guy is here? I didn't hear a car pull— *Oh no!*

I spring from my bed and rip open the curtains. He must see the rapid movement from his leaning position on my brother's truck, because his eyes instantly find mine.

Lucas.

I want to smile, wave, do something friendly, anything to wipe that blank look from his beautiful face. A chill races up my spine and the sting of inhaling cold water still burns in my nose. He cringes, as if he can read my thoughts, and his expression goes from blank to hurt. My arms long to comfort him, but I shake my head, slide closed the curtain, and drop back into the safe, warm cocoon of my bed.

Walk away from it all, Shyann.

Get the hell out of this town and never look back.

LUCAS

I can't pull my eyes away from the window. As if I stare at it hard enough I can get Shyann's face to reappear. Not that I need to actually *see* her to see her. Those light eyes, all that black hair, and those lips star in every dream I've had since we met. Every time my thoughts wander off, she's there waiting.

I'm obsessed.

Consumed.

Totally infatuated.

But that look, her lips pulled into a tight line, jaw set, and eyebrows pulled together. That's the face from the window, the hurt that twists her gorgeous features, and I put that hurt there.

"Yo, Lucas!" Cody jogs from the front door of Shyann's house to me. "Thanks for helping me out."

"No problem." I clear my throat. "What happened?" Mind off the woman inside and on the project. Stick to work, professional relationships only, don't get too close.

He jerks his head for me to climb into the truck. I do and he follows, firing up the four-wheel drive and pulling away from the house.

"Guess they vandalized the place."

My eyes stay glued to Shyann's window, hoping like an addicted junkie I'll get one more hit before we pull away. Not even a rustle of the curtains.

"We'll check it out, call Austin if we need to."

I drag my eyes away from the window and turn to him. "The sheriff?"

"Yeah, we'll need to file a report."

I swallow hard, nerves making me break out in a sweat even in the sixty-degree weather.

Would Shyann call the cops on me after what happened last night? I don't know the details, but she was wet, scared, and almost naked. God, what did Gage do to her? I swear if I could I'd confront him and beat him senseless.

I rub my temples, amazed still, even after all these years, how crazy I sound.

If it barks like a dog…

"Headache?"

"No." *Just regret.*

"That won't do."

I stare at him, confused.

He chuckles. "Just sayin', dude your age, single, you should be hungover as hell on a Saturday morning. Friday nights are for booze, your bros, and hoes."

"Oh…" I open my mouth to tell him I *was* out last night and kissing his sister. With tongue. But I think better of it and keep my mouth shut.

"Tonight. We're going out to a bar. You need to loosen up."

I shake my head, the idea of being at a bar with Cody making me want to throw myself from the truck. "No thanks, I don't—"

"Nope. I won't take no for an answer. You've been here two months. How many times have you gone out?"

Only one that I know of, thanks to Shyann. "I haven't."

He jerks his gaze to mine. "What? But you decked that Dustin prick at the bar the other night, right?"

"Oh, right. So once." *Thanks a lot, Gage.*

He lifts a brow. "One time in two months? What the hell is wrong with you?"

You don't want to know. My skin breaks out in a sweat and I roll my window down to free myself from the suffocating cab.

"Whatever, I'm dragging you out tonight."

"I don't—"

"You're going, if only so I can buy you a beer for helping me out on a Saturday." We pull onto the job site and already we can make out the jagged peaks of broken glass in the windows.

"Fuck me…" He throws the truck into park with force. "Punk assholes."

We move to the front door and he pulls the key from his pocket. I'm hoping the kids who did this just needed a place to hide and drink for the night and the damage is left to the windows.

One foot through the threshold and our feet are frozen to the unfinished floor.

The entire place is destroyed.

Holes the size of basketballs punched through drywall, insulation hanging from some of the bigger ones, and spray paint. Everywhere.

"Dammit to shit, those fucking pricks!" Cody storms through the house, ducking into bedrooms and releasing string upon string of curses, giving away the devastation lying within.

I move into the kitchen, the cupboards ripped from the walls, electrical wiring pulled and cut. I run my fingertips through a slash of black paint. Dry.

"Dude, come check this out!"

I head back to the master bedroom where I find Cody staring at a wall.

His eyes are filled with anger and they dart to mine. "What the fuck do you think this means?"

The black words are spray-painted in thick letters from one end of the room to the other.

DIE RETARD

I stare blankly at the wall and shrug. "No idea."

"I got a bad feeling, man." He pulls his cell from the pocket of his jeans. "This doesn't seem like your typical high school prank." He punches out a few numbers and presses the phone to his ear. "Hey, Austin? Yeah, we're at the house." He turns around in the space, shaking his head in disbelief. "You can try, but there's gonna be fingerprints all over this place from our crew alone."

My heart races. Fingerprints. If they run mine, my entire past will come up. What will they do if they know where I've been? I push that thought away and remember I'm a free man. I only have one thing to hide, and as long as I keep myself out of trouble, that shouldn't be too hard to do. If Shyann keeps my secret.

TWENTY-ONE

LUCAS

Tonight is the coolest night since I moved here. As soon as the sun dropped, there was a chill in the air and even a distant rumble of thunder. Lightning slices through the sky to the north, warning that a storm is coming.

I secretly hope for a downpour, a flash flood, anything that'll cut short my night out with Cody.

I squint and balance the wood just right on my thigh while I drive the chisel into the timber, slowly and delicately carving out small pieces that will soon become an elk. With the flashlight balanced on the banister, I'm able to work out here until late.

After spending almost six hours at the McKinstry place, cleaning up the mess of fingerprint dust and destruction the vandals left behind, my hands are already aching. I flex my fist a couple times just as headlights blast through the thick darkness. Tires crunch on gravel until Cody's truck comes into view.

He rolls down the window. "Come on, man! Jump in before it starts dumping out here."

With a heavy sigh I'm glad he can't hear, I grab my things and put them inside, making sure all the windows are shut to keep the rain out. I grab my hoodie sweatshirt and my baseball hat. The more cover the better chance I have of melting into the background tonight.

The first few drops of rain fall as I pull myself into Cody's truck. "Hey."

"I hope you're ready to let loose, man." He grins wide and for a moment I see a tiny bit of Shyann in her brother. It's in the pull of their lips, the way they— "Whoa, dude. Don't look at me like that. This ain't a date."

I sink deeper into my seat, hoping he can't see the embarrassment blaring on my face.

He floors it down the dirt road, and as we pass Shyann's house, I force my eyes forward, refusing to look for her truck, to see if her lights are on. Now that Cody is home, she's not mine to take care of. His job to keep her safe.

Protected from people like me.

The truth slices through my gut, and although I don't usually drink alcohol—my boozing experience consists of peer-pressured moments in group homes and the aftermath of Gage's nights out—I'm thinking that maybe a couple drinks tonight are needed. The numbing effect will help take the edge off the emptiness of missing Shy. Mourning the death of the dream I'd stupidly allowed myself to indulge in. Maybe the liquor will help erase the memory of her fear as she scrambled from my touch. Just one night I want to squelch the ache of the truth. I'm a monster; she deserves better.

It doesn't take long before we're jogging through the rain toward a barn with the name PISTOL PETE's in neon and the twang of country music filtering through the sideboards.

The double doors open to a crowd of people and a stage where a band plays and a man sings about his love of the South. I keep the hood of my sweatshirt pulled over my baseball hat while we move through the crowd. The space confining, people brush up against me, but I keep my eyes to the backs of Cody's legs and refuse to acknowledge anyone.

The room gets quieter the farther we head back and when Cody finally stops at a pool table, I look up. The majority of the hundred-plus people in here are around the stage, so except for a few other guys shooting pool, it's just us.

I shove back my hood and push my hands into the pockets of my sweatshirt.

"You any good?" He motions to the pool table.

"I'm all right." One of the group homes I lived in had a pool table. I wasn't interested in the *extracurricular activities* most of the other kids engaged in, so I spent a lot of time playing.

His gaze moves over my shoulder. "Great, I'll rack 'em." He moves around the table, the entire time keeping his eye on the crowded bar.

I head over to the wall behind him and pick out a pool stick. Staying busy at the table will make this night easier than I thought.

"Oh shit, there she is." The teasing tone in his voice makes my skin prickle with awareness.

I've heard him use that tone before. But only with one person.

As much as I want to whirl around and search her out, I don't. I keep my eyes firmly planted on the multicolored balls set up in a triangle on the green pelt.

"What the fuck?" His stick slams against the table edge.

My gaze jumps to his.

His lips curl back in disgust and his tall frame locks down. "What the fuck is she wearin'?"

Unable to avoid it any longer, I turn and— "Whoa," I whisper.

"Shyann Blue Eyes Jennings, get your ass over here now!" Cody's anger projects across the room, and even though Shyann doesn't turn to him immediately, her shoulders bunch at the sound of his voice.

He storms around the table just as she squares her shoulders and whirls to meet him, but something stops her dead in her tracks.

It takes me a second to figure out what it is because my eyes are glued to the healthy section of exposed skin around her belly button. I want to watch her legs move under her tiny skirt, see the soft flesh of her thighs rub together, but she's not moving.

My eyes dart to hers and she's staring right at me. I cringe at the way her muscles tense upon seeing me.

She blinks, a combination of shock and fear playing against her features.

I need to turn away, give her space to— I gawk at her breasts, which are pushed up and nestled in cups of black lace that show through her thin white shirt.

Cody rushes to his sister, pulls her closer to the pool tables, and glares at a few other guys playing as they stare at her appreciatively.

"Shy, what the hell are you doing dressed like…like…Sam?" Cody stands in front of her, using his body as a wall against, well, everyone.

Everyone but me.

"I…um…" Her eyes dart to mine, and I can tell she's searching for something in my expression. She dips her head to attempt to peek under the bill of my ball cap. "I'm working."

I know what she's looking for, so I hold her eyes for a few seconds until she visibly relaxes.

"Hey, Lucas."

"Shy."

She flashes a shaky smile and even that tiny show of affection has my chest warm and my lips aching to press against hers. Is it possible to be obsessed after one kiss? To get a single taste of her mouth, her warmth, and know if it were feasible to get it every single hour of every single day it would never be enough?

"Your tits are showing," Cody hisses under his breath. "Lucas, back me up here." He points to Shyann's chest.

I make the mistake of following Cody's finger and am reminded of how she felt pressed to my body, how she clung to my shoulders as I explored the sweetness of her mouth.

Her cleavage rises and falls quicker, and I blink up to find her face flushed.

"I think you look…" I lick my lips and push my hands deeper into my pockets. "Really pretty."

Her eyebrows drop low as if my words upset her.

"Are you out of your fuckin' mind?" He reaches over and tugs up Shyann's T-shirt by the shoulders, only to make the bottom half slide even farther up her belly. She smacks his hand away. "Dammit, Shy!"

"This is the best way to make money here, Cody. Now order a drink or leave me alone." She waits, and when he answers her with a scowl, she cautiously peeks over at me. "I didn't expect to see you here…" Her mouth gapes like there's more to that sentence, but she slams it closed.

"Never expected to see you either." My fingers burn to pull her to me, to bury my face in her neck and beg for forgiveness, promise I'll do better, try harder, all while drowning in her scent.

"Bring us beers so we can play!" Cody's harsh demand comes from across the table where he's picking out sticks and scowling. "And pull your fucking skirt down! Shit!"

She throws her brother the middle finger and I can't fight the laughter that bubbles up from my chest. She's speaking to me, which is more than I expected after Gage terrorized her last night. I haven't been arrested and Cody hasn't taken a swing at me, so she must've kept what happened a secret. My muscles relax and the knot in my gut unfurls.

Her friendship, her smile, the way I catch her looking at me like I'm not something nightmares are made of? It's more than I ever expected and enough to keep me going.

***

"Corner pocket." I point with my pool cue to the pocket I'm readying to drop the eight ball in to win the fourth out of six games we've played.

Cody seems to know every single person in this place; he's been cool enough to introduce me to them when they come say hi. It's a little awkward, bombarded with so many new faces, some I've seen before around town, but most are total strangers.

I've kept to our small corner of the bar, kept my hat low and my head down, and managed to have a pretty good time. I haven't had beer in a while and never really enjoyed the act of drinking or losing control of myself—God knows I have enough of that without the help—but with the promise of Shyann coming and going, I've drunk more than I should.

Leaning over the pool table, I blink in an attempt to clear my fuzzy vision and try to focus on the corner pocket. My body sways, as if someone tilted the floor without warning me first. I line up my shot, close one eye, and shoot.

"I give." Cody groans and drops his cue stick. "You win. *Again.*"

I tuck my smile and drop to a high barstool that lines the wall around the pool table. My beer bottle is empty and adrenaline makes my stomach tumble with the knowledge of what that means. I get to order another drink.

I scour the room for Shyann, a fiend looking for my fix. As the night has worn on and the bottles have been replaced with fresh ones, my inhibitions dissolved. I've managed to steal a few touches. When she leans against the pool table talking to Cody, I may have picked my next shot based on where she was so that I'd get to hook her around the waist and scoot her down the table. The first time she startled, but those light eyes conveyed something opposite of surprise. Relief. From then on it got easier. I've asked her questions about the band, questions I couldn't care less about but needed an excuse to pull her close and whisper in her ear. At one point Cody went to the bathroom and she must've seen me alone, as she came to sit with me. She talked about something I didn't hear because she sat directly across from me on a stool, close so that our knees were intertwined; her legs were slightly parted and for the briefest of moments I got a flash of black lace between her thighs.

My heart pounded so hard in my chest I'd have sworn she could see it through my shirt.

"Last call, guys."

My eyelids drop closed at the sound of her voice.

"Hey, you okay?"

I blink open heavy lids and smile. "I'm great."

She grins and shakes her head. "You're drunk."

With one eye closed to bring her beautiful face into focus, I nod. "I am."

Cody throws an arm around my shoulders, nearly knocking me off my stool. "Come on, lightweight. I'll take you home."

I shove his arm off me. "I don't put out on the first date."

A laugh that's half snort, half giggle falls from Shyann's lips and seems to catch her by surprise.

"After all those beers I bought you?" Cody feigns insult. "You're a lousy date."

I laugh, and damn, but it feels so good to just…laugh. How long has it been since I've been so at ease?

"Hey, baby," a female voice purrs in my ear.

Shyann's eyes go wide and move between me and the unknown female.

The heat and softness of a body presses to my side. Arms go around my neck like a python and the pungent scent of her perfume burns my nose. The scent is familiar but my booze-addled mind can't sort it out. I study the woman's face as she gazes at me with familiarity. Lust. Yeah, lots of lust, and a greedy need that makes me lean away from her touch. But she straddles my thigh, locking herself to me.

"Sam, back off. He's drunk." Shyann's on my other side, her lips pulled into a tight line as she shoots daggers from her eyes.

So this is Sam.

The woman with overly done eye makeup and bright red lips glares at Shy. "Think I can handle a man who's had a few drinks." Her gaze swings to mine and she rubs herself against me. "Handled him just fine the last time we were together."

"Damn, Lucas." Cody laughs and smacks my back in manly pride. "Not bad for a guy who never goes out."

Everything seems to move in slow motion, and my body is heavy along with my mind.

"Did you miss me?" Sam's hands move up my shirt to my bare chest.

Her fingers feel like bugs against my skin. I go to pull them away, but she's so close I end up gripping at her waist. "Miss you?" *I don't even know you.*

"Sam, leave him alone." Shyann's voice is laced with anger and maybe even fear.

"Stop cockblockin', Shy." Cody grabs his sister and pulls her away for what looks like a heated conversation.

Sam pulls my chin back to her and with my gaze firmly set on Shy, my eyes are the last to track so I'm helpless to avoid her lips when they swallow mine.

The sticky smear of gloss and taste of cigarettes threatens to empty my stomach. I rip my mouth from hers. Panic flushes the liquor from my veins, replacing it with adrenaline.

I don't like this. I don't want this.

She shoves her hand between us and palms the heavy length between my legs. "Mmm…"

Nausea curls in my stomach and black flickers in my peripheral. I push back and try to stand but unsteady I fall back. "Please."

Her mouth moves to my neck and she grips my dick so hard it hurts.

The veil falls.

TWENTY-TWO

GAGE

This bitch again?

I roll my eyes at her ridiculous attempt to jack me off over my jeans. Hell, my cock deflates with every pump of her desperate little hand. As entertaining as her efforts are to seduce me, I don't have time for this shit.

"Oh my God, Sam! Get off of him!"

The little slut dry-fucking my thigh falls backward with a yelp, and I almost fall forward along with her. Luke's drinking has my head foggy and my equilibrium all over the damn place.

I blink and focus. Aah, what do we have here but our own little Shy Ann. And from the expression on her face I'd say she's pissed.

Her chest heaves, drawing my gaze to her full cleavage flushed red with anger.

"What the fuck, Shy!" Slutty Girl pushes herself to her feet.

I sit back, cross my arms over my chest, and settle in for a good chick fight, only wishing I had a vat of Jell-O to throw them in and was sober enough to enjoy it.

They face off and I place my internal bets. My money's on Shyann. The woman is stronger than her five-and-a-half-foot frame lets on.

Shyann places her tight little body in front of me. Ha! Like I need this bitch's protection. "He's drunk."

Slut balls her fists. "Since when did you become his bodyguard?"

Shyann's back stiffens, but she holds her protective stance. I'm about to shove her forward into Slut just to speed up the process, get to the good stuff, when that Cody kid stands between the catfighting girls.

"Sam, don't!" He presses her back gently. "Walk away, all right?"

Party pooper.

"Fuck you, Cody!" She points at me. "We were hooking up and Shy went nuts!"

I hold up my hands in surrender, a gurgle of laughter rumbling in my chest. "In my defense, you were hooking up with me." Damn, it's been a long time since I've found something genuinely entertaining. I must be drunker than I thought.

"You wanted it." She holds up the hand she was groping me with. "I *felt* it!"

"Oh…" I stand up, try not to wobble, and advance toward her, but Shyann's in my way. My front hits her back, stilling my progress. I grasp her waist to steady myself. "You misunderstand, *Sam*. That hard-on wasn't for you." I flex my hips, rubbing my dick against Shyann's lower back.

No one seems to notice, but she hisses and tugs against my hold.

"You're an asshole!" Sam spits through clenched teeth.

I reach over Shyann to take the little bitch's throat in my palm and crush her fucking windpipe.

Shyann whirls, pressing both palms against my chest. "Gage…" she whispers. "Don't."

Slowly, I peer down at her.

She should be afraid of me. Terrified. I tried to kill her last night and now she's gazing up at me with those fucking witchy eyes and all the trust in the world.

"You fuckin' prick!" Sam rushes.

Cody snags her by the waist. "Get 'im out of here, Shy."

Shyann grabs my wrist. "Come on."

I allow her to drag me through the bar, down a hallway, and into some kind of a back room. She pushes me through the door, clicks on a light, then locks the door behind her and leans against it.

A slow grin curls my lips. "I'm your prisoner now, is that it?"

She juts up her chin, but I don't miss the way she presses deeper back against the door. *Aah, little Shy Ann, all alone with no one to hear you scream.* "Let's just wait until Cody calms her down; then I'll sneak you out the back door."

I take a step toward her.

"Don't." She holds up a hand, her fingers shaking.

"I scare you."

"You almost drowned me, so yeah, a little."

"Yet you lock yourself in a room with me." I tilt my head, studying her, as if it'll help me understand. "Why?"

She swallows hard but keeps her gaze to mine, refusing to show the fear she's so desperately trying to conceal. "For Lucas."

Her resolute answer sends me back a step, my booze-lazy thoughts trying to keep up. "What?"

"I'm protecting Lucas. Last thing he needs is you making trouble for him, Gage."

My eyes grow tight and the fire of anger flares in my gut. Who does she think she is? *"You're* protecting Luke now?"

She throws her shoulders back and nods.

"Weak, stupid, stupid whore."

Her hands ball up at her sides. "Call me whatever you want. You won't scare me away that easily."

SHYANN

I can't breathe.

Being stuck in this tiny room, surrounded by boxes and cleaning supplies, he could do anything to me in here. I've had a taste of what he's capable of; he warned me then not to underestimate him, which is exactly what I'm doing.

Maybe he's right. Maybe I am stupid.

I couldn't do it. I couldn't stay away. Watching Lucas play pool tonight, his head thrown back in laughter, it all seemed so unfair. He deserves to live a normal life filled with friends and the possibility of love.

Every time he brushed against me or whispered something in my ear, my whole body warmed and butterflies exploded in my belly.

I tried. I really did. But when Sam forced herself on him, I snapped.

Gage is the obstacle that stands between us and I can't let him screw everything up for Lucas. No one can find out about him. The people in this town wouldn't understand; they'd alienate him, ostracize him, make his life so difficult he'd have no other choice but to leave.

And I don't want him to go.

A little voice in my head screams that I'm selfish, that I'll be leaving soon anyway so I shouldn't care. I push the voice away and focus on the predatory stare of the man in front of me.

He stalks toward me, his head tilted, chin dropped. He looks like something out of a horror movie, but I force myself to see Lucas behind his cold stare. Strain to see the broken boy I've come to care about.

"You've got balls. I'll give you that." He steps so close the toes of his boots hit mine, and the smell of beer is thick on his breath. His knuckles run up my inner thigh, dipping beneath my skirt. "I think I better check."

I smack his hand away and he groans, his eyes practically rolling back in his head.

He presses the palm of his hand to the door behind me, leans in, and traces my hairline with his calloused fingertip. It's gentle, and for a moment I pretend it's Lucas. His touch glides along my temple, slides down my cheek, and I shiver under the barely-there caress. He cups my jaw, his thumb running along my quivering lower lip. "Scared, Shy Ann?" He purrs my name and it's like fire and honey dousing me in gooseflesh.

"No." My voice cracks on a whisper.

His hand moves to the front of my neck and he tilts my head back, holding me so my lips are just a breath away from his. "You really are one beautiful bitch."

"Stop it."

"Stop what?" He runs the tip of his tongue along the seam of my lips while his hand grows tighter around my throat. "This is what you want, isn't it? What I found you begging Luke for?"

"You're not Lucas."

He frowns and anger flickers behind his molten-gray eyes. His grip tightens. "*Lucas* would never hurt me."

He pulls back, his eyes flaring with heat. "You sure about that?"

My mind scrambles for something to say, anything that will remind him I'm human and not a source of torture for Lucas. That I'm worth protecting.

Gage protects Lucas. I need for Gage to see me as safe. As an equal. Someone strong and capable, yet harmless. My weakness seems to fuel his anger. I have to be strong if I'm going to get him to bring Lucas back.

"You never answered my question." I gasp as my airway tightens. "Why did you save me from Dustin?"

That seems to catch him off guard. He blinks. "Mistake."

"Liar."

He grips me tighter and my hands fly to his; fingernails claw his wrists to get him to release me. "Watch that mouth, Shy Ann, or I'll fuck it."

I blanch at the harshness of his words. His gaze darts around my face, lips curled back over his teeth, as if he can't decide to kill me or kiss me.

My vision swims and darkness closes in. He won't do it. He won't. Whatever Gage is, at the heart of him he's Lucas and he'd never hurt me.

Please, Lucas. Please…

He tenses. "Give in!"

My eyes flutter. Pulse roars in my ears. "No."

His jaw ticks before he releases the pressure but leaves his hand on my neck. I gasp, sucking in precious oxygen and trying to stay on my feet. His thumb rubs circles on my throat, his attempt to soothe. "What did I tell you about underestimating me?"

Victory washes over me. He's had the opportunity to kill me twice, and he hasn't. "You…are a coward."

His eyelids flicker and for a second I wonder if my insult was enough to send him away. "Yeah, well…I've been called worse."

He puts distance between us, an unspoken truce, even if only for the time being. I double over, bracing my weight on my knees. I breathe, allowing all the blood in my head to flow back into my body.

"We need to get Lucas home, Gage." I sound like a damn lunatic! "I can't leave until my shift is up and—"

"Not leaving you here with that crazy slut."

My head jerks up at the sound of his growled response and I catch him grimacing. His mouth twists in disgust as if the words were poison on his tongue.

A slow smile pulls at my lips as sanity escapes me and leaves me with a strange, crazed pride. "Aww, Gage. Are you saying you want to protect me from the big bad scary girl?"

"Hardly." He pulls off his baseball hat and runs a hand through his thick dark hair before popping it back on. "She causes trouble for you, it could blow back on Luke."

"Shy, you in there?"

My brother's frantic knocks sound against the door.

My eyes dart to Gage's, who seems totally unaffected.

"Yeah, Code, we'll uh…we'll be out in a sec." I rush to Gage, whispering, "If you're gonna stay…here…you better put on your best Lucas mask."

He smiles, but this time it's not the creepy evil kind but the amused kind. He nods.

I give Gage one more stern look before I turn and unlock the door, opening it enough for Cody to slip into the room. He eyes us both, speculation dripping from his gaze. "Everything good in here?"

"Of course." I throw my shoulders back.

He narrows his eyes. "Okay. I told the bartender lady that you got sick. She said you can take off. The mood Samantha's in, I'm not leaving you here with her."

Gage chuckles but covers his mouth and keeps his eyes to the floor.

"I need to get Lucas the hell out of here before he gets stripped and taken advantage of." Cody grins and slaps Gage on the back. "Fuck, man. Who knew you had that kind of game. I thought Sam was gonna rip me apart to get at you."

I catch the hint of a sly grin, but luckily Gage only shrugs.

"She was still fired up when I left her." He motions toward me. "Bartender chick said settle up. I'll drop your cash at the bar, and you can head home."

"But what about Lucas?"

Cody scratches his jaw. "Shit, that's right. You take him home."

Gage's eyes meet mine. Great, alone in my truck with Gage.

"Fine." I pull out my tickets, do a little math, and shove a wad of cash at Cody. "There."

"All right. Get Casanova here home safely." He pulls Gage into a playful headlock.

His body goes stiff and his fists ball.

Crap!

I tug the sleeve of Gage's sweatshirt, freeing him from my brother before Gage does something he'll regret. "Come on, let's get you home."

GAGE

I should just pull back and let Luke take over.

Here in Shyann's truck, the scent of her rain-soaked skin intensifies and surrounds me in the smell of her fruity girl shampoo along with a lingering hint of stale booze and smoke. After tonight I'm wondering if I misjudged the woman. Maybe she's safe? I peer over at her from the corner of my eye and internally slap myself for being a dumbass.

Who the fuck am I kidding.

She's a walking, talking, hell-on-wheels threat to everything Luke has managed to build here. A few weeks ago he'd never step foot into a bar, drink himself dizzy, and risk touching a woman, but that's exactly where I found him. What's worse is this agonizing tingling in my chest, the constant weight in my balls, and the throb of rushing blood that aches to touch her is driving me insane.

All bad.

Every-fucking-thing about this woman screams danger of epic proportions. A woman only has the power to destroy you if you give it to her.

That's not gonna happen.

Not on my watch.

The truck bumps through puddles of mud, and the visibility through the rain and the dark is next to zero. I grind my teeth. Sitting bitch in this truck, being driven by a woman like I'm some kind of invalid, I should cut my own balls off for the offense. I'd grab her by the throat and make her pull over if I thought she'd listen. Experience has proved she won't.

And I can't fight with her because her resistance makes me hard. It makes me want to break her, tear her down piece by fucking piece to make her compliant. That smart mouth, fake confidence she hides her terror behind, it's all hot as hell.

Damn her for making me feel something, anything.

Yeah, I don't want to fight with her.

I just wanna get the fuck out of the car.

I should've let Luke take over back there. Should've backed off and let him stumble through the rest of the night, but he's not strong enough to fight this witch's spell.

He's not.

But I am.

She clears her throat. "Can I ask you something?"

"No."

"Why not— Oh, wait. I don't care."

"Then stop talk—"

"Where'd you get the scar from?" So matter of fact when she's asking something personal and none of her fucking business.

"Shark attack."

"Oh yeah? I hear those San Bernardino sharks are insanely vicious."

Don't smile, you fucking pussy.

"It's cool. You don't have to tell me. I'll ask Lucas." There's a hint of challenge in her voice. A tone that says, *Dare me.*

"He won't tell you either."

She shrugs and her headlights shine on the cabin up ahead as we round the corner. "We'll see," she whispers.

I hide my smile into my shoulder. He might be able to tell her how it got there, but he can't share details because he wasn't there the night we got the scar.

I was.

I remember the entire thing, details etched into my mind like tattoos, imprinted and worn as a reminder to never forget.

Never trust.

And always keep my mouth shut.

She puts the truck in park but leaves it running. "How about this…"

I check her out from the corner of my eye, intent on keeping my eyes forward because, like Medusa, looking directly at her turns my dick to stone, and frankly I don't need that shit right now.

"Tell me why you protected me from Dustin—"

"Fuckin' hell." I shake my head.

"…and why you didn't want to leave me alone with Sam."

"This again." This bitch is like an alien, constantly probing my shit. "Let it go, Shy—"

"Why won't you just answer me?"

Why? Because I don't fucking know!

"Come on, Gage." Defeat laces her words. "I think I've proven I'm not a threat to you. I could've had you, er Lucas, arrested. Twice." Her hand absently rubs her neck and I swing my gaze away to try to lessen this stupid weight in my chest at seeing her do it. She hasn't the slightest idea of the power her femininity wields, luring poor saps like Luke into her arms only to crush and destroy them.

A low growl gurgles in my chest and my hand flexes around the door handle. I could tell her to fuck off and walk away. I'm *going* to tell her to fuck off and walk away. I don't owe her shit.

"Gage—"

"That's why."

She blinks and looks around, as if the cab of the truck hides the answer she's searching for. "Wait...what's why?"

Dammit to shit in a fuck basket!

"You protected him, all right? That's why." Laughter completely absent of humor falls from my lips. "Trust me, it wasn't something I thought about. It just happened." She reeled me in like all the other poor bastards, something I'd hoped I'd never have to admit.

She chews her lip. "So...when Dustin was teasing you, and when Sam was all over you—"

"You defended Luke and you've kept our secret. Used your body as a shield to protect him. I just"—*Fuck this shiiit!*—"reacted."

There, I said it.

"Wow." I don't have to look over to know her lips are fighting a satisfied grin; I can hear it in her voice. "That was really sweet of you, Gage."

I swing my gaze to her, using the bill of my hat as a barrier against the full force of her face, penetrating stare, and soul-sucking smile. "Right? Now take it for what it's worth and fuck off."

Jerking open the car door, I storm out into sheets of rain, heading for the shelter of the cabin.

"Have a good night, Gage!" She's laughing.

That bitch! She thinks she got to me, that she's won?

I toss a middle finger over my shoulder. "Go to hell!"

Her giggle is the last thing I hear before I slam the front door behind me.

TWENTY-THREE

LUCAS

The sun is barely up and I still haven't gone to sleep.

Last night, sometime around one in the morning, I came to standing in my kitchen. My hands braced on the counter and I was looking out the window as wave after wave of rain pummeled the earth outside.

I had no idea how I got there, no clue what happened after I blacked out. The only thing I knew for certain was Gage had come back.

He surfaced when a woman was kissing my neck. It's happened before, started back when I was living at a halfway house after I was released from the detention center.

Most seventeen-year-old boys would welcome a woman's touch. Sexual experimentation should've been on the top of my to-do list. But there hasn't been a single woman whose touch I could stomach. Not one I could trust. Who didn't abuse me or cast me out to be eaten alive by the system. None of them cared about me, not then, not until Shyann.

Using one of my fine-tip chisels, I put the finishing touches on the mantelpiece. I told Mr. Jennings I'd have it by the end of the week; technically it's Sunday, so I'm late, but Gage's appearance lately has set me back.

God, what did he do last night?

It's possible I no longer have a job or that he outed us at the bar, and now the entire town will chase me away with torches and pitchforks. But something inside, some deep-seated knowing tells me I'm okay, something I've never felt after blacking out in the past.

It's almost ten in the morning when I'm finally satisfied with the piece. I take a quick shower, forgo shaving—even though the stubble makes the bald skin of my scar under my jaw more noticeable—and throw on a pair of jeans, a white T-shirt, and my work boots.

I'm sure after all the commotion yesterday with the McKinstry house being vandalized that Mr. Jennings will be in his office dealing with insurance companies and police reports.

The quick ten-minute drive takes twice as long as usual. With the large mantel in the bed of my truck, I drive much slower to keep it from knocking around on the uneven dirt roads. When I pull up to the small portable, I don't see Mr. Jennings's car, but I see Shyann's.

My heart kicks triple time. She probably knows what Gage did last night and even with this newfound peace that my secret hasn't been exposed I won't know for sure until I talk to Shyann. I drop from the truck and jump up the steps.

I suck in a breath before heading inside, steeling myself mentally and emotionally before I set eyes on Shyann.

My gut flutters, proving my preparation pointless.

She has a cell phone pressed to her ear and holds up one finger to me.

I resist the urge to stare too long at her silky hair and full lips and instead drop down into the chair opposite her.

"I heard what you said, but I don't need your help." She sounds frustrated. Annoyed. "Just because you don't see the point of Oregon doesn't mean it's not a smart career move." She huffs out a breath and her chair squeaks. "Of course I researched it. It's not like I just c-closed my eyes and pointed and thought, 'Oh h-hey, I'll move to Oregon!'" She slumps in on herself a little.

She's moving? To Oregon? That excited fluttering in my gut turns to solid weight, crushing me with disappointment.

"Trevor, please, spare me the lecture on…Yeah, I know. Fine. I'll talk to you later." She doesn't wait for whoever is on the other line to even say goodbye before tossing her phone across her desk.

Trevor? Ex-coworker Trevor?

"Hey, Lucas." Her eyes are bright, smile perky, and all hint of irritation wiped clean. I relax a little. "How are you feeling this morning?"

"Oh, um…" I do a quick inventory. "Tired, a little headache. Other than that I'm okay."

"Good." She leans forward, her forearms resting on the desk, sending a cascade of ebony hair down her chest. "Remember anything?"

"No. But you're still speaking to me, so I'm guessing things were okay?" I frown and shake my head. "I was, I don't know, kinda hoping you could fill me in?"

When I woke up, I scented a musky perfume on my sweatshirt. I'm hoping Gage didn't take advantage of a woman with Shyann around. Hope he'd respect my feelings for her enough to keep himself under control.

"You and Cody went to Pistol Pete's."

I remember that.

"Sam, the woman Gage hooked up with before…"

I nod.

"She came back for more. She was getting pretty forceful. I told her to back off. She wouldn't…"

All sounds familiar.

"So Gage stepped in to help out." She flashes a hesitant smile.

"Did I...Did anyone get hurt?"

"No. Unless you mean ego. In that case, yes."

My chin drops to my chest. "Who—"

"Don't worry, Lucas. Most important thing right now is that you're safe, Gage is safe, and I'm still the only one aware of your secret."

"And us?"

"Yeah, we're good."

I exhale long and hard, relief calming my heart rate and my tense muscles. "Thank you. So, you still talk to your ex-coworker?" I suck in a breath at my own accusatory tone.

She drops back with a sigh. "Trevor was..." She groans and rubs her forehead. "How can I explain this without it making me sound bad?"

"Can't be worse than what you know about me."

"Trevor and I...he was kinda—"

"Your boyfriend." My stomach twists and my fists clench.

Her clear blue gaze meets mine. "No, but...kinda. We hung out off and on but it wasn't anything serious."

"And now?" It's none of my business, but I can't keep myself from wanting to know.

She chews her lip. "Hmm...now he still feels like he can tell me what to do even though I don't work under him anymore."

"He was your boss?"

"No, but he was my producer. I...uh...I worked in broadcast news for, like, a second before coming back to Payson. Trevor and I met in school. We had similar goals, so naturally we gravitated to each other, but we never had an emotional connection, if that makes sense."

I blink, thrown by the new information. "You were a reporter?"

"I wanted to be." She tilts her head, studying me, and I force a casual expression, trying not to give away my building anxiety.

Her probing questions, inquisitive eyes, of course she's a reporter. Is it possible she knows about me? It was years ago; she would've been in grade school at the time, but the story made national news. No, she was too young. Besides, if she did know, she'd know better than to be alone with me.

"If you wanted to be a reporter, why are you here, working for your dad?" She's the most beautiful and driven woman I've ever known, and there's no way she couldn't be a reporter if that's what she wanted.

"I got let go. Stupid, really. I let my emotions cloud my judgment. Now I'm no longer hirable in the industry." She shakes her head and waves me off with a sad smile. "Anyway, enough about—"

"You're moving to Oregon?"

The air between us grows tense and she stares for a few beats before breaking eye contact to fidget with a pen. "Um…that was the plan."

"Was…?"

Her gaze swings to mine and for the first time since I've known her she seems unsure. She wrings her hands together. "I don't know what I'm going to do now."

I stare silently, praying for the courage to ask what she means by "now." Is it even possible to dream she'd stay in town? My heart pounds furiously in my chest when I realize I can't willingly let her go. "Stay."

Her eyes widen and her lips part.

I clear my throat. "I'm sorry, I—"

"It's okay, Lucas. Things have been…" She blows out a heavy breath. "Crazy since we met. I planned to jump at the first opportunity to get out of here, but things have changed and I don't know what I'm going to do."

"Changed how?" The words fall from my lips on a whisper and I dare to hope for things I don't have a right to.

"I met you."

My breath catches in my throat. "Shy, no—"

"Don't list all the reasons why we won't work, Lucas. I know them all." She taps her index finger to her temple. "They run on an endless loop up here."

I'm broken.

Unstable.

Dangerous.

Her palm presses to her chest. "But what I feel here, when we're together, makes me believe anything is possible."

I swallow the lump forming in my throat. "Gage, he hurt you... If anything ever happened to you, I'd never be able to live with myself."

She leans forward, both forearms on the desk. "Last night Gage had every opportunity to hurt me and he didn't."

"That doesn't mean—"

"Don't you see what's happening? He's starting to trust me. *You're* starting to trust me." She pushes up from her seat, rounds the desk, and props a hip on its edge. "Gage is your protector, right?"

"I... yes."

"So all I need to prove is that I'm no threat and he'll leave us alone."

I adjust my baseball hat to avoid looking at her. This is all too much, more than I deserve. I should say no, push her away, go back to ignoring her completely, but she's offering more than I could ever hope to dream for.

Everything she says seems logical. If there's no threat, there will be no Gage. But what if she's wrong? Emotion isn't subject to logic. Gage has the capability to leave death and destruction in his wake. He's done it before. He could do it again.

I do my best to push the past from my mind.

It's selfish; it's more than selfish—it's cruel—but even still, I want her. "Okay, I'll try."

She lunges at me and wraps her arms around my neck.

"Thank you, Lucas." Her breath skates along my skin and my hands grip the armrests to keep from crushing her to my chest.

Seconds pass and a palpable heat builds between us. The joints in my hands ache as I refuse to release the chair and finally she pulls back, her neck flush and smile shaky.

Her focus zeroes in on my lips and then darts to my eyes, as if she's asking permission. I groan in blessed agony as the pull to her is just as powerful as my instinct to flee. Locked in the innocence of her gaze, I remain still as she presses a closed-lipped kiss to my lips. "Okay?"

I suck in a hesitant breath. "I'm good."

"See? It's working already." She steps back and props a tight denim-clad hip against her desk, putting the needed distance between us before I lock my arms around her and refuse to let her go.

"Shy, just promise me if things get...if they get to be too much... promise me you'll stay away."

"Lucas, I—"

"Promise me!" I cringe, lean forward and rest my head in my hands. "I'm sorry, I don't mean to yell at you. I just need you to promise me you'll stay away from me if Gage becomes...too much."

She crouches down in front of me and peeks up with tenderness. "I'll promise, Lucas, but only if you promise me the same. If at any time what we have causes you too much stress, you walk away. Okay?"

A humorless laugh bursts from my lips. "That's the problem, Shy. Don't you get it?" I dare a touch, reach forward and run a strand of her silky black hair between my fingers. "I can't. I've tried, and..." I lick my lips and force the words from my mouth no matter how pathetic they may make me sound. "You're *impossible* to walk away from."

SHYANN

I blink. For the first time in as long as I've been alive I'm rendered speechless.

He feels it too.

This whole time I've tried to talk myself out of wanting him, listed all the reasons—and there are plenty—why I should just forget about Lucas and focus on my plan to leave Payson, but as much as I've tried, I've failed.

You're impossible to walk away from, too, Lucas.

I roll the words around my mouth, staring into his eyes that have never looked more unguarded. The words freeze in my throat, because the fact is staying with Lucas means living in a town that, given enough time, will eat me alive and spit out my bones.

His brows drop low as he watches me and suddenly his expression falls in understanding. "I better go." He stands so abruptly I lose my balance and lean back against my desk to keep from falling flat on my butt.

"Wait!"

He shifts on his feet and tugs his hat lower over his eyes. "The mantelpiece is finished. I need to drop it off—"

"It's here?"

He jerks his head toward the door. "In the truck. Wasn't sure after the vandalizing if Mr. Jenn—er…Nash wanted me to drop it at the house or not."

"Can I see it?"

He hesitates, then nods, and as soon as he does I scurry out the door and to his truck. Lying in the bed is what I assume to be the mantelpiece covered by a blue tarp. He drops the tailgate and hoists his big body up with little effort, then pulls back the protective cover.

I gasp and lean forward as the intricate design in wood is revealed.

"Lucas…" I shake my head, words, again, locked in my throat along with the lump that forms from my pride.

"It still needs to be stained, but I need to get Nash to sign off on it before I do that." He sounds unsure, insecure of what I'd venture to call his best carving yet.

"He'll sign off, he will. How could he not? It's…Wow, Lucas, it's really great."

He shrugs one shoulder, humility tempered with a bit of well-deserved satisfaction. "Thanks."

The elk, bears, river, every texture and shadow make it look so real I almost expect them to come to life.

"You're going to give this to him now?"

He nods.

"You have to let me tag along. I can't miss the look on his face when he sees this for the first time."

A tiny grin curls his lip and my body heats, wondering if his lips taste even better when he's smiling. *Slow down, Shy. Don't scare him away.*

I rip my gaze from his mouth to shake my lust-driven thoughts. "I'll lock up."

"You know where he's at?" Lucas calls as I head to the door.

"He's at the McKinstry place."

With that, he covers the carving, hops in the driver's seat, and fires up the engine. I crawl in his truck and the smell of pine trees and a hint of man after a hard day's work slam into my senses. I roll down the window in an attempt to keep myself levelheaded, because at this rate I'd jump him in his seat.

"Here." He places the pajama bottoms I'd lost by the river into my lap.

They're clean, folded, and smell like soap.

"Thank you, but you didn't have to do this."

He throws the truck into gear. "I wanted to give them to you that next morning, but I didn't want to upset you."

I lean in, hating the distance between us, and press a kiss to his jaw. His body tenses, as if he's trying to restrain himself. "Thank you."

It's hard to pull away from the delicious scent of his neck, but when he moans and shifts in his seat, I figure I should back off. I'm going to have to take baby steps and pay close attention to his emotional cues if I plan on keeping Gage away.

We drive out to the McKinstry place just a few miles down the road. Some of the Jennings crew is on-site, putting in new windows and lugging in drywall.

"Guess they did a number on the place, huh?" I study the house.

"You haven't seen it yet?"

I shake my head.

"Yeah, they did."

Jumping from the truck, we weave through the work site and into the house. Dad's voice echoes from one of the bedrooms and we follow it back to find him glaring at a wall while Chris, his foreman, paints it.

"Hey, Dad." I sidle up next to him, but he doesn't take his eyes off the wall. Lucas stays in the doorway, leaning with one shoulder against the frame.

"Shy…"

"Am I going to have to have the sheriff cuff you to keep you away from the guys who did this once they're caught?"

"Understatement of the fucking year." His glare gets tighter and I follow it to the newly painted wall.

I squint and suddenly letters…no, words. Two distinct words show through the thin layer of paint. "Does that say…?" I walk to get a closer look.

"I don't care how many cans it takes," he addresses Chris. "Keep adding coats until you can't see a hint of spray paint."

Chris nods and continues to move the roller over the wall.

As I get closer, the faded letters come into view. *D…I…E…* I tilt my head and study the next word.

DIE RETARD

I gasp, loud, and swing my eyes to Lucas, who seems completely unaware. "Lucas, you and Cody were the ones who did the first walk-through, right?"

He nods, his lips in a tight line as if he's reliving the frustration of seeing the house for the first time.

"You saw this?" I point to the newly covered up hate words.

He nods again, but his expression registers nothing.

He has no idea, doesn't remember. Of course he doesn't. It was Gage there that night. Dustin called him names, teasing him and egging *him* on, not Lucas.

I swallow my nerves and tug on the sleeve of my dad's shirt. "Dad?"

"Right." He shakes his head. "I'm sorry, Shy. You came here for a reason." He waits expectantly, but Lucas is so close, he doesn't know the things Dustin said about him. I need to speak to my dad alone.

"Oh, um…yeah, Lucas has the mantel." I keep my voice light, despite the hysteria building within me.

My dad darts his eyes to Chris. "Be back." Then moves to Lucas. "Let's see it."

Lucas nods. "Sir." He turns and leaves the room with my dad on his heels.

I rub my forehead, the heat of anger slicing through my good mood. This is my fault. Who knows how much money this is costing my dad, how much potential pain this could cause Lucas if he found out. I know I didn't force Dustin's hand—he's the fucker who pushed the limits the other night—but I brought Dustin into our lives and because of that I need to straighten it out.

Dustin, that piece of shit!

Before I tell my dad anything, I'm going after that fucker myself.

TWENTY-FOUR

SHYANN

I was right. My dad's expression upon seeing the mantel Lucas carved was worth the trip out here. For a moment I saw the man he was before. Carefree, grinning like he used to before Momma got sick, and I fall a little more for Lucas for giving my dad that. There was a lot of back-slapping atta boys between the two of them, and seeing how the approval made Lucas blush and grin made me soften a little more toward my dad.

I would've loved to snapshot the moment, but I had shit to do. While Lucas stayed to help fix up the house, I hitched a ride back to the office with my dad.

I forced myself to sit through listening to him on the phone with suppliers and the insurance company, letting it heat and fester my anger. Once back at the office, after he assured me there was nothing he needed, I told him I was headed out to run some errands with only the slightest stutter.

He dismisses me with a flick of his chin and I force myself to walk slowly to the door until I'm out of sight. I run to my truck, fire it up, and peel out to Miller's Feed Store.

My fingers drum on the steering wheel and I fly through three stop signs before I finally pull up to the large warehouse-like building. It's a nice place, great location right on Main Street with a real parking lot, double doors, and a bronze statue of a long-horn steer out front.

I slam through the front door and beeline directly to the checkout girl, who jumps when she catches a glimpse of my face. "Can I help you?"

"Dustin." I spit his name as if it's a dirty word, my jaw sore from grinding my teeth.

Her eyes dart around before she picks up a phone and hits a button. "Yes, hi, it's Brittney. Um…there's a girl here to see you." Her eyes come to mine and she flinches, probably reading my thoughts, which sound something like, *You better not ignore me, you motherfucker.* "Your name, please?"

"Shyann Jennings." I cross my arms over my chest, daring him to refuse me.

"Yes, okay." She hangs up the phone. "Go on up."

She points to a staircase in the back of the store, but I already know where the offices, are so I'm already halfway there.

I stomp up the stairs and head straight for his dad's old office, but before I make it he appears in the doorway.

"Shyann, what brings you— Whoa!" He holds up his hands as I shove past him into the office. "What crawled up your ass?"

I whirl around to face him. "*You*, Dustin."

"I'd like to crawl up more than your ass, Shy." He chuckles, then shuts the door. "But something tells me you're not here to service me under my desk."

My lip curls and I feel dirty just standing in his presence. He moves to his desk in a pair of Wranglers and a brown button-up shirt, the picture of cowboy integrity. He may be able to fool the people in this town, but not me. The blinders are off. He drops into his chair and kicks his cowboy boots up onto the desk, flashing a salacious grin.

"I know it was you." My hands shake with fury at what he's done, what he said about Lucas, what he did to my dad.

"No clue what you're talking about, babe—"

"Don't fucking call me that!" I lunge toward him, wishing I were more like Gage, wishing I could intimidate him, wrap my hands around his throat and cut off his oxygen until he questioned his own mortality, but I freeze. "You fucked with the wrong family."

His eyes narrow. "Is that right?"

"I know you're the one who vandalized the McKinstry place. I saw your little calling card, Dustin. You make me sick."

He only stares at me with cold expressionless eyes. Shady fucking bastard.

"Confess, or I'll tell the cops myself."

He shrugs. "Got nothing to confess. My hands are clean."

"Liar! I saw what you wrote, the same thing you called Lucas in the bar before he put you on your ass."

His face reddens and his glare tightens.

"You called him a retard." I speak the words under my breath, the word so vile, just saying it makes me want to vomit.

"That's your evidence?" He lifts his brows. "Shit, Shy, everyone in town calls him that."

I jerk back and my mouth falls open.

He chuckles, one blond brow lifting to give his all-American-boy look a dangerous edge. "This comes as a surprise to you?"

Lucas is different, antisocial, painfully shy, and this town is known for prejudging newcomers.

"The guy practically puffs into existence and no one knows shit about him; he doesn't share. Hell, he barely speaks. Then he picks a fight with me outta nowhere. Come on, Shy. He's a freak!"

"He is not." The words come out on a whisper because everything

Dustin has observed about Lucas is true, except he didn't attack Dustin for no reason. "And you started that fight. He was defending me."

"You got a thing for this loser, don't you?"

"Don't call him that—"

"You fuckin' him now, Shy?"

"Shut up—"

"The reason you won't get back together with me is because you're suckin' retard dick?"

His words sock me in the gut and I step back to gain distance from his venomous mouth.

"That's what I thought." Dustin stands and braces his knuckles on his desk. His teasing smile falls and his jaw ticks. "Now, unless you got some evidence to prove it was me or have a cop with you to arrest me, get the fuck out of my store."

"I can't believe I ever cared about you." I turn on a heel, racing down the steps and into my truck. My skin is tacky with the sweat of adrenaline and my heart races.

Everyone in town calls him that.

Dustin's words run through my head on repeat. Is it possible I'm not the only one in town that knows about Lucas…knows about Gage? More questions run through my head than I have answers.

But I know someone who might.

* * *

I push through the front door of the diner and the little bell rings over my head. I seek out Dorothy. She's standing behind the counter wiping her hands on her apron and smiling at me.

"Hey, Shy. You here for a late lunch?"

I take the stool at the far end of the counter and she follows me down, placing a menu in front of me.

"No, I—"

"You okay, darlin'?" She presses the back of her hand to my forehead. "You don't look so good."

I force a grin and nod. "I'm okay, just…" *Sick and pissed at this stupid fucking town and the stupid small-minded assholes who live in it.* "I actually am a little hungry, thanks."

I order a club sandwich and wait for Dorothy to put the order in before I wave her back to me.

"Yeah, honey?" She smiles.

"Hey, Dorothy, can I ask you a question?"

"'Course."

"You know, Lucas, right? Newer guy in town, my age. He came in one morning to fill his coffee? Dark hair, always wears a hat—"

"Yeah, I know him."

"What do you know about him?"

She props her full hip on the counter and sighs. "Sweet kid. *Special*, ya know?"

The urge to roar is almost unbearable. I know exactly what "special" means, and it's not the same kind of "special" that Lucas is. Rather than spit fire, I simply nod.

"He showed up in town not too long ago. He was dirty, too thin, unkempt. Believe he was living in his truck, or that's what they say."

They. The townspeople. Suddenly I hated Payson for Lucas.

"People tried to help him, offer him food, take him to church and whatnot, but he refused." She shrugs. "Wasn't until he started working for your dad that people noticed he was being taken care of and left him alone."

"Do you, or does anyone know what's wrong with him?"

"He's a couple pancakes short a stack, but other than that I think he's harmless."

I take a long, relieved breath. They don't know.

"Can you, I don't know, think of anyone who might not like him? Have a reason to want to hurt him?"

Her face twists in disgust. "Lord, no. He's a good kid."

"Thing is, one of the houses Dad's working on got vandalized and whoever did it spray-painted some nasty stuff on the walls."

"Heard 'bout that."

Of course she did.

She scratches her head with her pencil, then sticks it back into its resting place behind her ear. "You know how people are, Shy. They hate different. That boy is different. There's something…" She motions to her eyes. "In here, makes me think he's got a story to tell. Not that he ever would. Boy don't say a thing but *please* and *thank you*, *sir* and *ma'am*."

He does to me.

"Right." Funny, sitting here thinking about it, I realize how very little I know about Lucas. As much time as we've spent together, I don't even know how old he is.

Maybe Dustin was right; anyone in town could've vandalized the McKinstry place. I still can't shake the feeling that my ex-boyfriend is far from innocent.

Dorothy slides a plate piled high with a triple-decker club sandwich and potato salad in front of me.

I peer up at her. "Can I get this to go? I just remembered I have somewhere I need to be."

"Sure thing, Shy." She smiles sweetly and slides the entire thing into a box.

I throw down a ten-dollar bill and run out the door. "Thanks, Dorothy!"

She waves and I jog to my truck.

I need more information, and to think it's been right under my nose this whole time.

***

"You're back."

"Yeah, I thought you could use some lunch." I thrust the to-go bag at my dad.

"You're an angel." He rips into the food. "I'm starving."

I point over my shoulder toward my desk. "There's some paperwork I need to sort, so I'll go ahead and do that." Not a lie.

"It's Sunday. You can do it tomorrow," he says through a cheekful of potato salad.

"Ha! Because my insane social life is calling."

He grunts and shoves a quarter of the sandwich in his mouth, his eyes on insurance claim paperwork. Between his food and his work, I hope he doesn't notice me pulling employee files.

My organizing over the last few weeks makes it easy to locate the folder I need. I cross to my desk with a stack of applications pressed to my chest. I flip through pages as quietly as possible, feeling half PI and half stalker slimeball.

There's a tiny voice in my head that says I could always just ask Lucas, but something tells me he won't be as forthcoming as his employee file will be. And there's always the risk that my questions will provoke Gage.

The files are in no alphabetical order, and I continue to move through them until finally my eyes land on the name.

Scribbled in blue ink.

Lucas Menzano

"His last name is Menzano," I whisper, as the heavy surname falls from my lips.

"What's that?"

I jump at the deep rumble of my dad's voice and drop the file of employee paperwork to the floor. "Shit! You scared me to death."

My heart pounds and I scurry to pick up all the loose pages.

His boots come into view. "Whattdya need with employee files?"

I peek up at him scowling down at me with a half sandwich in his hand. "Oh…um, just putting them in a-alphabetical order, Dad. They were a mess." I laugh nervously and right myself, dropping the gathered pages on my desk.

"Huh…good idea." He grabs his keys. "I'm headed out. Probably won't be back in, so I'll see ya at home. Thanks again for lunch." He shoves his mouth full of food, snags his keys, and he's gone.

I breathe a little easier now that he's gone and I can continue my skeevy snooping in private. I hate hiding things from my dad, but the truth would prompt too many questions that I don't have the answers for.

As soon as I hear his truck engine fade into the distance, I sort through Lucas's file, looking for his application. Guilt washes over me at this complete invasion of his privacy and my fingers still. I shouldn't be doing this. I got his last name. That should be enough.

The temptation to take one more look weighs against my conscience, making my fingers shake. Maybe just a quick peek, as long as it's on accident while I'm putting them in alphabetical—

My phone vibrates. I jerk and squeal like a little girl.

"Holy shit!" My hand covers my throbbing chest, hoping to slow my racing heart. "What the hell is wrong with me today?"

I grab my phone with my free hand. "Hello?"

"Hey, honey."

I groan internally at the all too peppy sound of Trevor's voice. "Hey, what's up?"

"Nice to talk to you too." He chuckles and I roll my eyes.

I find Lucas's name again. *Menzano*. Is that Italian? It sounds Italian. Why does that name sound so familiar?

"Hello? Did you hear what I just said?"

"Oh, sorry, no. I'm at work, got my head buried in paperwork." It's mostly true. "What was that?"

"I said I made the first cut for the job in Los Angeles!"

My heart plummets to my gut and my body sinks like dead weight into my desk chair.

"Isn't that amazing? They just called."

"Wow…" *That should've been me.* "That's great, Trevor. I'm…I'm really happy for you."

"Right? I'm happy for me too! They want me to bring in one unique work and if I pass that, I'm hired."

More good news about how Trevor is living the life I've worked my ass off for while I'm stuck back in the life I hate.

"This station is cutting edge, Shy. They're looking for dynamic people who're passionate and can put a new twist on news reporting."

Fucking awesome, Trevor. Why don't I go shove my face in a vat of horseshit to celebrate?

"I think, I mean, I don't know this yet, but I think they might find your on-air outburst pretty fucking cool."

I perk up, his voice suddenly coming in clear and chasing all other things from my thoughts. "Really?"

"Yeah, apparently one of the news reporters they just hired was fired by KSB for slashing the tires of a pedophile while covering the sicko's court hearing."

Wow, that means…"Are you saying…Do you think—"

"Yep, I think they'd love you. I'm going out there next week. I'll sniff around, drop some hints, tell them about you, okay?"

My heart leaps in my chest. "Trevor, thank you! Really, thank you so much."

"Sure thing, honey."

Could this really be happening? A real opportunity to get back my broadcasting career and in Los Angeles of all places.

My excitement quickly sinks as I remember my earlier conversation with Lucas. *Stay.* God, that single word tore from his throat with such longing that I wanted to wrap myself around him and promise to never leave.

Do I give up everything I've worked for to see where things go with a man I know next to nothing about?

I study the scribbled handwriting on his application and then realize he didn't list a high school or a college. Did he never graduate from high school? I trace his name with my fingertip.

Lucas Menzano.

"Who?"

Trevor's voice snaps my head up and I pinch my eyes closed. "Oh, um…sorry, I was just going through employee records. The name, it sounded familiar."

"Yeah?"

"Did we know anyone in college with the last name Menzano?"

He's quiet for a few seconds. "No, but NAU's a big school. Could've been a Menzano there."

I pluck my bottom lip, thinking. "Yeah, it seems familiar to me. I just can't figure out why."

"Ooooh, you're probably thinking of the Menzano Massacre. We were kids when it happened, but remember we studied it in Com Ethics?"

Menzano Massacre.

Yes, that's where I'd heard the name.

I stare at my desk, trying to remember the details of the case study.

"…professor that would fart every time he coughed." Trevor laughs.

"What was it again? The story?"

"It was about ethical decisions regarding minors who commit lethal crimes, felonies, shit like that. Fuck, Shy, did you sleep through that lecture?"

"Can you just remind me?"

He huffs out a frustrated breath. "The kid was a minor, thirteen or fourteen. I don't remember. We talked about how they released his photo but not his name to the public and then debated whether or not it was ethical to do so. Ring a bell?"

My breathing speeds; my heart pounds in my chest and it's hard to swallow. "Yeah, the kid he…"

"He killed his entire family, Shy. The guy was a fucking murderer. He shot his brothers and sister and his mom. Then the psycho killed himself, or tried to but he lived. I can't believe you don't remember this."

I lick my lips. My eyes feel like they're being held to open flame.

"The kid ended up getting off, some stupid technicality, fucking scary as shit to think he's somewhere out there, ya know? Our legal system failed big-time."

My hand shakes and I'm dizzy. "I'm…I'm sorry. I have to go, Trevor. I'll talk to you—"

"Wait…you said there's someone in town with that name? Someone who works for your dad. You think he's related?"

Fear lances through me, the urge to protect Lucas overwhelming. "Nah…this guy is…um…it's not—"

"Shy? You're stuttering."

Fuck! He thinks I'm lying. I am lying! "This guy is older. He's a friend of my...dad's."

I chew my lip, hoping Trevor buys my casual, if not too casual, tone.

"Okaaay...well, I should probably go. I've got a lot of work to do if I want to snag this LA job. Wish me luck."

"Right, good luck. California here we come." My heart squeezes painfully at the thought.

I don't question my reaction, just hang up the phone and pull up the Internet.

Using a search engine, I type in *Menzano Massacre* and hover the arrow over the search button.

With a deep, fortifying breath, I hit SEARCH.

My screen fills with lines on top of lines, all news stories from ten years ago.

I don't click on any of the links, but rather on the button that searches images related to the story.

With only a second to prepare myself, my screen fills with photos. One draws my attention immediately. There he is.

A teenaged Lucas.

His cheeks hollow, dark circles under his eyes, his thin, gangly body wrapped in a navy blue suit that looks four sizes too big, and a large patch of white gauze on his neck.

Right where his scar is.

I can't blink, can't look away as I take in the page of images before me.

Mug shot.

Him in a faded blue juvenile detention shirt.

Him following a woman in a red suit into the courthouse.

It isn't until a cool wind blows through the window by my desk that I feel the dry of my strung out eyes.

"Gage...what did you do?"

TWENTY-FIVE

LUCAS

I can't take any more of this distance.

It's eating at my skin and shredding me apart.

Why won't she talk to me?

It's been days since I dropped off the mantelpiece at the McKinstry place with Shyann. I can't imagine what happened between then and now, but we haven't spoken since. She left the job site that day a little preoccupied but still waved and flashed me that same Shyann smile.

Since then…nothing.

I cast out downriver, the gentle tug on my line and the racing water keeping me from pacing. Keeping me still. After Nash approved the mantel, I stained and installed it, but with the carving completed I have nothing to occupy my time. Silence and loneliness free my thoughts to fill with Shy.

I've gone by the office, but every time I do she's on the phone—or else she's pretending to be. She hasn't stepped foot on a single job site. And she hasn't been by to see me at home.

I've wracked my brain trying to figure out what I did wrong, what I said to push her away, and I come to the same conclusion. Gage. He hurt her before and she's finally come to her senses; it's what I asked her to do, so I can't be upset. We're not safe, and even though I'd love to have Shyann in my life, she may never be able to trust me. Not that I blame her. I don't trust me.

Life before Shyann was easy. I never knew what I was missing, so I didn't begrudge my lack of friends. But she spoiled me with her attention, gave me a taste of what it would be like to share my life with someone else. She looked at me like I was important, breathed new life into mine, and now she's taken it away.

My line tugs. I jerk back to hook the fish and reel in a trout. It flops around on the end of my line, its mouth gaping. Movement from the corner of my eye catches my attention and Buddy inches out from beneath the deck.

Unhooking the fish, the dog whines and creeps closer, tail wagging. "Can't eat him, Buddy. We're sending him back."

Which reminds me, I'm almost out of dog food. I can't stand the thought of him going hungry.

Gathering all my fishing supplies, I store them in the outdoor shed and Buddy darts back under the deck. The weather is getting colder at night as well, and the dog doesn't have anything outside of his coat to keep him warm.

I squat down and Buddy retreats deeper into the dark. "Cold in there?"

Deciding a trip into town for dog food and a dog bed is in order, I head in to grab my keys and some cash from my last paycheck. I study the stack of money and my face gets hot thinking about what I'd planned to do with it—to take Shyann out on a real date. To prove to her I could be normal. After our talk in her office, I was hopeful something was happening between us.

I was stupid to think it would last.

That someone like her would ever be able to stick around with someone like me.

Pulling on my sweatshirt and baseball hat, I hop in my truck and drive into town. The hustle of weekend guests fills the streets as the cooler temperatures bring tourists. Knowing there won't be any dog beds at the grocery store, I head over to the local feed store. I know they carry supplies for livestock, but I've seen painted advertisements on their windows boasting pet supplies as well.

A bell rings overhead as I step through the door, and I follow the signs that take me to a section devoted to dogs. Taking in all the different brands of food, I grab the bag that has a dog that looks like Buddy on it and move to a wall with beds. Circular, square, rectangle…even doghouses. Maybe I should build him a doghouse. All I'll need is a little scrap lumber. It'll get him out from under the deck, off the cold ground. He'll never survive through winter unless I can get him—

"Something I can help you with?"

A man's voice comes from behind me and panic floods my veins. Hostility triggers the dark, and this guy's tone isn't overly friendly.

"No thanks." I grip the bag of dog food under my arm. "Got what I need." A dog bed can wait until tomorrow.

I'm moving toward the checkout with my head down when a pair of brown cowboy boots step in front of me. "Got some nerve stepping foot in my store."

My gaze slowly moves up his wide body to his face. His jaw is tight and a vein pops from his forehead. "I'm…sorry?"

"A little late for an apology, don't you think?" His blond hair seems to get lighter as his face becomes crimson. "Your business ain't welcome here."

"Oh..."

"Get gone, boy."

I bristle at him calling me boy, and black flickers at the edge of my vision. I need to get out of here. I step back to the dog food aisle and slide the bag back onto the shelf.

"I see you here again I'll call the sheriff and have you arrested for trespassing."

Darkness bleeds into my vision, but I push it back and will my pulse to calm.

"You need an escort, asshole?"

I jerk at the hate in his words. "No. I'm leaving." I turn toward the door, my chin tucked deep into my chest.

"Hey, dumbass!"

My feet freeze and I slam my eyes shut as Gage claws to the surface. I wish I were a stronger man, the kind who could defend himself. I've always wanted to be brave but have fallen short. Always fall short.

"Stay the hell away from her, you hear me?"

My muscles tense and my shoulders hit my ears. "Her...?"

"Shyann Jennings. Stay away from her or you'll answer to me."

Defeat and anguish crush me from within. I shove my shaking hands into my pockets, fisting the flesh of my thighs to stay present.

"Now get on, boy. Get the fuck outta here."

I move as fast as my feet will carry me to the doors when I hear him mumble behind me. "Fuckin' freak."

A light sheen of sweat covers my skin despite the cooler temperature as I shuffle to my truck. My shoulders sag with the weight of betrayal.

How does Shyann know that guy? She promised me she'd never tell anyone my secret, but I got the distinct feeling whoever that guy was knew about me. About Gage.

He called me all the standard-issue names for a guy like me, names I grew up hearing more than my own given name.

If this gets out, if the town finds out who I am, what I've done, they'll want me gone. I'll be back on the road, jobless, hungry, cold and without a home.

A home.

This is the first place I've called home since…I push away the thoughts of my mother's house and focus on getting back to the river house. I squint and concentrate on the road ahead as a blackout presses in.

My pulse roars in my ears.

It was a mistake letting anyone in. Being friends with Mr. Jennings, Cody, and the closeness I felt to Shyann. I should've known better. I've learned this lesson before and I don't want to learn it again.

The pain of losing someone is more excruciating than never having someone at all.

I'm safer on my own.

We're safer on our own.

That's the way it has to be.

The way it has to stay.

The darkness looms beneath the surface. I need to get home. My foot presses the gas harder. *Please, Gage, wait until we're home.*

On that thought, I'm plunged into darkness.

SHYANN

"What do you mean *why*? I just told you." Cody huffs into the phone so loud I have to pull it away from my ear to avoid him blowing out my damn eardrum. "The guy delivered early and Dad needs to cut him a check. Just grab the checkbook and get over here before we lose our contract with these guys."

He hangs up on me and I stare at the checkbook on my desk. Chewing on my lip, I consider cutting my truck's fuel line to keep from having to bring the stupid thing out to them. I've managed to avoid work sites since finding out about Lucas. It's not that I'm afraid of him, or I judge him in any way…Okay, maybe that's not entirely true. I just realized I don't know Lucas at all, and everything I thought about Gage, all his threats came flooding back and it hit me. He was right.

I underestimated him.

I allowed myself to feel a false sense of security because I trusted Lucas, but if Gage would hurt his own family…my God…then what would he do to me?

So I threw myself into work. Made sure I stayed busy and when I wasn't doing that I was home taking care of my dad. I took over the shopping, cooking, and cleaning. Did laundry, cleaned out the refrigerator, the pantry, and ripped all the frilly crap from my old bedroom.

I did whatever it took to keep my mind off Lucas. Nothing worked. I've been hoping to forget the way it felt to make him smile, to feel his touch or be in his arms. And seeing him made it worse. Every time I see him, the ache in my chest gets worse.

The way he looks at me kills, because I'm avoiding him. And he knows it.

I need to move on from my feelings because whether or not I want to believe it, I can't deny the facts.

It's possible Gage killed his family.

It's taken everything in my power to stay in town. My feet itch to run, to put as much space between me and this town as possible. I could go to Los Angeles, live off what little I've saved; it'd be the easy way out. Also a coward's way out.

No more running, Shy.

I groan and scoop up the checkbook, then stomp to my truck, pissed I'm being forced to do this and risk possibly seeing Lucas. I suppose I could flag one of the guys down, throw it out the truck window without actually having to stop. I just…I can't face the man with the scarred neck and the broken soul.

His gray eyes flash in my mind's eye. Vulnerable, questioning…a shell of a man who seemed to come to life the more time we spent together. The more he trusted me, the more I saw bits and pieces of who he really is come forward. Even Gage, I started to believe that we'd forged a truce between us, that he realized I wouldn't hurt Lucas. Turns out we were both wrong.

The work site comes into view and it's surrounded by our crew working in various areas, some at the table saw, others lifting tile, and still others noticeable only through the windows working inside.

I quickly scan the area for my dad or Cody, making sure not to linger too long on any one of the men in order to avoid accidentally seeing Lucas, but with laserlike precision, my gaze is drawn directly to him. He's curled over a table, one long, powerful arm outstretched along a length of wood with a measuring tape in hand. He pulls a pencil from behind his ear and marks the wood before shoving it back between his ear and his backward baseball hat. His muscles bunch beneath his form-hugging tee and I'm captivated. His body stills, and as if he can somehow sense me, his head slowly lifts before his gaze slams into mine.

"Shit!" I turn away, pull my pickup to the side of the house, and force my racing heart to calm.

What is it about this guy? If I had any sense of self-preservation, I'd be running to the cops or at the very least to my dad, but something holds me back. Call it loyalty, or standards, or stupid, no matter how I work it all through in my head I can't and could never bring myself to expose him.

I just didn't realize how much I cared about him until I pulled away from him. Every time I see him, I hope my draw to him will lessen, that I won't feel the overwhelming urge to touch him in some way, to hug him, hold his hand, or press my lips to his, but I do. I feel it every single time.

I fist my hands in my hair and groan. "You're sick, Shy...sick, sick, sick."

A loud knock sounds at my window and I nearly jump out of my skin.

Cody's standing by my door glaring. "'Bout friggin' time." He pulls open the door to reach over me and grab the checkbook. "Hey..." He tilts his head. "You feeling okay? You seem, I don't know, pale."

"Fine. I'm good." I throw the truck into reverse, happy to get the hell away.

"Whoa, not so fast." Cody reaches in and throws the transmission into park. "Dad needs you." He walks away and I'm paralyzed, not with fear, at least not in the typical sense, but anxiety has me dreading leaving the safety of the truck.

I'm going to have to face him eventually. It's not like he'll even speak to me after the way I've treated him, ignoring his attempts to connect.

I push out the door and move to the house, thankful that my dad is the first person I see. I scurry up to his side. "Hey, Dad. Cody said you needed me?"

My hands tug impatiently on the hem of my T-shirt and my dad peers down at me through a narrow gaze. "Where's the fire, Shy?"

"Fire? No fire, just ya know, work to do back at the office." Male voices boom from behind me and I turn, thankful I don't see Lucas. "Lots of work, so what's up?" *Get to it, man!*

He doesn't seem convinced but ignores my edginess. "I want you to head over to the Dover house. It's a single level, end of the cul-de-sac. Four-seven-seven is the street number. Woman's name is Gabby Anderson."

"Sure, what do I do when I get there?"

"She wants to redo her kitchen and dining room and she's looking for some custom pieces."

My heart drops into my stomach like a brick.

"…need him to take a look at the space, get some ideas of what can be done…"

No, no, no!

"…get along so well, figured you could go with him."

"What? Why?"

My dad's glare grows impossibly tighter. "He ain't good around new people, Shy. You know that. You do the talking while he takes a look around."

"Have him take Cody, or"—I motion around the job site—"one of these guys. I really have too much to—"

"Go."

I blink at my dad's abrupt dismissal of my lame excuse. "But—"

"Hurry. She'll only be there till two." He turns back to what he was doing, not open to further argument.

What the hell.

I have no choice. He's given me no choice!

My heart thunders in my chest as I drag my feet outside and after a quick search find Lucas at the circular saw. His hat is still backward and he's wearing protective glasses that make most men look dorky, but with Lucas's powerful bone structure and model-worthy skin, they look like designer shades.

It's impossible to take a full breath as I move to him and brace for him to notice me.

He makes a quick cut, catches me out of the corner of his eye, and moves slowly to standing upright. Is he taller than he used to be or am I starved from not being near him? Ripping off the protective glasses, he stares at me with a blank expression.

I think back to the photos I saw of him on the Internet. Same blank stare. His emotions tucked deep, protecting himself.

"Hey, Lucas."

"Ma'am…" He shakes his head and drops his gaze to my neck. "Shyann."

I swallow hard. "I…um…My dad, he said you need to go to a house and give a bid for some custom—"

"Yes."

"He's asked that I go with you?" Not sure why that came out as a question other than the fact that although doing this is an order from our boss, I feel the need to gain his permission.

He pulls off his hat and flips it forward on his head, then pulls it low over his eyebrows. "Now?"

I nod.

"Oh…" He grabs his tape measure and brushes sawdust off his shirt and jeans. "Okay."

"I can drive."

His chin lifts, and even though I can't see them very clearly, I feel his eyes on me. "No. I'll meet you there."

"Lucas, you don't—"

"It's okay, Shyann," he whispers. "I understand."

I blink and shake my head. "Understand? Understand what?"

He looks away, rubbing the back of his neck.

"I'm sorry, okay. I know I've been distant, and it's probably been really confusing for you. I just…" *Did Gage murder your family?*

"I don't want to make trouble for you. Nash and Cody, they've done so much for me and I can't afford to…" He sighs. "Never mind."

My chest hurts at the rejection in his face and suddenly this week of silence between us feels pointless. I've promised him honesty and then tucked tail when I should've just talked openly about what I'd learned, but at the risk of provoking Gage. I was protecting myself and I dragged him through the mud to do it. Typical Shy. "Let me come with you, okay? You can drive, and we can talk."

"I don't know—"

"Please, Lucas." Now it's me who's fidgeting. "It's only been a couple of days, but…" I dart my eyes around, then study the dirt in front of my feet. "I miss you."

A hiss escapes his lips.

"Please…"

He doesn't answer, but his eyes grow intense, as if he's trying to read my thoughts. Seconds tick by until finally he nods.

We move in silence to his truck and with the drive to the house on Dover being less than five minutes, I never build up the courage to talk to him about what I learned. In typical Lucas form, he doesn't push to fill the silence with conversation.

At the house, I take the lead and knock on the door when a woman in her midthirties answers.

"Mrs. Anderson, I'm Shyann Jennings."

She smiles and offers her hand. "Nice to meet you, and please, call me Gabby."

"This is Lucas. We're here to take a peek at the kitchen and dining room you were looking to get some custom woodwork done for?"

She offers her hand to Lucas and he visibly tenses. I contemplate pressing my palm against his back to encourage him and hopefully offer him comfort but before I do he reluctantly offers his hand for a quick shake.

"Come on in." Gabby shows us the space and explains she has somewhere to be soon, so excuses herself to get ready. I stand back in the corner and watch in awe as Lucas moves around the space. Focused, his gaze slides along every surface in a visual caress while the creative wheels spin inside his head.

He stops at corners to do quick measurements, then moves to the next. In the kitchen it's more of the same. Study, move, measure. Study, move, measure.

Every time he lifts his arms, I get a flash of his firm stomach and a strip of dark hair that disappears into his jeans. The long, corded muscles of his arms flex with every pull of the tape measure and images of being held in those arms have me squirming.

"Okay." He doesn't face me but shoves his things into his pocket, indicating he's finished.

"Get what you need?"

He nods and quickly moves through the house, then outside to wait in his truck while I say goodbye to Gabby and let her know my dad will be in touch with a proposal.

The walk back to the truck is like marching to my own execution, because while I care deeply for Lucas, I can't be with someone capable of murder. I've read the news accounts of what happened to Lucas's family, but there are still unanswered questions, and before I walk away from this man for good, I will get the truth.

Just like Momma always said, like a dog with a bone.

TWENTY-SIX

LUCAS

If I didn't know better, I'd think Nash Jennings hates my guts.

That's the only explanation I can come up with for the torture he's putting me through. Having Shyann so close, stuck in my truck with her and that penetrating stare, all while knowing I can't have her.

The only thing worse is not seeing her at all.

She waves goodbye to Mrs. Anderson and I wipe my clammy hands on my thighs, forcing my pulse to slow. I blame my rapid heart rate on Mrs. Anderson. There's nothing wrong with the woman, but women of her age, especially those who are confident, remind me of a time in my life I'd rather forget.

"Hey, sorry that took so long." The corner of Shy's mouth hooks up in a shaky smile, making me want to press my fingertips against her lips and soothe her nerves. "Do you…uh…have some time so we can talk?"

"No." I don't want to hear her talk about all the reasons why whatever we had didn't work, don't want to hear her confirm all the ways I'm not good enough for her. I turn from my leaning position on the hood of my truck and slide into the driver's seat.

Her shoulders deflate and she climbs in beside me. I fire up the engine, hoping she'll leave it alone, not force me to confess how miserable I've been not seeing her, how much I've missed her friendship, how often I've dreamt of her lips.

She cocks her knee and turns, facing my side head-on. "Lucas, there's something I need to say to you and I'll say it while you're driving, but I think it would be better…safer…if we went somewhere to talk."

My hands grip the steering wheel tighter. "You don't need to explain. I understand."

I catch a glimpse of her confusion from the corner of my eye. "What do you mean, you understand?"

"I don't want you to feel unsafe with me, Shyann, but I can't change what I am."

"What are you?" she whispers.

"I'm split." I don't look at her but I can feel her eyes boring into me.

"Pull over."

"I don't think that's a good idea." The sooner I get away from her the better chances I have of not falling at her feet, begging for another chance.

Her warm hand touches my biceps and the muscle jumps in response. "Please."

"Don't. I can't…" I lick my lips, forcing any excuse I can find out of my throat. "I can't afford any trouble. You know I can't. Even the guy at the feed store has warned me—"

"Hold on. Who?" There's anger in her voice and my already amped up emotional state has me seeing spots. "What did Dustin say?"

"It doesn't matter." We stop at a red light and I chance a look. "I think it's best we stay away from each other."

Her eyelids flutter and she shakes her head. "No, Lucas—"

"You were right to avoid me. As much as it hurts to let you go, to see you and feel so far away, I can live with that kind of torture. I welcome it even, because I know the pain of not having you means you're safe." The light turns green and I'm forced to pull my eyes away from her.

"I'm sorry I've been avoiding you, Lucas. I want to talk to you about why, but first, let me straighten something out." The heat of her hand rests on my thigh and she leans in close. "Dustin and Gage have some bad blood between them. You remember I told you about that, right?"

"I remember you told me about the bar. I didn't know that was him." I think back to his words. *It's a little late for an apology, don't you think?* "Makes more sense now."

"Dustin knows how I feel about you."

"How do you feel about me, Shy?" I practically choke on my own nerves.

She sighs, and I can feel her looking at me, but I can't meet her gaze. "I feel more than I've felt in a long time when I'm with you. I'm scared, Lucas, because…"

I turn to her, hoping she'll finish that sentence and reveal she's just as freaked out about us as I am.

"You're right. I'm safer without you." She chews her bottom lip and then huffs out a breath. "But the thought of living without you is worse than my fears."

Could that be true? Could she possibly feel as lost as I do when we're not together? My hands shake and to be safe I pull over on an old road that leads to an abandoned mill. I shut the truck off. The air in the cab thickens between us and my mind clambers to sort the million questions that jumble my head.

"Then what happened? What did I do to chase you away?"

She groans. "You didn't do anything. I…" Her fingers fist into her hair. "Dammit, this is so hard."

Her silence weighs down the air in the truck and I'm tempted to open a door, stick my head out, and suck in much needed oxygen.

"I saw your employee paperwork, Lucas," she whispers.

My spine stiffens and I stare at nothing in front of me.

"Your name. I've heard your name before." As if every molecule of air between us swells, the space between us strings tight with tension. "Menzano. I know all about you, Lucas," she whispers.

No. She can't know; she'll hate me if she knows.

"I know about the Menzano Massacre."

I hold my breath, praying I imagined those words and she didn't just confess to knowing what I did.

"Lucas?"

My throat closes in and my head spins. She knows…but only knows what the news reported, the details released from my case, but still to this day, no one knows the truth. Not even me.

"Lucas, please talk to me."

The warmth of her hand hits my forearm and I recoil, trying to melt into the door. My hands shake as visions play out before my eyes like a bad dream.

The confusion, the blood, the voices of panic all around.

"You're shaking—"

Finding out my mother was dead.

"…scaring me, Lucas…"

My brothers.

"…breathe!"

My baby sister.

"Lucas! Breathe!"

Shyann, my only friend, the only woman I ever cared for, knows how sick I am. She trusted me once; even knowing about Gage, she accepted me. No way she'd believe in me now, knowing what I am, what I'm capable of.

"Lucas, please!"

"I think … I killed them."

TWENTY-SEVEN

SHYANN

I suck in a quick breath at Lucas's confession.

He did it. He killed his family.

Everything I read online said after a hung jury and a retrial the case was dismissed due to insufficient evidence. The entire family's fingerprints were found on the murder weapon. The angle of the gunshot entry wounds were sketchy, and eventually, after Lucas was held in juvenile detention for almost three years, it was determined to be a mass suicide and he was released. Controversy stirred around the case because of Alexis, the youngest victim. It seemed unlikely that a seven-year-old would willingly commit suicide, but nothing could be proven without witness testimony.

Whatever Lucas said, there's no way he's capable of murder.

But Gage, for Lucas's protection, I believe, would kill.

I study the man now, so different than the boy from the pictures online, and yet somewhat the same. He's pressed against the door, eyes cast out the window. I don't see a cold-blooded killer; I see a shattered soul who's pieced himself back together and despite his abuse has shown nothing but compassion and selflessness, putting his own desires aside by staying away to ensure my protection.

So I'll risk safety to give him what he needs.

I reach for him with shaky fingers and slide them behind his neck. "Lucas?"

"I can't...breathe."

My eyes burn as he becomes more and more like a boy and less like the man I've come to know. The man I've come to care deeply for.

"The air...I can't."

"Okay." I hop out of the truck and jog around the hood to the driver's side. Cautiously I open the door.

"Come on out." I try to sound strong, try to force a steady voice despite my anxiety. "You need fresh air, Lucas. It'll be okay."

I peel his fingers back from their clenched position at his thigh.

He's shaking and his palm is sweaty, but he grips my hand. "Why...? Why are you doing this to me?"

My heart fractures and shreds through me. I don't want to hurt him, I never wanted to hurt him, but I can't stand secrets between us. My job has always been to seek out information and search for the truth. That's all I want. I never expected what I'd learned about Lucas to tear him down so low.

I hold tight to his hand and tug. "Come on. You need to stand, get some air. It'll be okay." My voice cracks and I realize the lie in my words. It won't be okay; nothing about any of this is okay.

My conscience whispers that I am holding on to the hand that was responsible for ending the lives of four people, three of them children.

I'm in the forest alone with a self-proclaimed murderer and although I trust Lucas completely, I sense Gage just below the surface.

He drops out of the truck but only to lean back against it, his head bowed, his free arm wrapped around his body and tucked under his biceps. He tries to free the hand in my grip but I refuse to let him go. "I never wanted you to find out."

"I don't believe it was your fault."

He shakes his head. "How can you say that?"

"You tried to kill yourself. You"—my gaze darts to the angry scar on his neck—"shot yourself in the neck."

"Yeah, I...I don't remember that. I don't remember any of it because..." He lifts his chin and his gray eyes glisten. His eyebrows pinch together and he blinks slowly. "I wasn't there."

"Gage." The single name reverberates in the air around us, sending goose bumps racing up my legs, down my arms, and across my neck.

His chin drops. "Gage," he whispers.

"Tell me what he did, Lucas." I squeeze his hand, encouraging him to trust me.

"You read the news reports. That's all I know." His head rolls on his shoulders. "Only Gage knows the truth."

There wasn't a single mention of Lucas's psychiatric oddity in any of the articles I read. They all make Lucas out to be a loner, a decent student, a loving brother who neighbors said was always caring for his younger siblings. There was no mention of dissociative identity disorder. Matter of fact, according to published reports, Lucas passed all his psych evaluations and lie detector tests.

"Can't you just ask him?"

He shakes his head. "I can't communicate with that...side...of me. I can't reach him."

"So you'll never really know what happened that day."

His lifts his gaze. "No. When I was arrested, the entire time I was locked up, during the trial, he never surfaced. Not even once." His expression twists in agony as if the helplessness, the being left in the dark, is eating him alive. "But it doesn't take a genius to figure it out. Everyone died except me." He has no idea what happened that day, has to live with the fact that he could be responsible for the death of his siblings.

Gage might not be able to tell Lucas what happened; my guess is he wouldn't want him to know in order to protect him.

But he can tell me.

I can get the truth from Gage and release Lucas of the pain of not knowing the truth of what happened that day.

"He protects me; he's always protected me, regardless of the cost."

"Then why, why would he murder your siblings? They were younger than you, right? They weren't hurting you, but…" I swallow, terrified to bring up the inevitable. "Your momma, she hurt you, Lucas."

He nods again and his shoulders slump. "I'm afraid, I'm afraid that my brothers and sister got caught up in the cross fire, and that…that would be my fault. Gage protected me, but it was my job to protect them and I failed." He sets cold gray eyes on me. "Don't you see? Even if I didn't pull the trigger, and I very well could have, I didn't protect them and they're dead because of me."

"Don't do that, Lucas. Don't put this on yourself."

His body stiffens and he glares up at me. "Don't put this on myself? How can you say that? It's all on me. Gage is me! Who he hurts, I hurt!" His eyelids flicker and the rage building in his voice makes me step back. "He came and protected me, but he didn't protect them!" Jaw tight, he punches a fist into his chest so hard it thumps. "Me! I didn't protect them!" His shoulders tense and he breathes heavy through flared nostrils. "So stop saying it wasn't me!"

The pain in his voice constricts my chest. "I'm sorry."

"Why are you doing this, Shyann?" His voice cracks. "Why couldn't you just stay away?"

"I—"

"Why!"

I squeeze my eyes shut. "I'm sorry, I'm sorry..." I whisper it over and over and receive no reply. I avert my eyes to the ground like a submissive dog trying to gain favor. I can hear his heavy breathing slow to calm and slowly I peek up at him. "Lucas, I'm only trying to help—" A gasp shoots from my lips and I desperately try to school my expression. "Gage."

GAGE

This bitch is gonna die.

Right fucking now.

I rub circles into the tight muscles of my aching neck and lean back against the bed of Luke's truck. Keeping my eyes on the nosy whore staring back at me, a slow grin crawls across my face.

"Hey, Shy. Ann." I straighten and take a step toward her. "Just couldn't leave it alone, could you?"

Her icy-blue eyes widen. I can practically scent her fear. My strong Shyann is finally afraid. My blood pumps with excitement. I take another step toward her.

She holds up a hand and I smirk at the way her fingers tremble. "Hang on, Gage, just...hear me out."

I slide my head back and forth, then snap my eyes to hers. "Warned you plenty." I tilt my head. "Never listened."

"Let me explain—"

"Sick of hearin' your voice."

The column of her throat bobs with a thick swallow. "Gage..." My name shakes on her lips.

I groan and grip my raging hard-on. "Stop turnin' me on. Need to teach you a lesson, and you makin' me hard is gonna make this a lot more fun for me." I shrug one shoulder. "Not so much fun for you."

A whimper slides from her lips and fuck if it isn't the sexiest damn thing I've ever heard. Breaking her down piece by piece and now she's finally defeated. I. Win. "Please..." Her eyes dart around, as if she's looking for an escape.

"Run. I'll catch you." I fake-lunge and she stumbles but regains her footing.

A noise catches my attention. Humming, or...I study the source and find it when Shyann pulls her cell phone from her pocket and fumbles to get it to her ear. "Hello?!" She's breathing heavy and her shoulders sag in relief.

I ball my fists at my side. Dammit!

"Loreen, yeah..." Her eyes come to mine. "Listen, I need— What?"

I plant my feet, cross my arms at my chest, and wait. She's gonna tell whoever is on the phone to call the cops; I'll drop back and let Luke take over and no one plays innocent as well as the innocent. Luke won't remember shit; they could hook him to a lie detector and he'd pass with flying colors.

Worked before.

It'll work again.

"Oh my God, is she okay?" Shyann doesn't take her eyes off me, as if she's waiting for me to pounce. "Do they have any idea who did it?"

My little news reporter, always gathering information. Nosy bitch.

"Which hospital?"

Hospital?

A weird feeling comes over me but I squash it before I allow myself to question it too much while I pace, waiting.

"Okay, I'll do whatever I can to help. Thanks, Loreen." She hits a button and the second her eyes meet mine, she jerks. "Gage, I know you're angry, but we need to go."

"Like hell we do. I'm not finished—"

"Sam's been hurt. She's in the ICU." Her bottom lip quivers, but she blows out a long breath and stops it. "Someone hurt her bad, Gage."

She pushes past me and climbs into the truck while I stand there staring at the space she just vacated. What the hell? One minute she's scared shitless, and rightfully so; the next she's treating me like I'm her fucking chauffeur.

"Come on!"

I blink and turn slowly, only to find her staring at me impatiently from the open window.

"You're not scared anymore." The words fall from my stunned lips.

"I know you're mad, and we have so much more to talk about, but I need to get to Sam."

"But…" What fucking good am I if I can't scare away people who hurt Luke? This bitch just found out I murdered my entire family to protect Luke, and she's treating me like…a friend? Something about that bothers the shit out of me. "Do you care that little about your life?" Why does her lack of self-preservation make my chest feel tight? Damn, this witch!

"I care a lot about my life. But if your plan is to kill me, you've had and will have plenty of opportunity to carry that out. For now, please just take me to my truck."

Dumb-fucking-struck.

I numbly walk to the truck, turn it on, and take Shyann to her truck, parked at the work site. She climbs out, slams the door, but sticks her head through the open window, sleek and shiny black hair spilling in too. "Unless you plan on letting Lucas come forward, you better take off. I'll cover for you."

What the fuck! "I don't need you covering—"

"You may not know this but it's pretty obvious you're not him. It's…um…" She motions to her own eyes and a tiny blush colors her cheeks. "All in here. Your expressions, they're different."

Protecting Lucas. Again. "I—"

"We'll talk later, okay?"

Reassuring me?

I'm speechless.

She thumps the hood of the truck twice in goodbye and jogs away.

Who the fuck is this woman?

She's throwing up a big fat fuck you to every single thing I thought I knew.

For the first time in forever I feel…useless.

TWENTY-EIGHT

SHYANN

I slam through the hospital doors and skid to a stop in the waiting room. The place is filled with people, all quiet, and now staring at me.

The Payson Regional Medical Center is a hospital that matches its town: small, unimpressive, but functional. I spot the reception desk and move to it, eyes on a petite brunette whose friendly smile is aimed my way.

"Can I help you?"

"Yeah, I was told Samantha Crawford was brought here?"

She frowns. "Yes, are you family?"

"No, but—"

"Shy?"

I whip my head toward the deep male voice calling my name and my eyes narrow. "Dustin, I just heard. How is she?"

The whites of his eyes are bloodshot and the skin surrounding them is puffy. He jerks his head toward a section of the room that's mostly empty except for a man and an elderly woman who is engrossed in knitting a pink blanket. We drop down to a couple of plastic chairs in the corner.

"It's bad, Shy…" His voice is unsteady. "Her face, it's—"

"You were there?"

"No, she called me. I could barely make out what she was saying, so I called nine-one-one and raced to her house." His eyes fill with tears. "I beat the ambulance. Door was wide open and I could hear her moaning."

"Someone broke in?"

He shrugs. "Don't know. By the time I got to her, she took one look at me and passed out. She'd been there for a while; all the blood was old. Must've happened in the night." He leans forward, putting his head in his hands. "She'd been beaten pretty bad. Her face, her body, God…Shy, I hardly recognized her."

My throat swells and a shiver races down my spine. Could the Shadow have moved into Payson? It's always been a relatively safe town. Besides the bar fights and the occasional domestic disturbances, the crime rate is lower than the bigger cities that surround it.

"What do the cops think happened?"

"They're investigating. Can't get a statement out of her until she recovers enough to talk." He cringes. "If she recovers enough to talk."

I slump back in my seat and dig the heels of my palms into my eyes. I don't know enough about the life Sam lives to speculate who would've done this to her. As far as I know, she dates freely, has a few friends, but doesn't seem to have any real enemies. The more my mind attempts to come up with a logical suspect, the more related to the Shadow attacks this seems.

"Thing is, everyone knows everyone in this town and no one seems to have seen shit." He tilts his head to look up at me. "How is that possible, Shy? Not a single witness?"

There's so much pain in his eyes that I feel guilty for any anger I had at their being together. He clearly cares for her.

"Dustin, what if her attack is part of the ones happening in Phoenix and Flag?"

"Maybe. Although..." He blows out a shaky breath. "Girls at Pete's said they saw that kid Lucas with her."

My breath freezes in my lungs.

"That guy's a loose fucking cannon. Came by my shop to confront me 'bout you."

I jerk away from Dustin as if he were on fire. Lord knows he's hurting for Sam, so I try to soften what I'm about to say. "Lucas isn't capable of the kind of violence you're describing."

He fixes me with a glare. "How can you say that? He started a fight with me."

"Dustin, you had me locked to your body and wouldn't let me go." The high-pitched sound of my voice catches the attention of a man near us and he peeks over his *People* magazine. I smile at him, then clear my throat and pray to calm down. "You instigated that and you know it. And him going into your feed store to shop is hardly confrontational."

He sits up to his full height and angles his body to face mine. "That what he told you?"

"Don't do this, Dustin. I know you're pissed and you want to blame someone, but I'm telling you, Lucas is not responsible."

"Yeah? Would you bet Sam's life on that?" He shakes his head in disbelief. "Can't believe you're stickin' up for him."

"I know him, and he's not c-capable of what you're accusing him of—"

"You know him. You really know him? You blow in town for what? A few weeks and you know this guy? Don't be so naïve, Shy. You don't know shit about him."

Has it only been a few weeks?

I can hear the logic in Dustin's words, register them as making complete sense, and can even hear myself giving the same speech to myself in an out-of-body kind of way. Truth is, as much as I think I know Lucas, even claim to understand Gage, he spent time locked up for murder. Of his own family no less.

Is it possible that he's capable of hurting Sam too?

Every cell in my body revolts against the idea.

Not Lucas. No way.

But Gage…

Memories flash behind my eyes. His beautiful face twisted in rage and staring down at me while pushing me underwater. His clenched teeth and sickening smile as he held my throat while his fingers refused to let up despite my begging.

And even less than an hour ago, the way his arms shook with rage while he stalked toward me in the forest.

That is the kind of man who would commit murder.

Beat and maim to prove a point.

But why Sam?

That makes no sense. Gage didn't want Sam before; he flat out refused and even belittled her. What could she have possibly done to deserve getting beaten? What did I do that deserved coming within a few short breaths of being drowned?

Lucas. We're all a threat to Lucas.

Women seem to trigger it.

Lucas's words filter through my head.

I shoot upright and turn to address Dustin. "I'll be back later."

He snags me by the hand. "Stay away from him, Shy, at least until they figure out who's responsible for this."

"I will. I'll stay away from Lucas." I lie without stuttering because Lucas isn't the one I need to talk to.

The key will be bringing forward the one with the answers. I'll figure out how to get him to confide in me.

The problem will be staying safe while I do.

GAGE

I'm parked on the front porch of the river house, Buddy's head in my lap as I run my fingers through his mangy coat. He peers up at me through dark eyes that beg for me to keep scratching. "Get an inch, take a foot, is that it?" His eyelids get heavy when I hit his favorite spot right behind his ear.

If only women were as easy to control.

Feeling settled, I gear up to pull back and let Luke take over when I hear the sound of an engine and tires on gravel over my left shoulder.

Great. What now?

Never having been the type to give a shit about hospitality, I don't bother getting up.

A car door slams and seconds later footsteps crunch earth, growing closer, until they stop.

"Hey!"

I slide my gaze to Shyann, who's focused curiously on the dog before she squints and focuses on me. She lifts her chin, but I notice she keeps a safe distance between us.

"Good, it's you." She takes a few steps closer, but far enough away that it would take a great bit of effort to grab her. "Let's walk."

I tilt my head, lean back in my wooden chair, and prop my feet on the railing. "No thanks." I motion to Buddy. "I'm busy."

"He never comes out like that for Lucas."

My gaze drops to the near-sleeping dog in my lap. "So?"

"He feels safe around you."

Her brow lifts as if she's finally cracked my armor and damn proud of herself for it. She has no idea what I'm capable of. "What do you want, Shy?"

"We need to talk."

"We don't." I turn away from her and focus on the creek. "Not sure why you keep hanging around."

The sound of her shuffling closer makes me want to lunge for her throat.

"I want to show you something." Her voice loses its power, as if she's struggling for the right thing to say. "It's important and, just... *fuck*."

Her weakness sends a thrill down my spine, like dying prey in the ears of a predator. "I might be interested if what you wanna show me is in your pants..." I run my thumb along my lower lip and slide my gaze from her booted feet to her curve-hugging sweater. "On second thought, no thanks. You're not my type."

Her eyes flame with anger and her mouth forms a tight line.

I chuckle; I can't fuckin' help it. This woman has been more fun to torture than anyone I've ever met. She wants to know why I haven't killed her yet? I'm not done playing.

"You intend to scare me, belittle me, make being in your presence unbearable, and yet you can't stand to be alone with me." She props two delicate hands on her hips. "Looks like I'm the intimidating one, huh, Gage?"

My glare pulls so tight my eye twitches. "We go for a walk, only one of us might come back."

She rolls her eyes. "Ya know, real psychopaths don't openly threaten the person they want to kill. They disguise themselves as safe to lure in their victims. Come on, Gage. You can do better than that."

I drop the front legs of my chair to the wood deck, making her jump.

"Hmmm…" I lick my lips. "Excellent point, Shyann." I purr the first part of her name. "I'll go for a walk with you."

She exhales a shaky breath and I stalk toward her; every step seems to increase her breathing and for a ridiculous second I imagine what it would feel like to have her under me breathing like that. I banish the thought as quickly as it came and blame Luke and his pussy-whipped feelings.

Before I reach her, she turns toward the creek. "Follow me."

My teeth grind together, not at all appreciating being told what to do, especially by a woman, but watching her ass sway in a pair of sinfully tight jeans makes me think following ain't so bad.

She heads to the makeshift bridge over the creek, nothing more than a few downed trees pushed to cross safely over the water. Her steps are lithe and sure; clearly the bitch has experience in the forest.

"You taking me out in the middle of the woods to take advantage of me?" I step on the logs, jogging across and hopping off only to look up and meet her icy-blue stare.

"Maybe." She shrugs and keeps walking.

A laugh rumbles in my chest and I freeze. What the fuck was that? I don't laugh. I mean, not unless it's at the expense of someone else.

Blinking, I move to catch up to Shyann, who's keeping a pretty decent pace up a slight incline. We aren't following a trail, but the path is clear of bushes and large rocks. I mentally clock which direction we're heading just in case I do end up getting left out here and need to find my way back, but she doesn't even look up. It's as if this path is pulled from a map in her mind, one she's traveled often.

I don't know how long we've been hiking for, but by the time we stop, my T-shirt is damp with sweat and I'm breathing heavy. Shyann pulls an elastic band off her wrist and secures her hair into a ponytail, exposing the gentle slope of her neck, shining with exertion.

Not that I noticed.

She gives me her eyes but only for a second before looking away. "You okay?"

"Of course I'm okay." Irritation shadows my response.

"It's a little ways up here." She motions to the hill thick with shrubs and crisscrossed fallen tree trunks. "Let me know if you need me to carry you."

My hand flies on instinct and swats her ass so hard a flock of birds spook and scatter from a nearby tree.

Shyann squeaks and pins me with a glare that stirs my blood.

It's not hatred working behind her eyes; it's something else. Heated in a way that makes me aware of my own racing pulse.

The trance is broken when she whips her head around and takes off up the hill. The animal inside me can't stand to be run from, so I squash my thoughts and allow the hunter to take over.

I zero in on her back while my legs eat up earth at my feet. She must hear me gaining on her and cries out as I give chase. She zigzags through trees, pushing past overgrown bushes, but she's no match for me and the distance between us dissolves.

I reach out and snag the back of her sweater, pulling hard. She stops, stumbles, then slams back into my chest. My arms wrap around her stomach in a vise grip and I brush my lips against her ear. "Nice try." I'm breathing heavy and her entire body shivers against me. "I'll always win, Shyann."

She arches, just enough that her ass presses into my stiff groin. I groan and take a few steps, pushing her with me and pressing her into the trunk of a large pine. Her hands come up to shield the tender skin of her cheek against the rough bark. We're both breathing hard, my heart racing against her back, and the pulse at her neck flutters against my lips.

"Gage…" My name falls from her mouth on a needy whimper.

"What are you doing to me?" I don't know why I ask, other than it's the only question flaring in my mind, pushing at my skull, and I need to know the answer. Need it so bad I'd be willing to break her in half to find it.

I pin her hips with mine, making sure she can't get free, and dip my hand under her sweater. Her skin is hot and sticky with sweat and my mouth waters to taste it. I roughly drag my palm up her side, branding her with a heavy hand, until I reach the silky fabric of her bra. I pull impatiently at it, more desperate than I've ever been to capture the weight of her breast.

She pushes back, freeing space between her and the tree's trunk. "Yes, please…"

"Shhh…don't beg." No, I can't stand the sound of her begging, the weakness, proof that I broke her. "Fight." I rip the cup of her bra down harshly and she moans at the snap of stiches being torn. The heat of her tit falls heavy into my hand and I squeeze it hard. "Where's my tough girl?"

Her body stiffens. Muscles coil.

"That's it, baby."

She pushes back, rubbing me with her ass. My forehead drops to her shoulder on a moan. "Fuck…you don't fight fair."

"Gage, I—"

"Shhh…I'll give you what you want." It's what I've seen glowing in her eyes since the first time we met. The hunger, raw lust, simmering below the surface of a heavily controlled façade. As much as I want this woman to leave Luke alone, to stop fucking with his emotions, stop toying with his heart, I also want to taste her. I want to drive into her tight little body and hear her scream my name so loud the entire town will know who I am. I want to punish her for being irresistible and reward her for her silence, for her protection.

I pull at her stiff nipple, and she digs her nails into my arms. My hips roll against her ass, encouraging her to open her legs, while my free hand slides up to wrap her silky black hair around my fist. Once, twice, and I tug her head back. Her dark lips are parted, eyes closed, and she's writhing against me. Damn, never seen anything so beautiful in my life.

"Fuck, look at you." My mouth claims hers in a brutal kiss. Her head wrenched back and the long column of her neck so tempting that if I weren't toying with her breast, I'd wrap my hand around it just to feel the life blood pumping through her veins.

I pillage her mouth with my tongue, coaxing her to meet me with equal force and she accepts the challenge. Her teeth nip at my lips, chasing me down until she finally grabs my lower lip and bites. I growl, whirl her around, and slam her back against the tree.

Her hands go to my chest as I pin her between me and the trunk. "Gage, wait."

"What? No." I pop the button on her jeans and shove my hand between her legs, cupping her possessively over her panties. "Don't tell me to stop, Shy."

Her cheeks flush and she bites her lower lip, her eyes flashing with carnal need. My hand has little room to move in the confines of her tight pants, but I manage to create some friction that has her body falling limply against me.

"It's not right…this, us, it's…" A low moan vibrates in her chest as my palm zeros in on the sensitive spot between her legs. "It's not fair." Her hot breath ghosts against my neck. "To Lucas."

My body stills. Shit.

Luke.

He's the one she's into. Not me. She practically hates me.

I pull back and gaze down at her and the bitch has the decency to at least look embarrassed.

Suddenly I'm painfully aware of my body. The banging of my heart behind my ribs, the jolt of electricity I feel where her skin touches mine, my fingers aching to explore every inch of her naked flesh. And she's asking for Luke.

My eyes pull tight and I press hard between her legs. "This for him, Shy?"

"I…" Her eyes search mine, as if she's looking for Luke to save her. "I care a lot about Lucas, Gage. It's his body, he should be here."

"*His* body." My jaw hardens and I step back, pulling my hands free of her.

She scampers to cover herself and button her jeans. Her eyes avoid mine as she smooths loose strands of her hair back into place. A tick of pride at knocking her off kilter swells in my chest. "I'm sorry. I shouldn't have let that go on for that long."

"I was there, *Shy* Ann. Couldn't have controlled yourself if you'd wanted to."

She scoffs and brushes her hands off on her thighs. "Why, aren't we arrogant."

"Not gonna deny that, but the evidence was in my hands, baby."

Her cheeks flush a deep crimson and she storms off ahead of me. I chuckle, and follow after, not at all happy about the chafing of thick denim against my dick that's rock hard and oversensitized. This is her fault. She's an evil little temptress. Now I'm suffering with the world's worst case of blue balls all for Luke. Not the first time I've been put through hell for him.

After a few minutes and a lot of cold shower thoughts, the incline levels to a small clearing. I study the space, noticing nothing spectacular about it, certainly not worth the hour-long hike it took to get here. Not including the impromptu make-out, which would've made the hike perfect if Shy had put out. Prude.

She moves to the far end where there's a small tree that has no business in this particular forest. The thing is only about six feet tall, its branches drooping with long leaves that from a distance resemble hair. Shyann kneels at the base of the tree and turns to me, motioning for me to come over, before turning back to the small trunk.

What in the hell is she up to now? Nature worship? I internally smack myself upside the head, because staring at the strangely feminine-looking piece of horticulture, I can't help but feel like I'm on sacred ground.

"What is it?" I jerk my chin to the thing while feeling completely uncomfortable for some godforsaken reason.

"This is a willow tree."

"Huh—"

"And it's also my mom." She peers up at me with a shaky smile. "Gage, this is Annika Jennings." She turns back to the tree. "Momma…" she whispers. "This is Gage."

I squat down beside her. "You think your mom…is a tree?"

It's possible Shyann's just as fucked in the head as I am.

Her eyes twinkle with laughter and I force away the warm feeling her happiness evokes in my chest. "No. My mom is buried under this tree."

"What?" I shoot upright and take a step to the side. "Like, here…right here?"

"Yes. She believed that all life came from the earth and, when it ended, should be returned back to it."

I tuck my hands under my armpits. "So you just…tossed her body in a hole? Fuck, and you thought I was ruthless."

"No, we didn't just *toss her body in a hole*. We got a biodegradable coffin." She turns back to the tree. "Her body will decompose and nourish this tree along with everything around it for…gosh"—she picks a wildflower and presses it to her nose—"who knows how long."

"Why'd you bring me here? You said you wanted to talk. Is this what you wanted to talk about, your dead mom turning into worm food beneath our feet?"

She curls in on herself and I immediately wish I could suck the words back into my mouth, and simultaneously kick my own ass for caring.

"No, I guess I just wanted to trust you with something important." She feathers her hand over some wild grass. "I've never brought anyone up here before. The only people who know she's here are Cody, my dad, me…and now you."

What the fuck does she expect me to do with that?

"I know you don't want to trust me, Gage. You want me to prove to you that I'm a danger to Lucas, but you know deep down I'm not. The truth is, I've never cared for anyone as deeply as I do him. I know you want me to walk away, to turn my back on you guys and pretend we never met, but I can't."

You guys?

There's a spasm in my chest so powerful I grip my shirt over my heart.

Me and Lucas.

My pulse races as I consider what she's saying.

"What do you want from us?"

She pushes to stand and my fight-or-flight response flares. For the first time ever, I feel fragile, like thin glass, totally transparent and vulnerable. If she comes too close, touches me, I'll shatter from the intensity of her concern.

Of course she sees through me and stops, but her eyes, those soul-sucking, life-giving eyes, bore into mine. "I want you to trust me, Gage. I want you to tell me the truth. Was it you that hurt Sam?"

TWENTY-NINE

GAGE

The unease I saw back when she was grilling Luke about the past is back. It flickers in her eyes like a green light giving me the all clear to terrorize her. All this bullshit about trust and she's still scared of me.

I smirk, irritated and fucking over trying to understand this woman. "Maybe I did."

She studies me and whatever she sees causes a fraction of her fear to dissolve. "You still don't trust me."

"And you don't trust me. Guess that makes us even."

"What happened the night your family died?"

I stumble back at her complete one-eighty. I want to let Luke take over. I should let Luke take over. I've left him clueless on purpose so that he'll never have to pay for our crimes. The hideousness of what happened that night is enough to give even the strongest man nightmares.

Luke couldn't handle it.

"Why?" No, not why. The answer is no. Always no!

"Trust is a two-way street. You've got to give me something."

"Ask Luke."

"Lucas is…confused. He's lost these huge chunks of his life and—"

"It's for his own good. The things he doesn't know would destroy him if he did."

"You're not giving him enough credit."

I flex my fists. "You don't even know him!"

"Maybe that's true, but don't you think he deserves to have his life back? My gosh, Gage, he's running and he doesn't even know why. He lives with the guilt that you killed his little brothers and sister—"

"That's good. He'll be safer that way."

She shakes her head and frowns. "I don't believe that. Not even for a second."

Damn, this woman is relentless to make me fucking crazy!

"Who killed your siblings, Gage?"

I rip my hands through my hair and grip. "Stop talking."

"Was it your mom?" Her voice breaks on that putrid three-letter word.

I pin her with a glare. "Don't do this."

"She hurt you, didn't she." Her demands grow louder. "Tell me what happened. You were there. She hurt you and you couldn't take it anymore, could you? How bad did it get for you, Gage? What did she do to you?!"

"Shut the fuck up!"

"Who killed your brothers and sister? Tell me!"

"I did!"

She recoils and her eyes tighten.

Adrenaline explodes in my veins and I want her to shut up! "I killed them, all right! Are you fucking happy?"

She huffs out a breath. "No, I'm not fucking happy. Because you're a liar." She throws her arms out. "This was a mistake. Bringing you here…" Her eyes find mine. "I never should've trusted you with this."

The words are like a sucker punch to the gut.

She moves back to her mom's tree and kneels. Staring at the back of her head, I'm struck with her beauty, her strength, her unwavering fucking balls that would have her turn her back on an admitted murderer. A murderer of children!

I growl in frustration, so sick of denying what my insides are screaming. She is the most fascinating person I've ever known, and for the first time in my existence, I've met someone who makes me want to give away everything.

SHYANN

I sit with my heart pounding in my throat, the cool earth beneath my knees, and the fire of anger in my gut. Why won't he just let me in? I thought if I shared something deeply personal with him, he'd do the same. He'd understand I could be trusted if I opened up the most private part of my life to him.

Footsteps sound behind me and my muscles coil tight. He won't hurt me; I believe with every cell in my body that he'd never hurt me.

"She'd make him watch." His deep voice is rough with emotion, as if the words are being pulled from his throat over broken glass. "They were babies and…"

I exhale, close my eyes, and relief lightens the weight pressing in on my chest. He's opening up.

"She blamed them—her husband left and she blamed them." He clears his throat, but I don't dare look up, acting as still as the forest so he'll continue his confession. "One day she was holding Mikey's hand over the burner on the stove. He was so hungry he'd taken something out of the garbage and she caught him. The screams. I'll never forget the sound of his screams. Luke was crying, begging, offering himself up in Mikey's place, but every time he tried, Mikey would scream more. I snapped. I couldn't take any more of the screaming." A few beats of silence build thickly between us. "Ask me what I did, Shy," he whispers.

I swallow, my throat suddenly dry and clogged with tears. "What did you do?"

"I attacked her." There's a smile in his voice. "I shoved Luke into the dark and I tackled the bitch. I punched that stupid whore as hard as my eight-year-old body would allow."

I try to hold back, but a whimper falls from my lips. The things Lucas has seen, the extremes he was forced to endure. Would it be so shocking after years of this kind of treatment he'd want to end the pain? Send his siblings to an eternal peace rather than a lifetime of torture? Would I blame him if he did?

"I only got a few good hits in. She was bigger. Stronger. And, fuck, the bitch could throw down punishment as if she were Satan himself. I've had to bathe in boiling water, go weeks only eating whatever she left for me in the toilet—"

I gasp and cover my mouth to avoid crying out.

"—sleeping in a concrete room without a bed or a fucking blanket to keep me warm. I was sick most of my life. Fevers that got so high I'd hallucinate, vomit that would be so fierce it would break all the blood vessels in my face and eyes, break my ribs—"

My arms wrap around my stomach, trying to hold myself together.

"—the beatings that seemed to never end. The starvation. She'd finally feed me and when I'd bring the food to my lips she'd smack me so hard the food would fall to the ground and I'd see stars. You know what it's like to eat your food off the ground? To crawl on your knees with your hands held behind your back and have to lick your food off the dirty fucking floor, Shyann?"

"No."

"No, of course you don't." He shuffles closer, but I keep my head down. "Sucks your mom got sick and died, but don't expect an ounce of sympathy from me. At least you had a mom who didn't make it her fucking joy in life to torture you."

"I'm sorry, I didn't know how bad—"

"You wanna know?" His voice is at my ear, so close his heated breath is at my neck. "You really wanna know if I killed my family? Can you handle the truth of my life, Shyann?!"

I turn my head from his shouting and ask myself the same question. Can I? Can I handle any more of his truths?

"Y-yes."

He moans low and ends on a deep chuckle. "So brave, my Shy Ann." He wraps his hand around my ponytail and pulls my head back gently, but so far my neck strains at the angle. His lips move to my throat and he glides his tongue from my collarbone to my ear, slow and deliberate. "Mmm…I can taste your fear."

I squeeze my eyes closed and pray for courage. "I'm not afraid of you." My voice shakes as he continues the gentle assault of my throat with his lips. "I'm afraid *for* you."

His mouth freezes at my neck and his hand shakes where he's holding my hair, not a tremor of anxiety but of barely controlled rage. "Don't be afraid for me, baby. You want the truth, you got it." His breath is like fire ghosting my ear. "Yes, I killed my whore mother."

I suck in a breath, but blow it out just as quickly.

"Happy now?" He chuckles and releases my head. "You gonna run, Shy?"

I twist my shoulders to see him, his stance rigid and ready to pounce. My eyes heat, but not with tears. With a furious possession and fiery anger that

I've never felt before. Abusing her own babies, blaming innocence for the crimes of the guilty, making them literally eat shit.

A slow grin curls my lips and with his eyes narrowing on my mouth, he pales. "No, I'm not gonna run." I push up and stand and for the first time ever I see a flicker of fear in Gage's eyes. "Am I happy?" I take a step toward him and his hands fist at his sides. "Can you handle *my* truth, Gage?"

He doesn't answer verbally, but tilts his head. Good enough.

"The bitch deserved to die, and who better to deliver her eternity in hell than you."

GAGE

Never in my life have I been shocked senseless.

I've seen things, bore witness to the torture of children, experienced pain and mental abuse no human could fathom. Been cast out, treated as trash and spit upon by the one person in the world who is supposed to protect me.

I never lost my head, never struggled for ways to fight back. Always remained in control. But as I stare wide-eyed into the hateful glare of the woman before me, I'm stupid.

Completely incapable of a response.

Not only does she not hate me, judge me, or at the very least pity me…but she also supports me. The concept in itself is insane. Women like Shyann, her big heart and tender soul, should see me as a plague. Run for her life and never look back. The fact that she doesn't strips me raw and leaves me exposed.

"Tell me the rest of the story, Gage." She stalks toward me and I suck in a breath. "The part only you know. The part you never wanted Lucas to find out about."

"I…I can't." Fuck, I sound like a pussy.

She moves closer. "Did she kill your brothers and sister?"

Flashes of black blast behind my eyes and helplessness fills my chest.

I hold up my hand to stop her advancing both physically and with her words. "Stop!"

Her beautiful eyes narrow. "You were there; you would take over to protect Lucas. That day must've been worse than the others. Where'd the gun come from?"

I pinch my eyes closed, fighting the black. "I don't…I can't…"

"You can trust me. On some level you know you can. Don't fight it. Talk to me."

Tunnel vision squeezes in. I get dizzy and I squat to cradle my head. "Don't understand what you're doing, just…stop." I press on my temples in an attempt to push back the impending darkness.

"What happened the day you killed your mother, Gage? Tell me!"

A pathetic cry slides from my throat.

The curtain falls.

THIRTY

SHYANN

Gage snapped.

One moment he was there and the next his eyes slid closed and his muscles went slack. I wrap my arms around him, unsure of who I'm holding.

I attempt to comfort the man in my arms, his big body leaning against me as if he's lost all his strength. Lost his fight. My chest aches, my heart completely annihilated for this horribly broken boy.

Three words blare in my head as sure as my own name.

I love them.

Both of them.

God, and isn't that what they've been missing their entire lives? It's the absence of love that makes them guarded. The idea that they aren't worthy of unconditional affection that holds them back. With every part of my being, I want to fix that, to prove to them that they're exceptional. I don't want to fix them, get Lucas help with the intent of ridding him of Gage; that would only confirm what they already believe. What they need is to believe their worth not for who and what they could become, but for exactly who they already are.

Chaos breaks loose in my soul as I try to consider what this means. What it means to love someone who never had a chance at a normal life. He's so emotionally destroyed he can't even recognize love. Is a relationship between us even possible?

Visions burst behind my eyes. Lucas carving a piece of wood by the river with a small boy staring up in awe and a big smile on his face. Me watching from the porch, my hands on my swollen belly and a gold band on my finger. My mom smiling down on me from heaven, grinning because she always knew I was meant for big things, and those big things had nothing to do with my career goals.

I was meant for this. To love the unlovable.

A sense of rightness and belonging overwhelm me.

Taking every bit of affection that was poured over me by my parents and covering Lucas with it. Accepting him, all of him, as well as his past. Even the depths of hell and all his demons. I hold him tighter, unwilling to let him go now that he's finally found rest. The wind blows a soft moan through the trees and I close my eyes, feeling for the first time that I'm exactly where I belong.

Suddenly his body turns rigid in my arms. His breathing changes from that of sleep and calm to that of panic.

"Shy?"

I exhale and my muscles relax at the timid and confused tone of his voice. "Hey, Lucas."

He pushes up and out of my arms and I hug my knees to my chest. Sitting on one hip, his hand braced behind him, he takes me in with confusion. His gaze swings around the forest and then back to me. "You okay?"

"I'm fine." *Better than ever.*

"I'm sorry—"

I cover his lips with my finger. "Don't be."

A smile curves my lips and he watches in fascination.

He nods toward my grin. "Gage?"

"No." I lean in and when I get close, he jerks, but only slightly. I give him a second to recover and then brush my lips across his. "You."

He sucks his bottom lip as if he's tasting and savoring my kiss all while staring at my mouth. I lean in again, using my lips to coax him to release it.

"You're kissing me." His voice is soft and breathless.

"I am." I kiss him again, this time allowing my tongue to moisten his lips.

"I blacked out."

"I know." I sift my hand into the hair at his nape and pull him down to my mouth.

"Where are we?" His words feather across my skin.

Lost in Lucas, I'd almost forgotten. I turn toward the willow tree. "This is where we buried my mom."

A few beats of silence pass between us and finally he grabs my hand. "It's peaceful here. I like it."

I absorb the comfort of his gaze as it communicates more compassion than any string of words ever could. My chest is tight, so full with emotion, and for the first time in as long as I can remember, not one of them bad. The muted light of sunset gives the forest an almost ethereal feel and I'm reminded of the best part of this area. "There's something I want to show you."

Hand in hand, we move past the willow tree just up over the ridge and through the thick copses of evergreens to a patch of wildflowers that leads to the edge of a rocky cliff. The view is its own introduction and I turn to watch Lucas's reaction.

He stares in awe at nothing but untouched forest and mountain ranges. Sprawling hills covered in rock and green that seem to go on forever. The sun, vibrant yellow, sinks behind the purple-hued hills and paints the sky in a series of bright pinks and oranges. He blinks and squeezes my hand, then drags his eyes away from the view to set them on me. "It's a masterpiece." He blushes, as if the description came from somewhere deep inside, a place he's not used to showing others. "I mean, it doesn't look real."

I try to see the view through his eyes, through the perspective of an artist rather than the impassive view of a resident. The colors explode across the sky, contrasting against the gray background of an incoming storm. It really is breathtaking.

"Shy?" He cups my cheeks and his hands shake subtly against my skin. He stares at my lips and seems nervous.

"What is it?"

His eyes dart to mine, then to the view, and back to my lips. "I want to kiss you."

Running my hands up his chest, his muscles tense beneath my touch. "I want that too."

His lips tick for a second before he dips down and presses them to mine. I push up on my tiptoes and tilt my head. He accepts the invitation, his arms wrapping around my waist as he deepens the kiss. My legs wobble and I fight to remain upright, wanting nothing more than to give in to the gravity of his kiss and pull him with me to the bed of wildflowers under our feet.

He closes his eyes and his kiss turns from tentative to urgent. I groan at the demand and the way his hands splay across my back in a possessive and powerful hold. The sound spurs him on and he slips under my shirt, his fingertips trailing up my belly to my breast.

I suck in a breath. For a fraction of a second, I panic that Gage has stepped up and thrown Lucas back into the dark. In the beat of another second I relax because I don't care. Gage or Lucas. I'm in love with this man. All of him.

"I'm sorry. Is this okay?" His entire body quivers, even his breath.

"Yes, Lucas. It's okay. It's better than okay."

The corner of his mouth lifts and he tilts his head to sink into a kiss that has my head scrambling and hips thrusting to make contact. His long, powerful fingers slide under my bra and he runs the calloused pads along my nipple. I squirm, searching for more, and his breath beats against my skin. "You like that."

"So much." I need more. "I love it when you touch me."

His eyes flare and he steps back enough that cool air slides between us. "Lie down."

Without breaking eye contact, we kneel together; then Lucas pulls off his sweatshirt and spreads it out behind me. He nods and I drop back on my elbows, only to have him follow as his body chases mine. Lowering me down to the ground, my head hits the cradle of his palm. Our mouths mold together at a leisurely pace that scrambles my head and ignites my blood.

The skin on my belly is painted in goose bumps as he drags his fingers up my ribs to my breast. He pulls back and gazes up and down the length of my body, watching me writhe under his attention. The sweet torture of his barely-there touch and his open appreciation for my reaction is a heady combination.

Slowly his eyes make their way back to mine and he tilts to deliver a soft kiss against my lips that sends lightning down my belly. "You're so pretty. I can't believe you're letting me touch you."

"I want more, Lucas." I arch my back, searching for the friction of my jeans, something to cool the heat between my legs.

He slides his leg over my thighs, stilling me, and stares. Oh, if his gaze were a touch, I'd explode from the sensation. Those burning gray eyes, full kiss-swollen lips, and his apprehension works like an aphrodisiac. The solid length of his hard-on digs into my hip and I've never wanted anything more in my life.

"I've never done this before." His eyes search mine. "Show me what you like."

I nod and slide my hand down to pop the button of my jeans. He watches and his hand quakes against my breast. He lets me lift my hips just enough to slide down the denim and silk panties.

"Oh—" He bites his lip as he stares openly between my legs.

"Give me your hand."

He rips his gaze from my body and meets me with wide eyes before pulling his hand from my shirt. He doesn't break eye contact as I bring him, so warm in my grip, to where I need him most.

His eyebrows drop low as I cup his hand to me, allowing him to get used to the feeling of my body.

"Okay?" I whisper.

"Yes," he whispers.

His hand centered, I press his middle finger deeper and drag his hand up and down. His lips part and his expression morphs from nervous to awestruck. After a few passes, he bends his fingers, delving between my legs. I gasp at the sensation, and he flexes into my hip.

"I want that, Lucas."

He groans and drops his forehead to my chest while I continue to teach him how to pleasure me. My heart pounds behind my ribs, my insides throb to be filled, and Lucas is a barely contained animal at my side.

"What else? Show me more." His voice is like warm molasses, dripping with promise.

I pull up my sweater to expose the breast he had his hand on and arch my back, offering it to him. His eyes slide to mine and he dips his head and sucks my nipple into his mouth.

I cry out. The hand guiding him between my legs loses purchase and I grip the earth at my side. Thankfully he continues to explore and seconds later sinks one long finger deep into my body. The silken moisture of his tongue circles my breast in delicious ways as he learns how everything he does affects me. I'm on the edge, barely held together. My legs strain to fall open but are imprisoned by my jeans. Greedy, I roll my hips with every thrust of his fingers, reaching to fall over the edge. His teeth rake against my nipple and I'm gone.

Stars burst behind my eyes and my body convulses around him. He moans, a vibration so deep against my delicate skin it extends my orgasm in euphoric waves that endlessly crash over me. He doesn't let up until I'm squirming and oversensitized.

Stunned, he pulls back, his eyes on mine before a brilliant smile curls his lips. "You *really* liked that."

I giggle and nod, slightly embarrassed before I remember that with Lucas nothing is hidden between us. Every new experience we share is cherished.

His eyebrows pinch together and he frowns.

I cup his jaw. "What is it?"

"No Gage."

My thumb absently runs along his lower lip. "Nope. No Gage."

"Why?"

I shrug. "I think he's finally come to trust me."

Lucas grins, but I only catch a glimpse before he kisses me so deeply and reverentially it makes missing the grin worth it.

Besides, I plan on many opportunities to make him smile again.

LUCAS

I can't believe she's here, sprawled out before me and showing me how she likes to be touched.

By me.

Not Gage, but me.

I search my mind for him, seeking out the fog of black that hangs at the edges of consciousness, but there's nothing. He gave me this moment with Shyann, and if what she said is true and he really does trust her, then...we can be together.

The thought sends a thrill down my spine and my chest expands with a joy I've never felt before. I sort through it, trying to figure out what it is and all I can come up with is hope.

Hope for a future. A normal life.

A town I can stay in for longer than a few months, surrounded by people who know about me and want me anyway. A job I can excel at, and...a girlfriend.

It's almost too much to hope for. More than I deserve, but still...God, how I want that.

Shyann wiggles beneath my leg as she tries to pull her jeans back up.

My hand stills hers and she blinks up at me.

"Let me." I push to my knees and drop a kiss on her forehead, the tip of her nose, her lips, before moving down her body and pressing my lips to her breast before covering it back up with her bra and sweater. I slide farther down and practically explode at the feeling of her warm soft body between my legs. I pepper her flat belly with kisses. I'm hard and throbbing as I dip lower, overwhelmed by her scent. Gripping her hips, I press a kiss between her legs.

She gasps and pops her head off the ground.

"I'm sorry. Was that wrong?" I can't explain it, but I'm overcome with the need to taste her everywhere and not leave a single inch unexplored.

"No, it wasn't wrong. It's just…" Her cheeks flush. "If we're going there, we need a bed, in a room, with a door, because I won't be able to stop myself from tasting you too."

Her words shoot straight between my legs and I groan as the image of Shy's mouth on me makes me dizzy with want.

I pull her panties up her toned thighs and back into place, followed by her jeans. "Ya know, I have a bed, in a room, with a door…"

The light sound of her laughter makes my heart pound. I stand and grab both of her hands, hoisting her off the forest floor. She brushes herself off and redoes her hair that fell loose around her face while I snag my sweatshirt and pull it over my head.

I rub my fingertips together, still able to feel her on my skin and remind myself this isn't a dream. This beautiful woman wants me. Every single piece of me.

She stands there silent as I stare at her, wondering what on earth I ever did to deserve her. Even if we leave this place and things go back to the way they were, this single moment makes me forget the pain of my past. Makes me believe that miracles are possible.

"Lucas?"

I blink down at her and smile. "Yeah?"

"I want you to know that I talked to Gage about what happened."

It takes a second for my mind to catch up with her meaning and then the memory slams into me. The truck, we were talking and…my eyes dart to hers. "You know. About my family."

And she's here with me anyway.

She stands a little taller and holds my gaze. "Gage told me everything."

Everything? Even I don't know *everything*.

She reaches forward and picks up my hand, pressing it to her chest. "You know he'd never share that with me if he didn't trust me, and now I need to ask you to do the same, Lucas. Can you do that? Can you trust me?"

I search the recesses of my heart, my mind, and dig back to the depths of my soul. Do I?

I bring her hand to my lips and kiss her knuckles. "Yes. I do."

Her face lights up in a smile so brilliant it's almost too bright to look at, too much to behold. "Really? You usually say no."

I run my knuckles along her cheek and she sighs and leans into my touch. "Guess you could say you've proved yourself trustworthy."

"Thank you. That means a lot to me. I know you don't trust people easily, especially women." I lose her smile and miss it instantly.

"How do you know that?"

It comes back, but it looks forced. Shaky. "Gage told me about your mom. What she'd do to you and your brothers and sister."

He told her about my past. The disgusting things I was forced to do, and the even worse things Gage protected me from. Those aren't stories shared between lovers or friends. Those are tales of horror, the backbone of every nightmare, and meant to be taken to the grave. And I hate that Shy's been tainted by them.

My hand drops from her face and I step back. "Why would he tell you that?" My voice sounds void. Emotionless.

"Don't get mad, okay, I just…" She chews her bottom lip, her eyes skirting to the nearly set sun, then back to me. "Do you ever wonder what happened that day, the day you got that scar?"

"No." Gage took over that day, and I don't need to know the details of what happened to know it ended in four lives lost. "If I knew the truth, I'd probably hate myself more than I already do."

"You're not even a little curious to know—"

"No. Not even a little." All that matters is a jury found me innocent. What really happened is irrelevant.

"But—"

"Drop it, Shy!" I turn away, pissed at myself for snapping at her. She doesn't deserve my anger. "I don't want to talk about this with you."

"Why not me?"

Because I want you to like me, don't want you to see how weak I am, want to be deserving of you.

I turn and force myself to relax. "I don't want to know, okay?"

She shakes her head. "Okay, I understand." She holds out her hand. "Come on, it's getting dark. We should go."

I stare at the patch of earth where flowers are now crushed as evidence of what we'd done there and feel the frustration melt away. She tugs on my hand and after one last glance, I follow Shyann into the thick of the forest.

THIRTY-ONE

LUCAS

It's dark by the time we get back to the river house. We took our time hoofing through the trees talking about mindless things. She laughs when I tell stories about the guys at work, and she tells me stories about those same guys from when she was a kid.

Things are light between us, no talks about Gage or my past, not a mention of the murders. Thunder crackles overhead and we get the first few drops of rain as we hit the creek.

We hold hands as we maneuver the rustic-log bridge, and what started as drizzle quickly turns to a downpour. Her laughter permeates the air along with the powerful scent of pine and rain as we race to the front door.

Buddy barks at us from his spot beneath the porch, and Shy gives him a quick rub before pulling me to the door. She grins up at me, breathing heavy, her black hair wet and beads of rain on her eyelashes. "That came out of nowhere."

I open the door for her to go inside, but she stands for a few silent seconds before making a move to cross the threshold.

"If this is uncomfortable..." I rub the back of my neck, hating the words I'm about to say. "You don't have to stay."

She steps to me and pushes up on her tiptoes to press her lips against mine. Salt from her skin mixes with the cool rain and I lick my lips to absorb every drop.

Her eyes track from my lips to my neck, then dip to my chest. "You're drenched."

"So are you," I whisper, and don't know why, but it's like the volume has been turned down on everything but my pounding heart.

She dips her hands beneath my T-shirt and I lift my arms as she slides it up my body and over my head. Her gaze moves across my shoulders, my chest, and lower until her hands hook into my jeans. She fumbles with my belt but manages to get it open along with my button fly. I'm so hard, so ready for her that my erection strains the fabric of my boxers.

Her jaw falls open and her chest rises and falls erratically as she stares openly between my legs. Unable to control my need for her, I cup her jaw, tilting her head up, and crash my mouth to hers. I suck at her lips that taste of rainwater and only leave me thirsty for more. There's no gentle teasing, no silent requests for entrance. Our tongues lash violently together as if we'd finally let go of all restraint. I walk her back, moving deeper into the house while pulling at her sweater, pushing it up over her breasts while she struggles to free her arms, only then breaking the kiss long enough to pull it from her head.

My eyes burn to stare, to study her in nothing but jeans and a bra, but the competition of her mouth is too much. Later. I'll take time to worship every swell and dip of her body, learning her sounds and committing them to memory, but not now.

I pull at the straps of her bra, wanting the thing off but not having the slightest clue how to do it. She giggles against my lips at my clumsy attempt and I push her back against the wall in the hallway. "I wish I was better at this." My forehead presses to hers while she easily releases the clasp and it falls to the floor.

She hooks the elastic of my boxers with her fingers and brings my hips to hers. The heat of her bare chest hits mine. "You're better than you think."

The sensation of her warmth against me makes the urge to explode impossible to ignore. I'm shivering with excitement, raw desire, and a hint of nerves. I bend, cup her bottom, and easily lift her into my arms. Her legs wrap tightly around my waist and her heat grinds against my erection.

"Mmm...you feel so good."

Her tongue licks along my neck, the wet slide against my scar making me jerk behind my boxers.

I carry her into my room with uncoordinated steps and gently lay her down on the bed. There's a brief moment of insecurity, of what she might think of my stark room, the bare twin mattress with cheap sheets and sleeping bag blanket, but all that fear quickly evaporates when her hand grips me over the cotton of my boxers.

"Is this...really happening?" I pant against her neck, and she slides her hand beneath the elastic and wraps her fist around me. "Oh..." I moan, and she bows on the bed in a way that makes me lose my breath.

"Yes, but only if you want it to."

I reach down and cup her between her legs like she taught me earlier, running my fingers roughly over her until she's groaning in frustration.

"I want to feel you." She releases me to pop the button of her jeans and I hop off the bed to remove her boots, socks, and finally her jeans and panties until she's completely bared to me.

The visual hits me like an erotic assault and I step back in admiration. I record the moment to memory, hammering it into my head while swearing to myself that if Gage robs me of this with her, I'll never forgive him.

She props herself up on her elbows and my gaze follows the weight of her breasts, and the dark pebbled nipples that beg for my mouth. "Lucas?"

My eyes dart to hers and she relaxes a little. Maybe she's just as nervous about Gage stealing this as I am.

"I don't have a condom." Never really had any need for one before now.

"It's okay. We don't have to have sex."

My jaw drops open and I slam it shut, hoping she doesn't notice.

She laughs and holds her hand out. "Okay, maybe we do."

I can't trust my body with Shyann's unless I know I can keep her safe. If I were able to communicate with Gage, I could ask him if he has a stash hidden somewhere— Oh!

"Wait!" I hold up a hand and race to the bathroom, searching through drawers until—aha! A single square of foil.

Thank you, Gage!

Back in the room, I find Shy lying on her side, her black hair scattered around my pillow, and the feminine swells of her form calling for mine.

"You're the most extraordinary thing I've ever seen, Shy." My voice cracks with the emotion of it all, the lust driving through my veins, combined with something heavy that's new and terrifying.

I palm the condom and pull off my boots, allow my jeans to drop to my ankles and kick them off along with my socks. Her eyes drink me in and every feeling I have for her is reflected in her stare. Is it even possible that she could have a fraction of what I have going on for her, going on for me?

In nothing but my boxers, my hard-on punching through the thin white cotton, I cross to the bed. She rolls to her back, as if her body is reflexively opening for my intrusion. Standing—terrified of getting too close, for I know once our bodies connect, I'll be lost to her completely—I hang on to a little bit of my control.

I bring my hand between her legs and— My breath leaves my lips on a hiss. So warm and wet and perfect. I use my fingers like she showed me and find the parts of her body that make her writhe and moan, sinking one finger inside, then adding another until everything in me wants to crawl deep within.

"I want to kiss you here."

She bites her lip and nods.

I move to the end of the bed, putting one knee between her feet and pressing open her thighs. "You're so beautiful."

Her hands grip the bed, her hips rolling in invitation. "Please, Lucas. I can't wait any longer."

Bending forward, I use my tongue the way I did my fingers. A long cry bursts from her lips and I shoot upright. "Did that hurt? Did I do—"

She shakes her head impatiently. "No, hurry…more."

My chest swells and my lips twitch. "You like it."

"Yes, please, yes. So much."

I resume my position and kiss her between her legs the way I kiss her mouth, alternating between long swipes of my tongue, nips with my teeth, and gentle suction that has her moaning my name and begging. Her taste floods my mouth and feeds my addiction.

My stomach flutters with nerves, at what I'm about to do, but I fear if I don't do it soon I'll lose my chance. I push back and peel down my boxers. My body strains for her and she licks her lips, practically sending me to my knees with want.

Every time I look at her, the pressure of climax coils and threatens release. Breathe, do algebra, anything to avoid this ending too soon. Ripping open the condom with my teeth, I roll it on and meet Shyann's hungry, lust-fogged eyes.

"You sure?" I need to know I'm not imagining she wants me with the same desperation that I want her.

"Never been more sure of anything in my entire life."

I close my eyes at the rough tone in her voice and her words of acceptance sending sensations all over my body. Once I've regained a sliver of restraint, I crawl up and between her legs. She opens them wide and the heat of her core swallows me.

"Mmm…Shy, you feel so good."

Her hands guide my hips and she presses me forward. Inch by inch, I sink into the relentless grip of her body, stealing my breath. I still, unable to move as I allow myself a second to just be.

She encourages me to move, rolling her hips and gripping my ass. "Move, it's okay."

"It's not." I pull back and lazily slide in. "This is far, far better than okay."

Braced on my elbows, I can't tear my gaze away from her sly grin as I move inside her. The heated clutch of her body around mine sends the signal to drive into her to my muscles. I hold back, going slow so I can watch as every ridge glides against her softness.

I want to kiss her, to suck her lips so deep she becomes part of me, to drink in her essence, hold her captive, lock her away from the pain of the world and never let her go. Without the conscious decision to do so, I pick up rhythm and she meets me thrust for thrust. I remember how parts of her body would make her scream, so I tilt my hips with a long and languid roll. She sucks in a breath, her fingernails biting into my back.

Tension gathers at the base of my spine and pulls tighter than any orgasm I've ever felt. "I'm lost to you, Shyann." I suck her bottom lip into my mouth. "Gone forever."

Her back arches off the bed and a low and sexy groan falls from her lips. She tightens around me and the extra sensation shoves me off the ledge. I bury my face in her neck and thrust so hard I'm afraid I've hurt her, but my name falls from her lips on a heady groan of ecstasy, pulsing around me, milking me and taking my very soul with it.

She whispers something and I go still. No, I must've heard that wrong. I slide in and out of her, unable to give up the feeling of being deep inside her, wondering if I give her up if I'll get this chance again.

The thought cracks my chest in two.

Her hands run up and down my back, soothing the sting of her nail tracks, and a sick part of me hopes she marked me permanently. Left me with proof this isn't a dream and I had the most beautiful woman I've ever known in my bed and in my arms even if for only one night.

"…so much. I do."

I pull back and meet her eyes. Liquid blue staring up at me, her cheeks flushed and her full lips trembling.

"Did I hurt you?"

A tiny smile ticks her lips, but her eyes fill with tears. "No, you didn't hurt me."

One drop falls from her eye and I snag it with my finger, rubbing it into my own skin as if I could absorb her pain. "Shy…you're crying."

She laughs and shakes her head. "I know. I haven't cried since—"

"The night in the river."

Her smile falls, but she doesn't seem embarrassed at my bringing up my seeing her naked. I suppose having sex means we're beyond that now. "Yes, the night in the river. And before that it'd been years."

I run my thumb along her cheek. "Why now?"

She shrugs and smiles sadly. "Because I'm pathetic, weak…and madly in love with you."

Every muscle in my body turns to stone and I stare openly at her. There's no way she just said that…to me. "W-what?"

She sighs heavily. "Yeah, I do. I love you, Lucas."

I blink. "What?"

Her hand comes up to cup my cheek. "I. Love. You."

My eyes slam closed and I push away the thoughts that tell me I'm unworthy, that all this is too much to be true and I must be dead. Somehow, somewhere I was deemed good enough for heaven and I've finally made it because outside of heaven this would never happen to someone like me.

I rest my forehead against hers and hold my fingertips to her lips, needing to feel her mouth move to convince myself it's not a hallucination. "Say it again."

"I love you, Lucas."

I suck in a breath at the feel of her lips moving against my skin, the gust of her hot breath as she says the words I never thought I'd hear.

"Please…" *Let this be real.* My fingers tremble against her mouth. "Again."

"I love you, so much. All of you."

I rock my head from side to side against hers. "How is that possible?" I move inside her, this time more forceful, overwhelmed by her words.

By her acceptance.

My eyes burn, but I refuse to cry. Refuse to fall apart at the one time in my life when I've never felt more whole.

Her hands sift into my hair. "Kiss me."

I nod, knowing now and this day forward I'd give her anything she asked for. I'd pull my beating heart from my own chest if she wanted it.

Tilting my head, I kiss her with the emotion of a man who never believed in love but who with this one woman has learned that even the damned have a chance at redemption. Even the vile can find acceptance.

There are hearts big enough to love those who are different than them, who are hard to understand.

And I, by some freak accident, found her.

I'll die before I let her go.

THIRTY-TWO

SHYANN

Rain pummels the roof of the river house while Lucas and I lie naked and tangled in each other. The window is open and the smell of the forest is intensified as it blows over our heated bodies.

My cheek is pressed to Lucas's chest, and I find peace in the gentle rhythm of his pulse. He's relaxed, and if it weren't for fingers tracing a pattern on my back, I'd think he was asleep. I pretend he's creating one of his drawings, maybe an image of our future together or perhaps a recollection of our lovemaking.

"What're you thinking about?" He accents his words with a squeeze to my hip.

"Trying to figure out what you're drawing on my back."

He chuckles and the sound washes over me, sinking me deeper into his embrace. "You're so soft. Can't stop touching you." His fingertips continue to dance across my skin.

"So you're not creating your next masterpiece?"

His hand flattens against my skin and he kisses the top of my head. "You're the masterpiece, Shy."

I close my eyes and absorb his words.

"But I can't concentrate enough to draw right now."

I turn at his serious tone and rest my chin on his pec. "What's wrong?"

He blinks down at me. "You told me you love me." Confusion darkens his gorgeous face.

I lie back down and throw my arm over his belly. "That's because I do love you. And if it's hard to believe, I'll just keep telling you every few minutes until it sinks in."

"That could take a while." There's no smile in his voice, no hint of levity, but the weight of seriousness drips off his tone.

"You're gonna get sick of hearin' it."

"Never." He kisses my head, and a deep silence builds between us, his fingers resuming movement on my back.

This is the most time I've ever had alone with Lucas. Usually whenever we get close, Gage bursts through and rips us apart. A tiny grin ticks my lips; a relationship with Lucas seemed so impossible in the beginning, but it doesn't seem so impossible now.

"What're you smiling about?"

"How do you know I'm smiling? You can't even see my face."

He chuckles and the vibration rumbles against my cheek. "I can feel it."

I shrug. "I'm celebrating a small victory." I press a kiss to his chest, then push up to my elbows. "We've uncovered a lot in a couple hours and…no Gage."

He tucks a strand of hair behind my ear. "This is usually the kind of thing he'd rather…enjoy…for himself. And you telling me you love me seems like—"

"He'd show up to protect you."

He makes a noise of agreement.

"Well, I have a theory if you want to hear it."

He grips me to him and rolls so that he's on top of me. The weight of his big body presses into mine, and his erection lies against my thigh. I bite my lip and try to focus beyond my desire.

"Yeah, I want your theory."

I suck in a breath and nod. "It's simple, really." I stare at him for a few silent seconds, nervous about how he's going to take this. "Thing is…I love him too."

His eyebrows pinch together and his mouth pulls into a tight line. "You love Gage."

"I do."

"Why?"

"Because he's part of you."

His eyes dart to the side. "The bad part."

I pull his face back to mine and press a kiss to his lips. "I don't believe that."

"You said it yourself. He's not been good to you, Shy." He starts to push himself up and off the bed. I struggle to hold him close, but he's too strong and I'm left alone on the bed, watching as he pulls on his boxers.

Feeling suddenly vulnerable, I grab the sleeping bag and cover my naked body. "He's stubborn, and grumpy, and yeah, he's rough around the edges but he's also fiercely protective—"

"He hurt you." His jaw clenches.

"He threatened me, but he hasn't hurt me."

"Yet."

I push up and sit. "He loves you."

A humorless laugh bursts from his lips. "He hurts people—"

"Lucas, please." I reach out a hand, hoping he doesn't reject it. "Calm down."

He stares at it for a few seconds before moving to sit on the bed. I push up and wrap my arms around him, fitting my front to his back. "The only way things will work out between us is if I have both of you."

A long exhale falls from his lips and he drops his chin to his chest. "I hate this for you."

I run my lips along his shoulder blade, taking pleasure in the trail of goose bumps I leave behind. "I can handle Gage."

His elbows to his knees, he leans his head into his hands, gripping his hair. "I wish that were true. But if I can't control him, no one can. He's already pissed off women in town—"

"Sam got herself—" My body jerks upright. "Oh no, I forgot about Sam."

He turns to face me. "What about Sam?"

"Remember, we were talking and I got the call about Sam being—" *Oh no...that was Gage.* I purse my lips and bite the inside of my cheek. "She was beaten almost to death in her own home."

"By who?"

"They don't know." My cheeks warm and I find it hard to hold his eyes. "I thought maybe it could've been Gage." His body tenses and I scurry to explain. "But no, there's no way, I mean, he'd never hurt Sam like this." It could be the Shadow; I'm just shocked the story that destroyed my career would hit so close to home. "There are a string of serial assaults in Phoenix and a few in surrounding cities. So far it seems Sam's assault matches, but we won't know until they finish the investigation."

"Serial assault...?"

"The guy follows an MO. Never any proof of forced entry, and he never rapes. The cops are calling it a hate crime."

He's staring openly at nothing and his voice comes out a tiny whisper. "Hate? Against who?"

"Women."

He jumps from the bed as if he'd been electrocuted. "You need to leave."

"What? Why?"

"I'm not safe for you. The feelings I have for you, if Gage…oh God." He pulls on a pair of sweatpants, mumbling to himself. "I'd kill him if he hurt you."

With the sleeping bag around my body, I jump out of bed. "Kill who?"

He sets cold gray eyes on me, and if it weren't for the softness of his jaw, I'd think it was Gage. "Who do you think?"

"You can't kill Gage, Lucas. He's you."

He doesn't answer but turns and grabs a long-sleeved tee from the closet.

I cross to him and wrap myself around his waist from behind. "You can't kill Gage."

His muscles tense to solid rock. "What if he did it? What if Gage is the one who hurt Sam?"

"No, I don't believe that."

He peels my hands from around his waist and moves to the doorway. "Don't be stupid, Shy."

"He has every right to have trust issues with women, but that doesn't mean he'd beat them almost to death."

"You know that for sure?" His jaw ticks and he takes a step closer. "Sure enough you'd risk your life? Because every second we're alone together we tempt him."

My heart pounds in my chest and, craving his comfort, I reach for him.

"Please, stay back." He's panting, his fists clenched.

"Lucas, it's okay—"

"I can't trust myself around you…" He swallows hard. "You shouldn't trust me either." He dips to the floor to snag my sweater and tosses it to me. "Get dressed." His stormy eyes meet mine. "You need to go."

I blink and shake my head, then pull my sweater on and move to him, but he holds a hand out to keep me back. "Don't push me away."

He turns from me, his muscles prominent and straining his shirt. I want to touch him, to run my hands up his back, to ease him, but I fear that'll make him push harder.

"Okay, Lucas. I'll go." I snag my panties from the floor and tug them on, then rip my jeans up my legs.

He doesn't move and his gaze stays trained to the floor.

I cross to him while buttoning my jeans and cup his jaw, grateful he doesn't jerk from my touch. "Let me ask you this, Lucas. Besides earlier today, with me, in the last forty-eight hours, have you blacked out?"

Slowly, Lucas turns his eyes to me. Dread settles in my gut.

"Last night, after Dustin…on the way home I blacked out." His expression isn't panicked or even worried; it's worse. Totally blank. Void of any emotion at all.

The air in my lungs goes still. "Where did you go?"

"I came to in the shower." His eyes meet mine and although he doesn't say anything, I can hear his thoughts scream, *I did it!*

"That doesn't mean—"

"Go!" His eyelids flicker and he grips the side of his head. "Now! Get out of here!"

I jump and my boots stomp on the wood floor as I head out, hoping Lucas will call me back and beg me to stay. It isn't until I'm in my truck staring at the river house's front porch that reality sinks in. I've finally made some headway with Gage, but I'm back to square one with Lucas.

He's pushing me away.

THIRTY-THREE

SHYANN

My fingers drum against the hospital coffee machine as it spits premade vanilla-flavored coffee at an achingly slow pace. Impatient, I scoop the small paper cup out before it's done. "Ow, shit!" I wipe the scalding liquid on my jeans and head back to my seat, blowing to cool it before taking a sip.

After getting home last night, I fell into a restless sleep. My body ached in places that only served to remind me of Lucas. My heart clenches at what he must be thinking, that as amazing as he is, how tender he treated me when we made love, that he'd be capable on any level of the kind of violence that put Sam in the hospital. I tried to convince him but he's been trained to think the worst of himself. I push back thoughts of Gage and his unpredictability. He may have killed his mother, but is he capable of hurting an innocent woman? He has more incentive to go after me, and although he's had plenty of opportunities, I'm alive and well.

I drop down into a plastic chair, my mind swirling with doubt. I try again to push the thoughts far back into the recesses of my mind. I trust

Lucas as much as I've ever trusted anyone, and Gage, no matter how threatening, is part of him. I'll never buy into his own guilt.

My fingers drum against the armrest while I try to relax and sip my coffee. People filter in and out of the waiting room. Some are mournful while others embrace each other with hugs and happy tears.

The small television in the corner plays the Phoenix news and I watch for lack of anything better to do while I wait for the nurses to update me on Sam. Rather than follow the captions on the muted TV, I critique the anchor's choice to wear red, the station's use of a graphic to tell a story that a video would tell better, and the overly serious expression of one reporter while discussing gas prices. Commercials for toilet paper, laundry detergent, and a local Phoenix law firm that specializes in divorce, and then back to the news where a familiar image takes up the screen.

I sit up taller just as a person across the lobby says, "It's Payson."

Main Street lights up the screen, along with a woman in a bright yellow tailored dress and perfectly coiffed red hair that doesn't move an inch in the wind.

The subtitles tick across the bottom.

"...local police believe the assailant is still on the loose but locals are gripped with fear and the question, could this be another hit from the Shadow?" A video plays, still images of the outside of Sam's house, a drop of blood on her front steps highlighted by a crime scene number flag, and neighbors confirming that they didn't see anything. "Police encourage anyone with information about this assault to come forward." The story goes on to talk about the violent nature of the crime and compares it to the eight other assaults attributed to the Shadow. When the thirty-second time block is filled, they move on to talking about this year's football season.

I slide back into my seat, shock only intensifying my worry. Poor Sam. My chest cramps violently at the memory of the last time the Shadow hit and a woman lost her life, leaving her daughter motherless. Is it possible this sadist made his way to Payson? A shiver slides up my spine, and I rub my arms to fight back the chill. If only Sam would wake up and tell police what she knows, they could finally put an end to this.

My knee jumps in a furious rhythm.

Wake up, Sam…Wake up. A warm hand hits my shoulder and my body jerks.

"Whoa, sorry." Dustin comes around to take the seat beside me. "Didn't mean to scare you."

"Not your fault." I hold up my almost drained cup. "Too much caffeine and impatience."

He grunts and it's then I notice the deep circles under his eyes and his unshaven face.

"You just get here?"

"No, I was in my truck trying to catch a quick nap. Been here all night."

"Any word on how she's doing?"

"Her family let me sit with her for a bit. Think they felt sorry for me." He rubs his eyes. "God, Shy…she's so messed up. Eyes swollen shut, lips split to hell, most of her skin that I could see was bruised."

My heart hurts for what she's gone through. "Phoenix news just covered it. They're claiming it might be the Shadow. Won't be long before this entire town is swarming with reporters." I down the last of my coffee and crush the cup.

"The Shadow…wait, they haven't caught that guy yet?" His gaze darts to the window that leads to the parking lot, then back to me.

"No, unfortunately they haven't. It doesn't make sense. Payson is a blip on the Arizona map. Why here? I don't buy that it was him."

He nods and leans forward, putting his head in his hands. "This is all so fucked up."

I give in to my bleeding heart and pat him awkwardly on the back. "Why don't you go home and get some sleep. I'll call you if I hear anything."

He turns his head toward me, his expression soft with…something. "You'd do that for me?"

I shrug and pull my hand off his back before he gets the wrong idea. "Yeah." Grabbing my phone from my purse, I open my contacts and he rattles off his number. "Really, try to get some sleep. You're no good to her exhausted. When she wakes up, she'll need you strong."

He groans and rubs his eyes with the heels of his hands before sucking in a breath and nodding. "You're right." His eyes wander a bit before he hooks me behind the neck. "Thanks, Shy."

I watch in horror as he tugs me to him, his lips going toward my forehead before he quickly dips and presses his mouth to mine.

I wrench my head back. "Dustin…no."

He slams his eyes closed and nods. "Sorry, I…" He shakes his head. "I'm just tired and you're being so nice. Old habit I guess."

I hold off on using the back of my hand to wipe his kiss from my lips. The guy is clearly in emotional distress; I can give him the courtesy of waiting until he leaves.

He slides his hand from the back of my neck and the sound of car tires peeling against asphalt catches my attention. He doesn't seem to notice and stands, but my gaze swings to the large window that leads to the parking lot.

"Huh…looks like someone's in a hurry," I mumble to myself.

His eyes follow mine and the corner of his mouth lifts in an odd grin before he wipes it clean and looks down at me. "Thanks again and don't forget to call me if you hear anything."

I slump back into my chair and sigh. "No problem. I won't."

THIRTY-FOUR

SHYANN

A couple hours or so after Dustin left, I was allowed a short visit with Sam. Her mom had to grab some things and didn't want her left alone in case she woke up. I was able to confirm with my own eyes all of what Dustin described. I felt sick to my stomach. By the time her mom came back, I couldn't get out of there fast enough. I need air to try and curb the dizziness that plagued me while sitting in that cramped room with a woman who didn't look anything like my old friend.

I push out of the doors and into the parking lot, fishing my phone from my pocket along with my keys. Hitting Dustin's number, I head to my truck and suck in lungsful of precious fresh air.

"'Lo?" His voice is scratchy with sleep.

"Hey, Dustin. Sorry to wake you."

Rustling of sheets and a yawn sound in my ear. "Everything okay? Sam, is she awake?"

I huff out a breath and lean against the hood, suddenly exhausted. "No, she's still out. I just can't sit here anymore, so I'm gonna take off."

"Yeah, I understand." More rustling of sheets. "I'll be there in thirty."

"Call me if she wakes up, okay?"

"Sure. Thanks for being there, ya know, for both of us."

"Her parents are here. You don't have to come down."

"It's okay, I want to." There's a longing in his voice that makes me smile. They really are good together.

"'Kay, talk to you later."

I hit END and circle to my door, climbing inside and firing up the engine.

It's after three o'clock and I should probably check in with my dad but first I need to go talk to Lucas. A flash of Sam's swollen face, bruised neck, and busted lips flashes before my eyes. I told myself I'd give him time, and I'd planned on giving him more, but after today all I want to do is fall into his arms and make it all go away.

* * *

By the time I pull up to the river house, my heart is pounding with anticipation. I never knew I could be so attached to another person like this, but just seeing his truck, knowing he'll be holding me in his arms soon, sends butterflies exploding in my belly.

I hop down and take off toward the house but have to double back to shut my truck door, my mind hardly able to keep up with my body.

Buddy peeks out from the porch, his dark eyes assessing.

"Hey, Bud." I hit the front porch with force and knock on the door.

No answer, so I knock again. "Lucas, it's me."

Nothing.

I step to the railing and look to the side of the house, thinking maybe I missed him in my haste to get to the door. A light sound catches my attention and I turn back, realizing it came from inside.

A whisper of worry tickles my veins as I move to pound on the door again. "Lucas? You in there?"

Nothing.

I press my ear to the wood and strain to listen. Someone's talking. A man. Maybe he's on the phone? I knock again and hear the muffled voice, but this time I think he's talking to me. Is he telling me to come in?

This isn't right. Worry morphs to full-blown panic and the sense that something is off.

I reach for the handle and pray it's unlocked, all while telling myself if it's not I'll break a damn window if I have to. Luckily the door clicks open and I step cautiously inside.

The kitchen and living room are littered with empty beer cans and a half bottle of Jack Daniel's. My stomach clenches. Lucas doesn't drink like this.

"Lucas?"

Still nothing.

There's shuffling in the bedroom. Again my thoughts go back to Sam and my hands curl into fists, ready to defend myself against whoever is keeping Lucas from answering me. I strain to listen and tiptoe through the living room with my heart in my throat.

On light feet, I make it to his closed bedroom door. There are sounds coming from behind it. Sounds of a struggle.

I push open the door on instinct and prepare to swing at whoever comes at me, but freeze on sight.

"Oh my God," I whisper, all the air from my lungs expelled with the agonizing contraction in my chest.

It's Lucas, gloriously and beautifully naked.

And lying wrapped up in the arms and legs of a black-haired woman.

The scent of liquor and sickly sweet perfume turn my stomach and my arms wrap around my belly as crippling pain slices through me. My eyes heat and as much as I want to run from the room, I'm transfixed on the vision before me.

His sleek body moves in a punishing rhythm, his weight braced on his elbows, his biceps flexed, and his fist knotted in her hair. For a moment it's as if I'm standing outside my own body, watching in the light of day what we did together just last night. In this room. This bed. Where I confessed my love.

And he didn't return it.

As if in slow motion, his eyes move from the woman below him to me. The molten gray rages with a fury I've come to know well.

Come to love.

"Gage," I hiccup the single word.

A slow smile curls his lips and he thrusts hard into the woman beneath him. "I *love* an audience."

The woman doesn't seem to hear him, or care, only locks her ankles at his ass.

He slams into her, his eyes still fixed on me.

She cries out and rips at his shoulders with bright red fingernails. "More," she moans.

He blinks and looks down at her; the grin he was wearing dissolves. "You know the rules, baby." He dips low and plunges his tongue into her mouth, the wet sound of their connection blaring in my ears.

She rips her lips from his, catching her breath from his kiss.

"Come on, don't be *Shy*." He stretches out my name while drawing out a long slide into her body.

A single tear tracks down my cheek and my heart shreds.

His gaze finds mine and his eyes flash with concern for a fraction of a second before the woman beneath him cries out, "Fuck me, Lucas…"

Gage blinks and rams his hips forward so hard the girl would fall off the bed if it weren't for his hold on her hair. "Say my name again."

"Lucas," she moans.

He's an animal. Why did I ever think I could trust him? Or love him.

Whatever progress I thought I'd made with Gage was nothing but smoke and mirrors, the conniving behavior of a liar. He led me to believe we were past all this, that we'd found some common ground and our goals were aligned.

We both only want to love and protect Lucas.

But love isn't enough to endure this kind of pain.

Feeling rushes back to my legs as the reality crashes down on me. Lucas and I could never work because Gage will never allow me to get close enough. When I get within arm's reach of capturing Lucas's heart, Gage throws me back with a cruel reminder of where I stand.

My feet move through the house, down the steps, and to my truck and by the time I'm turned around and headed to my dad's house, I've managed to break into soul-racking sobs. Wiping the moisture from my eyes enough to see the road in front of me, I blaze past my dad's house and hit the highway with a skid of rubber and cloud of dust.

I can't go home.

Hell, I can't be in this town. I've saved enough money to get myself to Los Angeles; if Trevor can help me with a place to stay, it might not be too late to salvage my career, go back to the world of emotionless news reporting and surface relationships.

I got too close, let someone in, and paid the price. I need to put enough distance between us so that he can't hurt me.

I point the truck to the closest road that leads out of Payson and hit the gas.

GAGE

A little pain now is better than a lot of pain later.

That's the shit I keep telling myself as I drown my liver in booze. Hell, it's the mantra I kept chanting just so I could stay hard enough to screw that Shyann look-alike.

My plan couldn't have worked any better. Even though neither of us ended up getting off and I kicked her out of my bed the second Shy's tires disappeared down the drive, it's the illusion that did it. A finely played ruse that worked out better than I could've planned. Luke waking up to this mess would've been enough; he would've felt guilty, confessed, and Shyann would be out of his life for good. But no, she actually walked in and *saw* it. Perfect.

I'd pat myself on the back if I had the balls to do it, but there's one disturbing visual that's sucking all the fun from my victory. No matter how many shots of Jack I swallow, I can still see Shy's face. The subtle changes as I watched every emotion move through those big blues like a kaleidoscope. First shock, then confusion, devastation, and finally complete destruction.

I tilt the bottle to my lips, toasting to my success.

It's what I wanted.

Hell, I'd have been happy for her to walk in on any part of that impromptu date with the drunk I picked up in the bar.

What luck that she walked in at the best part?

Luck.

Right.

Then why the fuck do I feel like spooning my heart out and setting it on fire?

I tell myself this is what needed to be done. Shyann was fucking Luke, then had her lips smashed against that pet fucker's mouth in the middle of the hospital for the entire town to see.

She humiliated us!

Luke. She humiliated *Luke*.

I'm sure she's out there somewhere cursing my name, blaming me for breaking our newly fledged confidence in each other, but fuck her.

She broke it first.

How could she even speak to that asshole after how he treated Luke?

All Luke wanted was to be there for her, but to walk into the hospital and see her hands on that scumbag hours after she was naked in our bed? Fuck her!

I drain the rest of the Jack and toss the bottle across the wood floor, watching it bounce, then spin. My head feels exactly like that damn bottle but pain and dizziness is a motherfucking party compared to what's going on in my chest.

Right now she must be feeling betrayed, used, fucking walked on. Good. Now we're both in hell and miserable.

I groan and drop my head into my hands, refusing to acknowledge what my heart is demanding.

"She didn't love us. She didn't." The only bit of love I've ever felt from another human being is a long-forgotten memory of my siblings. Except what I felt from Shyann before she stabbed me in the back *seemed* like love. She accepted me, challenged me, and protected me.

She believed in me, not just me because I'm a part of Luke, but in *me*.

In Gage.

Oh shit…Did I make a mistake by throwing that drunken slut in Shy's face? A flash of her hand on that pet dick and then her lips pressed to his pours fire through my veins.

No, this had to be done.

It's not like I could've fought for her, stormed into the hospital and beat that fuckface senseless before dragging her out of there by her hair. Would she even want that, or would she finally see me as the monster I really am? Pretty sure practically drowning her exposed me long before today. Yet she never ran, always came back and even went so far as to try to understand. I didn't make it easy either. I put up a fight, pushing her away at every opportunity, and she never gave up on us.

She loves us.

Loved us.

"Shit, Luke." I rub my eyes, hoping it'll squelch the burn. "Think I may've fucked this up."

THIRTY-FIVE

SHYANN

It's quiet. And for the first time in my life I force myself to welcome the silence.

Staring at the small clearing in the forest they call "a park" because they've tied two swings to low-lying branches and threw in a few benches and a garbage can, I contemplate my life.

My breathing sounds loud in my ears as frustrated breaths saw through my lungs and eventually turn into defeated puffs of air.

Whatever was left of my heart after my mom died, Gage devoured it whole.

The memory of him with that woman plays through my head on a loop and I think of all the better ways I could've handled it. I see myself walking to the bed and ripping Gage off that woman. I envision her scampering for her panties and having to walk down the dirt road tugging on her clothing to cover her naked slut-whore body.

Aaaand I'm back to spitting mad.

This is all Gage. That poor girl did nothing more than fall for a handsome face, solid body, and a shitload of charm. She's not the whore. He is!

He will stop at nothing to push me away and he knows my feelings for Lucas are also my biggest weakness. I should've been on guard rather than opening my heart and freely offering it to be crushed.

Good job, Gage. You win.

What better way to hurt the woman who loves you than to fuck someone else in the bed you'd just made love in?

Love? Ha!

What a joke. I'm starting to wonder if Gage is even capable of the emotion. My guess is no.

Protection, sure.

Love, not so much.

He sure as shit wasn't protecting me today. Nor was he protecting Lucas. Clarity washes through me and my spine stiffens. His purpose is to watch after Lucas; how is sleeping with someone else helping his cause? It makes no sense. Everything Gage does is calculated, but this feels more like an emotional response. Rash and dirty. I shake my head and against my better judgment attempt to figure him out.

After contemplating the situation, rolling it around in my head and obsessing at all angles until the sun drops behind the mountains, I give up. Chilled and more confused than I was when I got here, I climb back into my truck for the trip home. My phone flashes with multiple notifications; missed calls, messages, and texts.

I swipe at my screen and see two missed calls from my dad, another one from my brother, and then another couple from Trevor. Perfect, now I can call him back and beg for his help. Yay.

I'm sure my dad and brother were checking on me. The text I sent saying "I'm headed to Strawberry for a bit" was probably more worrisome than me not texting at all. After all, no one just goes to Strawberry. I wouldn't be surprised if they're organizing search-and-rescue this very minute.

I groan and dial my dad's home phone, wishing his damn cell would get reception at his house so I can just fire off a text and avoid the awkward conversation.

"Nash here."

I clear my throat, hoping it doesn't sound like I've been crying. "Hey, Dad. Just letting you know I'm on my way—"

"Shy, where are you?"

"I'm just leaving Strawberry." I turn the key in the ignition to punctuate my words.

"What the hell are you doing in Strawberry?"

I chew my lip for a couple seconds, fighting the urge to break down and confess my shittiest of shitty circumstances with Lucas. "I was at the hospital most of the day, saw Sam…" My words trail off as if that alone is all the explanation he should need.

"Well…you need to come straight home."

I blink and my foot lays a little heavier on the gas at the seriousness in his voice. "Okay, what's going on?"

"You got a visitor," he mumbles under his breath.

"A visitor at your house?"

"Yeah, Shy, where do you think?"

In my head I rattle off the very short list of people who would care to even visit me at my dad's. But I come up with only one name.

It has to be Lucas.

My stomach churns, knowing full well what he'll be asking.

He wants to know what happened when he blacked out. He'll be begging for me to fill in the blanks. And I'm going to have to break him with the truth.

Gage had to know this was going to happen—matter of fact, this was probably all part of the torture. Having to relive what I saw in vivid detail and watch Lucas crumble under the guilt. Chances are Lucas woke up to a similar scene to what I saw and was confused. Surely he'd know he'd been used, and knowing Lucas he'd want to confess and beg for forgiveness.

God, this is all so fucked up.

If I were stronger, I'd keep what I saw to myself, pretend like none of this happened and smother Lucas with all the love I have just to piss Gage off and prove he can't break me.

A slow grin curls my lips and the sting of Gage's unfaithfulness dulls.

My heart throbs with excitement and a flicker of evil satisfaction melts the icy freeze of betrayal. Just because Gage is meaner doesn't mean he's better.

He thinks he can humiliate me, turn me away by using the man I love as a tool in his sick game.

Funny, I thought Gage knew me better by now.

"Shy, did you hear me?"

I snap out of my thoughts with the sound of my dad's growled question.

"Yeah, Dad. I'm on my way."

***

Twenty-three minutes later, I pull up to my dad's house. It's the second time today I've had a fire to race out of my truck and into Lucas's arms, and the second time today shock has me rooted in place.

"What the fuck…?" I sink into my seat as confusion and the weight of disappointment makes it impossible to move. "What the hell is he doing here?"

The kitchen window fills with the silhouette of my dad, and I wish the earth would open up and swallow me so I wouldn't have to face what's going on inside. But it doesn't.

I drop like dead weight from my truck, dragging my feet to the door. With a fortifying breath, I walk in to see two men. One big and looking way past the point of his tolerance. The other scrawny in comparison with an eager expression I haven't seen on the man's face since college.

"Trevor? What're you doing here?"

He sets down what looks likes a warm and barely touched beer—typical since the snob only drinks IPAs, not the good-ole-boy American labels my dad prefers—and hops off the couch. "Hey, honey."

I catch the look of disgust on my dad's face as it mirrors my feelings exactly.

He wraps his arms around me and kisses the side of my head. "Missed you."

I give him a weak smile but step out of his embrace, feeling somehow like I'm cheating on Lucas—even though Gage was fucking another woman just hours ago. I shake that off and look between the two men.

"What's going on here?"

Trevor shrugs. "Simple. You've got some psycho on the loose, and I need a story to blow LA away. I'm here to cover it." He puts his hands on my shoulders. "The Shadow story got you fired; together we can use him to bring you back."

"You want me to cover the story?"

His eyes light with excitement. "It's the break you've been waiting for. If we nail this story, it's your ticket to Los Angeles."

He's right. If I report it, the fact that this is my town, that I grew up here, should give me an edge the other reporters don't have. I could line up some interviews; the people here trust me.

"I guess it could work."

Trevor laughs. "Of course it'll work. With you we have a direct connection to the victim as well as a possible connection to someone related to the Menzano Massacre."

I step back as if I'd been slapped. "Lucas has nothing to do with this."

"Lucas?" Trevor's eyes pop open, wide and hungry. "You're telling me the Menzano who is here in town is the fucking killer himself?" He presses his palms to his forehead, absorbing the information and practically giddy with excitement.

My dad's eyes narrow on me. "Lucas ain't a murderer."

Trevor laughs. "The hell he's not!"

"Hold on!" I roll my lips between my teeth, searching for calm in a situation that's about to spin out of control. "Trevor, I'll help you if you keep the story about the Shadow. Lucas was already on trial and found innocent."

"Who cares? It's sensationalism, sure, but it's Los Angeles for crying out loud. They don't want the truth; they want a good story." His eyes get a faraway look and he scratches his jaw. "We need to talk to the victim. You can set that up, right?"

"No, no way. I'm not helping you frame an innocent man and exposing my friend to this bullshit."

His face gets hard and he steps in close. "You want the LA job? Get out of this dirt town for good? Because I'm telling you right now, Shy, this is your in."

A job in Los Angeles is tempting. I'd be free of Payson and its memories, make all my career dreams come true. Go back to a life of detached emotions and save my heart from being rebroken by Gage. The cost? Losing every single person I care about.

I can't do this. I can't continue to alienate myself, build walls so high I become the callous career-driven person I was on track to be. Become like Trevor, who no longer sees people as living, breathing, feeling beings but as stepping-stones that'll lead him to success.

I'd rather experience the pain of loving than be numb to human suffering.

My muscles tense. I move into Trevor's space, and even though he's taller, I feel bigger as he shrinks beneath my gaze. "Go home. There's no story here, at least not one you'll get from me."

"Shy, don't be stupid."

"Trevor." My dad's growled warning has my ex's eyes darting between us.

A knowing look hits his eyes and his lips twitch. "Mr. Jennings, you're aware that you're currently employing an accused felon."

"Trevor, don't—"

"Don't believe that for a second." My dad pushes up from his leaned stance at the counter and crosses to us, his eyebrows dropped low.

"Dad, he's lying." I turn to Trevor, pleading with my eyes and praying he'll let this drop.

Trevor crosses his arms at his chest as if they form a barrier between us, making him impenetrable to my nonverbal message. "Lucas was accused of killing his entire family when he was only fourteen years old."

"If that were true, he'd be in prison." My dad's voice is heavy with skepticism and for the first time since I can remember, I'm grateful he's stubborn as hell.

This will be easy. All I have to do is create enough doubt for my dad to dismiss Trevor and kick him out of the house, and we're all good.

"Just because O. J. Simpson is walking the streets doesn't mean he didn't commit double homicide."

My dad's jaw twitches, but that's the only reaction he gives away.

I could strangle this asshole. "Shut up and get out!"

Both Trevor and my dad ignore me.

"Did you know he was tried and only got off because everyone's fingerprints were on the weapon and the angles of the entry wounds were questionable?"

"Stop it!"

"That he managed to conveniently forget the murders, trick lie detector tests, and brainwash people into believing he had no recollection of the murder of his seven-year-old sister—"

I lunge to shut him up. "Stop!"

My dad holds me back.

"...ten- and twelve-year-old brothers..."

I struggle in my dad's arms and will Trevor to get lockjaw before the final words fall from his lips.

"...and his own mother before turning the gun on himself."

"Prove it." My dad's voice rumbles against my back.

"Google it, Mr. Jennings. Lucas Menzano is a mass murderer who was lucky enough to get off on a couple of technicalities and is now living in your town. Working for your company and cozying up to your daughter."

My dad's grip loosens and I sag against him, absorbing his strength. "Leave my house. Now."

"Shy, don't kill the messenger." Trevor has the fucking nerve to smile.

"Get the fuck out of my house!" I go after him again, but my dad holds me back.

"You heard her, City Boy." Barely controlled anger drips from my dad's words. "Get gone."

He laughs humorlessly and throws his flabby arms into the air. "Fine. I'll get the story without you." He moves to the door, swings it open, and turns back, glaring. "Missed your chance, Shy. Guess you're not as driven as I thought."

"I'd rather have the respect of my family and this town than some stupid, lonely job beside a piece of shit like you. Now leave before I grab my daddy's rifle."

"Fucking hillbilly." He slams the door behind him.

THIRTY-SIX

LUCAS

The black recedes and catapults me into the light. I'm sitting on my chair in the middle of my living room and although it's much brighter than the thickness of my blackout, it's still dark. Nighttime. The single blub isn't on.

My head throbs and I blink to clear my wavering vision. Beer cans, an empty bottle of liquor combined with the stench of booze in the air confirm what my body is already telling me. I'm drunk.

I rip my hands through my hair and my heart gallops in my chest. I crank back to my last clear memory. It was Shyann inside the hospital. All I wanted to do was comfort her, apologize for pushing her away.

That's when I saw them together. Dustin had his hand around her neck and had pulled her in for what looked like a quick hug, only dropping his lips to hers at the last minute. Seeing them like that, his fingers threaded into her hair, lips that he'd used to bad-mouth her pressed to her lips. I knew what he was tasting, the sweet flavor of her mouth still so fresh on mine, and a fear like I've never felt before exploded inside me. She'd pushed him away—I know she didn't want the kiss, but he took it anyway. I felt the dark close in; the thought of him taking what she wasn't willingly giving snapped the last bit of my sanity. It was on that thought that the veil fell and Gage plunged me into darkness. That was hours ago.

My trembling fingers absently move to the scar on my jaw.

Whatever Gage did here, he clearly wanted me to know about. If only I could reach him, find him in the recesses of my soul and ask him why he continues to keep me in the dark.

I push up from my seat and head to the shower, swaying slightly and gripping my throbbing head. Once in my room, I kick off my sweatpants and the scent of unfamiliar perfume and sex socks me in the gut. I brace my weight against the wall and flip on the light. Beer cans on the floor, my sleeping bag tossed to the ground, and…My stomach lodges in my chest. No…

A used condom.

I breathe and slam my eyes closed. Please, no. He wouldn't do this to me. Heat springs to my eyes. My arms wrap around my stomach, refusing to accept the obvious. The stench of perfume teases me and I'm reminded of similar times in the past.

Gage screwed one of his skanks in the bed still warm from Shyann. I'll never forgive him.

Never.

I stagger to the bathroom, turning the shower on hot enough to scald my body. Punishment for what I am, what I've done…the trust I've destroyed. I'm disgusting. Insane.

My mom's voice comes flooding in.

"You're no one. Do you hear me? A dog deserves more respect than you. Now you'll eat like one."

I squeeze my eyes closed, remembering the way I'd cry, beg her to be nicer, plead for her love.

"No one could love a bastard. Now eat!"

Saliva floods my mouth as the vivid memory brings me back. I'd hunch over the toilet, my stomach growling as I was forced to eat her feces. My body would revolt with the burn of stomach acid and tears would pour down my face.

"You ungrateful bastard! Now you'll have to eat that too!"

She'd crack my skull against the toilet, screaming how unworthy I was, and I'd pray I was someone else. Someone stronger who would fight back, someone she'd be afraid of. Pray for the darkness to veil me in safety.

And eventually, it would.

He'd take the punishments, be the stronger person I couldn't be.

Then why this? I'd finally found someone I could trust. Someone who made me feel human, worthy. Why wouldn't he want that for us?

I step out of the shower and peek into my bedroom, hoping what I'd seen earlier would no longer be there. That somehow what I saw was a figment of my imagination, a delusion conjured by a mind that can't be trusted to reality.

It wasn't.

Bracing my weight at the sink, I stare into the mirror. The eyes reflected back at me convey the weakness I feel.

"What did you do, Gage?" It seems so ridiculous, but I know he can hear me. "I love her and I know you do too. Why won't you let us have her?" Unable to stare at my own reflection, knowing my body had been given to another woman, my lips pressed to a stranger's, makes me sick. "Let her love us, please. We don't deserve it, but it doesn't mean we shouldn't accept it."

I sigh and turn to my room to grab a clean pair of sweatpants and start picking up the aftermath of what Gage left behind. Some of the beer cans are rimmed with bright pink lipstick, increasing my shame. By the time I'm finished, my shoulders feel like they're carrying a load of two-by-fours as the need to confess to Shyann smothers me. I take the reeking garbage bag out to dump it and find Buddy standing in the drive, alert and fixated on the dense forest.

I drop the bag into the Dumpster and step toward him, expecting him to run back to his shelter under the porch, but he stays still, his eyes trained on nothing.

"What is it, Buddy?" Maybe an elk or a deer nearby?

His head jerks to the long dirt road and he growls low.

I follow his gaze and hear it before I see it. A vehicle of some kind. My heart leaps in my chest that it could be Shyann. It's probably close to nine o'clock at night, not too late for her to still be awake.

Headlights come into view and Buddy's body is unmoving, a fierce growl rumbling in his throat. I approach him cautiously, risking a touch, but he's never let me this close before. I squat and pet his head, hoping to calm him down. He spares me a quick glance and turns back to the oncoming headlights that are too low to the ground to be a pickup truck.

Disappointment settles in my chest as a sedan pulls up and parks. I stand, wishing I'd put a shirt on, as a man folds out of the driver's side. Buddy repositions so that he's standing at my left, his dirty fur pressed against my knee, and I scratch behind his ears.

The man walks toward me and lifts his hand in a friendly wave. "Hey, there, sorry to bother you."

"You lost?"

He steps closer and Buddy leans into me, for support or out of fear, I'm not sure.

"No, not lost, but I was hoping you could help me." He offers his hand and it's then I notice this guy doesn't look like he belongs in Payson. He's driving a city car, wearing city clothes—shirt with a collar and shorts with pleats; he's even wearing some kind of slip-on shoe that looks like it belongs in an office, not out here in the dirt.

I shake his hand and his eyes fall on Buddy. "He friendly?"

"Don't know. He's never met an outsider before." It's not a lie, and the slight flare of fear I see in the man's expression brings me a tiny bit of satisfaction.

He narrows his eyes, studying me. "Lucas, right?"

A burst of adrenaline speeds my pulse. How does this guy know me?

"You are...?"

He chuckles. "Sorry, how rude. I show up at your house and don't even introduce myself. I'm a friend of Shyann's. We went to college together."

The heat of possession floods my veins at hearing her name from a man I don't know. "Got a name?"

"Trevor Peterson."

Trevor...her ex-coworker kinda ex-boyfriend.

"If you're looking for Shy, she's not here."

He turns to look up the road toward Nash's house and nods. "Yeah, I know. Spent some time with her and Nash earlier."

My pulse races and I ball my fists.

"I was hoping you'd give me a chance to talk to you about Shyann."

I shake my head, my body answering before my mouth can form the words. "Don't have anything to say to you about Shy. I don't even know you."

"Huh..." He rubs his chin. "Funny, 'cause she swore you'd be happy to help us out with a little research."

Us?

"What kind of research?"

He nods toward the house. "Mind if we go inside and talk?"

"No one's going to hear you out here, Mr. Peterson. We're miles from the nearest house."

Irritation colors his expression, but I ignore it. I can't figure out why but this guy gives me the creeps.

He swings his arm to the porch. "Mind if we have a seat?"

He doesn't wait for me to answer but shuffles through the dust and pine needles to the steps, where he drops to sit. I lean against the railing and Buddy goes back to staring blindly back into the trees.

"Here's the thing, Lucas…there's a woman in the hospital right now fighting for her life after being brutally beaten."

Sam. My pulse pounds a little faster and I'm grateful this guy can't see my unease.

"I know about the attack. The entire town does."

He frowns. "Of course. Did you also know there's a man on the loose who's been beating women? Eight women to be exact."

Shy had mentioned that, so I nod.

He flashes a patronizing smile. "Shyann and I are covering the story here in Payson."

"You and Shy are…working together?" She never mentioned that to me, and whenever the guy's name came up, she never spoke about him fondly. All she said was he still thought he could tell her what to do.

"We are. She's a driven woman and she wants this job in Los Angeles—"

"Los Angeles?" She told me Oregon. Never mentioned LA.

"Yeah, this story would put her on the map." He swats a bug on his arm, then flicks its carcass away. "That's where you come in. Tell me what you know about Sam."

My jaw locks down tight.

"Oh come on, you knew I'd do my research."

"I don't know her. I mean, I don't know her very well."

He lifts an eyebrow. "That's not what I heard. I heard you two had a few very public displays of…affection. Then a very public fight at the bar she works at." His face pinches in thought. "I even heard you went for her throat."

Who told him that? Shyann wouldn't. She'd never sell me out…unless. Does she know Gage slept with someone else? Would anger drive her to expose me?

"I didn't hurt anyone."

"Aah…" He shakes a finger at me. "See, that's where you're wrong." Pushing himself to the railing, he leans toward me. "I heard you beat up her boyfriend. You've got a jealous streak, huh?"

"I have nothing to say to you."

"You don't have to say anything. The evidence speaks for itself. All I have to do is connect the dots." He moseys along down the porch, grinning. "Guy like you…"

Like me?

"…your record."

My skin breaks out in a cold sweat.

He tilts his head. "You seem surprised." His eyes narrow. "I know all about you, Lucas. I know what you did, that you killed your entire family before turning the gun on yourself."

Black flickers at the edge of my vision.

"But things didn't turn out for you the way you'd hoped, did they? You didn't die that day after you killed your family."

"I don't know what you're talking about." I curse the waver in my voice.

He chews the inside of his lip, then smiles. "You're smart, I'll give you that. A teenage boy who can pull this off, fool lawyers, a judge, hell a jury…it's impressive." He takes a few steps toward the river and my feet burn for escape, to hide out until all this goes away. But that's the old me, turning my back on confrontation. I know I can be a better man, the kind Shy deserves, and I'm determined to start now.

"I'm not surprised you'd be capable of hiding what you did to Sam too."

"I didn't—"

"A violent mass murder, a house vandalized, a girl beaten within an inch of her life, you know what all those things have in common?"

I don't answer.

"You. They all have *you* in common." He steps closer.

"You can't prove anything."

"Ah-ah-ah…I don't need to. I'm not here to convict you. I just want the story, on record, and I want exclusivity."

My eyes narrow and my stomach rolls with sickness.

"They're gonna arrest you eventually anyway, Lucas. Might as well get your story out there. Hell, you may even get book deals while you're in prison, have a movie made about you. For all I care you can disappear and never be heard or seen again. All I want is for you to tell your story, to me, on the record."

My hands shake and I fight the black as it demands to take over.

"I can't. I—"

"Oh, sure you can. Come on, tell me your story and I'll leave Shy here in Payson rather than drag her to Los Angeles with me. I'll let her stay here with her family instead of making her my wife."

My teeth grind together and every muscle in my body tenses.

A slow, knowing grin curls his lips. "That upsets you, doesn't it? You being separated from Shy, that makes you want blood." He takes a few steps toward me. "Does it make you want to kill?"

The veil drops, but I hold it back just before complete darkness falls.

"Between us, I'll have to have a few girls on the side. Not sure if you've tasted the little Navajo yet, but she's not all that good in bed. She can stay home and raise our kids while I become the number one news reporter in LA." He chuckles. "The thought of her, so strong and fierce, barefoot and pregnant, makes my dick hard, ya know? On second thought"—he pulls his keys out of his pocket—"keep your story. I'll take Shy."

I roar, "No!" just as the curtain falls.

THIRTY-SEVEN

SHYANN

"How're you doing?" My dad drops down next to me on the couch where I've been staring at the blank television since Trevor left.

"Been better." I give him a small, most likely unconvincing, smile. "I need to go talk to Lucas. I just..." Don't want to walk in on him and his *date*. "I need to warn him Trevor is sniffing around. This is all my fault. If I'd never come back, he'd be living a quiet life."

"How long've you known?"

"Dad..." I exhale, trying to hold on to the sliver of calm I'd managed to gain since that asshole left. "Trevor's a prick. Lucas, he—"

"Never would've let you go anywhere alone with the kid if I thought he was dangerous."

"He's not dangerous. He's..." Shit. My throat aches at the memory of him with another girl. "Complicated."

"Shit, Shy..." He drops his head to the back of the couch and rubs his eyes. "Lucas on trial for murdering his entire family? I'd swear that boy was the closest thing to pure we had on this earth."

I stare at my dad's profile, wondering if I should just share Lucas's secret with him. He'd understand, remembers what it was like to see people judge my mom when her body stopped working and she was a prisoner in her own head.

"He is. Lucas is the closest thing to pure." I want to yell that Lucas didn't kill his family, but I know it's a lie. Is murder any less of a crime if there's a reasonable explanation to do so? Whatever he did he did for the safety of himself and his siblings. "There's a lot about Lucas you don't know."

I can't help but feel like I'm betraying his trust, but keeping his secret is too heavy a burden. My dad's expression stays impassive and he waits.

"Thing is...um...Lucas has some mental issues." I peek up at my dad, only to see his eyebrows pinch together. "He suffered, Dad. He was abused by his mother and after time, in a last-ditch effort for his brain to cope with it all..." I sigh and push the word from my lips. "He split."

"Explain."

"They call it *dissociative identity disorder*." I tilt my head to peer up at him and find him intently focused on me. "One body, multiple personalities."

He blinks and shakes his head. "So Lucas..."

"Lucas is the main identity. He's the one you know, the artist, the quiet man you hired." I clear my throat. "Gage is the other."

"It has a name?"

"Not an it, Dad. A who. And, yes, Gage is Lucas's protector. He surfaces when Lucas is in a situation he can't handle emotionally."

"He violent?" There's panic in his voice.

"He'll protect Lucas at any cost. I've seen him angry and he's threatening, but at the heart of Gage is Lucas, so—"

"Lucas wouldn't hurt a fly."

"Exactly."

He runs two hands through his salt-and-pepper hair, and the worry in his eyes makes him look older than his fifty-five years. "Poor kid."

I lean over and squeeze my dad's shoulder. "We're the only family he has now and I refuse to let Trevor exploit him when he's finally found a home. A place where he belongs."

"You trust him, Shy?"

"With my life." Although maybe not so much with my heart.

"All right." He stands and tosses his empty bottle into the trash. "Only known the kid for a few months, but he's given me no reason not to trust him. That says a lot seein' as that Trevor guy makes my skin crawl just standing in the same room with him."

"I need to go talk to him, Dad. Things between us are…in a way they're…"

"You two been dating?"

"Yeah."

He nods. "Let's go to the river house, make sure things are okay with Lucas."

"Dad—"

He holds up a hand. "I'll give you guys space, but after hearing all this I need to see the boy for myself."

"'Kay."

He grabs his keys and I snag my coat before heading out to my dad's truck. It's so cold out I can see my breath, but seeing Lucas again has me sweating with nervousness. What if Gage is there? How will my dad react? I exhale and climb into the truck, hoping that Lucas has proved himself enough that my dad will accept Gage just as easily.

We head down the dirt road that leads to the river house in silence. My mind mulls over what needs to be said, as well as the things Lucas and I need to talk about in private.

"Whoa!" My dad slams on the brakes, sending a plume of dirt into the air.

"Buddy?" The brown and white dog is pacing in the middle of the road. "What's he doing?" I hop out and cautiously approach him. "Hey, Bud." He looks up at me with his sad doggie eyes. "Everything okay?" He goes back to pacing. I turn back to my dad and shrug, then walk the rest of the way to the A-frame house. Once the place comes into view, I squint at what looks like a dark vehicle parked close to the water's edge.

"Are you *fucking* kidding me?" I take off running, and Buddy barks, chasing after me. I faintly register the sound of my dad's truck door slamming and as my foot hits the bottom step of the porch, two arms wrap around my waist from behind.

"Shy, calm the hell down," my dad growls in my ear. "Don't go storming in there with guns blazing."

My breath hits in sharp bursts, but he's right. I hate that Trevor got to him before we did, but I need to calm down. "Okay, I'm good."

My dad releases me and I take a calming breath but notice Buddy is back in the middle of the road, staring out into the trees.

Together we climb the few steps up to the porch and my dad knocks on the front door. "Lucas! Son, you in there? Open up!"

"Help!"

"Shut up!"

Two male voices.

Shit!

My dad pulls me behind him and pushes open the door. "What the hell…?"

I peek around and there, in the middle of the living room, is Trevor. He's sitting on a chair, his arms pulled behind his back and secured with duct tape, his ankles the same.

"Nash, please, call the police!" Trevor's voice is weaker than I've ever heard it.

"I am *so*..." Gage is sitting in the corner, his knees cocked, forearms resting on them, his hair loose and wild, hanging over eyes that are glaring at me. "Disappointed."

"Lucas—"

I grip my dad's biceps. "That's Gage," I whisper.

Gage chuckles. "I cannot believe you'd be attracted to a man like *this*." He motions to Trevor, disgust twisting his gorgeous face. "He's already cried twice." A maniacal laugh bursts from his lips. "I don't even have a weapon!"

My dad steps deeper into the room, closing the door behind us. He stares between Trevor and Gage but finally addresses Gage. "What's going on, son?"

Gage's eyes flicker with emotion at the fatherly tone in my dad's voice. "Mr. Nash..." He pushes up from his seated position but doesn't move any closer. He runs a hand through his hair to smooth it down in what seems like an attempt to look more presentable. "It's nice to finally meet you."

"Gage." My dad nods.

Gage's eyes find mine and his eyebrows lift in a silent, *You told him.*

I nod back. As much as I want to hate Gage for what he did, how badly I want him to know the hurt he put me through, I can't. I have to believe he acted out of self-preservation, some inherent defense to avoid any kind of emotional abuse. God, I'm sick, but I still love him.

"This fucking psycho is holding me hostage!" Trevor breaks the silence.

Gage rolls his eyes and saunters forward. My gaze devours his shirtless torso and the way his gray sweats hang loose around narrow hips. He's the walking definition of dangerous and sexy. His eyes fix on mine. "Was he *always* such a drama queen?"

My dad stabs a finger in the air. "Someone better start talking or I'm calling the sheriff."

Gage glares at Trevor, making my ex's face drain of what little color it had. "This piece of shit showed up on my doorstep to fucking interrogate me. He was asked to leave. Multiple times. He wouldn't." He shrugs. "So I dragged him inside, tied him down." He flashes me a wicked grin. "We had a little chat about his intentions with the lovely Shy Ann."

This gets both my and my dad's attention and Trevor shifts uncomfortably in his binds.

"Seems he had plans to drag you to Los Angeles, but not to help you with your career goals." Gage smacks Trevor on the backside of his head, making him yelp. "He was going to make you his whore."

"Ha! Yeah, well, he could've tried." I glare at my ex-friend. "Like I'd ever let him touch me again."

"You fucking liar!" Trevor's face screws tight and a vein bulges from his forehead. "You would've done anything I asked to get to Los Angeles. Don't go acting all self-righteous now. You fucked me all through college just to get a job, and don't—"

"Heard enough." My dad crosses to Trevor and pulls him up from the chair. Keeping his wrists and ankles bound, he tosses him over his shoulder. "I'll be outside. Callin' Austin to come pick up this sack of crap. You two talk about whatever you need to talk about before the sheriff gets here. And you?" He stares down at Gage. "I'm trusting you with my daughter. Don't make me regret it."

Gage stands a little taller. "Sir."

Satisfied with Gage's response, my dad heads out with a wiggling and irate Trevor over his shoulder. Once the door closes, I face Gage. Silence builds between us, both of us daring the other to talk first.

"You hurt me."

He rocks back and his shoulders slump, his gaze dropping to the floor. "I know."

"Why?" The single word comes out like a cry from my soul.

"I thought...fuck. I saw you at the hospital. He kissed you."

I suck in a sharp breath. "You were there? It wasn't what you think—"

"Luke knew it wasn't. He understood." He shifts on his feet and finally brings his eyes to mine. "It was me. I was...scared. Thought we'd lose you."

"So you pushed me away first."

His eyelids drop in a slow blink. That's a yes.

"I'm not used to feeling this"—he digs his fingertips into the space between his pecs—"deep. It's fucking scary." His molten-gray stare meets mine. "I don't get *scared*."

I wish like hell his explanation could erase the memory and take away the heartache of what he did. "You'll never trust me enough to love me."

He takes a step forward but must see something in my expression that makes him stop. "That's not true. I trust you. I do. I can't bear to lose you, that's all. We can't live without you and that's..." He blows out a long breath. "How can I prove it to you?"

I swallow hard, hoping what I'm about to say doesn't take us two steps back in the progress we've made. But I have to know he trusts me, and it's the only way. "Tell me what happened the night your family died."

His face blanches. "You'll hate me when you hear."

I move closer until we're almost touching but I refuse to make the first move. He'll reach for me when he's ready. "I could never hate you, Gage."

"Thought I ruined everything."

"You almost did, but lucky for you I don't give up easily."

"You should let us go, find the life you deserve, Shy." His eyes shine and he dips his chin. "I can't promise I won't hurt you again."

"Of course you can."

"I can't. This is all so new and I'm so fucking afraid of messing it up."

"Take a chance, Gage. Trust me. Let me carry some of this weight for you. Tell me what happened the night your family died."

His arms wrap around me and he buries his face in my neck, the skin of his cheeks cold and clammy against my heated throat. His big body sags against me in what feels like welcomed defeat. "Why are you intent on destroying me, Shy?" He's dropping his walls and my chest floods with warmth as his trust envelopes me like a warm blanket. His lips dance across my skin. "Why?"

"I don't want to destroy you." My pulse pounds in my ears at the shakiness in his voice. I've never heard him so undone. I wrap my arms around him, holding him to me. "I want you to let me love you."

He pulls back, his eyes flickering, and I don't know how I know, but I feel Lucas trying to get through. I cup his jaw with both hands. "I love you, Gage. I do."

His face twists like he's in pain. "I hurt you." His voice takes on a child-like tone.

"You should've talked to me. I would've explained."

His features turn cold, distant. "No man puts his lips on you."

"Gage, please. Listen to me. Dustin made a mistake, all right. He apologized. He knows where I belong and it's not with him." I search his eyes, imploring him to see the truth in mine. "I don't want anyone but you."

A small smile curves his lips. "And Luke."

"Of course, and Lucas." I run my thumb along his lower lip and he drops his eyes closed.

"I didn't kill them," he whispers.

Relief washes over me like the warmest caress. I knew in my heart Lucas and Gage weren't capable of murdering children, but hearing it directly from the only person who survived that night squashed the trickle of doubt. He didn't kill them.

"The night they died…" He stares at his hands. "Mom, she…had a way with punishment. It was always a mental game with her. I don't even know what we did that day to piss her off so badly." He laughs, but it's far from funny. "Not that she ever needed a reason to fuck with us." His expression turns dark, like a switch has been flipped. "She called us all in the room and handed Mikey a knife."

I roll my lips into my mouth, holding back my words, my sobs, and my breath.

"She put a gun to Mikey's head. I remember it was silver." He blinks, then scowls as if it's all playing out before him. "She told him if he didn't stab our sister, she'd put a bullet in his brain."

I want to beg him to stop, to save me from the nightmare of his past, but I know he needs to tell it just as badly as I need to hear it.

"Mikey cried; he begged not to be killed." His head lolls to the side, his cold, haunted eyes on mine. "You ever heard a ten-year-old boy beg for his life, Shy?"

I shake my head, incapable of words, all while my soul is screaming for his pain.

"He couldn't do it. Every time he brought that knife to her little neck, she'd scream that she didn't want to die, beg for her life." He thumps his temple with his fist. "I can still hear it!"

Tears build in my eyes and threaten to spill. "I'm so sorry…" I whisper.

"Mom told him to open his mouth. He listened." His eyes drift away to focus on nothing. "He always listened to her. He was a good kid." Snapping out of whatever memory he was in, his gaze shifts to mine. "She slid his shaking fingers onto the trigger, took the knife, and held it to our sister's throat. Gave him a second option. Kill himself or she'd kill Alexis."

"Oh, Gage—" I cover my mouth as a sob rips from my chest.

"He blew his own brains out to protect her." His hands fist into his hair so hard I'd swear he was pulling it from his scalp. "So much blood. And crying. God, the fear in their cries was the worst."

A few seconds of silence pass before he regains the control to continue. "I thought that might be it, that my brother's suicide would be enough for her to scare us into submission." His eyes meet mine. "I was wrong. She gave that gun, splattered in our brother's blood, to David. Alexis was hyperventilating. He didn't even hesitate, probably looking forward to dying because it had to be better than living. Then it was my turn. She knew I'd shoot myself before I let her touch my sister, so with me she got creative. She made me choose." He holds out shaking hands, palms up. "Slow death by knife or a quick shot to the head." His eyes shine with tears. "My baby sister...I had to choose."

"Oh God..."

"By then she'd gone quiet. Maybe it was shock, but I knew she was gone somewhere deep inside her head. One by one, she watched with sick satisfaction as all three of my siblings took a bullet to the head. But it was me...it was my job to keep them safe. I didn't pull the trigger, but I was responsible for their deaths."

"Gage, no. You had no choice; you were a child and she was an animal."

A slow, twisted smile crawls across his face. "Then it was my turn."

"What happened?" I swallow, not sure I want or can handle the answer.

"She put that gun in my mouth, but she held the trigger. Everyone was dead; she had no one to threaten me with. 'You're the worst of them. You won't be missed. You're no one,' she said. Her eyes were almost black. I remember that. It was like...like she was high on the anticipation of spilling my blood. I knew I was gonna die. Hell, after what I'd seen, I was ready. Welcomed it. She pulled the trigger. It knocked me back and as I was lying in a pool of my brother's and sister's brains and blood and then…" His gaze comes to mine, bringing him back from the nightmare. "I realized I was still breathing. Luke learned later at the hospital that it was the angle that saved us. Shot under my tongue, and here." He points to the scar under his jaw. "She dropped the gun on my chest, and I remember her laughing." He coughs out a chuckle but his face twists in pain. "Surrounded by the gruesome mess of her children's dead bodies, and she was *laughing*. I lost it then; I couldn't help it. I joined in. I was choking on my own blood, but I was happy. I picked up the gun, excited about what I knew I was going to do next."

"Gage…" Fear rolls through me and as desperate as I am for the next words to roll from his lips, to hear what I already know, I'm shaking.

He cups my jaw with both hands and holds my head tight so I can't look away. "I was spared to accomplish this one thing, to get revenge. I pushed myself up"—a languid grin pulls at his lips—"and shot the bitch between the eyes."

I suck in a breath, and strangely there are no tears. "You didn't murder your family." No fear. Not even revulsion. Only relief. Respect. And the feeling of justice. "But…you killed your mom."

"She killed me first." His hands release me and he takes a step back, putting distance between us. "And, Shy?"

"Yeah?"

The sound of voices yelling outside is followed by boots stomping across the porch. Oh no, the sheriff. Our time is up.

He turns to me and smiles softly as a single tear falls from his eye. "I love you too."

The door bursts open and deputies with guns drawn pour into the living room.

"No!" I move on instinct to protect Gage, to cover him with my body.

"What is this? What are you doing?" I'm snagged from behind by a deputy and pulled to the far end of the room.

Deputies surround Gage, but he doesn't run or take his eyes off me. They jerk his arms behind his back. "Lucas Menzano, you're under arrest for—"

"Arrest?" I kick to free myself from the deputy's hold. "For what? He didn't do anything!"

He blinks and confusion tightens his expression. "What happened?"

Sorrow drags me to my knees. "Lucas! Oh God, Lucas!" Finally, the tears come.

"I don't understand," he says to one of the deputies. "What's going on?" His gaze searches mine and he takes a second to study my face, most likely seeing the leftover emotion and tears from Gage's confession. "What did you do to her? Why are you holding her?" He fights in their hold, the muscles of his upper body straining beneath his bare skin.

"Lucas…"

LUCAS

Pain I can take. The burn in my shoulders as I struggle to get free, the ache in my legs as I push to get to Shyann, all of it is a party compared to the slicing agony at seeing her cry.

Her eyes are puffy, bloodshot, and tear-soaked.

What happened?

Confusion makes everything sluggish. As if my thoughts can't catch up to real time. But nothing matters except soothing Shy.

"Stop fighting, son." I ignore the deputy and try to wrench my arms free when I'm shoved between my shoulder blades to move. "Calm down and we'll get this straightened out."

Nash pushes his way through the human barricade to Shyann and I breathe a little easier knowing he's with her. He'd never let anything touch her. He swings his cold blue gaze to me and I resist the urge to tuck my chin.

I didn't do anything wrong, at least not that I remember.

Last I remember was that Trevor guy making comments about Shyann and then Gage shoved me into the dark.

Fear ripples through my veins as a thought hits me hard.

Did Gage hurt Trevor?

I do a quick inventory and my knuckles aren't sore, no aches that would give away there was some kind of physical fight. I don't own weapons, so...?

The police pull me out to the front porch and Buddy barks at me feet. "It's okay, Buddy. It'll be okay." The front of my house looks like a parking lot filled with a couple sheriff's Jeeps, Trevor's car, a van, and Nash's truck. "What happened?"

"We were hoping you could tell us," the deputy leading me to a Jeep says.

I wish I could.

Headlights shine as another truck pulls up, this one brown with SHERIFF written in gold letters on the side.

Just then, Shyann appears in front of me and throws her arms around my neck. "It's gonna be okay, Lucas. I promise. I'll figure out a way to get you out of this."

If I had the use of my hands, I'd hold her to me, but I don't, so I nuzzle her hair at her neck and breathe as much of her in as I can.

Nash pulls her away, but she rips her arm free. "Stop, I just want to say goodbye."

I look between Nash and Shy, hoping to decipher her meaning. She pulls my face down to hers.

"Why goodbye, Shyann?"

Her lip quivers, but she's strong and fights back the tears. "Don't worry, okay?"

I shrug, but my body screams I should be more than worried. "Okay."

"Do you trust me?"

The twitch of a smile tickles my lips. "Yes."

She sighs and pushes up to her toes. "I love you."

My eyelids drop closed as the warmth of her words spread through me and breathe life into my soul. The soft heat of her lips brush against me in a slow kiss before she rests her forehead on mine.

"I love you too."

"Lucas Menzano?" Sheriff Austin steps up to me, his face grim. "You're under arrest for the assault of Samantha Crawford."

The sound of Shyann's roar slices through the night and straight to my chest.

THIRTY-EIGHT

LUCAS

"You're telling me you were home the night in question?" Gary, the deputy interrogating me, stares with disbelief.

We've gone over this multiple times already, and no matter how many creative ways he tries to ask it, my answer is still the same. "Yes, sir, as far as I can remember."

He leans across the table, his forearms bracing his weight. "And you don't have anyone to corroborate your story?"

"No, sir."

He falls back into his chair with a huff and shakes his head. "Witnesses say you were seen leaving the victim's house just after six in the morning."

"No, I've never been to Sam's house." Nausea crawls through my gut. Someone saw me, or rather Gage? After the blackout receded, I didn't feel any different. My muscles weren't weak or sore; there wasn't evidence of a fight left on my body, no blood on my clothes, but I was in the shower. I suppose any evidence could've been washed away.

"Is it true that you and the victim had some kind of sexual relationship?"

I drop my head and search for the courage it'll take to be honest. If I want to stay in Payson, have a shot at being a good man, the kind of man Shy deserves, I need to own who I am. I peer up at him and hope what I'm about to say doesn't get me locked up in prison, or worse, an institution. "Yes and no."

"Care to elaborate?"

I shift in my seat, my hands completely numb from the handcuffs and my arms well on their way. "I…um…I was abused as a child. My mind isn't like most people's and because of that I black out. It's like sleepwalking, only I'm awake, but I'm…not there. So I myself can't remember having any kind of a sexual relationship with Sam, but I've heard we…hooked up."

He doesn't say anything but I sense shock in his silence.

His eyes narrow. "Employees at Pistol Pete's who saw you together, they said the two of you got into some kind of fight and that you"—he flips through a few pages on a small spiral notebook—"threw her to the ground." He makes eye contact, daring me to lie. "Is that true?"

I swallow, knowing how bad this must look. "Yes, sir, I think it might be."

He lifts his eyebrows.

"I'd had a few beers and Sam started kissing me. I didn't like it and wanted her to leave me alone. I…um"—*blacked out*—"I don't remember what happened after that." I huff out a breath. That was harder than I thought.

The deputy's judgment is evident in his glare. "According to people in the bar, after your altercation with Sam, you left with Shyann Jennings."

I nod, not because I remember, but because that's the story Shy told me.

"You and Shyann seem pretty serious."

My eyes tighten and again, I nod. "I'm in love with her. For me, that's as serious as it gets."

"You know Shy and Sam were friends a long time ago. Sam's now with Shyann's ex." He shrugs. "Jealousy's a powerful motivator."

"I didn't beat up Sam." I just can't prove it.

He slaps his hands on the table. "Right. Okay, it's late and I need to get home. I'm going to put you in a cell and we'll figure this out in the morning."

A cell.

My heart pounds as he guides me out of the questioning room and into one of six or seven holding cells. The barred door swings open to a padded bench and a single toilet. I freeze, my body rejecting my command to move. With a firm press from Gary, I step inside and my skin pricks with anxiety.

The door closes and I jump at the loud clank of metal on metal.

"Back up, stick your hands out, and I'll remove those cuffs."

I do as I'm told and the blood flow returns to my fingers.

"Lucas." Gary tilts his head, studying me. "The thing with your mind, is it something you can't control?"

"I can't. When it hits, I'm helpless."

He nods and avoids my eyes. "Get some sleep."

The lights go off and I'm able to calm just a little at being alone in the dark. The smell of disinfectant and stale air swirls around me, and claustrophobia pricks at my skin. I lie down on the bench and throw my forearm over my eyes and imagine I'm in bed at the river house, and it helps to ease the panic.

No matter what I do, I can't seem to keep myself out of trouble.

Witnesses say they saw me at Sam's and I can't deny it because my memory is a blank spot.

Whoever said they saw me at Sam's has to be lying, but it's my word—the word of an accused and acquitted felon—against eyewitnesses.

Once the news gets out that I'm split, not even my innocence will save me.

SHYANN

I push through the door to my dad's house well after midnight to find him in a familiar spot in the kitchen. After Lucas was arrested, I hung back at the river house with Buddy, made sure he was fed and warm before I sat talking his fluffy little ears off. I pretended I was talking to the dog, but I was really talking to my mom. Asking her for guidance and praying she'd hook Lucas up with some divine intervention to get him free of this ridiculous charge.

My dad is leaning into the table on one elbow, his head in his hand and a short glass of amber liquid in front of him.

"Hey, Dad." I toss the keys onto the kitchen counter and drop into the chair across from his.

"Shy, you okay?" He pushes back and slumps into his seat.

"No."

"Mind telling me what's going on between you and Lucas?"

I blink up at him and for the first time it doesn't take all my reinforced walls and steely attitude to tell him exactly what's on my heart. "I'm in love with him, Dad."

"See that." He picks up his glass and takes a mouthful down his throat. "Seems he feels the same, not that I blame him."

My lip quivers and my chest throbs as his quiet compliment.

"You're so much like her, ya know."

I flinch and squelch the hope blooming in my chest. *You're nothing like your momma.* His words ring through my ears and I shake my head. "Like who?"

He sighs and a soft chuckle falls from his lips. "You know your grand-daddy wasn't too happy about his daughter falling for a pale face. He made it damn near impossible for us to be together."

I grin, remembering the stories my mom would tell about her and Dad having secret meeting places, how she spent time with a boy she grew up with on the reservation, paid him to act like her boyfriend so her dad would get off her back. "She told me."

"The woman was stubborn as hell." He rubs the back of his neck and drops his chin. "God, I miss her."

My instinct is to say something to comfort him, words of strength that'll hold him together, but I'm choked with sorrow. I miss her too.

"I know when you left for college I said you were nothing like her." His eyes shine with a vulnerability I haven't seen in him since the day we lost Momma. "I lied. You're so much like her it scares me to death."

"Dad…" My breath catches and a single tear slides down my cheek.

"I hated losing her. Then I lost you. Now you're back, and"—he shakes his head—"I can't lose you again."

"You won't lose me, Dad. I'm not going anywhere."

"Can you promise me that boy is safe?" He tilts his head. "I'd bet he's all right, but I won't gamble with your safety."

"I…yeah, I mean—"

"I don't like that Trevor guy, but fact is Lucas tied him up."

I open my mouth to defend Lucas but slam my lips shut without a single defense. "He deserved it. You can't ambush a man at his home in the mid-dle of the night, especially a man like Lucas."

"I feel terrible about the life the boy was forced to live. Understand how that would mess a kid up. He's always seemed like a decent guy. And now you're in love with him." He drains his glass and stands up. "Your mom was blind to my faults. I felt like the luckiest man in the world and took advantage of her not seein' 'em. Don't make the same mistake, baby. You see red flags, you run." He dips and presses a kiss to the top of my head. "I won't lose you too."

I watch my dad amble down the hallway like a man pulling the weight of a thousand lives behind him.

Red flags. You run.

Not this time. I'm done running.

THIRTY-NINE

SHYANN

"I'm sorry, Shyann, but visiting hours don't start for another thirty minutes." Diana, the receptionist at the hospital, gives me a sympathetic smile.

I have to see Sam. I have to wake her up, plead with her to push through so she can give me the information that'll free Lucas.

My fingers clasp together on the counter in front of me and I try to remain calm. "I know, and I'd never want to get you in trouble, but do you really think anyone's going to balk over thirty measly minutes?" I've been waiting to get in to see Sam since before the sun came up, and with every passing hour I could see Diana's resolve dwindling. "Please, if anything happened and she didn't wake up, I'd..." A lump forms in my throat at the very thought that Sam might not come away from all this okay. That I'd never get a chance to say how sorry I am for being a shitty friend.

"Sorry, Shy—"

"Please. I'm going crazy here." Only she can free Lucas and I must get through to her and at least try to pull her out of this.

She sighs heavily and leans toward me. "I'm going to run to the bathroom." A tiny lift of her eyebrows is all she gives before she turns her back and walks away.

With her out of sight, I scurry toward the double doors and pray like hell I don't get caught. Once through, no one seems to care that I'm there except for a few questioning looks from nurses that I brush off by acting like I belong there, walking the halls of the hospital.

I follow the numbered doors until I reach Sam's. Her door is cracked and I peek inside to see her lying in the dark alone and still unconscious. I tiptoe inside, close the door, and take the seat closest to her bedside.

I expect her parents will be here the second visiting hours open and I don't want an audience for what I need to say.

Gently grasping her swollen fingers, I dip my forehead to our joined hands. "Sam, please wake up. I know I don't deserve your friendship. Don't deserve your help, not after the way I left things between us. I'm so sorry. I should've been a better friend to you."

My words fade into the rhythmic sounds of the medical equipment as it beeps and hisses around us. Nausea rolls through my stomach as guilt and shame eat at my insides. I left Payson to avoid feeling, closed myself off to every single person who killed the numbness I refused to emerge from. It's never been about this town; it's always been about the people in it. About their love for me and my family, their concern, and even their pity. After Momma died, I was suffocated with it. All of it too much to internalize and more than I could ever process. So rather than even try, I took off.

I hardened myself against *feeling* anything. No friends, meaningless sex with someone I couldn't stand, I even chose the most emotionless job available. Then I got fired and who did I turn to when I needed help? The people I abandoned without ever looking back. They should hate me. At the very least ignore me.

But they didn't.

They embraced me.

Taking a deep breath, a sense of calmness comes over me. I stare at Sam as her chest rises and falls with the ventilator. "Come back to us. Don't let this be the end." My nose burns and my eyes fill with tears. "I know it's selfish, but I want the time to make up for ditching our friendship." I lean my elbows on the bed. "I'm sorry about what happened at the bar the other night with Lucas. If I hadn't messed things up between us a long time ago, you would've known I had feelings for him." I blink back tears as I imagine him locked in a cell. "I love him, Sam. And he loves me too." I drop my forehead and sniff back tears as they rush to the surface. "He's never had anyone to save him, and I won't be another person on the list of people who've let him down. I won't abandon anyone I love ever again."

Silent minutes pass and fall into the next and for the first time since before my momma died, I pray. I send up heartfelt requests and plead with God that Sam will survive this. That Lucas will finally catch the break he so desperately deserves and get a chance at living a life free from fear and filled with peace.

Lost in my prayers, I startle at the sound of my name being whispered.

Blinking open my eyes, I see Mrs. Crawford pulling off her purse and setting it on the floor before she comes to me.

"You're here early." Her gaze moves from me to Sam and she frowns.

I follow her eyes and my heart cramps at what she must feel seeing her daughter like this. "Yeah, I had to see her."

She moves to the other side of the bed and sits on the edge. "Suppose you heard they arrested that quiet boy for questioning."

I nod. "He didn't do it. I can't prove it, but I just…something doesn't feel right."

She hums. "Everything about this is far from feeling right." Her hands hold Sam's free one and she leans over and kisses her daughter's bruised forehead.

"Yeah. I better go." I want to stop by and sit with Lucas as long as I can. I flash what I hope is an encouraging smile at Sam's mom. "Call me if she wakes up?"

"Of course."

I press a gentle kiss to Sam's head and send one last silent message. *Wake up. Help me save him.*

LUCAS

Time passes slowly when sleep refuses to come. I've been staring at the ceiling of this small cell because every time I close my eyes, all I can see is Shyann. Her face tormented as I was taken into custody. The sound of her hollered protest rings in my ears even still, and knowing she's out there hurting is killing me worse than the possibility of me serving jail time for a crime I didn't commit.

"Menzano."

I cringe at the sound of my last name but sit up and swing my feet to the floor. My back cramps from lying on the thinly padded steel platform.

"You've got a visitor." A deputy I've never met swings open the door.

A flash of black hair has my heart pounding and I rush to the bars just as Shyann's eyes find mine. She thanks the deputy and comes to stand just behind a bright yellow line painted on the concrete. Her eyes move over my face, neck, chest, and to my feet.

"They said I can't get close enough to touch you." The pain of her voice makes everything behind my ribs ache.

"It's okay. Seeing you is enough."

She tilts her head, squinting. "Are you all right?"

Heat creeps up my neck at how I must look behind bars in my sweat-pants and a borrowed T-shirt after a night without sleep. "I'm good. Yeah."

A rush of air comes from her lips and her shoulders drop a little. "This is all a mistake, Lucas. It has to be."

"I know. I mean, I know I didn't hurt Sam, and Gage..." Is it presumptuous to say he'd never hurt her either?

"She wasn't a threat to you, Lucas. He didn't do it, but..." She studies the room, clearly spotting the few cameras strategically placed and pointing our way. "They know about you now."

I nod.

"They're going to think the worst of what they don't understand."

"Shy, don't worry about me. They'll investigate and the truth will come to light. Everything will be okay." I'm not sold that it will, but I lie to make her feel better.

Her eyes water and redden around the edges. Dark flickers in my peripheral vision. I shove it back, but it nudges again, this time accompanied by a feeling that constricts my throat. *Huh, that's new.* I blink and try to relax, but a twitch of my lips gives me away.

"What?" She sniffs. "Why are you smiling?"

I reach deep into my mind and am flooded with a fierce concern for Shyann, similar to what I already feel, but somehow more...possessive. "He's protective of you too now."

Her eyebrows pinch together and she studies me. "How do you know?"

I shrug one shoulder, amazed that for the first time I'm able to understand what Gage is feeling and recognize it as him. "He doesn't like that you're upset." More dark tunnels my vision, but I hold it back. "He's trying to push me into the dark."

"Lucas...you can communicate with him?"

I search my thoughts, explore the deepest caverns of my feelings. "No, but when you get upset, he tries to take over. At first I thought he was protecting me from your anger or whatever but now he's letting me feel what he's feeling. I think he's trying to"—our gazes tangle together—"comfort you. We love you, Shy."

A single tear rolls down her cheek to her parted lips. "I love you guys too." I grin and a crazed smile stretches across her beautiful face. "We're quite the fucked up couple, Lucas."

My smile falls as I study the woman before me, capable of more love than I've ever seen and more beautiful than any man deserves, especially us. But we're keeping her and never letting go. "I wouldn't have it any other way."

"I want to hold you."

Heat explodes in my chest. "I want to kiss you."

She blushes and jumps as the large metal door that leads into the police station opens and Sheriff Austin walks in. His deep frown makes my gut twist with anxiety and he takes in Shyann before moving toward us.

"Austin, what is it?" Shy moves toward me but stays on her side of the safe distance line.

The sheriff's gaze slides to mine and he squares his shoulders, which makes me unconsciously stand taller, preparing mentally for him to deliver what I assume to be bad news.

"Son, wanted to stop in to let you know Sam's awake and her doctors have cleared her to talk."

I exhale hard and nod.

"That's great. When will you go question her?" Shy's voice drips with excitement.

The sheriff checks his watch. "Gary should be pulling up over there now." His eyes find Lucas. "I'll be back in a few to let you know what we get."

"Thank you."

He nods and turns from us, calling out over his shoulder that Shy only has ten more minutes.

Her bright smile turns toward me. "This is it! This could get you off the hook!"

"Yeah, but if it was the Shadow, will she have any information to give to get me off? I mean, if she didn't see his face, or hear his voice, and there wasn't any evidence, won't that leave me on the chopping block?"

Her smile falls and I instantly regret my words.

Sam's testimony will seal my fate, one way or the other.

SHYANN

"Time's up!" a deputy calls from the doorway. "Say your goodbyes."

I straighten my spine and throw as much power behind my words as I can. "I'm not leaving."

Lucas smiles, actually smiles!

"Shy, you have to leave." Lucas's long fingers are curled around the bars of the door, his grin that melts my insides flashing adorably.

"This room maybe, but I'll be waiting in the sheriff's office. I want to be here when they get back and you'll need a ride home when they release you."

He frowns, his expression growing serious. "I think we have to be prepared for the worst. They've done their research, Shy. They know my record, that I was tried for murdering my family."

"The jury found you innocent."

His eyes snap to mine. "On a technicality."

I swallow hard and resist the urge to move closer and grasp his hands in mine. "Do you think you killed your family, Lucas?"

"No. I loved my brothers and sister. I can't image Gage hurting them."

"And your mom?" I need to know, finally, the truth of what he knows, or at least what he believes happened that night.

His expression turns hard. "I'd wished she would die, yes. But I can't see myself killing anyone, no matter how evil they were. Gage is a different story, though."

I nod to his scar. "And that?"

He shrugs. "I believe my mom killed them, tried to kill me, and then killed herself. That's what the jury decided, so that's what I believe."

Safe, keeping the bad guy evil and the innocence of children pure. Even if it's not the truth, Lucas could never live with himself if he knew he'd taken a life. If the authorities ever found out, would they drag him through a retrial?

It's better he remain clueless.

The door swings open, jarring me from my thoughts, and my stomach leaps into my throat. Is it them? Do they have answers?

The deputy walks in and waves me forward. "Time's up, Shy."

"Five more minutes?" I flash my poutiest pout.

"Not a chance. Already gave you more time than I should've." He motions to the door. "Let's go."

I sigh and look at Lucas, wanting so badly to touch him before I go, comfort him and myself even if only for a second. He seems to read my thoughts and steps away from the bars. "Go on, Shy. It'll be okay."

"I love you, and I *will* see you soon." My stomach drops and I hope to God I'm telling him the truth.

"Shyann, let's go!" the deputy yells, and I walk away from Lucas, each foot of distance between us increasing the dread building in my gut.

LUCAS

There are no windows in the cell I'm being held in, so the passing of time is relative and it feels like it's been days since Shyann left. I've counted the bricks on the exterior wall, the number of rivets in the metal dividing walls, and the bars in the door. Multiple times.

After what seems like a lifetime, the door finally opens and I push up to see Sheriff Austin and Gary walk in; their faces are unreadable. I remain silent as they step up to my cell, my pulse pounding in my ears. My eyes widen as he pulls keys from his pocket and unlocks my cell door.

"Mr. Menzano." Austin's gaze is dark and set on mine. "Appreciate your patience through all this." He swings open the door. "Seems we were led astray by false witnesses. You're free to go."

The opening is right there but I hesitate to walk out, as if this is all some tease to intensify my punishment. "I don't understand."

"Samantha was able to identify one of her—"

"I swear to *God*..." We all turn to the door at the sound of Shy's voice. "If you try to stop me, I will send your nuts into your body cavity, Tom!"

She storms into the room and Austin's lips twitch as he nods to a pale-faced Tom to go ahead and allow her in.

Her eyes find mine but quickly dart to the open cell door. "What's going on?" She looks up at Austin. "Where are you taking him?"

He steps back and motions to me. "I was just explaining to Lucas that Samantha positively identified—"

She gasps and covers her mouth.

"Lucas was not the man who attacked her."

She darts toward me and I have just enough time to brace myself before her body barrels into mine, knocking me back a step. "I knew it! I knew the truth would surface."

I wrap her up tight in my arms, feeling like it's been years since I've held her. Her soft, warm body melts into mine and she buries her face into my neck, her lips dancing kisses against my jaw and scar. My blood powers through my veins with the need to get her alone, and darkness clouds my vision as Gage pushes for his chance with Shy. Too bad. I nuzzle her neck, breathing in the heady scent of her shampoo and my muscles relax. He'll have to wait.

The clearing of a throat drags us from our reunion and I release Shy only enough to tuck her under my arm.

Austin grins and jerks his head toward the exit. "If you two have a minute, we can go to my office and I'll explain."

Hand in hand, we follow him out of the room of cells and through the station to his office. I take a seat but grab Shy as she moves to sit too far away from me and pull her into my lap. She squeaks and looks at me with wide eyes and a smile. I don't know what's come over me, but now that I have her close, it doesn't feel right if we're not touching.

Austin sits behind his desk, shuffles around a few papers, and leans back. "Here's what we know. Samantha Crawford finally woke up late this morning."

Shy's back goes straight. "Is she okay?"

"Looks like she'll make a full recovery physically. Mentally is a different story." He fixes his eyes on Lucas. "You were set up."

"Set up?" Shy's hand fists on her lap. "By who!"

I shift in my seat and run my palm along her thigh until her muscles release some tension.

"The man who attacked her told her his name was Lucas Menzano. Now, I've been doing this for long enough to know that most people committing crimes don't give their full names to their victims. Then we got the anonymous tip. We noticed the tip came from a number associated with pay phones. When we tracked it, we discovered the call was made outside the Quicky Q off I-87. Gary went and got a copy of the video surveillance and the guy who called in the tip didn't look like a local as he claimed." His jaw ticks. "Sam shared that it was obvious the man who assaulted her wasn't comfortable beating a woman. He'd finished what he came to do, and, thinking she'd passed out, he pulled off his mask and gagged or vomited into it. She got a good look at his face and when she described him, well, we thought it sounded familiar." He leans back, rocking once in his chair. "We showed Sam close-ups from the surveillance film and she positively ID'd her attacker."

"Oh my God..." Shy whispers. "Lucas was set up."

I stare back and forth between them. "By who?"

Austin's eyes harden and he practically growls the man's name.

She gasps and swings a stunned gaze to mine. I watch in fascination as her shock morphs to fury. "*Trevor*."

"Trevor Peterson." Austin repeats it, and only then does it finally sink in.

She shakes her head and her body stiffens again. "He framed you so he could create a story for that stupid LA gig! I can't believe it!" Her tone is a high-pitched shriek. "That motherfucker!"

I sink my fingers into Shy's hair at her nape, hoping to relax her. As annoying as all this has been, Sam's the real victim here and all I lost was a night of freedom. I'm just glad they found who did it and that he'll be punished. "What about the other witness? You said there were two?"

He flips through another couple pages. "We traced the second call to a burner cell that was purchased in—"

"Let me guess," Shy grumbles. "Flagstaff."

"You got it." Austin shakes his head. "We confiscated all the video footage from the van we found parked in the trees outside Lucas's house. Got Trevor ambushing Lucas at his home on tape. From what we can see, it seems he forced Lucas to defend himself when he wouldn't leave after being asked *repeatedly*. It's my belief that Mr. Peterson's cameraman is responsible for that second call."

She turns toward me, a frown tipping her lips. "This is my fault. I never should've mentioned your name to Trevor. I'm so, so—"

I press my lips to hers, silencing her immediately. "Don't." After all the things Gage has done to hurt her, to push her away, she's the one who deserves an apology. But not here, not with an audience.

"Is that all?" I'm ready to get the hell out of here, take my girl home and hold her until they send someone to pry us apart.

Austin pushes up from his chair and holds out his hand. "Again, I'm sorry about keeping you overnight. We had to take the tips seriously."

Shy stands, but I snag her hand in mine while giving the sheriff my other.

"I understand. Thank you."

We move to leave but Shy turns back. "Please tell me you got 'em, Austin. I need to know Trevor is off the streets."

He moves past us and opens the door into the small booking area, then grins. "Oh, we got 'em."

FORTY

LUCAS

"Don't touch me!" Trevor slaps at the deputy's hand as he guides him in front of the blank wall where a mugshot will be taken. "I'll sue this Podunk town for everything it has! I'll call every media—"

Shy lunges toward him, but I grasp her around the waist and hold her back, burying my face in her neck. "He's not worth it."

She tenses in my arms, her body radiating unbridled anger. "He's a sick bastard. I hate him!"

I shrug. "He's not my favorite person either."

The room is small enough that he not only sees us, but probably hears us too. He glares our way when I press a kiss to her temple. He sneers and a slow twisted smile that feels so foreign, and yet somehow familiar, curls my lips. My vision blacks out for a few seconds. When it comes back, Trevor's face is pale.

I can't help but laugh and give Gage an internal high five.

The front door of the station opens and in walks two deputies with an infuriated Dustin Miller in handcuffs.

We turn to the sheriff, who is shaking his head and frowning. "Turns out Dustin Miller is responsible for vandalizing the McKinstry place. He was bragging about it to Sam before the night she was attacked." He clicks his tongue and mumbles, "Strange pillow talk."

"No way…" Shy whispers. "I knew it! That fucking prick!" She lunges again, but I turn her around to face me and hold her to my chest. "Let me go, Lucas."

"No."

She tilts her head up, her teeth clenched and eyes spitting blue fire. "Two minutes. That's all I need."

My mouth twitches and I actually consider letting her loose on Dustin, but I drop a kiss to her jaw and whisper in her ear, "Just got out of jail, Shy. You lose it on Dustin…Gage'll wanna play. I'll end up back in that cell when all I want to do is get you home."

A quick burst of her breath plays against my neck and I pull back to see her fighting a smile. "Good point."

"Can I please get you out of here before you get us both arrested?"

She nods and her expression gets soft. "Probably smart."

We move through the police station and push out the glass door and into the midday sun.

Huddled in the parking lot around an old pickup truck are a few guys from Jennings, including Stilts and Chris, along with Nash and Cody. They all grin and meet us at the bottom of the stairs.

"Son." Nash hooks me around the neck and pulls me in for a back-pounding hug. "Good to have you back."

And suddenly without warning, Shy and I are smothered in arms and words of appreciation. All the guys tell me they're proud of me, and my eyes burn but I force it under control. Now that everyone knows about Gage, there's really no reason not to let him take over—after all, Gage has always handled the emotional situations. Taken the moments that bring out the more intense feelings. But not this time. Rather than duck away, I welcome the intensity rushing through me because it doesn't hurt or scare me anymore. For the first time in my life, I feel like I belong.

SHYANN

At a quick stop at the 87 Café, I watched Lucas hesitantly stare at his pancakes before I reached over and took a bite, then melted into the faux-cowhide seat when he flashed me that smile I'll always feel in my toes. Cody and my dad joined us and things got a little awkward when they asked Lucas about Gage. He was generous with his answers, and my family was good enough not to pry too deeply.

Out in the parking lot, Dad gave both me and Lucas the day off and we decide to spend it at the river house together. There's a freedom that surrounds us now and I can't wait to take advantage of it. I'm just sorry it took Trevor's involvement in our lives for us to get there.

We pull up the drive, only to be met by a barking Buddy as he jumps around the truck and leads us to the house. Lucas hops out and gives the dog a rub behind the ears. "Good boy, Buddy."

I lean against the hood and watch the man and his dog, admiring how far they've both come. Guiding each other from the dark.

Lucas tilts his head and brings his eyes to mine. He flashes a smile, and I realize he's done that almost every time he's looked at me since the police station.

My heart flutters in my chest. "What?"

He pulls his top lip with his tongue, trying to tamp down his grin. "Nothing." He stands to his full height and plucks at his shirt. "I need a shower."

Inappropriate images of my body pressed against a naked and very wet Lucas flash through my mind. My skin heats and I press my thighs together to try to stifle the fire burning between them.

"Hey..." His hand cups my jaw and his eyebrows are low over his slate-gray eyes. "You okay?"

I try to laugh but his closeness has me practically breathless. "It's weird; I keep thinking my feelings will mellow a bit, but they don't."

"Is..." He studies my face. "Is that what that is? When your face gets serious like this and your eyes turn...I don't know...intense?"

"It is. Sometimes I get overwhelmed with it and I just have to touch you." I run my palms up his abdomen, over his pecs, up to his shoulders, and suck in a stuttered breath. "You're so beautiful, Lucas."

He drops his forehead to mine. "This doesn't seem real to me yet. You're out of my league, Shy." He tilts his head and runs his nose along my cheekbone in a slow drag, inhaling the entire way to my ear. I tremble as his hot breath teases my sensitive flesh. His muscles tense under my hands before he sinks his teeth into my earlobe and pulls with a growl.

Gage.

I don't have to see his eyes; I can feel the difference in demeanor. As if our souls have connected and I can sense the change. My legs wobble and he holds me firmly to him. "You're here."

"Of course. Where else would I be?"

He presses against me, nuzzling my neck with a soft moan that ghosts across my skin. "You know it all now, Shy. And you still want us."

I sift my hands through his hair, hoping to erase the insecurity that coats his words. "I do."

He pulls back, his eyebrows pinched together, and he frowns. "I love you." His fingers fork into my hair at my nape. "But I'd understand you not wanting to be with someone like me."

"You said you love me."

"I do."

"Let's just start there."

He rests his forehead against mine, breathing together, inhaling and exhaling, filling each other with the unspoken promises of forever despite the obstacles in our way.

"You have the ability to break me." His voice is raw, causing me to sink deeper into his embrace.

"Then we'll shatter together, because without you I'm not whole."

"Fuck, Shy, you want us." His words drip with disbelief.

"More than I've ever wanted anyone or anything."

"I need you." He rakes his teeth along my skin, sending a delicious shiver up my spine.

I drop my head to the side, exposing my neck and offering myself to him. "What are you waiting for?"

He chuckles and pulls away enough to give me his eyes. His forehead lowers, predatory glare bores into mine, a slow smile pulls at his lips. "He gave you over to me." His eyes flutter and dart as if he's hearing something in his head and trying to understand; then his grin widens. "He's warning me to be good to you."

I lock my hands around his neck and a thrill races through me. Whereas Lucas is tender and coaxing, Gage is powerful and demanding. I know I'll always be safe with him, but that doesn't change the fact that this is new and the unknown is a little terrifying.

"I'm nervous."

His thumb brushes along my jaw. "Don't be. I'll always take care of you, Shy." His eyes move from my lips to my eyes. "I'll never hurt you again. Promise."

"Okay, Gage. I trust you."

His eyes flare and he leans in. His lips cover mine and command my compliance. Tender, but firm enough to communicate he's in control, his tongue lashes against mine. Our hands grasp at each other and can't seem to get close enough. He rips his mouth away and dips to grab my ass and pull me up around his waist.

"Gage!" I giggle and wrap my legs around him while he strides to the house, through the front door, and straight to the bathroom.

"Shower, baby." He releases me, our bodies brushing together the whole way as he slides me to my feet. "Now."

I shake my head, grinning. "I took one already." I point over my shoulder. "I'll just wait out there—"

His arms come around me so quickly I lose my breath and he whips my shirt off over my head. "No, I need you right this fucking second, Shy."

Ruthless.

My skin explodes in goose bumps as Gage lovingly but effectively strips me naked until I'm standing before him with nothing to cover me except my hair that drapes over my shoulders to cover my breasts. His gaze moves over me in a visual caress from my feet, to my thighs, to my hips. He tilts his head and licks his lips and continues to travel the length of my body until he's at my eyes. His expression is soft and I'm trapped in the intensity of his stare. I shudder in anticipation, and his eyebrows pinch together. "You're cold."

I open my mouth to tell him I'm a lot of things, and cold isn't one of them, but he flips on the shower and tests the water until steam fills the room.

With one hand he reaches behind him and pulls his tee off, then holds his arms out. "C'mere, baby. Let me take care of you."

I've been naked with this body before, but not with this man. I move to him and he swallows me in his embrace. Our bare chests press together and

I can feel his heart beating against mine. So intimate, gentle, the opposite of what I'd expect. He rubs my back and then puts his lips to my ear. "Get in."

"Not yet." I walk him back to the toilet and sit him on the closed seat.

He quirks a brow and the look is so confident, sexy, and I realize how lucky I am to have this incredibly complex man, so sweet and vulnerable, and also so dangerously beautiful it's too much to ever hope for and more than I can comprehend.

I kneel at his feet and unlace his boots, pulling them off and tossing them aside along with his socks. When I stand, he pulls me between his open legs. His arms come around me, holding me in place while he covers my bare stomach in tender kisses. Running my fingers through his hair, I watch as he skates his lips over my skin, tasting and breathing me in until I'm squirming with want.

Sensing my restlessness, he stands, cups my jaw, and pulls my mouth to his. "You're perfect." His lips lightly brush against mine and I'm awestruck as he treats me with a gentleness I didn't think he was capable of.

"Perfect for you."

He tilts my chin up to meet his eyes, now molten with desire. "Perfect for us." Kicking his sweatpants off, he half leads, half carries me to the shower. I'm barely in when he pushes my chest to the tiled wall. I arch at the sensation of the cold tile against my heated breasts and he holds my hips in place.

"Please, Gage…"

"Love you." He slides his fingers into my hair and twists my head to the side; his mouth on mine he swallows my gasp of surprise.

He grinds against me and his hands shake as if he's holding back, afraid to lose control. My breath saws in and out of my lungs in anticipation. He must sense it and releases his hold on my hair to turn me around. His mouth moves from my lips to my neck, then down to my breasts, and he sucks each nipple so hard it shoots bolts of sensation across my skin. He explores every inch of me with precision, as his tongue leaves nothing neglected. A powerful grip holds me captive to keep me from bucking uncontrollably in his hold.

He drops to his knees and tosses my leg over his shoulder, opening me to him. He stares in between my legs until insecurity has me wiggling away.

"Stop." He stills me with a firm grip on my thighs. "You're gorgeous." He groans against me as he dips to taste me there. I cry out, my head slamming back against the tile. His sensual assault is relentless as he coaxes my body to bend to his will. His powerful lips play against my sensitive flesh. Sounds I've never heard before fall from my lips in a symphony of need and when I can't take another second, he's gone.

I blink open my eyes to see him standing before me and I startle at the ferocity of his stare. "I'll never forgive myself for hurting you."

My lust-fogged mind struggles to comprehend, but the way his eyes shine with unshed tears tells me all I need to know.

"I know you won't." I press a kiss to his mouth. "But I have." After another kiss, I close my eyes and whisper, "I forgive you, Gage. I forgive you."

His eyes search mine with confusion etched into his beautiful features and he must find what he's looking for when he slams his body to mine in a hug that steals my breath. "I don't deserve you, but I'm going to keep you."

With my face buried in his neck, he reaches for something in the soap tray, then separates our bodies enough to roll on a condom. He hoists me up, pressing my back against the wall as my legs lock around his hips. I expect him to power into me, but he holds me just out of reach and cups my cheek. "Tell me this is real."

For a second I wonder if Gage pulled back, but the low set of his brows and firm set of his jaw give away that this isn't Lucas. "I hope so; if not, then waking up from this dream will be torture."

He nudges against me and slowly inches inside. His eyes never leave mine and we watch each other in fascination as our bodies come together, to connect physically the way we already have emotionally.

He pins me against the tile in an unrelenting hold. "We're never letting you go, Shy. This is it. Run, we'll find you. Hide, we'll sniff you out." He thrusts forward in what I'm sure is supposed to be threatening, but it only works to pull my orgasm closer to the surface. "You'll never be rid of us."

"I'm not going anywhere." His threats should scare me, but instead they make me feel safer, more secure, than I've ever felt before. Because that's been my fear all along, my reason for keeping distance from those who mean the most to me, because I'd never survive losing someone I love again.

His face twists in agony and he drops his forehead to my shoulder while pushing and pulling inside me. "Promise me."

I can't imagine life without Lucas. Without Gage. All my hopes and dreams paled the day I met them and since then have fizzled into something so much bigger than a job and notoriety. Now all that matters is us. Our love, a life together.

I was meant for big things. My momma knew it. And loving Lucas is bigger than anything I could've imagined.

"I promise." I nuzzle his hair, pulling him deeper into my embrace. "You're stuck with me."

"Fuck, yeah." His thrusts quicken and things turn frenzied. Hands grip, nails bite, and when he yanks my head to the side, he whispers in my ear, "I love you, Shyann."

As if our bodies are in tune, my orgasm rips through me seconds before he thrusts one last time and groans into my neck. We hold on to each other, panting for breath through the steam, our hearts pounding against our ribs.

He leans away so that his mouth is at my ear. "I'm yours. From here on out, nothing will touch you. I'll never let anyone hurt you."

"And *I'll* never let anyone hurt you, Gage."

With a shuddering exhale, his body stills. "Thank you," he whispers, and his muscles soften against me as his death grip on me loosens. After a few deep breaths, he pulls back, blinking, and a shy smile curves his lips. And there's a little cockiness there too.

I giggle and cup his jaw. "Hey, Lucas."

He rests his forehead against mine. "I missed you."

My eyes dart to where our bodies are joined. "Don't think I can get any closer."

He laughs, and the sound cocoons me in acceptance and love. "Let's get dry. I want you back in my bed."

He lowers me to my feet and gets rid of the condom before holding a towel out and folding me in his arms. We dry and crawl into his bed naked, wrapping ourselves up in each other and nose to nose.

"You changed the sheets." These are dark gray and smell like soap.

He blushes. "Tossed the old ones." His fingers twirl a long strand of my hair and his expression grows serious. "I'm going to make it my life's mission to make you happy, Shy." He tries to hide it, but I see the fear work behind his eyes. "I'll do whatever it takes. Therapy, medication, whatever—"

"You've spent most of your life trying to earn the love of a woman."

"We're not easy to love."

It's not the words that shatter my heart; it's the way he says it, as if it's the gospel truth. Hooking my fingers under his chin, I force his eyes to mine. "Nothing has ever been easier for me, and I'm not going to make this hard for you, Lucas. Just being with you is enough."

He shrugs one shoulder. "I'm broken. Split. I'll never be normal."

"I know things won't always be easy, but I don't want to change you. I love you the way you are, everything about the way you are and you're who I want. You've never given yourself the freedom to just be. You don't have to hide who you are anymore, Lucas. Ever again. Especially not from me."

"I don't deserve you." He blinks and his eyes focus just over my shoulder before coming back to me. "He's pretty full of himself, isn't he."

"He is the perfect yin to your yang."

His lips brush against mine. "Would you rather…" Another kiss. "Leave Payson and chase your dreams?" His tongue dips into my mouth and I open to him, tasting his apprehension, his vulnerability, and I kiss him with a passion I hope puts all his concerns to rest. "Or…" He kisses the tip of my nose. "Throw it all away for a guy going nowhere fast?"

"Hmm…" I tap my chin. "Leaving Payson means walking away from everyone I love, and I don't have to go far to chase my dreams because they're all wrapped up in the man who's currently wrapped around me."

His eyes slam closed. "Shy…"

"So I pick stay in Payson and chase down my future with the man who owns my heart." He doesn't respond but watches me thoughtfully. "So? What do you say? Can you live with that?"

"We can."

FORTY-ONE

SHYANN

I'm sweating, but not because I'm hot. Hell, it would be impossible to reach a temperature that would make me sweat with the hospital blowing sixty-degree air-conditioning through the halls.

I'm nervous. Leaving the warmth of Lucas's arms this morning, I headed home only to find out that Sam has been asking for me. Unable to reach me by cell, her mom called my dad—aaaand suddenly we're eight years old again—to request I stop by to see her as soon as I could.

So here I am, standing in the hallway, building up the courage to face my old best friend and fully expecting her hate. This must be what it feels like before walking in front of a firing squad.

My stomach bottoms out as I think about all the reasons she has to despise me; after all, I'm the one who brought Trevor and Leaf into her life, even if unintentionally. Sam's anger is justified. I'll take my punishment like a good girl and move on.

I shake my hands to get my circulation flowing and throw my shoulders back, so ready to get this over with and get back to Lucas.

Pushing open the door, I'm welcomed by a stream of sunlight through the window, the beeping of a heart monitor, and that weird smell hospital rooms have—some mixture of bleach and blood.

Sam's alone, but rather than lying flat on her back like the last time I was here, she is in an upright position in bed. Her face is still heavily bruised, one eye swollen mostly shut, but her stitched up lip lifts a little when she looks at me.

"Hey, Sam." I move to the chair at her bedside but don't sit, not sure if I'm welcome to stay long. "How're you feeling?"

"I'm okay, better I think." She blinks with her good eye. "Thank you for coming."

"Of course." I hesitate but eventually sit, as it seems looking up at me is more of a strain on her. "I figured you'd have some things to say to me. Before you get started, I want you to know how badly I feel about all this. You have to know I had no idea—"

"Please." She does her best to hold up a hand to silence me. "This wasn't your fault."

I feel my eyes widen and my lips part in shock. "It kinda was. I mean, if—"

"Stop, Shy." She shakes her head and drops it back against her pillow as if the movement took too much out of her. "You know what it's like in this town. I never locked my door. I'm surprised something like this hasn't happened sooner."

With the knot in my chest unwinding, I lean over and place my hand on her forearm. "This isn't your fault."

"It doesn't matter; it happened, and honestly…" Her bloodshot eye meets mine. "I'm happy it did. I mean, I'm not, but I am. Coming close to death makes you see things differently. It's like putting your life under a microscope, ya know? I've wasted so many years, Shy. It's time to grow up."

"What does that mean?"

She shrugs and faces into the sun, as if the rays of light hold the answers. "A better job, thought I could take some classes at the satellite school, settle down...eventually start a family."

"You'd make some man very happy."

She barks out laughter and winces, but her lopsided grin stays in place. "Not yet. I mean, look at me." She sobers. "But someday."

"Listen, there's something I need to talk to you about." I chew my lip, worried bringing him up will taint her opinion of me. "It's Lucas."

"You guys are together."

My cheeks heat with a blush that seems to come out of nowhere. "I'm in love with him."

"That's great, Shy." There's sadness in her voice. "Just...be careful."

"Right, um..." I fidget in my seat. "That's what I wanted to explain, see..." Damn, I knew I'd eventually have to explain Gage to Sam; I just hadn't prepared to do it now. "Lucas has DID, uh...dissociative identity disorder."

Her eyebrows drop low, and with all the bruising, it looks painful.

"You've probably heard it referred to as *multiple personality disorder*."

Her expression changes to understanding, and I take that as my cue to explain the last month of my life in great detail. She's quiet and nods that she understands.

"It wasn't Lucas you were...um...hooking up with. It was Gage." There. It's all out there now.

"Wow." Her lips open and close as if she can't find the right words.

"It's a lot to take in; just know that Lucas is a great guy and if Gage did anything to hurt you, it was only to protect Lucas." The sentence that just fell freely from my lips should sound absolutely insane in my own ears, but it doesn't. Not anymore.

"Anyway, I hope it's okay, but your mom gave Jennings your house key. Lucas is over there with a crew now, replacing all your locks, adding window locks and a security system."

"You're kidding?"

I shake my head. "Nope. He feels terrible about the way Gage treated you and went to my dad about doing whatever it takes to make you feel safe again."

Her eyes tear up and one drop of moisture falls from the slit of her swollen lids. "He's a good guy."

"He's a great guy." I swallow back the emotion I feel at seeing her break down but give her a second to regain her composure. Once she does, I breach the subject I hope won't piss her off. "Thank you for telling the sheriff about what Dustin did to the McKinstry place. I know you really care about him; it had to have been hard to turn him in."

She doesn't meet my eyes. "I felt like shit not telling you sooner. I mean, hell, your parents were like second parents to me. After everything Nash has gone through, I hated that Dustin did that to him." She picks at a loose thread on her blanket. "I don't know if you've noticed, but whatever he felt for you in high school only intensified after you left. He was so drunk, jealous of Lucas, that he told me later what he'd done. I think he felt bad about it after, but that doesn't make it okay. I would've said something sooner, but Lucas wasn't my favorite person at the time either so…"

"I understand."

"You do?"

I sigh, long and hard, so over all this drama between us. "Do you think we could start over? You know, put all the hurt feelings and animosity behind us and just go back to being friends?"

I watch her swallow and she nods. "I'd like that."

After getting all the heavy stuff out of the way, we catch each other up on the last five years of our lives. She tells me about a secret crush she's been harboring for the young dentist who moved to town a few years ago, and I tell her some of the better stories of college life, making sure to leave Trevor out of every one of them. After a while, she loses steam and I take my cue to leave.

"Get some sleep, okay?" I fold over her and kiss the matted hair above her forehead.

"Thanks for coming." She squeezes my hand. "I missed this."

"Me, too, but we've got a lifetime to catch up."

She yawns and the way it stretches her battered face makes me cringe. "So you're staying in Payson?"

My mind cranks back to Lucas, all the plans we talked about between making love last night, and yeah... "I'm staying."

She grins and her hold on my hand goes slack as her good eyelid slides closed. "Good."

And with that, my future just got a whole lot brighter.

EPILOGUE

SHYANN

Three years later…

"Where do you want this?" Cody's standing in the doorway to my new office, holding a box labeled with my name and *HEAVY: Don't let her lift this.*

I swivel around in my brand-spankin' new ergonomic desk chair and point to the corner next to my new file cabinets. "Over there would be great."

He drops it down with a thunk and I take another rotation in my seat, checking out the one-hundred-eighty-degree view from my picture windows. Even though it's winter and there's snow covering everything from treetops to blacktop, the office is warm due to the woodstove we had put in the lobby. I love this place.

It only took two years and eight months to convince my dad that Jennings needed a better office space, a more visible location, and a structure that would exemplify the product we produce. It took another four months for the place to be built, and today is moving-in day.

"You gonna unpack all that?" My brother motions to the boxes he's been bringing in and leaving where I direct him to.

"Eventually."

"I love it here!" Sam calls from her office located directly across the lobby from mine. "I can see Star Valley from my desk!"

Shortly after Sam recovered from her injuries, she took some accounting classes at the satellite school and my dad hired her on. It's been so much fun working with her. We chase my dad out most days with our incessant chatter, so he's on job sites more, which only helps business.

In the last couple years, Jennings Contractors has doubled. Not only did Payson open a fancy new country club and resort in town, but also the housing prices in Phoenix have gone up, so many have left to seek out the more affordable lifestyle that Payson can offer.

"Hey, I brought you a decaf. That fancy pod coffeemaker is the bomb." Sam puts a mug on my still-empty desk and props her legging-covered hip on the arm of my chair. She sighs long and hard, mirroring my feelings on the place. "So much better than the portable. I could live in here."

"I know, right?" I blow on my steaming cup of coffee. "Although, what would Doctor Smile say?"

She blushes and shakes her head. "He'd drag me back to our place, still smiling of course."

"Of course."

Sam and the town's hotshot dentist, Dr. Gregory Post, just got engaged after living together for over a year. He's a great guy, always happy, which is what earned him his nickname. She's suffered from night terrors and panic attacks after what Trevor did to her. A few months after her attack, Phoenix police caught the Shadow—an ex-con from Texas who got a rush from beating up women—when he attempted to attack a woman who also held a black belt in the martial arts. The man got a taste of what he'd been putting women through and is now serving a life sentence in state prison. Although Sam was inspired by the woman's story, she still hasn't felt safe. Until Dr. Greg insisted she get therapy. Even though she still struggles with the attack, I've never seen Sam happier or more settled.

I take a sip of my coffee just as Cody brings in another box, this one labeled *Shy's Desk* with a big *FRAGILE* scrolled on the side.

"Oh, here! I'll take that." I reach to grab it, but my brother moves past me and sets it on my desk.

"Nice try," he mumbles.

I roll my eyes and ignore him, digging into my box.

Cody motions to Sam. "Once you two are done chitchatting, maybe you could start getting some actual unpacking done." He flashes a teasing smile.

"Eh…he's probably right." Sam skips off. "I'll be in my suite if you need me." She giggles and slaps Cody in the gut as she passes him.

My brother's footsteps shuffle toward the door, but he calls out, "Be careful," before he leaves.

"Overprotective much?" I mumble.

"Ha! I'm nothing compared to—"

"Puleaze! Don't even say it. All you men are equally as bad!" I slide my hands under the box to move it to my seat so that I can pull things out and place them on my desk.

"Who is equally as bad— *Whoa!*" Firm hands grasp my hips from behind, the touch as familiar as my own. "Put the box down, baby." Those warm hands slide around my waist to my belly, rubbing circles on the six-month baby bump that stretches the fabric of my sweater.

"Lucas, I'm fine. I can lift a box to my—"

"No." His lips skate up my neck, kissing and tempting, until he nips at my earlobe.

I shiver in his arms and press my thighs together as desire rushes through my veins like a flash fire. His chuckle vibrates against my skin. I tilt my head to expose more of my neck, a silent plea for more. "You love teasing me."

"Mmm…" He moves his attention from my neck to my jawline. "Our baby's doing beautiful things to your body. I think it's *you* who loves teasing me." He flexes his hips into my lower back and I gasp at how hard he is.

"I think, I wonder, if we could take a break? Ya know, just um…" I lick my lips, unable to concentrate past what his mouth is doing against my skin to string together a complete thought.

"Nash is in his office; probably not smart to do dirty things to his daughter with him in the next room."

"Well…" I'm panting now as his teeth run the length of my neck. "As your wife, I will take control of our Netflix membership and torture you with historical biographies every night for the next year if you don't put out this fire you've created between my legs."

Another chuckle, this one deeper, darker, dangerous.

"Gage…" His name falls from my lips on a moan. "Take me home."

"Like you have to ask." He swoops me up in his arms and crashes his lips to mine in a kiss that robs me of breath. Our tongues glide together and he sucks at my mouth as if it's the last drop of water in the desert.

I slide my hands around his nape, fisting the hair that sticks out beneath his ball cap, and moan when he sinks his teeth into my bottom lip. "Home."

"Fuck, yeah." He carries me from my office and through the lobby, past my brother carrying a box, and some of the Jennings crew doing some last-minute finishing work.

"Be back in an hour, Dad!" I holler over Gage's shoulder.

"Hey! Careful going down the stairs with her!" my dad yells from his new executive office. "She's in a delicate cond—"

"She's safe on my watch, Nash," Gage calls back.

"You guys, I'm *fine*!"

"I thought the honeymoon was over." I can hear my dad's grumbled laughter as I'm carried over the threshold and across the snow-covered earth.

"Not even close!" Gage nips at my lips.

I claw his shoulders, pulling myself in tighter to protect myself against the icy cold. My breasts, now bigger and a lot more sensitive, brush against the firm plain of his pectorals and we both groan in anticipation.

He manages to open the passenger side of his new truck, this one complete with seat warmers and four doors to accommodate our growing family. He slides me inside, reaches over me to fasten my seat belt, and pulls back, his dark gaze boring into mine. "We're gonna share this one."

To anyone else, those five simple words probably seem meaningless, but they warm and cramp my heart all at the same time. Ever since I became pregnant, neither one of them have managed to stay away for long. Gage is more protective than ever; the tiniest thing, like me carrying in groceries or pulling out a stepladder, triggers the change. They flip back and forth daily, whereas before the baby I'd only see Gage about once a week. As hard as I know this is on Lucas, having Gage take over when Lucas would rather stay close, I love spending time with both of them. Each one has managed to offer a kind of beauty I never knew existed. Lucas's tender, artistic, gentle side is what I crave. He's the one I want to curl up to watch movies with and fall into the safety of every night. When we're together, he loves with a passion that has brought me to tears, with a dependence that aches so deep it's almost painful. Gage is our guardian. He's fierce, loyal, brave, and demanding. When we make love, it's without boundaries, without shame or record of the past. It's free and rough and so intense it shakes the very foundation of my soul.

I cup his jaw and drop a gentle kiss to his lips. "Whatever you need."

He blinks, and his eyes dart to the side before he focuses back on me. "He's worried this is too much for you."

"Never. But honestly, Gage, if you don't get me home and in our bed—hell, at this point I'd settle for this truck, anyplace warm will do—I'm going to explode."

His eyes flare and the corner of his mouth lifts. "Done."

GAGE

My *wife*.

My fucking wife!

Will it ever sink in?

Staring at her now, her black hair fanned out around her face, those lips that've brought me more pleasure than should be legal for any man to enjoy, relaxed and slightly tipped up on the ends. Her naked body sprawled out before me, swollen in the middle with the baby our love brought to life growing strong inside her. There's not a single inch of her that I don't love, that I wouldn't worship. That I wouldn't die to protect.

And she's mine.

"Stop staring and come hold me."

Her words call me to action. I crawl my naked body over hers until my chest is seated between her thighs, my arms braced on either side of her belly.

I run my lips from one hip bone to the other, taking the time to nip around her belly button and leave a trail of wet kisses in my wake. "You feelin' okay?"

"Mmm…" Her hips roll against my chest and I bite my lip against an animalistic growl. "Feels really good."

I grin against her skin. "Not what I asked, baby."

"I'm fine, I feel fine, we're all fine, I promise. If anything were wrong, you'd be the first to know."

"He's getting so big." I palm her belly like a small basketball. "He's not hurting you, is he?"

She pushes up on her elbows and forks her fingers through my hair. "No, he's not hurting me."

I try to relax, but ever since I found out about the baby, I've been a nervous fucking nightmare. *Congratulations, you're pregnant. Here's an injection of psychopath with a dose of homicidal tendencies.* I can't believe she hasn't told me to fuck off and banished me from her life yet. I've become the world's most obnoxious helicopter husband. The worst part is, I don't know how to stop. I've wanted to rip people's arms off for touching her belly, caught myself growling at the ultrasound appointment, twice. Considered very strongly gutting her doc during a very routine exam.

It's Luke who's saved me. I've tapped in to the calm he feels every time he's around Shy. I've managed to harness the tingling warmth that envelops his chest when they're together. I've paid attention to the way he talks to her, the soothing tenor of his voice when she's freaking out about something like dust mites in the baby's clothes. He's great with her, so much better for her than I am right now, and yet she looks at me, like the way she is now, as if I could do no wrong. Like the earth ends and begins with me.

"Have you decided on a name yet?" Her fingers continue to rake across my scalp.

I push up the last foot and a half to drop down to her side, throwing my thigh over hers to keep contact. It looks possessive, but it's really a weakness.

I need to touch her. "I'm leaving it up to Luke. After all, I owe everything to him. I'd never be here, with you, like this, if it weren't for him."

Her eyes fill with tears. "Don't do that! You know I always cry when you get sweet."

I kiss away a single tear that slides down her cheek. "You cry when Buddy's sweet. And he's a dog. He's not capable of anything else."

She sighs, and another tear falls. "Aww, Buddy…" Her face screws up and a sob rips from her. "He's such a good dog."

Okaaay, that's my cue.

I brush my lips along her ear. "I love you, Shyann. I'm gonna keep loving you until we're both long gone from this earth. You *and* the babies you give us."

"I love…" She sniffs. "You…" Another sob. "Too."

LUCAS

I come to with my face buried in Shyann's neck. I breathe her in and start to grin when I hear the not-so-quiet sound of her crying.

Thanks a lot, Gage. Always ducking out when things get sticky.

"Baby…" I wrap her in my arms and pull her to my chest. "Shhh…it's okay." I try to soothe her with my touch, but with us both being naked, my hands have minds of their own.

I cup her backside and she wiggles in deeper, her legs straddling my thigh and the firm bump of her belly at my hip.

"I'm okay. It's just…"

"Gage bein' sweet again."

Another loud sob and then hot tears hit my throat. "Yes! I liked it better when I couldn't cry!"

A laugh rumbles in my chest. "I don't."

She pulls back, her puffy eyes meeting mine. "You don't?"

"Nope." I run my thumb along her full lower lip.

"But...I'm a mess!"

Sifting my fingers into her hair, I pull her down so her lips are just a breath away from mine. "Yeah, but I love cleaning you up."

Our lips come together in a sensual touch. She breathes against me, "You're too good to me."

I roll her to her back, taking care to shift my lower body to the side to keep from crushing her belly. "You always say that."

Her tongue slides into my mouth, and it's just like that first kiss. My stomach leaps into my chest and butterflies explode behind my ribs, because finding Shyann was like opening a door to a different life. We've found acceptance, not only in her love and loyalty to us, but also in her family. In this town. She's given us more than we'd ever dreamt we could have, and no matter how unworthy of us she feels, she has to know that we're the grateful ones.

Her hips thrust against me and I rip my mouth from hers. Ravenous for her taste, I slide down, sucking her swollen nipple and circling it with my tongue. Her back arches off the bed and the sound of her cries echoes off the A-frame walls of our newly added loft bedroom.

I scoot farther down her body, ravishing her with kisses until I'm between her legs. Her hands grip the comforter at her sides and her knees fall wide open in invitation. I take a second to appreciate her form, her body spread out like a buffet for my senses.

I run a firm hand up her inner thigh, pressing it to the bed to open her more. "You're so beautiful." Gliding my tongue up her thigh, I don't hesitate before plunging it deep inside her. Her taste floods my mouth and I growl into her.

I'm lost to every sound that falls from her lips, every groan that vibrates her entire body, and every pinch of pain from her fingernails. It all shoots straight to my hard-on with a hunger that refuses to be ignored.

She whimpers when I pull away and drop beside her.

"Come here." I reach over and scoop her up to guide her on top of me.

The second her legs spread wide over my hips, I almost lose myself to the wet heat that swallows me. She grips me and guides me to her, then sinks down slowly until we're completely connected.

"I love you so much." Tears still brim in her eyes as she braces herself with her palms pressed flat to my chest, then rolls her hips in waves.

The visual of her moving above me calls to me on a primal level and the sudden urge to have my tongue filling her mouth overtakes me.

I hook her behind the neck and bring her lips to mine. "You *own* me, Shy. Take what's yours. Everything good in me, it's all for you."

"If that's true…" Her forehead drops to mine on a long moan. "Let me have the bad too. I want it all."

I'm panting, holding back the orgasm that's about to blow through my body, but I grin. "Greedy."

"For you? Always."

We drop over the edge in unison, free-falling with our hearts hammering together behind the press of our bare chests.

What we have isn't conventional, it wouldn't be considered ideal, but it's perfect for *us*.

Because love never discriminates.

Even when you're split.